Frankie and Stankie

BARBARA TRAPIDO

BLOOMSBURY

First published 2003
This paperback edition published 2004

Copyright © 2003 by Barbara Trapido

The moral right of the author has been asserted

Bloomsbury Publishing Plc, 38 Soho Square, London WID 3HB

A CIP catalogue record for this book
is available from the British Library

ISBN 0 7475 6814 6

10 9 8 7 6

All papers used by Bloomsbury Publishing are natural,
recyclable products made from wood grown in
well-managed forests. The manufacturing processes
conform to the environmental regulations of the
country of origin.

Typeset by Hewer Text Limited, Edinburgh
Printed in Great Britain by Clays Ltd, St Ives plc

www.bloomsbury.com/barbaratrapido

Praise for *Frankie and Stankie*

'Occasionally you come across a story you really don't want to end. Barbara Trapido is one such storyteller. You find yourself devouring enormous chunks at one sitting until all too soon, goddammit, it's finished . . . Trapido balances the light and dark with a story that maintains a vibrant optimism'   *Glamour*

'Trapido is a wonderful storyteller, mixing menace and humour with fine balance. Through the appealing character of Dinah, she pinpoints all the tragedies of South African society' *Sunday Mirror*

'Barbara Trapido has always juggled light and shade, comedy and tragedy, but in *Frankie and Stankie* her narrative pitch finds the perfect subject'   *Observer*

'Sparks and crackles . . . Trapido tours the suburban landscape, observing a culture where the strenuous cultivation of conformity masks a multitude of individual dramas . . . Trapido writes wonderfully about giggliness and the ardour of girls' friendships, about childhood illness and the excruciating clumsiness of grown-ups'   *Sunday Times*

'Wry and ironic . . . The tone serves to underline the horrors of a society that sets out to rob an entire people of its dignity and power. But this is the grim background to a story that has the characteristic Trapido energy and sparkle'   *Independent on Sunday*

'Marvellous . . . an inspired amalgamation of personal, national and international history, a *tour de force*, a joy to read' Shena MacKay

'This is an absorbing and deeply felt novel . . . Most of all, it serves one important purpose: to reconnect the deformities of white South Africa with Europe's own twentieth-century convulsions, and, in so doing, put the British, among others, firmly back on the hook'   *Time Out*

'The story of Dinah's childhood and anecdotes from the lives of her family and friends are interwoven with events from this cruel period of South Africa's history in a strange and delightful tapestry that spans most of the twentieth century. Trapido explores issues of racism, family, friendship, loyalty and the discovery of self with an impressive lightness of touch in this whimsical yet thought-provoking novel'   *Irish Independent*

Brother of the More Famous Jack

Noah's Ark

Temples of Delight

Juggling

The Travelling Hornplayer

For my father

ONE

Dinah knows that she's weedy: she's always been little and thin, and she has no meat on her bones. She has permanent black smudges under her eyes and, because she's asthmatic, she breathes through her mouth, which is always open. This makes her look daffy as well as weedy. In addition, her parents tell her she's edgy; *zänkisch* her mother calls it. There are various anecdotes about her early life that testify to this. Dinah is edgy because her mother is edgy during the pregnancy, and she's born premature because her mother has got over-excited on the day. First of all she's had a pleasant surprise because Dinah's father has got a letter declaring him unfit to serve in the Dutch Army in the war against Hitler. This is because his eyesight is too bad, which ought not to have been a surprise, since he's as good as blind without his glasses. Dinah's dad is from Holland, though he's been in Cape Town for nearly five years. That's why it's the Dutch Army that can decide whether or not to call him up. In the South African Army you can't get called up. You have to be a volunteer. But there are lots and lots of volunteers, because some of the recruitment posters have been so snappy:

DON'T BE LEFT OUT OF THE GREATEST ADVENTURE OF ALL TIME!

WAS THERE EVER A GIRL WHO DIDN'T PREFER A MAN IN UNIFORM?

Quite a few black men are volunteering as well but they're not allowed to carry guns – though if you come from Basutoland you'll be given a stout wooden stick. Or sometimes you'll get an assegai. Meanwhile the women are saving on light bulbs and they're knitting balaclavas for the troops.

1

Dinah's mother has never learned to knit. And just a few hours before Dinah is born, she has a really nasty shock, because, while Dinah's dad is out teaching one of his evening classes, a man, having first tried to break down the front door, has gone tramping round and round the garden of their ground-floor flat. He's been shouting abuse at her in the darkness and he's banged on the bedroom window.

'Open up there, Dolly!' he bawls. 'Come on now, Dolly, for Christssake!' Then he tramps around and bangs about some more. 'Give us a kiss, now, that's my girl,' he bawls. 'Let me in, you bitch! Wazza matter with you?'

Dinah's mum thinks he must be the multiple rapist currently on the loose in Cape Town and, since she's got no telephone in the flat, she takes a big risk in making a dash for the phone box, clutching Dinah's elder sister to her bosom, while the rapist is busy trampling the arum lilies to death around the back. She dials the police, who come at once, only to discover a drunken Australian soldier asleep in one of the flowerbeds. His troopship's docked in Cape Town for a few days and he's been trying to make his way back to a woman who's been very free with her favours on previous nights.

Right now there are lots of Australian soldiers docking in South African ports. And most of the local citizens think that the Aussies are really wild. In Durban, way up the Indian Ocean coast, the local Vera Lynn has been offering up special renditions of 'Waltzing Mathilda' from the quay, which has the Australian soldiers rushing eagerly to the wharfside of their troop ships. This is because the singer in question is just like a great white whale. She can manage two hundred and fifty songs a day which she belts out through a megaphone and she's always dressed in white. So she's known as the Woman in White. Her real name is Perla Gibson.

Dinah is born later that night. It's the night of the Australian soldier. She's born in the lift during a wartime power cut because her mother can't hold on any longer, even though the nurse tells her she's got to.

'You've *got* to hold on,' the nurse says. 'I've never done a birth before.'

The poor girl is a wartime stand-in. Next morning, the regular day-nurses all remember Dinah's mother from her previous child-birth. They groan at the sight of the new baby, who weighs just a fraction over four pounds and looks exactly like a shrivelled yellow monkey because she has infant jaundice. But Dinah's mum is quite taken with her baby's yellow complexion and imagines it to have something to do with her husband's Netherlandish family, who are all unknown to her – trapped as they are in occupied Holland – but she does know there's a Dutch connection with Indonesia. She fancies that her baby's looks are exotic. The same nurses saw Dinah's older sister into the world fourteen months earlier and they right away called her Angel-face. Now, with a flash of originality, they call Dinah Tiny-mite.

'Tiny-mite is going to give poor Angel-face a very hard time,' they say.

Angel-face by this time is a healthy, smiley, auburn-haired cherub with four pearly incisors, two up, two down, who gurgles and bounces so charmingly from her cot on the balcony of the apartment that total strangers come by and bombard her with presents. They throw stuffed toys up on to the balcony for her and little jerseys they've knitted out of their scratchy wartime wool rations. What the nurses don't know is that Tiny-mite is already giving Angel-face a hard time, because, once the waters have broken, Dinah's dad has just leapt straight into the taxi along with his wife. He means to drop her off at the hospital and hurry back at once, so he's left poor Angel-face sound asleep and all alone. And then, of course, he's stuck in the lift. Plus, given that he's a fairly recent immigrant and not yet all that *au fait* with English popular culture, he's forgotten that it's Bonfire Night, so when he gets back two hours later, Angel-face, who's been woken by the neighbourhood rocket display, is standing at her cot bars in paroxysms of terror with her poor little face caked in snot and her beautiful gingernut curls all spiky with sweat.

> Remember, remember
> The Fifth of November,
> Gunpowder, treason and plot.

Treason and plot are uppermost right now, because pro-Nazi elements among the white population are stockpiling their arsenals of hand grenades and guns. Plus the government is anxiously gearing up for a possible Japanese invasion, now that Japan has entered the war on Germany's side. General Smuts has just announced that all South Africans, black and white, must learn to pull together. Segregation measures will be relaxed, he says. That's while the war's on, anyway. Afterwards the segregation measures will all come back again. Meanwhile, a mad lady in the hospital foyer is telling Dinah's dad that Scorpios will always have the rockiest journey through life. Unfortunately Dinah isn't even meant to be a Scorpio, so maybe it's no wonder she's not all that well equipped to deal with its several astrological disadvantages.

Angel-face is called Lisa. Tiny-mite is supposed to have been called Amaryllis, after a song her dad sings while her mother accompanies him on a borrowed piano. *Amarilli, mia bella.* It's in a collection of antique love songs that he's got in a book from the Accademia di Santa Cecilia in Rome. Instead, Dinah's dad changes his mind on the way to the registry office next day. He finds himself whistling a pop song that goes, 'Dinah, is there anyone finer, in the state of Carolina?' He likes to make decisions without consultation because it's quicker that way and, anyway, he always knows best.

Dinah's mum has the girls so close together because she doesn't always know best. She's been told that you don't get pregnant while you're breastfeeding and to her credit she's been breastfeeding Angel-face for fourteen months on demand, since she hasn't read Truby King, who has created a fashion for formulas and four-hourly regimentation. She does so even though Angel-face, who has a hearty appetite, frequently bites the nipple. In between feeds Angel-face even takes bites out of the bath soap, leaving behind little telltale semi-circles serrated by her teeth. Her favourite soap comes a dark, marbled green and it's called Cuticura. Angel-face finds it irresistible.

Dinah is kept in a cardboard box at first and wiped down with olive oil because she's too small to have proper baths. This is at a time when olive oil is still strictly medicinal. It's well before Elizabeth David has brought the good news from Aix-en-Provence to the British Isles, courtesy of Penguin Books, and then all over the Empire including Cape Town. Angel-face goes stiff with terror

4

when she first hears Tiny-mite's unearthly mewling cry, and she won't go near the cardboard box for days. For two years afterwards, she's even afraid to approach lifelike dolls. Unlike Angel-face, Tiny-mite is not a good eater. She drops off at the nipple and will not suck.

'We had to smack you to make you eat,' her dad tells her in years to come.

He's always been a ready smacker. Her dad is called Ta, which is a corruption of Da, though Dinah's mum has diminutised this to Tächenherz because she comes from Berlin. His real name is Fred.

Dinah continues to be a non-eater throughout her childhood. When one of her dad's colleagues visits with a packet of biscuits, he says they're 'for Lisa to eat and for Dinah to play with'. The biscuits are called Iced Zoological but the girls call them Animal Biscuits. Each biscuit is a scalloped rectangle with pastel icing on the top and an animal piped on to it in a contrasting colour. There are yellow giraffes on rose-pink icing and white tigers on sky-blue icing. Dinah loves to play with the biscuits. She's always been good at playing, while Angel-face isn't introspective enough to make up games. She likes visitors and outings and treats. Best of all she likes Toffo-lux. She hangs around saying, 'I'm bored. I've got nothing to do. What can I do now? What's there to eat? What's for pudding?' So, right from the time they're about three and four, it's Tiny-mite who thinks up all the games.

Sometimes she leads Angel-face into the garden shed, where families of daddy-long-legs live on the walls. If she touches their fragile, umbrella-spoke legs with her index finger they scurry up the walls so deftly that it leaves her feeling heady. She already loves to climb walls and trees herself but she knows she'll never be able to climb like that on sheer vertical walls. For some reason Angel-face hates the creepy-crawlies, especially when they move. When Dinah makes them scurry up the walls she yells and screams in panic. This makes Dinah keep on doing it because, being so much smaller than her sister, it's one way to redress the balance.

Mealtimes are hell for Dinah, when she clamps her mouth shut against the approaching spoon.

'This one's for Teddy,' her dad will say. 'This one's for Panda. This one's the last one. This one's the very last one.'

She knows it will never be the last one until the bowl is empty.

Sometimes he eats a spoonful himself to encourage her, and because, like Angel-face, he has a hearty appetite. Then, once she's turned six, he always finishes up by saying, 'This one's for Co.' Co is Dinah's rag-doll that she's had for her fifth birthday. Her name is really Ro. Ro is short for Rosema, which is not short for Rosemary. When grown-ups suggest it, Dinah says firmly, 'No. Her name is Rosema. Just Rosema.'

Dinah only gets to know one real-life Rosemary, but this is only once she's started school. Rosemary is a girl in the neighbourhood who has high status in the child community because she's excessively blonde. Rosemary is white-mouse blonde with a small whiffly nose and little see-through ears. Lots of the children are blonde-ish but not so blonde that the light shines right through them as it does with Rosemary. This whiteness is associated with purity. Rosemary's dad is immensely rich, even though he can't read and write. He is said to sign papers with an X.

This is an achievement that Dinah's mum remarks upon, a little pointedly, from time to time, since the girls' dad is not at all rich even though he can read and write in eight languages, having been rigorously taught between the wars in one of those gymnasiums they have in Holland for clever boys and girls. His best thing, along with teaching himself to play musical instruments, is maths. For a while he works as an actuary in a bank but he finds it boring so he now works for a pittance as an untenured junior lecturer in the maths department at the university in Cape Town. The girls' mum calls his mathematical activities puzzling. She uses the word as if it was from the verb to puzzle.

'Tächenherz is puzzling,' she says.

It's just one example from her range of Germanic verbal peculiarities.

The flat doesn't have a lot of space and if he's marking exam scripts at the only table then the girls' dad has to clear them away at mealtimes. Dinah's horror times. Sometimes, presumably to blot out the girls' chatter going on in the same room, he'll start to puzzle out loud. Angel-face and Dinah are amused by his mathematical gibberish and chant bits of it at each other.

'Pi to the curve,' they say. They say it as they take turns to climb on to a big wooden box called the *Klappkasten* and jump off. 'Pi to the curve.'

Dinah envisages triangles of gooseberry pie with crimped edges, because there are gooseberries growing in the garden of the flats.

They do the same sometimes when their dad sings his Italian songs to their mother's accompaniment. There's one about a beautiful mouth: *O bocca bella. O bocca, bocca bella.* For years the girls think it's about malted corn porridge because one of Lisa's many culinary favourites is a chocolatey porridge called Maltabela which she likes to alternate in the mornings with Aunt Jemima's Cream of Wheat. The song keeps repeating the phrase so they giggle and sing along in silly voices: 'Oh Maltabela, oh Malta, Maltabela!'

They suffer a similar misunderstanding with an Italian worker song that makes reference to comrades who have died in the struggle. One of the comrades is called Carlo Franchi and, since the struggle has worn him out, there's a reference to the Italian word for being exhausted. *Stanchi.* It rhymes with Franchi. Dinah envisages it as a song about two clowns called Frankie and Stankie and she explains this to Lisa. She pictures them in orange bloomers and very small orange bowler hats. When Frankie is the right way up, then Stankie is upside-down and vice versa.

Aunt Jemima's Cream of Wheat has a medallion on the box with a smiling Southern black lady on it who wears her hair tied up in a red-and-white-spotted handkerchief with a knot at the front. Dinah likes this picture almost as much as that of the shiny black cat on the Black Cat peanut butter label. She also likes the label on the Camp Coffee bottle and wishes her mother would buy it when they go shopping, because the man in the turban is saying to the man in the kilt, 'Ready, ay ready,' which sounds just like the repeating refrain of a poem. Ay is a poetry word for always.

The absence of money is a trial to Dinah's mother, whose family used to have lots of it, but now the money's all gone up in smoke – some of it literally, because the family houses in Berlin and Furstenwalde and Frankfurt-am-Main have been bombed to dust along with the businesses in which they had their investments – and the rest of it vanished when Dinah's mum's parents got cheated out of it as not very clued-up immigrants during their period of relocation to Cape Town before the war. It's hard for Dinah's mum to be always thinking about saving tuppence on vegetables and biscuits, or to get her head around the idea that the world she grew up in isn't there any more. Not even the streets in Berlin are in the same place, even though they've still got the same names.

And she's often sad about her favourite aunt, Tante Ella, who is currently living like a pauper in one room of her own villa in East Berlin – or what had been her own villa until she was 'invited' to make it over to the state and watch it turn into a doss-house. Tante Ella never married, having in her youth broken off her engagement to a Danish count whom she suspected of being after her money. She decided to spend her life as an independent single woman and she became Dinah's mum's favourite relation.

The aunt made herself responsible for her niece's coming-out and took her to the opera and on trips to Copenhagen on a boat called the *Schleswig Holstein*, where Dinah's mum sometimes won at deck quoits. She still has a china sailor doll with a hat that says *Schleswig Holstein* in gold Gothic script on the hatband. And she still has one of the winning rope deck quoits. She keeps these in her knicker drawer and she sometimes lets the girls play with them. Dinah who loves poking about finds that her mum periodically hoards dark Swiss chocolate and Nescafé and Lux Flakes in her drawers along with little bottles of 4711 cologne. She does this whenever there's a whiff of further trouble in the world. Korea, Suez, Cyprus. This is from having lived through the First World War in Germany. Swiss chocolate, Nescafé, soap flakes and cologne are this life's greatest necessities. That's if you're German.

Dinah's mum has lots of stories about her childhood, unlike her dad who only has five. At the drop of a hat she will tell stories about skiing holidays in the Harz Mountains and about her two boy cousins, the skiing champs, whose mum was Tante Berthe and whose dad was a judge. She'll tell about her cousin Gunther's wedding where the bride was a White Russian ballet dancer on the run from the Bolsheviks who had a tantrum at her own wedding reception. A grown-up woman in red lace, kicking and screaming with her legs in the air. She'll tell about the seafaring trips she took with her father and her three brothers on the family's motor launch called *Sophie*.

Sophie is Dinah's maternal grandmother's name, but she never went along on the boat that was named after her, because she didn't have sea legs. She had no head for heights either, because when she was chosen, as the auburn-haired beauty of Wiesbaden, to represent the new century on New Year's Day in 1900, she fainted while waving regally from a specially constructed obelisk and her huge feathered hat wafted slowly downwards into the square from a great height, like a winged angel. In all the photographs, she's shown to have a fine hourglass figure and a thick mass of wavy hair. She doesn't look at all like Dinah's mum who is tall and thin with high cheekbones and widely spaced blue eyes and fine baby-blonde hair.

Dinah's mum looks just like her father who comes from the Friesian Islands, but got sent to school in Berlin where the boys called him Bahne Banana, because his name is Jacob Bahne Jacobsen. The two things that Dinah's mum tells the girls about her visits to the island are that, when you posted a letter, you didn't need to buy a stamp, because you just posted your money into the box along with the letter and the postie knew it was your money. She also tells that, when you went to church, there was a plaque that said all the families on the island, except for the Jacobsens and one other family, had been wiped out in a flood in the sixteenth century. This was useful for the Jacobsens when it came to proving their grade A Aryan blood when the Nazis came to power. Dinah's mum looks like a star candidate for the Hitler Jugend, except that she's always hated uniforms.

The girls' mum tells stories about the orphaned baby owl that her brother Otto reared in the stables at Lindenstrasse vierundachtzig by feeding it pieces of raw meat on the end of a stick. She tells stories about the family dog, who was called Deena, but spelt just like Dinah without the 'h'. She tells about how Dina had been taught not to kill the chickens but couldn't resist taking them in her mouth and giving each one a little squeeze, so the chickens in the garden at Lindenstrasse vierundachtzig all walked with a limp. She tells about how her dad had bought the rambling old Lindenstrasse house from the estate of a reclusive army colonel who'd lived out his decline surrounded by dogs and cats; and how the overgrown garden of the house was a mass of animal gravestones as far as you could see.

'Dogs to ze right, cats to ze left,' Dinah's mum tells the girls.

She has stories about the Tiergarten and the Berlin Opera House where the boat carrying off the Wagnerian lovers got derailed on stage on account of the singers' immoderate combined weight.

Once the war is over, occasional letters get through from the Eastern Zone in which Tante Ella, old and sick, pleads for parcels of smoked bacon. Dinah's mum sends these wrapped in linen sewn up with a darning needle, though she doubts whether they ever arrive. Dinah watches her write the address in marking ink with a tiny dipping pen that she longs to have for her dolls to use at their pretend school. Dinah has lots of dolls, the favourites of which, other than Rosema and the baby dolls, are Deborah, Naomi and Jennifer. Rosema is closest to her heart, even though she has the look of a candidate for facial surgery and Dinah has replaced her original hair, which went matted and couldn't be brushed, with some unsightly black knitting wool. She's sewed this on with backstitch along the line of Rosema's centre parting so that, if she turns Rosema upside-down, the doll looks like a Mohican doing a headstand. At first Dinah despises Rosema because she is a rag-doll and proper dolls are made of china or celluloid or Bakelite, and they can open and shut their eyes, click-clack. So for a year Rosema always dies when Dinah and Lisa play hospitals. They pick her up by one of her lanky limbs and hurl her into the corner.

Dinah, unlike Lisa, becomes obsessed with her dolls. They begin to exist in real time. And from the time she starts school herself, all the dolls have school as well. They are in their classrooms every day and Dinah makes them all miniature school books and school uniforms. Each chair in the living room is a different classroom, depending on the dolls' ages, and their home time has to be staggered. So for the dolls in the younger classes, Dinah's mum has to fetch them home. Home is on Dinah's bed. The neighbourhood boys who spy on her doll games manage to pick up that Rosema is an abuse victim, so they promptly start knocking her about. Everything about poor Rosema's body language is screaming at them to abuse her. They barge in and kick her round the garden like a football. They toss her high into the tallest trees so that she hangs for a moment in the branches by her hair before falling on to the red earth in a heap, like a broken spider. Then, one day, a boy called Donald Carter gets into a frenzy. Dinah watches as he shakes Rosema violently between his teeth, tossing his head from side to side. Then he throws her into the air and catches her in his mouth. He growls at her like a tiger and suddenly he's ripped off the end of her nose. Dinah's eyes are opened. In a fit of guilt she takes Rosema to her heart and swears to love her best for ever. Having rejected her child, she now adores her with an extreme devotion. She sews up Rosema's nose with a needle and some of the flesh-coloured thread that her mother uses to cobble together holes in silk stockings.

'Rosema is my favourite,' she says. 'Rosema is my best doll.'

She and Rosema become inseparable.

The reason Dinah can sew from an early age is that her mother can't. Sewing follows the law of alternating generations, so that if your mum can't sew then you can. Dinah's mum's idea of sock-darning is to work a tacking thread round the hole and pull it tight into a ruched lump. This is one reason why Dinah and Lisa have blisters on their heels. The other is that their shoes are much too clumpy. Their dad, who is independent-minded and holds strong opinions on most things, has grown up in a household without sisters. He thinks girls' stuff is silly and inferior and he's got no time for it. He buys his daughters boys' toys and boys' shoes, so they have a red-and-green Meccano set and Bayco building blocks and a Hornby and several gyroscopes, and sturdy laced shoes called Knockabouts. But when Dinah is six, precisely because she's so skinny and weedy, a shoe-shop attendant measures her as AA width, and says that her feet will be ruined unless her parents put her in ultra-narrow, girly Startrites which just happen to come with a T-bar and a buckle and petal patterns cut out on the insteps. This is the happiest day of Dinah's life and poor Lisa is terribly jealous.

Dinah is a cry-baby and she has a bleeding heart. So one day she won't stop crying because she's accidentally washed a small spider down the plug-hole. Her mum, who has a Gothic streak, tells her that much more terrible things are happening every day. There and then she tells Dinah about a court case in that day's news-paper. It's all about a mother who's been tying up her children and making them eat their own sick. Because Dinah's mum is anxiety-prone, she likes to off-load gruesome stories. This is why she tells Lisa and Dinah about the multiple rapist in Cape Town for whom she mistook the Australian soldier. He could get through any locks and keys, she says. So the rapist would get into a house or a flat while the woman who lived there was out, and then he'd hide, so that when the woman came home, she'd lock the door safely behind her and, just then, the rapist would step out of a cupboard.

This anecdote makes Dinah start checking all cupboards on entering a house, including small flat wall cupboards. And she always looks under beds, chests and dressers in case of very small rapists – sometimes even two-dimensional rapists. Only then will she think of locking a front door. Dinah's mum calls the rapist a murderer, so that she doesn't have to explain what rape is, because Dinah and Lisa don't yet know anything about sex, not until they are nearly ten and eleven. This is when Dorothy who lives in Manning Road takes them into a cupboard and whispers to them one by one what their mum and dad do together in bed.

When their dad gets a proper tenured lectureship in the maths department at the university in Durban, he has to go on ahead for the first day of term, so it's just the three of them that take the train together the day after the girls' mum has finally finished the packing. Dinah's mum has found a home for the family's cat, but not for the last two of her kittens, so, on the night before they leave, she sneaks out after dark without telling the girls and she pushes the kittens through the fence of the nearby Cecil Rhodes Estate. She's always liked the gardens there and she hopes that the kittens will dig in and manage to have nice lives.

The Rhodes Estate is called Groote Schuur which means Big Barn. It's got a small pride of lions that Lisa and Dina can sometimes hear roaring at night. Cecil Rhodes was once the Prime Minister of the Cape, but now he's forty years dead. There's a bronze statue of him in The Gardens in Cape Town, pointing heroically towards the north. This is because, as well as owning twenty-nine Cape wine farms and most of the Transvaal goldfields, he also owns lots of Rhodesia in the north, because Queen Victoria has given him rights to rule all the territory there – that's any territory where his mining ventures are venturing. Cecil Rhodes is famous for the Glen Grey Act which is designed to create extra land shortage among blacks, because having land has always made black people far too idle to go and work for whites. And, until now it's been only white farmers who've wanted cheap black labour. Now Rhodes and his friends are needing far more of it, because mining has become the big thing. Cecil Rhodes is a man of vision. He believes in making money for Empire and in white boys having adventures. He's got his own sort of personal boy-scout pack, but it's made up of boys who are grown-ups. Dinah knows that Cecil Rhodes is famous because he wanted to build a railway line all the way from Cape to Cairo. Everyone knows that this is a very inspiring idea, because it's not only ambitious, but it's alliterative as well.

The train journey to Durban takes days and days, so the girls settle in happily to seventy-two hours of cutting out paper dolls with breaks for eating ham-and-pea soup from thick china plates in the dining car. Outside, the telegraph poles dip and rise in the wide landscape. The waiters enchant Dinah by their virtuoso method of dispensing tea and coffee. Holding nickel-plated coffee pot and milk jug, one in each hand, they pour two streams from a great height, swaying with the train's motion as they do so. It's a wonder to her how they always get the coffee and the milk to reach the top of the cup at exactly the same time. Their mum merely comments that the coffee is *Dreck*. She shakes her head and grimaces. '*Schrecklich*,' she says. '*Schrecklich*.' All the waiters are white Afrikaners and all the bedding 'boys' are Cape Coloured.

The original pale-brown people of the Cape had called themselves the Khoi, but the Dutch settlers called them Hottentots. The early Dutch had made so bold as to land, because the Portuguese had recently proved to them that the seas around the Cape didn't boil. So the Khoi lost all their territory to the Dutch and were turned into landless labourers. They also lost their language. That's except for those peculiar clicks that got taken over by the Xhosa. Finally the Khoi stopped being the Khoi and became the Cape Coloured people. They'd got mixed up with the whites and their slaves – slaves who had come from everywhere – from Guinea, Angola and Madagascar; from India, Java and China. But the top-notch slaves were always the Malays and they built the old Dorp Street Mosque. So if a Cape Coloured person says to you that his daughter looks like a Muslim, what he means is that she's got straight hair, which is a top-notch thing to have. Plus his daughter's probably also got those beautiful green eyes.

Durban is all sweaty heat and banana palms and huge succulent plants. The girls step out into the Victorian Gothic of the railway station to be met by their dad, who steers them through the surrounding bustle of Indian fruit vendors and Zulu rickshaw men to settle them in a taxi. Both girls are in new kilts for the occasion: Lisa's is plaid, Dinah's is pink. Lisa and Dinah have neither of them ever seen a rickshaw man before and so they can't stop staring at first, even though these are just the plain-Jane rickshaw men in grubby, colourless head rags whose job is to pull sacks of maize. They haven't yet seen the fancier rickshaw men on the beachfront who wear ten-ton ornamental head-dresses with lots of horns and beads. The headgear fans out, two foot both ways, in a parody of an Aztec priest, and the rickshaw man's job is to pull around white tourists in their swimwear so that they can have their pictures taken. Holiday Snaps. Everybody Dinah knows calls a photograph a snap, except for her dad who is a serious amateur photographer – which is why he always spends half an hour taking your picture. Dinah's dad says that the rickshaw men are usually dead by the time they're forty, because you shouldn't be pulling four tourists in a cart with a ten-ton thing on your head.

Their house is a small prefab bungalow, one among many erected hastily for ex-servicemen in the grounds of a vast, exotically landscaped estate. It's called the Butcher Estate and it's owned by one of the local sugar plantation aristocracy, but now it's on loan to the university as a place to house academic staff and students. A jacaranda tree sheds mauve, bell-like flowers just outside their kitchen door.

There's an island of giant bamboo inhabited by a colony of grey vervet monkeys with black faces and black doll-sized human hands and feet. They leap and chatter and munch bananas, holding their babies upside-down on their bellies as they fly through the air, and sometimes they swing from their own tails just for fun. From the living-room window, just beyond the undergraduates' cricket pitch, you can walk through a shady green pergola covered with passion-fruit vines and bougainvillea, because in Durban bougain-villea grows over everything. Most of the trees are umbrella-shaped and have varieties of big red flower. Sometimes they have seed pods as big as dagger sheaths that crack open on the ground, spilling out fat speckled beans. There's a flower in the garden called chinker-ing-chee and lots of bushes called yesterday-today-and-tomorrow because they have flowers in three colours all on the one bush. Yesterday's flower is violet, today's is blue and tomorrow's is white.

The war is over and there's been a mass of emigration from Europe, so lots of the academics are from somewhere else. Most have been busy breeding, so that clusters of children peek out from the other bungalows and young university wives with babies in bouncy carriage prams are visible on the communal green. There's always somebody to play with and somebody's baby to mind and somebody to gang up against in the child community of the Butcher Estate. Dinah's favourite person is Harry Stent and very soon everyone is teasing her about him.

'He's your boyfriend,' the children say.

Harry is a skinny boy with tight blond curls, but his small sister Margaret is plump and olive-skinned with big black eyes, because she takes after their mother who is Spanish. Margaret is too small to talk properly, but she always stretches out her little dimpled right hand and says, 'More,' in the presence of biscuits. All the other children laugh at her and tell her she can't have more when she hasn't had any yet, but she just says it again. 'More.'

Sometimes, when all ideas for games dry up, the child pack will go and sit on the wall in a long row and watch the undergraduates practising cricket, because it's fun to giggle and point if a batsman is wearing his groin guard on the outside of his trousers and to shout out 'Hard cheese' and 'Hard luck' in groany voices when someone's been given out. It makes the batsmen get really narky.

'You kids clear off!' they say. 'Go on. Scram! *Voetsek!*'

Then Dinah's family furniture comes. There isn't all that much of it and, in the kitchen, they just have wooden orange boxes for cupboards with cheap cretonne curtains strung across the fronts, but there are the two ornate, throne-like chairs – Grandfather Gieseke's chairs – which are definitely not bungalow chairs. They were carved by Dinah's mum's grandad for whom woodcarving was a hobby and they date from the 1870s, but their style is sort of Jacobean-baronial and they look as though they could be used for the banqueting scene in *Macbeth*. They are large and square, with heavy arms and stretchers, and they're made of dark, heavily carved oak. Their arms and legs and tall backs are transformed into a mass of vine leaves, barley-sugar twists and Gothic inscriptions from the Lutheran Bible. And then there are three new consumer items that cause excitement. There's a fridge called Frigidaire, and a small brand-new upright piano for their mum.

And there's a radiogram like a cupboard for their dad whose growing collection of classical-music records is stored in big flat boxes with file-reference numbers. But the best thing about the new radiogram is that it comes with a rogue demo record that's completely unlike the rest of their dad's collection and Dinah and Lisa love it to bits. This is because all of one side is taken up with a song called 'Little Piggy'. So they ask for it over and over, and they always sing along:

> Every little Piggy has a curly tail
> And nobody knows the reason why.

Dinah loves having all the trees to climb on the Butcher Estate. Some of them grow so close to the bungalow roofs that she can picnic on a variety of staff rooftops. She rigs up a pulley system with a large fire bucket to haul up her dolls. She and some of the boys even haul up Lisa, who doesn't like to climb but wants to join in. Then, when the monkeys come on raids to steal their bananas, all the children retreat in haste, leaving poor Lisa wailing on the roof that she's stuck. Dinah always has to run home on these occasions and call their mum.

'Ma!' she yells. 'Quick! Lisa's stuck!'

This becomes a very frequent refrain.

About the monkeys, there's a big divide on the Butcher Estate and it's usually immigrants versus native-born South Africans. The foreigners think the monkeys are exciting but the locals, including most of the students, think they're a pest and talk about them as if they were rats to be got rid of. Plans for monkey pogroms are hatched from time to time so that the Butcher Estate can be purged of them and stories are swapped about monkeys attacking women and children.

There are several folk remedies proposed for getting rid of the monkeys. One is to nail a dead monkey to a tree, which will drive all the others into exile. Another is to dip a live monkey in a bucket of whitewash and then let it go. The whitewashed monkey will then frighten off all the other monkeys, who will run away and set up house somewhere else. Dinah thinks the second idea is even more horrible than the first because she feels so sorry for the whitewashed monkey who will be left all alone after the others have gone, just like the lame boy on crutches in 'The Pied Piper of Hamelin' who got left out of the magic hill.

Angel-face starts school just one year ahead of Tiny-mite. It's the year in which she turns seven. The school is called Berea Road Government School for Girls. She wears a grass-green sleeveless pinafore dress over a white blouse, and grass-green bouffant knickers to match, with a pocket on the knickers for her hanky. Every morning all the girls have to lay an ironed hanky on their desk before assembly and put their hands on the hanky to display clean fingernails. The dress and the knickers are made of regulation fabric called Tobralco, and Lisa has to wear white ankle socks with her black Knockabouts. She also has to have a leather satchel with two shoulder straps and a panama hat with a badge.

Angel-face isn't lucky with her reception-class teacher. On her first day she is herded into the assembly hall with seventy-five other new girls, all dressed in grass-green, and they are made to wait and wait. Eventually a pretty, smiley young teacher with auburn hair like Maureen O'Hara and a bias-cut skirt and cork-heeled sling-backs comes in and calls out lots of names. The lucky little girls line up one by one in front of her and are borne away to a classroom, while Lisa's half wait and wait some more. Lisa is caught short and piddles discreetly on to the lino, standing up. Some of it runs down her legs and into her socks, but most of it makes a puddle on the floor, from which she walks away. Eventually an old battleaxe comes in, with pale, watery eyes and with her hair done in sausages under one of those hair-nets made of human hair. She's called Miss MacLean. She gets the children to line up two by two, before tapping at Lisa's puddle with a billiard cue.

'And who is responsible for this?' she says, but Lisa doesn't own up.

Miss MacLean is a witch, and she victimises Lisa, who writes with her left hand and smudges a lot. When they graduate to dipping pens with G nibs, bad girls fill the inkwells with blotting paper so that, when you dip your pen in the inkwell, you get a midnight-blue jellyfish on the end of it. The jellyfish are used for ink fights.

One day a girl called Tilly Boston lobs a jellyfish which splatters on the wall, but Miss MacLean blames Lisa and demands that she

17

ask Mother for a picture in a frame to cover the blots. This is timed with the arrival of a batch of lithographs sent to Dinah's mum by her one-time boyfriend at the Berlin art school where she herself was a student a long time ago. But the girls' mother is determined that Miss MacLean is not getting one of those. So she cuts out a photograph of Swiss mountains from *Life* magazine and puts it in a frame. Miss MacLean is pleased with the picture and hangs it over the jellyfish mark on the classroom wall.

The only other picture is of King George VI, because Durban is terribly royalist. Everybody knows that the English are best and Lisa learns to sing 'Rose of England thou shalt fade not here' and 'There'll always be an England down every country lane'. She also learns a hymn about not letting her sword sleep in her hand until she's built Jerusalem on England's green and pleasant land. Dinah is already longing to be English, although she hasn't even started school yet. Tilly Boston is huge and scary because she's much older than everyone else in the class. She's been kept down two years running because she can't pass the Class One end-of-year exams.

Lisa, having learnt to write her letters, writes lots of letters at home. Then she teaches Dinah, and every afternoon they busy themselves writing letters to their mother. The letters are always the same, because Lisa has misunderstood the purpose of letters. She says that, after you've written the address and the date at the top right-hand corner, in a neat slope, and after you've written the salutation, what you do is you copy out sentences from the Beacon Readers. When you've copied out as much as you want to, you write, 'From your loving friend' and you put your name at the bottom. Then you draw pictures in the margins. After that, you make an envelope out of a sheet of paper which you stick with Gloy and you draw a stamp in the corner with a smiley king face on it.

One day, towards the end of her first year, Lisa has learnt to do invitations as well, so they write out lots and lots of invitations for people to come to tea the next afternoon, and post them through all the neighbours' doors. It takes them all day to make the invitations and the envelopes. They draw flowers on all the envelopes. Everybody comes to tea. There's Paul and Alice Carter from Manchester with their three boys, and the Notcutts and their sons, Simon and Martin, and John and Dornacilla Peck from Canada who have a

DIY built-in wonder-kitchen in their bungalow because John is a handyman and Dornacilla can make Baked Alaska. There's Dr Garjinsky from Poland and Dr Leberman from Germany, and Ken and Jean Hill, and Peter Bullen in his stripy blazer, and Professor Raymond Sands from Nottingham via Sweden, and Wendy Jones with her pregnant Welsh mum and her little brother Owen in baggy rompers. And there's Mrs Taylor the Estate housekeeper who says she's Swiss when she's really German, because that way people don't refuse to give her a job – and Mrs Taylor needs a job because nobody has ever clapped eyes on Mr Taylor.

The girls' mother has nothing in the house to feed anyone, except for half a packet of plain biscuits and a pound of Five Roses tea, but all the visitors sit on the grass and chat while the girls' mum tries to hide her embarrassment and sends Lisa flying out to the Overport grocer's shop. Lisa comes back with milk and Romany Creams and two big chocolate Swiss rolls.

At the Overport shops there are two grocers, but their mum always makes them go to the same one because she once saw a cockroach in the other one. On the way to the shops you nearly always pass Ralph who lives in one of the big houses along Ridge Road. Ralph used to go to the daffy school. Now he's got too big, but he's still a member of the local Scout Cubs, so that when they have processions Ralph marches along at the back in full regalia, swinging his long arms, even though he's two heads taller than all the other Cubs in the pack, who, year by year, move upward and onward to become proper Scouts.

By the time Dinah starts school she is weedier and more asthmatic than ever, and so is her mum. It's Dinah's infant asthma that first triggered her mother's asthma because she was trying so hard to carry her tiny baby's burden instead. Now she finds the humid Durban climate doesn't suit her. She's lost some of her bloom and she's got as thin as a stick. Her pretty blonde hair has gone a bit matt from ill-health and also from all the obligatory post-war perms. These are hit-and-miss affairs and sometimes Dinah's mum comes back from the hairdresser in tears, with the ends of her hair all burnt and yellow. Sometimes she tries to perm her own hair with a kit called a Toni, that has two bottles of stinky ammonia solution and a re-usable bag of little plastic shapes like cartoon dog bones. Dinah is very frail and catches everything. Then, whatever it is, it always turns to bronchitis. Ill-health makes a bond between them. For her mother, Dinah is always Poor Little Dee, an endearment which is accompanied by anxious looks and the wringing of hands.

'I am so worried about you,' she says.

Dinah learns to love all her mum's smothering concern and special treatment. She hates the feeling of waking up in the night not able to breathe, but she reaches out for the pills on her bedside table: one tiny Ephedrine tablet and half a Luminal. The Ephedrine dilates her bronchial tubes but leaves her heart banging violently against her ribs. The Luminal is a tranquilliser to stop the palpitations. What she likes is to be tucked up in bed with her mum on days when she can't go to school – that's once they've both stopped struggling for breath. Sometimes they have bronchitis at the same time and they spend days and days together in bed. It's the beds that are helping to give them asthma, of course, because the undiscovered housedust mite is rampant in Dinah's mum's ancient German pillows and feather beds. Microscopic creepy-crawlies are having parties in the Kaiser's bedlinen – because Dinah's maternal grandmother was in at the bidding when Kaiser Wilhelm's household items were auctioned off at the beginning of the Weimar Republic. For some reason that has never been explained to Dinah her mum's family – though they brought precious little out of Germany except for money that got impounded and jewellery that got stolen – still had the Kaiser's bedlinen when they sailed into Table Bay, the Kaiser's bedlinen and the two ornately carved Gieseke thrones.

Nobody knows about housedust mite when Dinah is a little girl. So asthmatics are thought to wheeze at night because that's dream time, Freudian time, unconscious time. If you're asthmatic, it's because you're daffy. It's all in your head. Dinah's dad doesn't get asthma. He's a physically superior specimen – that's except for his terrible three-day-long migraine headaches which leave him groaning feebly in a darkened room. Otherwise, he'll always take flights of stairs three treads at a time and he goes for vigorous day-long hikes in the Natal countryside at weekends, stamping in his sturdy boots to discourage the green mambas. But he still likes to contemplate the possibility of terminal illness. He does this with spirit at mealtimes while tucking into great quantities of bread and cheese, though he always keeps his slim, boyish physique.

'It's a shame to leave such a little scrap on the dish,' he'll say, about a quarter-pound of mortadella, or a wedge of Danish Blue. Then he'll proceed to his burial arrangements. 'No fuss; no bother,' he says. 'Just throw me on to the compost heap.'

'*Ach nein*, Tächenherz,' Dinah's mother says, because she gets easily upset. '*Ach nein. Nein, nein.*'

To correspond with her daffy, mouth-breathing image, Dinah develops a range of facial tics. She screws up her left eye and then her right. She does it alternately, twisting up her face in a grimace. This is partly because she's edgy, but mainly because she has one eye that's a lot more short-sighted than the other eye. She does close work with her left eye and distance with her right. Her dad doesn't believe in giving her glasses. He thinks they'll only make her eyes worse. Plus he can't help thinking that, compared with his own eyes, her eye deficiencies are chicken feed. Dinah's dad lived all his pre-school life in a beautiful cloud of unknowing, a swirl of light and dark tinged with pink and gold, until he went to school. Then, just as the teachers were about to write him off as subnormal, the school nurse came round and tested his eyes and gave him glasses.

Along with the housedust-mite feather beds are Dinah's mum's tasteful handwoven dust-impregnated bedspreads. She likes these because she is artistic. So is Dinah. She draws all the time and she draws quite well.

'Dinah is artistic,' her mum says, 'like me.'

Lisa is labelled practical. She is not artistic. She is tidier than Dinah and she likes to bake cakes. Plus she always keeps her eyes open. These respective characteristics are blown up into long-term personality traits. Lisa, says their mum, should be a reporter. She is always first with news. This is true. She knows that Mrs Spinks has had her baby. She knows the moment that Babs has broken her leg.

When they draw pictures together of houses and trees, Lisa's pictures are not as good as Dinah's. Their mum always likes Dinah's best. Lisa says that this is because Dinah is her favourite.

'Let's swap pictures,' she says. They take in the finished products to show their mother. 'Which one do you like best?' Lisa says.

She always makes their mum choose. Their mother points to Dinah's picture, which is currently in Lisa's hands. Lisa is furious. She throws down the picture and stamps off.

'You're the pet,' she says. 'She likes you best. That's because I'm adopted. I know I'm adopted.'

Sometimes Lisa, who is a good organiser, rallies the neighbourhood children into a gang. They stomp round and round the bungalow, banging on saucepans, while Dinah and her mum are having their lovey-dovey wheezy little rests together in bed.

'Dinah's the pet of the fam-er-ly,' they chant, over and over.

Being the pet disadvantages you with the other children. Dinah is aware of this, but it's a role she clings to, a role she can't give up. And it's true that they are both artistic, even though her mum is limited to expressing her talents in exclusively domestic contexts, so that Dinah remembers a birthday party when her mum made every child a ballerina table decoration with a filmy layered skirt made out of pastel tissue-paper. She remembers a farmyard birthday cake with a pen of marzipan pigs and a little coop of marzipan chickens.

Dinah's father is as fed up with all the sickbed bonding as Lisa is. He bangs about and swears in Dutch, especially at mealtimes when Dinah's mum gives her the special Poor Little Dee treatment. He and Lisa are both first-borns. They are both strong, forceful and assertive personalities. They identify with each other. Dinah and her mum are shrinking violets. Dinah is still a non-eater, and her mum strains her freshly squeezed orange juice through a fine sieve because Dinah whinges if it has 'bits' in it. Her dad thumps the table and makes everything jump.

'You're not straining that child's orange juice AGAIN!' he says. 'She'll come to a sticky end, you mark my words.'

But Dinah carries on whingeing. 'I'm not hungry for potatoes. I'm only hungry for gravy.'

At breakfast she eats one-sixth of a dry Weetabix biscuit, but only if she's allowed to glue each separated crumbly flake to a small slab of cold butter. Sometimes she'll eat nine raisins after having arranged them in a pattern on the cloth. One day, her dad is so incensed by it that he rips off the tablecloth. It makes the jugs and bowls crash to the floor along with Dinah's raisins.

'She'll end up on the gallows, that girl!' he says.

Mealtimes are often high drama.

But, in the street, when Lisa and Dinah are out together, they are united in sisterhood against adult busybodies who go in for personal remarks.

'All her strength is going into her hair,' they say.

They tend not to flatter Dinah by addressing her direct. They maintain a third-person mode, as if they were simply stage-whispering among themselves. But they make free contact with her skimpy blonde plaits, which tail off somewhere near her shoulder blades.

'She should get all her hair cut off,' they say.

The busybodies have just as much fun with Lisa, who was born with a malformed right arm. She has only one proper hand because the umbilical cord wound itself round the limb early on in the uterus and starved the hand of blood. The girls' mum attributes this misfortune to a big wave that knocked her over when she went swimming once while she was expecting. So Lisa's funny arm is all her fault. Lisa was born on mid-winter's day and handed to her mother at feed-times so effectively swaddled that she didn't discover the funny arm until the nurses told her about it two days later. But it helped that by then everyone in the hospital had been so charmed by Angel-face, who weighed eight pounds at birth and had a cloud of soft orange hair and a smooth creamy complexion.

'What happened to your arm, little girl?' say the busybodies. Something about Lisa's greater forcefulness makes them talk to her direct. 'Did a shark attack your arm?'

This is a favourite suggestion for a few months after killer sharks have made a sudden, unexpected appearance on one of Durban's beaches and they've ripped the arm off a child called Julia Painting. Then the shark nets are laid with a great fanfare and everyone feels safe again, except that you still have to watch out for the jellyfish and the currents. You always have to swim between the lollypop signs and the lifesavers are there all day, watching from their latticework tower, or practising manoeuvres with a rope. The lifesavers are all men, but they wear girls' bathers that come up over their chests and girls' bathing caps with the strap dangling. After the lifesavers have gone home, the evangelicals come and do clappie stuff on the beach.

I met Jesus at the crossroads
Where the two roads meet.
Satan too was standing there
And he said, 'Come this way,
'Lots and lots of pleasures
'I will give to you today . . .'

The beach is only for white evangelicals because blacks aren't
allowed on the beach except to sell popcorn and toffee apples. But
there are lots of black breakaway churches that do stuff alongside
inland rivers. Sometimes Dinah sees black people go off wearing
beautiful blue-and-silver robes, so that suddenly one of the gardeners on the Butcher Estate will pass the bungalow looking like
Sorastro. Plus all the black Methodist ladies have a special smart
uniform in red and black which they wear with white cotton hats.

Lisa and Dinah don't mind the busybodies all that much.

'Walk on my Born Arm side,' Lisa will say, when she spots the
approach of any potential busybody. 'Walk on my Born Arm side
so that the lady won't ask.'

And Dinah will skip to Lisa's right side to obscure the malformed
arm. Lisa calls her left upper limb her Born Arm, because she's
forever having to say, 'I was born like that. No it wasn't a shark. I
was born like that.'

Other than the Born Arm, there is never anything wrong with
Lisa, except that she has cuts under her ears. She has a sensitive
redhead's skin and gets a sort of athlete's foot where her earlobes
join her head. Then she won't let anyone wash them. She covers her
ears at bathtime and she shakes and screams.

'No!' she yells. 'I've got CUTS under my ears!'

So their mum has to swab her ears with Olive Oil BP before
anointing them with cream.

'Lisa is strong as an ox,' their mother says, employing her grasp
of English idiom in a manner not designed to improve the self-
image of a little girl who is over-large for her age, since Lisa is at
least a head taller than all of her classmates except for Tilly Boston
and she's quite solidly built.

'Big bones,' people say.

By eight Lisa is judged too big for the sleigh-ride through Santa's
grotto in Greenacre's department store, and has to walk around to

the exit to collect her present from Santa, just as Dinah comes helter-skeltering to conclusion in a cloud of fake snow and piped jingle bells. Lisa likes to eat chocolate sprinkles on bread and she spends all her pocket money on Crunchie bars, while Dinah is a miserly hoarder whose money all goes into a red tin money box whose contents she has to extract with a knife. They are Fattipuffs and Thinifers.

TWO

S CHOOL IS UNSPEAKABLE. Dinah arrives in floods of tears on
her first day. Parents are not allowed beyond the gate and,
since poor Lisa can't do anything with her, she starts to cry as well.
Some older girls come up to them to ask Lisa what's wrong.

'I'm crying because my sister's crying,' she says.

The big girls take pity on her and relieve Lisa of the burden.
They lead Dinah to the assembly hall where her teacher, as luck
will have it, is the auburn-haired Maureen O'Hara lookalike, with
lipstick and cork wedge-heeled shoes. Her name is Miss McNeil.

'But you're a big girl now,' she says nicely.

This brings on a crescendo of tears and snot.

'I want to be a small girl,' Dinah snivels with feeling.

Miss McNeil puts her in the left-hand half of one of those all-in-
one double desks with spaces for your things in the lift-up seat and
under the writing surface.

The girl next to her is called Delsia Dovey. All the girls have the
weirdest names. Shelmadir Sanderson, Damaris Livingstone, Trevlyn Noel Barham, Vinora Salvesen, Hyreath Carrick, Rayleen
Fisher. Rayleen explains to interested parties that her dad is called
Ray and her mum is called Eileen. Trevlyn's name is the same. Her
dad is Trevor and her mum is Lynnette. Phoebe van Jarsveldt has a
name that you'd think was pronounced 'Phobe' when you saw it
written down. Moira Davey has a dad who keeps the funeral
parlour near the railway station in town, which is next door to an
ironmonger's called C. Argo. Dinah always has to blink when she
passes the ironmonger's to make the full-stop go away, because she
knows that it should really say 'Cargo'. That's a proper word,
whereas 'C. Argo' doesn't make any sense. There is another shop

26

that sells furniture nearby called Chicks. It has three lovely cartoon chicken cut-outs on the first-floor balcony with a cut-out speech bubble. The chickens are telling people, 'It's C-H-E-E-P-E-R at Chicks.' You're meant to understand that the chickens are singing, because the words are arranged on five lines with a treble clef and some semi-quavers.

Miss McNeil gives them all really fat pencils and jotters. When the pencils go blunt, you sharpen them at the teacher's table in a sharpener clamped to the desk that looks like Dinah's mum's mincing machine. Some of the girls like using the pencil sharpener so much that they keep on sharpening their pencils until there's nothing left of them by the end of the day.

Delsia Dovey is a quiet girl, but after an hour she puts a finger to her lips and lifts the lid of her desk just slightly.

'Shhh!' she says to Dinah, to indicate a secret.

Inside Dinah can see a small white-bread sandwich wrapped in greaseproof paper. She doesn't know why this is a secret, but later on, at home, her mum explains that it's because the post-war food restrictions don't allow the milling of white flour. And, two months later, when the restriction is lifted, her mum buys a honey spoon with a long handle to celebrate and she gives them white bread and honey for their after-school tea.

There's a camphor tree in the school playground that Class One girls discover during morning break. They snap off little twigs and give them to each other to sniff. This is a lot of fun, but after the bell goes it's hygiene. Hygiene is a subject on the curriculum and it's very important because, not only is it polio time, but all sorts of germs are everywhere. Mobile X-ray units come to the school to show you photographs of your own chest. Paramedics give you serious talks so that you'll understand all the dangers. Lots of blacks have got TB and it's blacks who are washing your dishes. Blacks will be handling the food in your kitchen and blacks could be spitting into your sink. Vegetables must be soaked in a purply solution of permanganate of potash. This is especially important, because of the market gardeners being Indians. If you look at some of the older Indians you'll sometimes see a person whose face is pitted with smallpox scars. And when Lisa and Dinah go Saturday shopping in Durban's town centre, they will always see those legless black beggars who swing along on their hands. One day the girls are at the Overport shops when they see a man with no nose. The man is black, but the flesh around where his nostrils should be has gone a horrible, wet-fish white.

At school, as well as hygiene, there are special Health Education films for Africa that show giant flies with evil eyes being sick over giant slices of bread. The girls' bodies are depicted in these films as areas of ongoing civil war. Personified blood corpuscles, red and white, are slogging it out in your innards. There is never a birthday party without at least one child in callipers, and polio has carried off one of the new babies that used to bounce on the green in the university compound. Iron lung is a concept that everyone has grasped and some children at school wear cloves of garlic round their necks to ward off disease. This is long before anyone has thought about cooking with it.

The Health Education films are shown in the Durban Museum in town, which adjoins the City Hall. It's opposite the Royal Hotel and the Playhouse Cinema and, to get to the projection room, Class One has to walk in a grass-green crocodile through the library and through a room full of huge stuffed rhinos and elephants that also has illuminated niches like caves all around the walls showing 3D scenes from native life. The library is great because you can borrow five Bobbsey Twins books all at once and bring them back two weeks later. All the library books in Durban are bound with a special stippled leather and on the flyleaf, under the town crest, there's always a sticker that says, 'Readers making returns via a native servant must enclose all books in a wrapper.' If you're a black person, then you're not allowed to use the library.

On that first school morning, Dinah finds out, to her horror, that it's not Miss McNeil who takes them for hygiene. It's Miss Cowper, who is a large, ferocious old person with brutally cropped hair. Plus her neck is wider than her head. Her neck is dissected by a narrow gold chain which only serves to emphasise this anatomical oddity. Miss Cowper begins her lesson by extolling the virtues of porridge. She does this so extensively that it nearly uses up all the lesson, but finally she throws the subject open to the floor.

'Hands up all those girls who had porridge for breakfast,' she says.

Dinah observes a sea of eager hands that wave in the air all around her, including that of Delsia Dovey. In fact everyone's hand is up except Dinah's. It doesn't cross her mind that perhaps not everyone is being truthful and she trembles with fear when Miss Cowper's stern glance fixes on her.

'You, girl,' she says. 'WHAT did you have for breakfast?'

Instead of replying, Dinah starts to cry.

'WHAT is the matter?' Miss Cowper says.

Dinah's voice is a whisper. 'I didn't have porridge for breakfast,' she says.

She has to say it three times before Miss Cowper can hear her. By this time there are faintly audible titters behind her.

'WHAT did you have for breakfast?' the ogre says.

'Rice Krispies,' Dinah squeaks as she remembers the five grains of puffed rice she lined up on the breakfast table three hours earlier. Two for Snap, two for Crackle and only one for Pop.

Miss Cowper sighs impatiently. It's a sigh that's halfway to being a grunt. 'GO to the cloakroom and wash your face, you silly little girl,' she says.

Dinah goes off to the room with the row of little low wash-basins and miniature lavatories with no lids and fixed wooden seats. In one of them an unflushed turd is bobbing darkly. She is appalled by this and knows that she couldn't possibly drop a turd in a public lavatory. She and Lisa will even run home from a friend's house if ever they feel the call. Peeing is all right, if you're caught short, but it's difficult in public lavatories, because their mother makes them swathe the seats with ribbons of lav paper that always stick to your bum. Plus she tries to make the girls hover in the air above the bowl, which is difficult when your legs aren't long enough for your feet to touch the ground.

Dinah remembers how once she and Lisa hesitated anxiously in Professor Eileen Krige's lavatory during a tea-time visit to the house, because they'd torn the paper at an angle of forty-five degrees from the lateral perforations. Professor Krige is the head of the anthropology department and she's a widow with two little boys. Lisa and Dinah don't have perforated lav paper at home, because their dad makes them have those interleaved sheets of scratchy Jeyes, like tracing paper, that come in a flat box. He has a theory about soft lavatory paper, but Dinah has never quite worked out what the theory is.

The school wash-basins are all furnished with shiny pink chunks of slimy carbolic soap that look like sections of human lung. Dinah sloshes water on her face and dries it on a soggy roller towel that seems anything but hygienic. Then she returns, cowed, to Miss Cowper's lesson. She coincides with the return of Miss McNeil, and another sea of waving hands.

'Miss McNeil, Miss McNeil,' the girls say. Everyone is eager to be first with the news. 'Miss Cowper called Dinah a silly little girl.'

Miss McNeil has the kindest smile. 'I expect we're all a bit silly,' she says.

At big break Dinah discovers all sorts of things she's never heard of before, but she tries to pretend that she has. The girls of Class One have taken their lunch-boxes into the playground and they sit in a ring on the grass under a lychee tree that drops its pink armour-plated fruits, like small hard-boiled eggs. She learns about comics, because some of the girls have been to afternoon children's cinema at the Playhouse in town and they talk about what comics they've swapped for which, in the foyer before the show.

And they talk about a radio show called *Mister Walker Wants to Play* where people phone in and ask Mister Walker to play their favourite pop music. Mister Walker will ask the callers what their hobbies are and whether they'd like to send a message to anyone over the radio before their music is played.

So the caller will say, 'My hobbies is picot-edging and crochet, Mister Walker, and I'd just like to say hello to my Auntie Ida and all the kids – hello there and keep smiling through – and for my record I'd like "Deep in My Heart" by Bing Crosby – *thank* you, Mister Walker.'

Mister Walker is Australian, but he puts on an American accent for the show. Dinah has never heard commercial radio, or seen a comic, and the only film she's been to see is *Nanook of the North* at the Roxy bio-café where she went with her dad. At the bio-café they show the same film over and over all day, so you can come and go any time. Plus you get a cup of tea or a mug of lemonade included in the price of your ticket.

Then Dinah learns about natives and koelies.

'Would you rather have a native girl or a koelie to make your sandwiches?' a little girl asks.

Dinah doesn't know what the girl is talking about, because she's never heard a black person called a native girl before, and she's never heard of a koelie. A koelie is an Indian and there are lots of Indians in Durban. Dinah's family don't yet have a maid and it's her dad who has made her sandwiches. He does lots of the cooking and domestic work, especially since her mum has got so frail. Dinah has salami and gherkin in her sandwiches with home-made mayonnaise and some fresh orange juice in a washed-out Dettol bottle. The others all have Edam or purple jam. Not melon-and-ginger jam, because that's just for the native girl. Ughh! And the native girl always has her own special tin plate and mug. Every child has a story about how one day their mother went out and came back home to find that the native girl was drinking out of one of the family's china teacups. Ughh! The native girl always gets the sack if she's caught and it serves her right. Because if you give them an inch they take a mile. That's what natives are like.

Native girl or koelie? The question is taking quite a while to reach Dinah because of her position in the circle, so she is able to suss that everyone would prefer a native girl to make her sandwiches rather than a koelie.

'I'd like a native girl to make my sandwiches,' Dinah says.

Koelies are inherently more threatening than natives. Koelies are a plague in our midst. The girls talk about koelies just as if they were like cockroaches. Squash them and they're yellow inside. Natives are all right. They're just more stupid, but you can train them to be more hygienic. Everyone has a story about what thick skulls natives have. Everyone, except Dinah, has actually *seen* a bus driver knock down a native and drive right over his head. Afterwards the native always just gets up and walks away.

In history nice Mrs Hale explains that we have Indian immigrants in Natal to work on the sugar plantations because a native's idea of hard work is to sit under a tree with his hat over his eyes. And, one Wednesday, when it's the day to bring in extra sandwiches for the poor children in the native location, the headmistress holds up two huge doorstep sandwiches from the charity basket and asks which girl has brought them. Then, when Hilary Barber puts her hand up, Dinah thinks that she's going to get into trouble for bringing such horrible wedges of bread with a scrape of jam and no butter.

'Look at Hilary's sandwiches, girls,' says the head. 'These are the sort of sandwiches that a native likes.'

She doesn't tell the girls what Indians like because we don't bring sandwiches for them. Ughh!

Hilary's dad is a lawyer and one day, in class, when the teacher says does anyone know what a lawyer does, Hilary puts up her hand.

'My dad's a lawyer,' she says.

'And what does he do?' says the teacher.

'He does lawyer work,' Hilary says.

Dinah's dad plays tennis on Sunday mornings with an Indian lawyer called Veejay Pillay. Dinah is terrified that someone at school will find this out.

'Your dad plays tennis with koelies. Ughh!'

Dinah's mum is a bit exercised about Mr Pillay as well. They quarrel about it at home. Their mum isn't against Mr Pillay but she thinks their dad shouldn't be sticking his neck out. Lisa and Dinah copy their dad and laugh at their mum for being such a coward, but Dinah's mum is right in thinking politics can get scary. She's the only one in the family who has seen Hitler with her own eyes. And as a child after the First World War, she can remember seeing a Communist demonstration being broken up on her way home from school. She saw Rosa Luxemburg address a crowd in Berlin, but the police came and banged people on the head with truncheons and threw them into police cars. Dinah's mum saw blood spurt from a man's nose when a policeman banged him on the head. So she knows that if you're a Communist then someone will bang you on the head and make blood spurt out of your nose.

She knows that where politics is concerned you should keep your head down – and sometimes quite literally. She can remember the time when her own father quickly pushed her brother Otto's head down on the balcony that overlooked their Berlin street. Her brother had stuck his hand out and called out '*Heil Hitler!*' in a piercing joke voice when a troop of Nazis went by, all marching in step. Her father saw one of the officers look up and scan the balconies, but by that time Otto wasn't visible because he was on the floor. All the same, when Alan Paton comes to tea one day Dinah's mum brings out one of the Kaiser's damask tablecloths. This is because, although he's political, he's written a book that has made him famous in America. It's called *Cry the Beloved Country* and it's going to be made into a film.

Dinah's dad goes on playing tennis with Veejay Pillay, and one day the whole family is invited to a Hindu wedding. This requires them to cross the great divide into an area of distinct otherness where Indians live. The roads have more potholes and there are more banana trees. They descend from the ridge of the Berea into the valley behind. Indians must not live or work or have their shops in our parts of town, although, for the time being, they are cheek by jowl. Whites have the cooler ridges and Indians have the muggier valleys that the mosquitoes like best. Dinah's dad says these geographical demarcations are thanks to General Smuts, our leader. Where Indians live, or have lived, can always be charted by the density of the mango trees, lychee trees and avocado trees they planted. And later, as people are more rigorously moved from one area after another, as the system moves from imperial-racist to criminal lunatic, the trees become a sort of memorial to them, a sort of trail, like Hansel and Gretel's stones.

The wedding takes place in what Dinah's classmates call a koelie temple, though she doesn't tell them about the wedding and, anyway, a koelie temple is sufficiently remote from her classmates' experience to mean that any reference they might make is exclusively metaphorical. It means something gaudy and trashy. So a girl will say, 'She was all dressed up like a koelie temple,' if the person's clothes were too shimmery and brash. The koelie temple is amazingly gaudy. So are the saris and the dresses of the little Indian girls. They are all made of purple and shocking pink and saffron-coloured silk with an overlay of scratchy lace and lots of sparkly trim and silver braid. The bride and groom, lavishly garlanded, sit for what seems like all day in a sort of bower at the altar end of the temple while the guests are served food on banana leaves. The banana leaves are their plates. Dinah is amazed by the temple's ornate interior because she has never been in a Catholic church – or in any church – and has had no contact with the baroque. All the churches she passes on her way home from school are Presbyterian or Methodist. They are all built of red brick, except for the one that has a sort of peanut-brittle pebbledash. The newer ones look like petrol stations or like giant 1940s gramophone cabinets. Some of the Dutch Reformed churches that she's seen in newspaper pictures look quite a lot like grain silos. Dinah's father is against religion but, once a week, on Sunday mornings, she hears the tail-end of the Dutch Reformed Church service in Afrikaans, because it comes just before a classical music programme that her dad always listens to.

The church service frequently overruns its time, and this is because the dominie likes to pray and sermonise for ever. He intones his words in a slowed-up, stretched-out monotone, as if he were trying to make each one last as long as possible. This drives Dinah's dad into a frenzy. He swats the radio with a rolled-up newspaper as he waits for whatever Haydn or Palestrina is being promised in the weekly radio guide, and he rants at the dominie in fluent Afrikaans. Once the prayers are concluded it's time for the final hymn. This is nearly always a slowed-up version of one or other of the hymns that Dinah knows in English from her school assemblies. The Dutch Reformed hymn singing has a bullish, male-dominant sound and the hymns are sung strictly in unison. Harmonising is what natives do and who wants to be like them?

From almost every bus ride in Durban all through Dinah's early childhood, gangs of Zulu road builders, stripped to the waist and shining with sweat, are to be seen at work. They raise picks and lower them to unspoken rhythms and they sing so perfectly in exquisite harmonies as they do so that Dinah is transfixed. She doesn't know if they are prison gangs or ordinary day labourers, but there is always one white foreman to about twelve of the black men. The white man is also stripped to the waist and burnt lobster red. And he is always screaming at the men with such intense and apparently inexplicable ferocity that it makes him sound raving mad. Then one day there's just one black man and he's got a pneumatic drill. The gangs and the foremen are gone for ever and, after that, whenever Dinah asks, nobody can seem to remember that the road-gang songs ever happened.

Scripture happens after lunch, and it's taught by Mrs Garson, who looks just like a picture-book granny, with funny half-moon specs. Her hair is parted dead-centre, just like Rosema's, and she has a bun at the back which is made out of her own hair arranged around a doughnut. Mrs Garson wears her bosom hanging over the belt of her shirtwaister dress and her face is strangely matt with powder. Her eyebrows and eyelashes as well. She looks as though she must immerse her face in a bag of flour every morning and then blow hard. Mrs Garson is so religious that she has a biblical quotation for every occasion. So, if any girls are chattering as they are putting on their gym shoes, she'll write on the blackboard, 'Let all things be done decently and in order.' And then she'll write in brackets after it, 'II Corinthians, chapter 6, verse ix' – or whatever the reference is.

Mrs Garson runs the weekly optional bible class in the lunch-hour and she calls the gospels the Good News. She brings the Good News in Scripture as well and she has exciting visual aids. She's got a green baize board that she rolls down over the regular blackboard like a roller blind and a whole lot of shiny cut-out pictures that stick to the board. These are all the people in the Bible stories that she tells. Dinah has never heard about any of them before, so the shepherds and the wise men and the raising of Lazarus and Joseph with the many-coloured coat – well, it's all very Good News to her.

Mrs Garson teaches them how to say the Lord's Prayer with their eyes shut and their hands together. Dinah learns it off by heart that very day and she dashes home after school to show her parents. She longs for them to praise her for her new accomplishment. Dinah makes them wait outside the door of the bedroom that she shares with Lisa until she is in kneeling position beside her bed, with her eyes closed and her hands together. Then she calls out, 'Ready!' Her parents come in and she starts to recite.

'Ourfatherwhichartinheavenhallowedbethynamethy –'

She gets no further before her dad bursts out laughing. Dinah is mortified. It's probably one of the worst moments of her life. She hates him. She feels so bad that she wants to wither away. But she knows that what Mrs Garson says about the Good News is true – every word of it. Yet Mrs Garson has told all the same stories to Lisa for the last two years without them making any impact. Lisa is a natural materialist and the Good News never gets to her. Some-times the girls have religious arguments together at home.

'Well, if there is a God, why can't you see him?' Lisa says.

Dinah thinks of all sorts of reasons. 'He's hidden behind the clouds,' she says.

'Well, what if there aren't any clouds?' Lisa says.

'It's because he's so big he takes up the whole sky,' Dinah says. 'What you can see is just a little part of his blue cloak.'

Sometimes she takes the opposite line and argues against God's unimaginable largeness.

'Well, Lisa, you see,' she says. 'You can't see God because he's just like a teeny, tiny flea in the carpet.'

'But I *can* see a flea,' Lisa says. 'I'll bet you anything I can see a flea.'

Dinah's mother has spiritual leanings as well, but she's too timid to be assertive about them in front of the girls' dad, who has a much more forceful personality. For a while she goes off on Sundays to play the organ for morning service in the Congregational church in Aliwal Street, but even then Dinah's dad suspects this as a cover for her leanings. He interrogates her on theological matters whenever she comes home and, naturally, he always knows lots more than she does about the Trinity and the Virgin Birth and the House of David and the Sermon on the Mount, et cetera, so after a while she stops going because she doesn't like having arguments.

Dinah's mum always thinks that an argument is the same as a fight. She's not really a very talkie person, in spite of all the family stories. She likes reading books about plants and animals best, because plants and animals don't talk. She has a conservationist instinct long before it's in fashion and she gets very agitated about felled trees and whaling fleets. Whaling is an outrage to her and she passes on these feelings to the girls, so that the day Dinah's class gets taken on a school outing to visit the local whaling station it's a memorably horrible experience – especially as they get made to have their photograph taken standing on the body of a dead whale that's gone sort of phosphorescent. The whole class is in Wellington boots, standing on a lump of dead mammal. And the smell is making Dinah gag.

Otherwise, the only school outings Dinah remembers – that's other than the ones to see the Health Education films – are the one to the sugar refinery when the whole class is photographed standing on a mountain of white sugar, and the one to Durban Airport when they all stand on the wheelie staircase that's hooked on to the plane they've just been allowed to see inside of. Dinah's mum's favourite books, other than *The Kon-Tiki Expedition*, are those written by Albert Schweitzer and Laurens Van der Post. Both authors commune with Darkest Africa, but only one is any good at playing the organ.

One day, Dinah asks her mother about God when they are alone together.

'Of course there's a God,' says her mother, speaking in whispers. 'Of course there is. God is in the trees and in the flowers. He's everywhere. But please don't tell your father.'

36

So Dinah and her mum have a God conspiracy. God is a secret for them to share. Dinah loves it that they have a secret. It makes her feel even closer to her mum – just like when they go into town together and have tea in Anstey's Tearoom, but they never tell about it back home.

'I fiddle a bit on ze greens,' her mum says.

Ta is very good at sums and he likes to keep tabs on the household outgoings. He's very good at everything. This is because his own father was the opposite. Ta's dad was a tall, swashbuckling, brainy rebel who ran away from a strict Calvinist home in Utrecht and married the daughter of a family of one-time diamond cutters in Amsterdam. The diamond cutters were pale, auburn-haired Sephardic Jews and most of them, by then, were unemployed and on the skids. The daughter worked as a shop assistant: a tiny, dainty red-head. Having no qualifications, and having got three boys upon her in quick succession, the Brainy Rebel then spent the next two decades drudging as a teacher for unskilled wages in a slum school in The Hague.

Since the university students in Durban are always saying that Dinah's dad is a brilliant teacher, the Brainy Rebel was probably the same, except that he had no option but to teach children with knuckle dusters whose dads were on and off in jail. But he gambled away his wages on the horses and, being a gregarious type, lent money whenever he had it to needy half-acquaintances. This meant that Dinah's dad's childhood was a succession of humiliating events like having the furniture dragged out on to the street by creditors, or like being sent out by his mother to borrow cups of rice from neighbours when the food cupboard was empty. This is the second of his family stories. And it was the same need for ready cash that is responsible for the third. It caused a visit one day from a rough giant in cracked boots who came to take away Dinah's dad's pet rabbit. With a fist as big as a cabbage, the rough giant crammed the pet rabbit into a grimy sack that was already full of other people's rabbits.

'He'll be going to the farm, sonny,' said the giant, leering toothlessly at Dinah's dad.

Then he winked at Ta's mother and gave her a coin. After that he tied up the sack and left. Tramp, tramp, tramp.

By the time Dinah's dad was thirteen and had won his place in the gymnasium, his own father's headmaster called him in.

'You're a bright boy, aren't you?' he said. 'You've got your head screwed on? From now on I'm paying your dad's wages to you. You give him his beer and cigarette money, OK? And you dole out the rest of it, day by day, to your mother. Do you understand? Day by day.'

Dinah's dad understood perfectly. It was a system that worked until Ta left home, and after that his dad disappeared in the Dutch Resistance throughout the Occupation. Missing Presumed Dead. This is his fourth family story. Then, one day, Dinah's dad gets a black-edged telegram while they're all having breakfast in Durban. It's from an elderly heiress whom the Brainy Rebel had met in the Resistance. He'd been co-habiting with her ever since. But the Brainy Rebel had done his wife one huge favour. He'd caused her to lose her Jewish identity, so that, though the Gestapo came looking for him as a listed Communist, though they ripped up all her floorboards, though they carted off her sisters who died in Nazi concentration camps, she herself survived the war and now, without knowing any English, she sends Lisa and Dinah all their favourite English children's books.

Guided by the owner of her local bookshop in The Hague, she sends all the Flower Fairy books and all the Beatrix Potters. She sends *The Lord of the Rushie River* and *The Tale of Perez the Mouse*. She also sends Lisa and Dinah the most wonderful mouth-watering sweets: flat, dark-chocolate discs the size of half-crowns and covered in hundreds and thousands. They come in a blue-and-white oval tin with a Delft pattern and on the outside it says Drosdy. She sends some intensely sweet black-coffee bonbons textured like glacier mints in little twists of paper. These are called *Raademaker's Eenichste Echte Haagschse Hopjes*. The Hague's Only Authentic Little Jumps. Dinah loves the bonbons' names almost as much as their flavours.

The reason why Dinah's mum has to 'fiddle a bit on ze greens' when they go out to tea in Anstey's is that, because the girls' dad has been keeping household accounts since he was thirteen, he's very good at it. He issues Dinah's mum with a small notebook, and in it she has to write down every penny she spends. Then at the end of each week she and Dinah's dad sit down at the table and check over their incomings and outgoings. Dinah's mum's figures never add up right – she's always got too little money left over or too much. The girls' dad gets really cross about this and bangs on the table either way, even though Dinah's mum is delighted when she's got too much money left over. Lisa and Dinah cower in their bedroom during these sessions, which nearly always end with Dinah's mum in tears.

Another two things that often end with Dinah's mum in tears are the songs at the piano, or when she buys herself a new dress. They'll do romantic love songs together for hours, not only those from the Accademia di Santa Cecilia, but Schubert *Lieder* and Schumann. Dinah's mum plays the accompaniments and her dad sings in his nice tenor voice. They go through all the song cycles and everyone who hears them thinks they sound great, but Ta will suddenly stop. She's getting the timing all wrong again, he says. It makes him so angry that he'll start yelling. Usually he yells in German which is their predominant medium of exchange.

'Can't you SEE, *Popchen*, it goes "ta-TA ta ta ta ta?"' he says. 'You're playing "TA ta ta taa TA"!'

About the dresses, he'll always say that what she's bought is not only wrong, but so way-out wrong that it makes him despair of the human race. Sometimes he'll slap his forehead with the palm of his hand because his sense of despair is so intense. One dress Dinah remembers is made of lovely yellow linen and it has a full, swirly skirt with a sort of apron across the front that is swept up to one side and caught in a knot, so that the effect is asymmetrical. The swirly apron drives Ta into a frenzy. He cannot credit his own wife's bone-headed stupidity that she could have come home with such a thing. So she takes it back next day and changes it for something else.

He never minds about Lisa and Dinah's dresses, so their mum can express her creativity through her daughters. She designs little numbers for the girls which get made up for them by Mrs van der Walt. Mrs van der Walt is a parrot-voiced Afrikaner woman who lives in a poky flat off Umbilo Road where the flour mills are and to get to her you have to go on the bus and then climb a flight of scary concrete stairs that are stuck to the outside of the building. Mrs van der Walt talks with a cigarette in her mouth and she likes to wear her slippers all day with the backs trodden down. She pokes the girls in the ribs and calls them lovey in loud parroty squawks.

39

Their dresses are usually the same, only where Dinah's have two short puff sleeves, their mum whispers to Mrs van der Walt to make Lisa's sleeves a little longer so that her Born Arm will be covered.

Mrs van der Walt nods and says, 'Ach shame!' about Lisa's arm and she directs an extra puff of ciggy smoke at Lisa in sympathy.

When she says shame, she doesn't mean 'It's a disgrace', because in the local idiom shame means a combination of 'What a pity' and 'Isn't she sweet?', so people will always say shame to babies in prams and to cute little puppy dogs. That's as well as to people with funny arms.

The reason Lisa and Dinah know about fleas in the carpet is because of Punch the dog. Punch sometimes has fleas and even ticks, but he's worth any degree of infestation because Punch is a dream dog who comes in answer to wishes the girls haven't dared to express. He arrives unexpectedly, in the year Dinah starts school, and it's all because of her dad's maths walks. The girls' dad is in the habit of going on walks with his colleague Peter Bullen. A big favourite with Lisa and Dinah, Peter is younger than their dad and he's, as yet, unmarried, which makes him extra generous with his time. He's a lanky blond who lets the girls tease him and sit on his knee and torture his hair into bunches and ribbons. Peter is always gracious about watching their amateur theatricals, for which the girls get into costume and announce each other in turn.

'Miss Lisa de Bondt will now sing "Blow The Wind Southerly".'

'Miss Dinah de Bondt will now recite "A Birdie with a Yellow Bill".'

'Miss Lisa de Bondt and Miss Dinah de Bondt will now dance "Beetles and Crickets".'

Peter appreciates that making the illustrated programmes for the theatricals has taken all afternoon and, unlike Ken Hill, their dad's other colleague, he will sit patiently in the centre of the row of dining chairs and study his programme respectfully. He never criticises their spelling – not like Ken Hill who says out loud, 'Beetles and *Cry*-kets?' in a sniffy sort of way, just because they've spelled it 'crikets' by mistake.

One day Peter and the girls' dad go walking. They do a lot of puzzling as they walk and they forget how far they have gone. They walk all along Musgrave Road, as far as Mitchell Park where the air is thick with screaming mynah birds descending on their appointed roosting tree. Only then do they realise that they've been followed by an eager little black dog – a Scottish terrier cross-bred with something a little more elongated – though in the years to come Lisa and Dinah will always say firmly, 'He's a pedigree,' whenever people ask. Peter and the girls' dad retrace their steps hoping that the dog will go home at some point, but he follows them all the way back to the Butcher Estate and walks in through the front door. He's wagging his tail expectantly. Lisa and Dinah are ecstatic. They hug him and roll around on the floor with him, while their dad says, 'Don't encourage him.' The dog has a drink of water out of a pie dish and he spends the night on a folded blanket on the kitchen floor. In the morning he's still there, wagging his tail and running his tongue along his muzzle most charmingly to suggest that it's time for some breakfast.

That afternoon the girls' dad and Peter Bullen retrace their steps once more. They do this for three days running, and each time the eager little dog just walks along with them all the way to Mitchell Park and all the way back again. Each time Dinah and Lisa are in a fever of anxiety, lest their dad should return without the dog. Finally, on day four, he does. The dog has heard a faint whistle from within a house on Musgrave Road. He's pricked up his ears and scurried off inside. Lisa and Dinah can't stop themselves from crying. They just know that he's meant to be their dog and now he's gone. They are still crying an hour later, when there's a familiar scratch at the front door, and there is the little black dog, panting and smiling and wagging his tail fit to burst.

Next day, Ta walks the dog back to the house on Musgrave Road, where he introduces himself to the occupants and tells his story. The occupants are an old retired doctor and his wife, who thank him and promise to keep the dog locked up for a few days until he changes his ways. The dog's name is Punch, but it should really be Houdini because, by the time Ta gets home, Punch has already made it back to the Butcher Estate before him. For two weeks the girls' dad goes back and forth; Punch is tied up and locked up, until the elderly couple finally admit defeat. Punch has always been very fond of children, they explain, and now that their own children have grown up and flown the nest, Punch has got itchy feet.

'You'd better keep him,' they say.

So they hug him goodbye and hurry inside.

The girls are celebrating. Punch is theirs. He loves them best in all the world. He's proved it. He's chosen them. He has singled them out from the multitude. For years Punch is the girls' best friend. They take him everywhere, though he's a demon for dog fights and can't leave anything in canine form alone. He aborts every picnic outing by needing stitches as a result of canine spats along the way – incidents always initiated by himself. And at the vet he lets it be known that he doesn't approve of residential care, by frequently escaping from the surgery to return home trailing bloodied bandages. Lisa and Dinah's mum always tries to stop the girls from taking Punch for walks, but they whine and plead so much that she relents.

'Don't let go of his lead,' she says, but, faced with Punch's invariable assaults on other dogs twice his size, this is what they always do. They drop the lead and run screaming home in panic.

'Ma-aa! Punch is *fighting*!'

Punch has no idea of his own limitations and one day he attacks a bull mastiff. The dog tries at first to retain his dignity by ignoring the little upstart, but, finally, when Punch's taunts, growls, nips and exhortations become too irritating, the bull mastiff simply leans down and takes Punch's left ear in his great jaws. And there Punch has to stay, with his head twisted sideways, trying all the while to balance on his stumpy little hind legs. He is whimpering pathetically, but the mastiff's jaws have locked and he can't or won't let go. Passers-by all have helpful suggestions.

'Twist his tail,' says one.

'Light a match under his nose,' says another.

Finally, a helpful householder comes out with a zinc bucket full of cold water, which he throws over the head of the bull mastiff. It works. The dog is so surprised that his jaws unlock and he lets go.

Punch is a sociable and greedy little dog, so the Butcher Estate suits him well. He joins in all the children's games and, in the evening, when a range of supper-time smells issues from all the stable-type kitchen doors that open on to the green, he lifts his nose in the air and makes his choice about which family to visit. Liver is a big favourite with Punch and, since this is a carnivorous era – an era of brisket and offal and innards; of tripe and trotters and stuffed hearts; an era before Anglo-Saxons have thought to fill red peppers with couscous, or to throw white wine over arborio rice – Punch is often in luck. Dinah even forgives him when a budgie goes missing and Punch is to be observed with blue feathers around his mouth. She writes a poem about the episode, with a mournful repeating refrain:

> Sing woe for Joey
> Eaten by a dog.

Dinah can't bring herself to name the dog in question.

At school, Sally is Dinah's best friend. This is because Sally says so. Sally is much bigger than Dinah and her dad is the butcher at the Overport shops. She has short hair because her mum won't let her grow it. Sally says that, because Dinah is her best friend, she can't play with anybody else. Class One spends most of its playtime rustling up numbers for games that never happen because the bell goes before they've had a chance to begin, but it's the preparation for the games that always looks the most fun. It begins with two girls linking arms and skipping through the playground.

'Who wants to play *Nau-augh-ty Babies*?' they chant.

Anyone wanting to play joins the line and the skipping chant continues. The line gets longer and longer, and the chorus gets louder and louder. Often the line gets so long that an intermediate game develops which involves sweeping into all the other smaller games and swallowing them up. Sometimes the chorus line stops in front of Dinah and someone will ask her directly to come and play, but Sally always puts out a hand across Dinah's chest.

'She's not playing with YOU,' she says, 'because she's MY friend.'

Dinah looks longingly at the chorus line because the skipping and the chanting look so jolly. And being Sally's friend means letting Sally undo her plaits every day and then do them up again. Dinah knows that Sally's efforts make her look silly because she always gets too much hair in one plait and not enough in the other. Plus she makes a zigzag parting all down the back. Sometimes one plait is a lot higher than the other. One will sprout from above her right ear while the other will be coming from the left side of her nape. And Sally tweaks while she's about it. Dinah tries to protest but Sally is always too forceful for her.

'I don't want you to do them,' Dinah whinges, 'because last time you did them all funny.'

'That's because I was small,' Sally says. 'I'm bigger now, so I know how to do them prop'ly.'

'You did them yesterday,' Dinah says, but Sally is already pulling out the regulation grass-green ribbons that match Dinah's regulation grass-green pinafore dress.

At lunch-break Sally does swapping.

'Swap your sandwiches for mine,' she says.

Sally guzzles all Dinah's blue cheese and celery on nobbly health bread and all her roast beef and piccalilli, even though piccalilli is one of the few things Dinah likes to eat, and she likes the bits of cauliflower best of all. Then Dinah goes home with her lunch-box full of Sally's sweating plum-jam sandwiches. The jam is always oozing through the bread in the humid heat, dyeing it purple. The sight of Sally's sandwiches drives Dinah's dad to distraction, because he thinks the brand-new health bread is such a delicious innovation and he buys it all the time. But it's not really meant for him. The health bread has recently been devised as a way of injecting some nutrients into the terrible carbohydrate diet of the black urban poor. But the black urban poor are refusing to buy it – they, who were once such successful pastoralists with a varied agriculture. The poor are now committed to a debased industrial diet of maize meal, white bread and Coke. That's along with the occasional lump of gristly flyblown meat. 'Boys' Meat Two Shillings. Dogs' Meat Two and Sixpence.' Dinah wishes that she could dump Sally's sandwiches in the litter bin. But, after school, Sally always walks her home. Then Dinah walks Sally home. Then Sally walks Dinah home and then it's time for supper.

Dinah can't remember ever actually entering Sally's house, but she knows Sally has a much older sister, because Sally tells horrid stories about her sister's monthly periods. She says it makes her sister go smelly and that at dinner time her dad will sniff the air and then he'll say, 'What's that nasty smell? It smells like bad meat in here.' Sally has a wild tale about how once the doctor had to come and chop her sister out of her sanitary pad because she'd got stuck to it. Dinah hasn't much of a clue what Sally is talking about, because her own mum is always so discreet about what she calls her visit – '*Mein Besuch*' as she says – though daffy blue-baby Bev, who goes to the open-air school, has a live-in auntie who launders her re-usable sanitary towels and pegs them up on the washing line complete with blood-brown stains. Dinah has always vaguely imagined that the stains are Bev's auntie's poo.

Bev's dad has a hobby which is to keep on building more and more stone walls in the garden and her big brother Barney's hobby is to smash milk bottles in the road and to knock out streetlights with stones. Bev's family has a dog that's fixed to a chain which runs along an iron bar that's riveted to one of the stone terraces, so that the dog spends all day running the length of the bar and barking itself into a frenzy. The chain makes Dinah feel crawly inside, but it's not as bad as the house she has to pass on her way home from school where there's a monkey in a collar fixed to a tree stump by a three-foot chain. All the monkey can do is jump from the ground on to the tree stump and back again. It's in the garden of one of those blue-collar white households where to border your flowerbeds with arched sections of rubber motor-car tyre counts as a style statement and to flick a bull-whip in the yard counts as a hobby. A bull-whip is called a sjambok and you can buy them from the vendors on the beachfront.

At the end of Dinah's first school year, Miss McNeil has a Christmas party for her class, and she gives them each a balloon out of a big multicoloured cellophane bag. Every balloon blows up to about ten inches in diameter and comes red, green, yellow, blue or orange – that's except for Dinah's. Her balloon is the only silver one in the bag, and it blows up to double the size. It doesn't occur to Dinah that this blessing may have been random. She knows that it's because Miss McNeil loves her best. She treasures the balloon. She becomes anthropomorphic about it. While some of the girls play wild games with their balloons and have popped them before the end of the afternoon, Dinah takes hers home and ties it to her bedpost and keeps it for months and months. Gradually it gets to look like a shrivelled grey kidney on a string. Then it loses its remaining air altogether. Dinah stashes the damp grey rag in a drawer with her knickers and vests. She loves Miss McNeil and she knows that Miss McNeil loves her. The end of Miss McNeil is the beginning of hell.

THREE

Mrs Vaughan-Jones takes Class Two. You have to watch out every second, because she's like one of those malicious firecrackers that keeps on jumping about all over the place. You never know where she's going to land or when the bang is going to come. Mrs Vaughan-Jones is like a drunkard because she's both belligerent and unpredictable. Her teacher's table is on a little platform and she stands on the platform making speeches in her own praise.

'I may be strict but I'm kind,' she says.

This is her favourite utterance and she always says it just before she moves off down the aisles to start hitting out to left and right with her metal-edged ruler. She goes raging up and down the aisles, cutting and slashing with the metal edge. But there's a teacher's pet in the class who never gets hit with the ruler. Then another thing she likes to do is make jeering remarks about some of the girls she's especially taken against, because that way she gets the rest of the class to copy her and pick on them as well.

Mrs Vaughan-Jones frequently hints at an out-of-hours connection with the teacher's pet's family.

'And how's Auntie May?' she'll say. 'Please give her my love, when you next see her, won't you, dear?' Or she'll say, '*Do* thank your mother for her hospitality, dear,' just as if she and the teacher's pet's mother are always meeting up over the weekends.

The teacher's pet has come up from Miss MacLean's Class One and Dinah tries to feel sorry for her because, like Lisa, she's had a year of Miss MacLean which is now being followed by a year of Mrs Vaughan-Jones. Yet it's hard to feel sorry for the teacher's pet, because she looks as if she's smirking all the time. Or it may be just that her face doesn't help because it's so much like a pudding. She always looks smug when she gets chosen to go outside and clap the chalk out of the blackboard dusters – which is all the time. Or when she's allowed to take messages round the school to the other teachers. And, even when everyone else in the class has got their hand up to answer a question, Mrs Vaughan-Jones always chooses her.

'Yes, dear. *You*, dear,' she says to the teacher's pet.

Then she says it's because the teacher's pet is sitting up the straightest. Or she'll say it's because the teacher's pet's hand isn't waving about in the air like everyone else's. Sometimes Mrs Vaughan-Jones will even change the answer to a question so that the teacher's pet can always be right.

Then suddenly one day the teacher's pet has left Dinah's school, halfway through the year. She's gone off to a new school that's been built nearer to where she lives and Mrs Vaughan-Jones is bereft. Now there's no one to be teacher's pet until Yolande Berry joins the class from Manchester. For months Mrs Vaughan-Jones tries to say Yolande is best at everything, just because she comes from England.

'Stop. Look, everybody,' she'll say. 'Look at Yolande.'

This always happens during eurhythmics and PT because Yolande's classwork is so bad that Mrs Vaughan-Jones doesn't want to draw attention to it.

The girls do eurhythmics in the hall. They wear short Greek tunics and pretend to be butterflies, or trees, or goblins when the music plays. Dinah's tunic is black, because it's Lisa's hand-on, but, from the beginning of that year, the school rule has changed about eurhythmics tunics, so they don't have to be black any more. If you get a new one it can be any shade of pastel so long as it's made of a material called Moygashel. Lisa's new tunic is lemon-yellow, but some girls have baby-pink, or hyacinth, or sky-blue. Yolande's tunic is crumpled jade with a beige, unwashed edge, because she keeps it in her gym-shoe bag and never takes it home.

Mrs Vaughan-Jones is always so cringey about her that it takes the rest of the class nearly four months to work out that Yolande is really just a slob. She always has greasy hair and her teeth have a greenish film. Plus she chews with her mouth open and she doesn't change her socks all that often. Enid Palmer sits next to her and one day she says right out that Yolande smells. She tells a joke that she's got off her dad who was demobbed in England after the war.

'Where's the best place to hide a ten-shilling note in England?' she says and the answer is, 'Under a bar of soap.'

This is because Enid's dad says the English only have a bath once a week. The girls giggle about this, but no one really believes it, because it's so hot and humid in Durban that you've got to have a bath every day. Sometimes twice. And people are always saying to each other, 'It's not the heat, it's the humidity.'

Mrs Vaughan-Jones calls Dinah the Cow's Tail instead of by her proper name so that very soon the whole class is doing it as well. She does this because Dinah is always last getting changed for PT. Sometimes, for variety, Mrs Vaughan-Jones calls Dinah the Snake because Dinah is so scared whenever she speaks to her that all Mrs Vaughan-Jones can hear are the voiceless sibilants at the ends of Dinah's words. Then she'll push her big scary moon face right into Dinah's face, so that Dinah can see her bluey wrinkled skin all speckled with liver spots. She'll go 'Hisssss!' so that she spatters Dinah's face with flecks of foamy spittle. Dinah dares not wipe it off until Mrs Vaughan-Jones isn't looking, but somehow she's always looking. It's as if she has those compound eyes, like flies have, that can see in all directions at once. Her eyes are a darting, washed-out blue with a sort of egg-yolk film over the outer corners.

When it's mental arithmetic you all have to stand at the front of the classroom while Mrs Vaughan-Jones shouts out, '– and thirty-two, take away seven, times five, add fourteen, take away six, times two and –' She says it all much too quickly and she goes on for ever. At first everyone is a bag of nerves, except for Janet Camperdown and Jennifer Wilson who always get the answers on time, but soon enough everyone realises you don't have to work anything out for yourself. You just use Janet and Jennifer as prompts. That's until Mrs Vaughan-Jones decides on the odd random pounce.

Mrs Vaughan-Jones has a rule about packed lunch. She's the only teacher in the school who makes her girls eat their lunches in the classroom and she won't let anyone out to play until their lunch-box is empty. This is torment for Dinah, who can't possibly finish her lunch and anyway she's so slow that even to get halfway through means that she's never got any playtime left. She can't dump her lunch on Sally because Sally doesn't sit near her and she can't tell her parents to give her less lunch because that way her mum might come up to the school and talk it over. She'll explain why she thinks Dinah shouldn't miss out on her playtime and why she thinks it's much nicer to eat your lunch under a tree with your friends.

Dinah knows that Mrs Vaughan-Jones hates her already, not only because she's asthmatic and prone to illness, but because of her sister Lisa. Dinah's mum once complained about Mrs Vaughan-Jones always whacking Lisa on her left hand, especially because Lisa's only got one proper hand. And she used to make Lisa come and sit at the teacher's table all day, instead of at her desk with the others. She used to tell Lisa that this was because she had to be always correcting her left-handed writing, but really it was so that she could whack Lisa every time she smudged, without even having to get up out of her chair. All this was just making Lisa smudge more than ever and she was missing not sitting with her friends. But after their mum had come up and complained about it, Mrs Vaughan-Jones just whacked Lisa more than ever. Plus she never stopped making sarcastic remarks about 'certain people's mothers' always coming up to complain. And especially about 'certain people's mothers' having a German accent. It teaches Dinah, right from day one, never to tell about anything that has happened to you at school.

Lisa has now moved on to nice Miss Vaizey's class, but Mrs Vaughan-Jones still makes sarcastic remarks to Dinah about her sister and her mother – even about her dad – so the whole class can hear. This is how Dinah knows she thinks their dad is a clever-dick, too big for his boots, and their mum is just a Hun foreigner who can't speak English properly. Plus both the girls are physically sub-standard. They should both be at the open-air school. Mrs Vaughan-Jones despises physical weakness and she has a special badge that she pins on whichever girl has a full attendance record for that term. The teacher's pet used to wear it all the time, but now it's Enid who wears it – and she just thinks it's a giggle.

Because of the packed-lunch policy, Dinah is always the last one left in the classroom, so she sits there chewing and gagging all on her own under Mrs Vaughan-Jones's beady eye. This is a form of slow torture which evidently gives Mrs Vaughan-Jones such a lot of pleasure that she doesn't mind not having any lunch-break herself.

She just watches Dinah all year. Sally is furious about it and she jumps up at the classroom window from time to time until Mrs Vaughan-Jones chases her away with one of those long poles you use for opening tall sash windows. Not only does Sally now have to eat her own lunch instead of Dinah's, but in the playground she hasn't got anyone to play with, because nobody else likes to play with her.

Anointing Top Girl is one of Mrs Vaughan-Jones's more gruesome rituals. The monthly tests mean that every four weeks the girls have to change where they sit. Every month Mrs Vaughan-Jones calls out all the results from Top Girl to Bottom Girl. She makes everyone empty their desks and then, when their name is called, they have to come and stand in line at the front of the class holding all their things. So if you're Top Girl that month, then your arms have nearly dropped off from holding all your books by the time she has finished berating the people who have come near the bottom. Finally she makes all the girls go to their new places. There is the A1 row, the A row, the B, C and D rows. Each row has eight girls. Top Girl wears a huge red rosette all that month, and she has to sit at the very top of the A1 row.

Each month Mrs Vaughan-Jones says the same thing to the A1 row. 'You girls are my A1 ice-cream girls,' she says.

Nobody knows why she says this, until Janet Camperdown's mum explains that there used to be a brand of ice-cream in Durban that was called A1 Ice-cream. Only you can't get it any more. It was something from before the war. Now all the ice-cream is called Rondi's and it's sold by black men bathed in sweat who ride around the streets ringing a bell. They have a big tricycle with a cold box on the front which is full of dry ice and you can choose between a Vanilla Wafer and an Eskimo Pie.

Dinah nearly always comes first, second or third in the monthly tests. She takes turns with Jennifer Wilson and Janet Camperdown. When she doesn't come in the first three, she's Bottom Girl. This happens when she's been off sick during the monthly tests. Then Mrs Vaughan-Jones gives her nought out of a hundred and makes her sit at the bottom of the D row all month, next to Patsy John, who is always last except for when it's Dinah.

Patsy is nice. She's popular because she's so small that the other

50

girls can baby her in the playground and carry her around. She's always really glad to have Dinah next to her because then she can be second to bottom instead of bottom. Patsy is a sweet, dark-eyed girl whose head is a slightly funny shape, but it's quite pleasing in a Kewpie-doll sort of way because her eyes are so big. Or maybe they just look very big, because her head is quite small. Later on, when they're having medical examinations, the school nurse writes 'foetal alcohol syndrome' on Patsy's form. Dinah knows this because she's lined up behind Patsy in her vest and pants and she's quite good at reading upside-down. They are in a little group of sub-standard specimens that have been drawn off for special category, open-air-school consideration.

The other girls in the D row are Marion and Penny-Lou Headley, who are identical twins with sticky-out teeth who behave as if they were sharing one brain between the two of them, which tends to slow them up if they have to answer questions or work on their own. And there's Sandra Gibson, who has sores on her legs and sometimes stays away when it rains because she has only one pair of shoes; and then there's squinty Melanie, who gets into trouble all the time because her mum keeps making her have home perms when it's against the school rules and also because she's had her ears pierced. There's Aletta Engelbrecht, whose dad drives a crane in the docks, and there's a girl called Joyce van Tonder who always has a phlegmy cough. Her posture is all hunched up, because her spine is too curved, and she's got such hairy legs that it's hard not to keep on staring at them. The D row children are all really poor. They are the children of poor whites. That's except for Aletta Engelbrecht, who is obviously not white. She is a glaring example of racial misclassification.

Aletta is a pale-brown, mixed-race Afro child who ought to be classified as Coloured. She has black ringlets done in cute bunches and small dazzle-white teeth and high cheekbones. Aletta has a fantastic body like a dancer or an acrobat. She is one of those unusual children who always looks squeaky clean, trim and grace-ful – but these things count for nothing, because whenever the other girls gang up on her they say that she's a 'chut'. This is a word Dinah's classmates use for a Coloured person.

Aletta will defend herself as best she can. 'My skin's only this colour because my mother used to bath me in olive oil when I was a baby,' she says, but nobody believes her.

And Dinah knows that it can't be true, because her own skin is always deathly pale in spite of all the olive-oil baths. She hates it when Aletta is being taunted. She hates it especially because she always just pretends that nothing is happening.

Dinah's classmates say that Coloureds are worse than blacks, because God never meant the races to mix, so Coloureds are a mistake. It's like mixing blood and water. That's what people often say. And Dinah's dad, if he hears this said, likes to quip that if God hadn't intended the races to mix, he would have created their offspring sterile. 'Like the mule,' he says. But people always just gawp at him, because what have mules got to do with it when you're having a moan about chuts? Anyway, everyone knows that maths bods are all nutty professors who talk to lamp-posts by mistake and forget to take off their pyjama trousers when they go out of the house.

Aletta is probably the girl in the class who dislikes natives most and she holds her nose just that much longer than the other girls when a Zulu gardener passes the classroom window. She does this so that everyone will know that she thinks that natives smell. But everyone already knows that natives smell, so they aren't at all impressed.

Once, when one of the chattier teachers is on playground duty, she tells the girls all about an exciting night-time break-in she and her husband have had.

'I opened my eyes and I said to my husband, "I can smell boy!"' she says.

This was because a native boy had got in through the french windows, but then his boy-smell woke her up and so he ran away.

By the end of Class Two, once the Afrikaner Nationalists have won the 1948 general election and they've begun to tighten up the race laws, suddenly Aletta Engelbrecht isn't there any more. Nobody says anything about it. It's as if she was never there in the first place, except that she's in the front row of the Class Two group photograph, smiling broadly and showing her pearl-white teeth. Sometimes, to tell if you're white or not, a special government committee will put a pencil in your hair and, if it falls out, then you're classified as a white person. Also, you can tell if somebody's not really white, because they don't have half-moons at the base of their fingernails. Everyone at school says this, but Dinah knows that it isn't true, because Lucy's got beautiful pale half-moons and she comes a dark-brown.

Lucy is the domestic servant. Dinah's dad has always been adamant that he doesn't want a servant, but it's hard to keep on resisting when unemployed Zulus go door to door asking for work all the time. Or sometimes they knock on the door wanting to sell you old-fashioned witches' brooms they've made, or wooden verandah chairs and a table that are all laced together so that they can carry a whole set on their heads. Lucy comes to the door one day in the company of her father, who is a wizened old man, though Lucy is a blooming, plump, busty girl, no older than fourteen. She wears a navy-serge school gymslip and girdle over a snowy-white school shirt and she has bare feet. Her father has a head ring and a gnarled walking stick and those elongated earflaps where plate-like insertions have been removed. Lucy has Zulu initiation marks on her face – inch-long vertical incisions in her cheeks, which only serve to enhance her prettiness. And Lucy is very pretty. Most Zulus are fine to look at, either thanks to their benign DNA, or because they still bear the signs of having been, within living memory, a people in control of their own lives. Lots of them don't yet have that look of centuries of settler depredation.

Both Lucy and her father speak almost no English, but manage to indicate that Lucy needs placing as a domestic worker. Once one of the Butcher Estate gardeners has been called in to interpret, Lucy's dad embarks on a speech extolling his daughter's industry and obedience. If she is not obedient, then Dinah's dad must beat her with a stick, the old man says – and he shakes his walking stick to underline this point. Meanwhile Dinah's dad is looking extra myopic and uncomfortably egalitarian. All the same, Lucy stays. Her father goes.

There is a barrack-like room for her in the servants' quarters which requires a constant supply of candles and a Primus stove that blackens the walls, since there is no electricity supply for the servants. Even the white people's bungalows are on a somewhat rickety grid, so that Lisa and Dinah are accustomed to being plunged into darkness as the sound of their dad's newest 78 r.p.m. recording – Kathleen Ferrier doing Gluck's *Orfeo*, Elisabeth Schwarzkopf in *Der Rosenkavalier* – spirals strangely into silence.

Lucy is everyone's favourite. Dinah's mum, who tires easily, loves her, not only for her radiant smile and her sweet, bubbly nature, but for her amazing stamina. She polishes shoes. She polishes the red-tiled stoep. She never shows signs of exhaustion. She peels and chops. She's a big sister to the girls and, in the mornings, she gives weedy Dinah piggy-back rides all the way to the school gate. Or sometimes she'll hold Dinah's hand while carrying Dinah's school bag balanced on her head. Dinah loves the pale undersides of Lucy's long brown hands and asks her about them, but Lucy always just laughs. Zulus are forever laughing at things white people don't think are funny. It's sort of like a more dynamic way they have of smiling.

Lucy chases monkeys from the kitchen, stamping her feet and shouting '*Hamba!*' and making loud click noises with her tongue. She crushes cockroaches with her bare feet and thinks nothing of it. Enormous cockroaches are a feature of Durban life. They will appear suddenly from nowhere, waving their feelers and making bold eye contact. They come three inches long, dark-brown and armour-plated. They manage to live anywhere. They subsist on anything, including the plaster on the walls of people's houses. They appear, feelers first, from the waste pipes of sinks and bath-tubs and are more reviled than the flying ants that come in sudden swarms at nightfall, filling the air like snow in a blizzard.

And next morning the flying ants are no longer flying. They are writhing on the ground en masse. They have all shed their wings and become termites that can eat at high speed through the foundations of houses or through the roots of passion-fruit vines. They're so fast that you can see your plants actually withering as they munch. Piles of papery wings lie in the gutters and clog the storm drains. The storm drains have always fascinated Dinah, who is, in general, likely to take up challenges with regard to climbing and crawling. Because the rains come heavy and tropical in Durban, the gutters are deep and the pavements high, so the concrete ramps from pavement to street that cover the storm drains leave just enough room for a scrawny child to crawl through. Dinah can remember several times taking up dares to crawl on her belly through the triangular, eight-foot-long concrete tunnels created by these ramps which are open on the wide side to torrents of gushing water.

Every year Lucy goes home to what locals call the kraal. She goes home to Zululand and she returns with gifts for her employers. These are always one excessively scrawny dead chicken and a handful of oranges that come the size of golf balls. The girls' dad explains to them that the size bears witness to the over-use of over-populated land. But at school, Lisa and Dinah learn that the smallness of the oranges is because the Zulus cause soil erosion by refusing to engage in contour ploughing, much as we have tried to educate them in this matter. The eroded crevices are called dongas. Zulus have got a word for soil erosion but they haven't got a word for thank you. This is what white people say. 'There is no word for thank you in the Zulu language.' This is why the Zulus are never grateful.

In geography the girls are required to draw pictures of the erroneous way that Zulus plough: vertical furrows, running down the hill. Then, alongside, they draw pictures of proper ploughing, with the furrows going in concentric, horizontal rings around the hill. They do these with their Lakeland coloured pencils that come in a tin with a water-colour painting of Windermere on the lid. Dinah's mother will pressure-cook Lucy's chicken and then make a big pot of soup. She always refers to the chickens as 'ze zousand-year-old fowl', but only when Lucy isn't listening.

Then one day, five years on, there's a kerfuffle in the servants' quarters and Lucy is in floods of tears because her father has arranged a marriage and he has come to fetch her home. She weeps and clings to Lisa and Dinah, just as the girls are weeping and clinging to her. But as the old man has pointed out earlier, Lucy is an obedient girl. She soon succumbs and allows herself to be stripped of her housemaid's overalls and headscarf. Then she is elaborately prepared for marriage.

By the time the wedding party is ready to leave, Lucy is bare-breasted and has a tall hairstyle moulded with red mud, and lots of beads on her neck and wrists and ankles. Plus she's wearing a sort of sporran covered in beads, like a little apron over her crotch. Then she is encased in a blanket cloak for the third-class train ride home. Lucy's appearance ought not to be a shock to the girls, since the centre of Durban is still dotted with bare-breasted young Zulu women with mud-sculpted hair, moulded into shapes like the tall, exotic hats in Piero della Francesca paintings. They're adorned with elaborate beadwork and tinkly seed anklets. These are the country girls come to town to visit their menfolk who are working at jobs in town. But once Lucy is dressed in her bride's gear, Lisa and Dinah keep their distance – just as Lucy does from them. It's as if she isn't quite Lucy any more and they feel shy to reach out and touch her.

Then Lucy's gone and, though they long for her, they never see her again. After a while there's a new maid called Maria. She's very efficient and townie and she's very fluent in English. But poor efficient Maria has a permanent downside, because there's a violent drug-addicted boyfriend who comes by quite frequently at night and he attacks her with a knife. And once the screams in the small hours and the police raids get too much for everybody, including all the other servants, Maria is paid off with two months' wages and given a glowing reference so that she can start the doomed cycle all over again somewhere else. 'To Whom It May Concern.'

Lots of blacks smoke cannabis, which is locally called dagga. The papers are always full of pictures of police raids in rural Natal. Police anthropology maintains that dagga makes 'the natives' violent. But this is decades before white students have taken to smoking it as a means of invoking peace and love.

The reason why the Zulus whom Dinah sees in Durban are less townie than the indigenous people she remembers from Cape Town is not only because whites have settled in Natal much later. It's also because the Zulus are stronger. In the Cape, the Khoi have lost all their land before the end of the eighteenth century – by which time the settlers are bumping up against the Xhosa's land in the east. The Xhosa clans are thriving farmers and they've got some fabulous pastures but, on their own, the Dutch settlers aren't strong enough to grab it for themselves. So it's only when the British take the Cape that the Xhosa lose their land. The British have recently defeated Napoleon, so now they can whistle up any number of redcoats who haven't got very much to do. So the project is total onslaught and it continues for thirty-five years. In her school history, Dinah's forever having to learn about the eight Xhosa Wars but, always, in the history lessons, the wars are the Xhosa's own fault. Plus one of the wars has got something to do with somebody stealing an axe. A lot of the war stuff has got muddled in her mind with white people having to teach the Xhosa about wearing trousers and also about how they should start to build their houses square – because the Xhosa's houses are round.

The British officers in her history book's pictures all have that pretty, effeminate look that she's seen in oil portraits of Lord Nelson. They've got wide-spaced eyes and sucked-in cheeks and those wafty puffs of silver hair. But what they're saying is that they will not cease, 'so long as a single kaffir remains alive'. So the Xhosa get their land sold off as white-settler sheep farms. Plus their cattle and their social structures are screwed. And those Xhosa who are left alive have started to eat out of dustbins.

The Zulus have a different story because, by the time the British set up their little trading post in Durban, it's twenty years into the nineteenth century. And the Zulus have stopped being a group of clans because by then King Shaka has come along and has welded them into the Zulu nation with an effective military dimension. So, although they concede significant chunks of land, they don't become a serious target until the end of the century when the mines are rabid for more labour. Blacks with land are a thorn in the flesh of those wanting cheap migrant mine workers. Plus other black migrant mine workers will need to be moved across the Zulus' territory and that could pose a problem. So the British High Commissioner decides to stoke a war. He makes wild demands of Cetshwayo, the Zulu king, knowing that these can't be met. Cetshwayo's response is to keep things cool. He won't start a war with the British, he says, since he considers them his friends. But if they choose to start with him, then his armies will be ready. So the British march into Zululand, whereupon the unthinkable happens. Twenty thousand highly disciplined Zulus with assegais demolish the British forces at the Battle of Isandlwana.

After that, honour requires that the Zulus get defeated next time round, but the victory doesn't come particularly cheap and the memory of Isandlwana never quite goes away. So total onslaught is not an option. Instead the British abolish the Zulu monarchy and divide the kingdom into thirteen chiefdoms, saying that they are 'restoring' Zululand to its rightful, traditional structure. That is to say, to the structure it had before Shaka came along and spoilt it.

Cetshwayo is imprisoned in the Cape Town Castle, but, being an active letter writer, he finally secures a passage to London and a lunch date with Queen Victoria. He charms the queen, he charms fashionable London, especially the female contingent, because Cetshwayo is a tall black *Übermensch* and he's quite incredibly good-looking. From his six-month billet in Kensington he at last secures the right to go home, but within the year he's dead.

Nonetheless, for all their new, somewhat pseudo chiefs, plus a medley of punitive taxes, the Zulus, unlike the Xhosa, are never quite eating their own sandals. And, more than any other defeated group, they manage to hang on to something. They hang on to an idea of themselves. And, while this proves both a strength and a weakness, it accounts for Lucy's allure – that she carries around a sense of herself: a sense of being who she is.

All that year in Mrs Vaughan-Jones's class, Dinah is so miserable that her health goes steadily downhill. She faints in assembly three times and, each time, gets carted off to the sick room. She gets asthma so badly nearly every Sunday night that she can't go to school on Monday mornings. She develops four consecutive bouts of bronchitis. Once she gets a high fever that makes all the skin come off her hands and she stays in bed for so long that her parents buy her a Fairy Cycle as a lure to get her up. So Dinah gets up for just long enough to fall off the Fairy Cycle and rip open both her knees. Then she goes back to bed with two thick pus-y scabs that grow a kind of fur which is nice to pick at. After that, the Fairy Cycle becomes the property of the child commune. All the kids on the Butcher Estate learn how to ride it, except Dinah.

One Monday morning she is screaming with pain after a night of wheezing and she says she can't pee. Her abdomen is hard and distended. By the time the doctor comes and recommends immersion in a hot bath, it's too late for her to go to school. Oh bliss. In the bath, Dinah's sphincter muscles relax. Her pee flows copious and dark, dyeing the bath water amber.

Dinah is by now quite phobic about school and prays for lightning bolts, twisted ankles and asthma attacks. Anything. *Anything.* And there is something increasingly seductive about bed. She sits propped up in bed and sews throughout her days off school. Her mother buys her squares of felt. She sews a whole range of miniature three-dimensional animal toys, which she cuts out from patterns of her own design. She blanket-stitches the seams together with embroidery thread. The animals become family heirlooms and hang from the Christmas tree each year. There is a monkey and a giraffe, and a lion with an orange-wool mane. There's an elephant and a deer and a hare, and a sheepdog with a pink felt tongue hanging out of his open felt mouth. Dinah always remembers the satisfaction she got from working out how to make the sheepdog's open mouth. And she makes paper dolls to her own designs too, with wardrobes of paper clothes that hook on to the dolls' shoulders and hips with tabs.

She writes stories in little home-made books with lots of illustrations – books that are always tribute for her mother. *The Strange Little Dog Who Only Ate Tomatoes*. Then there's *The Kitten Who Had No Tail*. One day she starts writing her most ambitious story. It's about a mouse who saves an old Dutch sailing ship from capture by gnawing through the ropes that are binding it to a pirate ship. The mouse's name is a pun. He's called Hieronymous.

Sometimes she creeps out of bed to play with her big home-made doll's house. This is an ever-increasing collection of wooden margarine crates that her mother has painted for her. The doll's house is inhabited by pipe-cleaner people who've been sent by her grandmother in The Hague. Each time Dinah has a birthday, people on the Butcher Estate give her more and more items of doll's-house furniture – and kind Mrs Notcutt, who keeps a present cupboard for birthdays, has more than once supplied the pipe-cleaner people with whole suites. Whenever Dinah gets another set of furniture, then her mother has to paint another margarine crate and soon the doll's-house people are living in a fifteen-roomed mansion with a music room, three bathrooms, five reception rooms and a nursery. And while her parents – the Gieseke thrones excepted – incline towards post-war Swedish birchwood interiors, the pipe-cleaner people have a more traditional style. Their house is all mahogany and Chippendale and the grand piano has a red Chinese-y lacquer. Dinah also has a Dryads miniature weaving loom, eight inches by ten, which is just big enough for her to weave carpets for all the doll's-house rooms.

Sometimes her mother weaves the dolls a carpet too, since in her heart she longs for a proper weaving loom all for herself. Dinah's mother worked as a dress designer in Berlin before the war. She designed ball gowns for a small couture house until one day the head of house asked her to model the gowns herself.

'You have a fine figure, Marianne,' he said. 'You'd look beautiful in the clothes.'

At home, as far as her parents were concerned, this suggestion was tantamount to an assertion that their daughter had loose morals, and Dinah's mum was made to resign the job immediately and be a stay-at-home girl from then on: an old-fashioned young lady waiting for a suitable husband. Now she likes to make dresses for Dinah's dolls, but because she's so hopeless at the practicalities of sewing, Dinah has to match up all the seams herself.

Dinah's mum has some old books in which she once collected smoothed-out sheets of silver paper from chocolate wrappings. So the silver paper is fifteen years older than Dinah. Each sheet is different. Each has a period look. Some have star patterns and some have a sort of tumbling-block effect when she holds them up to the light. Dinah loves to play with them.

It's bliss to be alone in the house with her mother. Her only rival is the piano. Dinah's mother plays Scarlatti and Bach and Brahms all morning. She plays Haydn and Mozart and Chopin, which Dinah finds a trial. She calls out for drinks, but her mum can't hear her. Sometimes she whistles along so persistently that it makes her mother stop. There are days when nothing will stop her mother's piano playing except for a dramatic tropical thunderstorm, which drives them into each other's arms. One day Dinah and her mother are cowering in the tiny passage after a deafening crack of thunder, when a zigzag bolt of lightning runs down the opposite wall three feet from where they are standing. Dinah has no idea that the lightning could have killed them, though she always remembers the crackle. She remembers it as the day God sketched a lifesize gold Christmas tree on the passage wall just for the two of them. Not for anyone else.

Whenever Dinah returns to school after a patch of illness, Mrs Vaughan-Jones always prods and pinches her. She picks her brain about the details of the illnesses, without ever reading her parents' notes. When Dinah tries to answer, she gets mimicked and contradicted. By the end of the year Mrs Vaughan-Jones is making Dinah take her sick notes straight to the head who always colludes with the teachers. The open-air school is their joint favourite threat. It's a terrifying prospect for Dinah: an institution conceived by fresh-air fascists in which all the local dafties and cripples are lumped together. If you're at the open-air school, you have to go off every morning in a special white bus with writing on the side. And you have to do things like make wicker baskets all day long instead of doing proper work, even if you're brainy, because proper work might make you much too tired. Dinah knows that to be sent there would be the end of the world.

Then, one astonishing day, Mrs Vaughan-Jones Goes Too Far and Dinah, and all future generations, are saved. It's the final week of the school year, just coming up to Christmas and it's Toy Day. Dinah has been away with bronchitis just before Toy Day, but she knows, when she goes back, that it's the day on which you're allowed to bring a favourite toy to school. Because she knows better than to bring Rosema, with her darned nose and wool hair, she brings Felicity-Jane, a new doll that has plastic button-over shoes and can stand up all by herself. Felicity-Jane is a present from one of Dinah's dad's grateful students. He's knocked at the door the previous weekend with two identical dolls in cellophane boxes. The dolls are wearing silk and lace dresses very like those worn by the little Indian girls at the Hindu wedding. One doll is for Lisa and one for Dinah.

Although it's still coming-to-school time, Mrs Vaughan-Jones makes Dinah stand Felicity-Jane four-square in the open classroom doorway. Then she orders Dinah to come and stand at the teacher's table with her back to the door while she goes through her usual sadist's routine over the sick note.

'Was the sickness in your hair?' she says and she tugs Dinah's plaits. Next, she stamps on Dinah's feet. 'Was the sickness in your feet?' she says.

As she proceeds, the inevitable happens. Poor, squinty, permed Melanie dashes in, hoping not to be late, and she sends Felicity-Jane flying. The doll is not broken, but Mrs Vaughan-Jones decides to cut short her interrogation of Dinah in order to set about Melanie. She is beating Melanie about the head with the metal-edged ruler in time to her own rhythmic ranting.

'How-many-times-have-you-been-told-not-to-run-in-school?'

Then she starts telling her off for being careless with Dinah's new doll, which is worth 'such a lot of money'. It's all making Dinah feel terrible. Mrs Vaughan-Jones makes Melanie say sorry to Dinah out loud in front of the class. By this time Melanie is crying and so is Dinah.

Then, once both girls are snivelling and humiliated, Mrs Vaughan-Jones breaks into one of her scary, moon-faced smiles.

'But we've got a surprise for Dinah, haven't we, Class Two?' she says.

'Yesmrsvaughanjones,' the class chants in reply.

She plucks the large red Top Girl rosette from her teacher's drawer on the podium and pins it, for the last time, to Dinah's wheezy little concave chest. On this occasion, Dinah has managed to complete the monthly tests just before she got bronchitis, so someone else has had to move all her books from the bottom of the D row to the top of the A1 ice-cream row. Dinah is sent to her new place, but she's still so scared that someone will smash Felicity-Jane that she can't enjoy her elevation. This is because Mrs Vaughan-Jones has made her put the doll right back in the open doorway.

Just then a new girl comes in on a visit with both her parents. They are a trio of beautiful, small-boned Italian immigrants – part of the post-war immigration boom. Mamma, Papa and Bambina. Lots of Italians are coming to live here right now, because the men have been prisoners-of-war in South Africa and they've decided to return with their families. Claudia Tucci looks just like a child film star in a white muslin party dress and she wears her hair in ringlets tied with ribbons. Her mum wears red lipstick and peep-toe shoes and gloves and a white dress to match Claudia's only with a wide circular skirt, and a hat of white straw, like a plate with the crown cut away. Signor Tucci is wearing a smart black suit and very shiny black shoes. His hair is parted dead centre and he's got a nice little black moustache. None of them can speak a word of English. They skirt delicately round Felicity-Jane, looking at her with some surprise, and they approach the teacher's table, where Mrs Vaughan-Jones gabbles and spits at them, pushing her mad woman's moon face right into Claudia's face and giving her a poke in the ribs. Then she sees fit to take the family on a tour of the classroom. She leads them straight up to the top of the A1 row.

'This is Dinah,' she says, 'our Top Girl. Snivelling, as usual.'

Dinah knows that she looks hideous with her red swollen eyes and her red swollen nose and her asthmatic's black smudges around her eyes. She wishes the floor would swallow her up as the angelic trio beams down upon her.

None of the Tucci family understands a single word of what Mrs Vaughan-Jones is saying, but they can see that the Class Two Top Girl is not a happy little creature. Signora Tucci opens her white straw handbag and plucks out a little wrapped bonbon which she slips into the pocket of Dinah's hideous grass-green uniform. Signor Tucci mimes a little cheering-up routine, which involves persistent waves and winks, while Mrs Vaughan-Jones is talking. When they leave, Claudia goes ahead, doing skippety little dance steps down the aisle. Her feet are two dainty little mice.

Claudia Tucci never turns up at Dinah's school, but Dinah sees her, two years on, at the Durban Beach Baths. It's the inter-school junior swimming gala and, like Dinah, she isn't swimming. She's cheering on her team from the tiered stands that rise up in front of the Cuban Hat drive-in restaurant. Dinah can't help noticing that the bold red-and-black blazer of the girls' convent school is looking very good on her.

Meanwhile from everywhere in the school the sounds of Christmas carols are floating into the classroom. Everyone in the school is doing Christmasy things, special-treat things, except for Dinah's class, because Mrs Vaughan-Jones is making them keep on copying notes from the board. Suddenly she makes one of her lunges at Patsy John and she's armed with her metal-edged ruler. The only difference this time is that she seems to have forgotten that she's still standing on her podium. She misses her footing and falls flat on her face. Literally flat on her face. The class, which is already silent, falls so silent that it's eerie. Dinah thinks that maybe Mrs Vaughan-Jones is dead – or then again maybe not. It could be that she's like a wicked witch in a fairy-tale who's just playing dead in order to trick them.

Finally, after ages, Mrs Vaughan-Jones gets up very slowly and, with the ruler still in her hand, she advances on Patsy without a word. Her jaw is sort of wobbling and there's dribble on her chin. She drags Patsy out of her seat by the hair without a word and pulls her along until they are on the spot where Mrs Vaughan-Jones fell. Silent tears have started from Patsy's Kewpie-doll eyes, because the pain in the hair follicles on her scalp must be unbearable. Then Mrs Vaughan-Jones shakes Patsy, back and forth, before forcing her to the floor and planting a foot in the small of Patsy's back. She gets Penny-Lou Headley to empty Patsy's desk and make a pile of all her books and pens on the floor.

'You'll do your work down *there*, Patsy John,' she says, in a slightly lisping voice. 'You deliberately caused me to fall. Now let this be a lesson to you.'

And Patsy has to spend the rest of the day doing her work like that, lying face down on the floor. Then, the next day – and the next and the next – Mrs Vaughan-Jones isn't there. And then it's the Christmas holidays.

Once it's the holidays, Dinah forgets all about Class Two, because when she gets back she'll be upstairs in Class Three with Miss Vaizey, who smiles and chats and sits on her desk swinging her legs. Sometimes Miss Vaizey wears a polka-dot dress with a full skirt and cap sleeves, or she wears a tight pencil skirt with a kick pleat at the back and a trim white blouse with a cameo brooch. And she lets her girls do really fun things, like making 3D maps of all four provinces of the Union of South Africa on pastry boards with Plasticine. The Cape, Natal, the Orange Free State and the Transvaal. She gets you to do all the forested areas with bits of bath sponge that you dip in dark-green paint. Dinah knows all about these things from Lisa who's had a great time all year and she's made lots of friends.

Plus, once you get past Class Two, you do cookery and sewing in the special domestic science annexe with Mrs Stewart, but everyone calls her Stewpot behind her back. The girls have been preparing for cookery all through Class Two, because, on one afternoon a week, they have had to work at making their cookery aprons by hand. The aprons are white poplin but they have checked gingham waistbands and matching blue or red gingham borders and pockets. On all the gingham bits the girls have to do cross-stitch patterns. If your gingham is red then you do your cross-stitch with blue embroidery thread and, if it's blue, you use red. You have to embroider your name on the white bit of the pocket as well, in chain-stitched cursive.

At home, over Christmas, Lisa and Dinah make peg bags and needle books for their mum and they buy their dad some very tight brown socks that are quite hard for him to get on and off. They buy the socks with all the money Dinah's got saved in her red tin money box and it has to be a together-present, because Lisa hasn't got any money left. She's spent it all on Toffo-lux and Crunchie bars. Their mum bakes special plaited doughnuts and cream puffs, and she makes biscuits in different Christmasy shapes, like fir trees and bells and stars. She decorates the Advent *Kranz* with greenery and hangs it over the dining table with tall candles and red ribbons.

Because Dinah's mum does German-style Christmas, it's Christmas Eve that is the big time and the girls always open their presents by candlelight after supper while the radio is relaying the Nine Lessons and Carols from King's College Chapel in Cambridge. Dinah loves the pure, posh-voiced treble of the choir-school boys – and especially that of the one who reads the lesson into the darkness of her living room, against the nightly siren-scream of the grasshoppers. For supper they have home-boiled ham and asparagus out of a tin and shredded carrot salad and potato salad with lots of mayonnaise. Dinah's dad always makes the mayonnaise in a bowl, adding the oil drop by drop with a wooden spoon. Mayonnaise and piccalilli are about the only things that Dinah really loves to eat, so she'll eat almost anything if it's smothered in mayonnaise.

Back at school Mrs Vaughan-Jones has been dispatched as if by spontaneous combustion. Or perhaps she's just dissolved, like the Wicked Witch of the North in *The Wizard of Oz* that Lisa and Dinah have just been taken to see. But no! She hasn't, because Dinah sees her one more time and it's about two years later. Mrs Vaughan-Jones is doddling down West Street, right in the town centre. She's making strange niddy-noddy head movements and talking gibberish to herself. Her mouth is wearing a madder version of the scary moonfaced smile and she's dressed in a plaid skirt and a cable-stitched cardi. Dinah can see that, at the back, Mrs Vaughan-Jones's skirt has got all tucked up into the waistband of her bloomers, so that from behind you can see all the way up her lumpy, gnarled old legs.

A bit of Dinah wants to go and sort out the old woman's skirt, but she can't for fear that Mrs Vaughan-Jones will suddenly spin round, dextrous and triumphant. And Dinah will be back in Class Two, gnawing her way tearfully through a mountain of packed lunch. Or she'll be stuffed, snivelling, into the hot seat at the top of the A1 ice-cream row. Besides, Dinah finds that her legs have turned to jelly and she can't seem to move an inch. Mrs Vaughan-Jones walks right on past her, because the increasing egg-yolk film in the corners of her eyes has clearly done for her fly's-eye vision. Then, once she's moved on by, Dinah's heart leaps inside her and she knows that she is glad. Free for ever of Mrs Vaughan-Jones and so glad that she wants to dance and sing.

FOUR

THE GENERAL ELECTION IN 1948 is being fought between one white party and another white party. Black people and Indians can't vote. Coloureds can vote, but only in the Cape, because the Cape still has that little vestige remaining of its one-time colour-blind franchise. So blacks used to have the vote in the Cape, but they don't any more. Not since the Act of Union at the end of the Boer War. At school Dinah is taught that this elimination of the Cape's black franchise was a Good Thing, because it means all four provinces of the Union of South Africa now have the same Native Policy. And UNITY IS STRENGTH – that's the Union's motto. In Afrikaans it's just the same. *Eendrag Maak Mag.* Dinah is taught that anything which brings the two white-language groups together is always a Good Thing, because it proves that both groups have put the enmity of the Boer War behind them and that Afrikaner and English South Africans are now the best of friends. Meanwhile, the two groups go on hating each other like poison. The only rule is that any gestures of unity between them will come at the price of short-changing the blacks.

The two white parties are called the United Party and the National Party. The United Party is the one English whites like best, even though its leader is the former Boer War general, Jan Smuts. But these days the General is big friends with all the captains of industry – and, for the moment, they're all English. Plus he loves to hobnob with the British royal family and, since the Windsors seem to love him back, his photo-opportunities are many. With his dapper little naval beard and his regal bearing, you might think that the General *was* one of the Windsors, were it not for the occasional presence of his wife, Ouma.

Ouma Smuts is much loved by the nation – or, at least, by that part of the nation that can vote – and she has black, un-styled Afro hair that would have a hard time passing the pencil test. Plus she wears old tennis shoes without any laces decades before this can be interpreted as a fashion statement. Unfortunately, by the time of the 1948 election, the General himself is well past his prime. He's over seventy and it's obvious to anyone with eyes that the brilliant guerrilla leader who went on to become the friend of Quakers and the darling of several North Oxford salons is now wearing his hair in a silly bald man's comb-over.

Because the English whites live in the cities and work in business, they want a political party that will make sure blacks have just enough freedom to be able to move from the native reserves into the towns to work for knock-down wages in the mines and factories, just so long as they can be shunted back to the reserves again, once they're too old or too disabled, or in any way extraneous to requirements. Afrikaner whites tend to live on farms and in one-horse country towns, so they want a political party that will make sure blacks can't move into the cities. That way they'll have to stay in the countryside, working as serfs on white farms and getting paid in bags of maize. The two parties are colloquially known as the Nats and the 'UP' – the latter pronounced 'you-pee' – which gives rise to several popular wee-wee jokes at school.

At Dinah's school all the girls are UP because they're English-speaking. Everyone at school knows the English are Best, even though lots of the girls have surnames like Van Jaarsveld, du Plessis, Tonetti, da Souza, Levy, Engelbrecht, Herschel and de Bondt. Everyone in the melting pot has read those books about the little English princesses, Lillibet and Margaret Rose. Everyone knows that Crawfie is the royal nanny. Everyone, even Dinah, has had a bash at joining the Brownies and learning to gabble the oath:

> ipromisetodomybesttodomyduty
> togodthekingandmycountry
> tohelpotherpeopleatalltimes
> especiallythoseathome

– though Dinah, who can plait, knit, sew, boil an egg, lay the table and make hospital corners in bedsheets as well as anyone else in the

Elf pack, who invariably produces the most shined-up, Brasso-buffed penny for her weekly subs, never advances beyond the tweenie stage; never gets her hands on the coveted brown uniform, having somehow been sniffed out by the pack sixer at the St Thomas's Anglican Church platoon as Quite the Wrong Sort.

This is an assessment much assisted by her dad who arrives to collect her one evening and, finding himself inadvertently trapped before the Brown Owl *Anschluss* on Show Day, cannot contain either his irritation or his mirth, as he's forced back into the seating area and suffered to sit through the proceedings. This mortifying event is one which he afterwards incorporates into his public anecdote collection as 'the night on which a mad woman rushed at me shouting "Tweet-tweet-tuwhit-tuwhoo"'. He likes to embellish it with an account of how one of the Brownies faultlessly demonstrated her table-laying skills to the assembled throng, extracting all the implements from a cardboard box – only to find, after she'd finished, that the tablecloth was neatly folded right at the bottom of the box. One of his favourite routines is about Dinah's Brownie efforts at 'helping at home'. These, he asserts, consist entirely of her leaving a trail of spilled Brasso and blackened copper tarnish all over the kitchen table in the hour before the weekly pack meetings.

Everyone takes out Enid Blyton books from the school library and knows that proper children call their mothers Mummy. They have buttered toast for tea, which they eat in front of crackling log fires on winter afternoons. Proper English children have real snow at Christmas instead of cotton wool and glitter stuck to the windows. And they have a person in the kitchen called Cook, who is definitely not a native girl. She will do a 'splendid spread' for a picnic or an outdoor adventure if you approach her diplomatically. And she doesn't have bare feet like the native girl. She's an awesome white crosspatch who commands respect and she comes complete with a uniform not unlike what nurses wear, including the sturdy laced shoes.

Cook is always scary, but in Durban nobody is scared of the native girl and, once, when Lisa is helping to make rock cakes in Bugs Gourlay's kitchen, she stands on the native girl's foot by mistake so she says sorry, but Bugs's mum says to Lisa that she must never say sorry to a native girl.

'You mustn't lower yourself,' she says.

Bugs's mum says this right in front of the native girl, so Lisa is really embarrassed.

Bugs's real name is Beulah, but she hates it and she hates being a girl. She makes everyone call her Bugs, and she wears boys' khaki shorts with a snake belt. Bugs is school swimming champ and she always has a pink peeling nose from spending so much time at the Beach Baths. She's older than Lisa and, when she's thirteen, Bugs suddenly becomes the biggest flirt in the neighbourhood. She manages this without ever wearing a dress and without giving up on her locker-room style, though sometimes Bugs will wear a puff-sleeved broderie anglaise blouse with her khaki shorts and her snake belt.

At school, everybody hates the Afrikaans lessons and resists learning anything, even though it's quite an easy language because it doesn't have verb conjugations, and even though Mrs van Heynigen is very strict and makes the class chant their vocab every day while she claps out the rhythms with her hands. By the next day half the class will have forgotten it all. If any girl can't find her vocab notebook in class, Mrs van Heynigen always does the same thing. She strides up the aisle and flings back the girl's desk lid on to the head of the girl in front.

'The only way to find a lost book is to shake out all the books and throw them elsewhere,' she says, with her rich rolled 'r' sounds. As she speaks, she begins to toss the girl's books in all directions across the room. She does this until the missing book is found, or until the desk is empty. Girls duck and suppress giggles as books come hurtling towards them, and they use their hands to protect their heads. Since these moments of theatre are all that anyone ever enjoys about the Afrikaans lessons, some of the bolder girls begin to hide their vocab notebooks on purpose, but Mrs van Heynigen soon smells a rat.

Dinah has never been into the rural hinterland of the Transvaal or the Orange Free State where most white Afrikaners live. Her family can't afford holidays, and anyway her dad always says he is too busy. He prefers to spend his vacations staying at home and puzzling, or plucking at his new second-hand Spanish guitar which has begun to displace his mandolin. So the only three countrified places she has been to are all just around the corner and all of them are a little bit aberrant. There is Mrs Hall's smallholding on the edge of Durban. There is Henrietta's parents' farm near the Howick Falls – a scenic spot where people go to get engaged. Then there's the Marianhill Monastery, which is about ten miles away in the beautiful Natal midlands.

Mrs Hall is a kind lady in the university administration who throws an annual children's Christmas party and, one year, Lisa and Dinah get invited for the first time. She has a huge Christmas tree loaded with little wrapped presents and the children are told to choose one each. Then Margaret Carpenter and her brother, who are both older than Lisa and Dinah, spread the word that really Mrs Hall said you could take as many presents as you like. And, because Lisa and Dinah are first-timers at the party who hold back a bit while the rest of the infant gannets go to work with alacrity, it is they who are last at it, still stripping the tree of its few forlorn remnants when Mrs Hall re-enters the party space.

She tells them to stop it at once and, for a kind lady, she's sounding really cross.

'I'm disappointed in you two,' she says. 'And I'm really surprised. Those presents are for the native children on the farm. Their party is tomorrow.'

Lisa and Dinah want the earth to swallow them. They're so ashamed that they leave their legitimate presents behind, even though Dinah's is a tiny, jointed ceramic doll, her absolute heart's desire. And then, on the way out, when a goose takes bites out of Dinah's head, it's none other than one of the despoiled native children who comes and rescues her.

'Let's never go back,' Lisa says in a whisper, but Dinah can't seem to speak at all.

Henrietta is a beautiful young politically dissident school teacher who works at the Indian Girls' High School in Durban and specialises in having all the men in the university fall in love with her. She's turned them all down, one by one, and transformed them into friends, watching with apparent equanimity as they go off and get married to other women. Sometimes she has weekend parties at the farm and everyone takes the train three stops down the line and sleeps over at the farmhouse where her mother makes pancakes and porridge for breakfast. What Dinah remembers most is refusing point blank to sleep in a baby's cot, even though Henrietta's mum is pressed for beds and Dinah's still easily small enough to fit in it.

'I won't sleep in a baby's cot,' she says.

So Henrietta's brother has to go off and ferret for ages in a medley of outbuildings until he comes up with a roll-up khaki army bed with lots of metal rods that get slotted into corresponding canvas pockets.

Henrietta's current suitor is a comparative newcomer, a physicist called Ted, who shares his name with the farm sheepdog. So when Henrietta tells the girls' dad that Ted is putting on weight, he agrees with her because it's true – especially after Ted's orgy of breakfast pancakes that morning. But then Henrietta really confuses him.

'He's been accused of stealing sheep,' she says.

'Really?' Dinah's dad says. 'Surely not?'

'Oh yes,' says Henrietta. 'I'm afraid it's true. He's been doing it in broad daylight from all the neighbouring farms.'

'Never!' says Dinah's dad.

Henrietta sighs. 'We might have to have him put down,' she says. 'And I've always loved him so dearly. Ever since he came through distemper as a puppy.'

At Marianhill the monks and nuns run a craft school for local Zulus and a farm with pigs and chickens. Plus the nuns run a really cheap guest house that has some permanent old people there as well. Whenever Dinah's family goes there, Dinah and Lisa delight in watching Mary, the Coloured maid-of-all-work, who yells encouragement into the ears of assorted deaf and toothless residents at mealtimes.

'Ach, come on now, Mrs Thomas,' she says. 'It's just slip-down for pudding today. It slips down like anything, Mrs Thomas, I'm telling you now. Just try a little spoonful and see how easy it just slips down.'

Their mum buddies up to Sister Pieta who has painted a new altarpiece for the chapel and their dad is very soon highjacked to go on walks with a deaf old monk who's fond of birdwatching, but he can't any longer hear the bird calls. Since, among all the things that the girls' dad is best at, whistling is definitely one, he spends his mornings productively at Marianhill, whistling bird calls into the ear of the deaf old monk whose face lights up with each new sound.

One day, Peter Bullen comes with them and, because he's a fidgety person, he clicks his camera shutter on his last exposure by mistake, just as Sister Pieta is taking them all to see the new mural she's painted in the chapel.

'Bloody hell!' he says. But then he remembers he's walking with a nun and the back of his neck goes bright red. 'Oh Christ Almighty!' he says.

Sister Pieta is trying not to laugh, but the girls just keep on giggling about it all through the trip – all the way to the chapel and all the way back.

The real country, the terrifying country, as Dinah envisages it, is somewhere beyond the Vaal and the Orange Rivers, where she knows that Afrikaner farmers have dominion over earth-coloured peasants dressed in rags and sacks. And she knows that the farmers keep guns in their bedrooms and that shooting is a popular hobby. She knows this because occasionally the farmers shoot their own wives or their children by mistake, and then it gets into the papers. Sometimes they'll shoot the black housemaid who's coming in with the morning tea, because they think she's an intruder. Or their children will get hold of the guns and shoot each other while playing Cowboys and Indians. Now and again the odd farmer's son will go gun crazy after a coming-of-age spree with his mates on too much cheap Cape brandy. Then, instead of having his fun lobbing empty Castle beer cans out of the car windows at black pedestrians, he'll take a pot shot at one of them instead. She remembers a man being quoted in the paper.

'I always wanted to shoot a *kaffertjie* for my twenty-first, your honour,' he says.

Kaffertjie is the diminutive of kaffir, which is the most in-your-face offensive way of referring to a black person, just as hotnot is the most offensive way of saying Coloured. But lots of Afrikaners still use kaffir just as if it were the regular word for a black person. Kaffir isn't that much used by the English these days but, instead, white Durbanites call all male Indians Sammy and all female Indians Mary – or sometimes, to be pejorative, it'll be koelie-Mary. So they'll say to the Indian fruit vendor, 'Have you got a nice water-melon for me today, Sammy?' – just as if Sammy was his name. Or they'll say, 'Who does that koelie-Mary think she is – sitting on the bench there like Lady Muck on Toast?' That's if they see an Indian woman sitting on a park bench, just like a white person, instead of squatting on her haunches as Indians usually do.

And when Sally's mother takes a Union Castle boat to visit her relations in London and she sees two Indian women in saris coming out of the Ladies' Room in Selfridge's – the very Ladies' Room that she's about to use herself – she's so knocked back that she goes and complains about it to the manager.

'There are two Marys in the toilets,' she says, but the manager doesn't understand her. Sally's mother gets quite agitated, which causes her to mix a metaphor. 'Two Marys,' she says. 'In the toilets. Behaving just like the bee's whiskers.'

Once back in Durban, she reports the incident by way of a humorous anecdote. It's humorous because everybody knows that bees don't have any whiskers.

'Europe's OK,' she says. 'But it's nice to be back in SA.'

People in Durban call England 'home', but they think it's going to the dogs these days, because of all the Marys in the toilets and because of the way some people just shuffle out of the cinema right in the middle of 'God Save the King', instead of standing to attention as we always do at the Durban Playhouse. The Playhouse has got a ceiling that's made to look like the night sky with electric twinkly stars and it looks just like the Globe Theatre as reconstructed by Walt Disney. You can buy paper cups of that orange squash that always makes your throat close up and, in the interval, there's an organist who rises from the orchestra pit by magic in a swirl of coloured lights. He's there to accompany you while you do community singing by Following the Bouncing Ball. The Bouncing Ball is there to point the lyrics for you on the screen. In Durban the cinema is called the bioscope. That's how it's written down, but everyone pronounces it 'bi-scope'. Or mostly it's 'bah-scope'.

Dinah's dad can speak really good Afrikaans because he's spent three years at the University of Stellenbosch being a graduate student. After he'd finished his first degree at the University of Leiden in Holland, he had no money to go on studying there, so he applied for a scholarship at the Cape just because he happened to see it advertised. He knew nothing about South Africa, so he was quite surprised, when the application form came, to find that it had

74

a box on it where you had to fill in your race. He had no idea what his race was and he had never thought about it before, so he set about finding out all about it as best as he could. He took several anthropology books out of the university library and – since this was the 1930s – he discovered that they all had lots of diagrams of skulls and jawbones, with measurements. For several days Dinah's dad did head measurements. He measured the circumference of his cranium, and the width of the bridge of his nose, and the angle at which his jaw protruded, and the depth of his eye sockets, and the distance between his eyes. He wrote down all the measurements and made careful drawings, using his mother's hand mirror for doing the back of his head. Then he compared all his figures and drawings with the ones in the anthropology books.

'It was perfectly clear to me that I was descended from the Beaker Folk,' he tells the girls, 'so I wrote, "Beaker Folk" in the box.'

This is the last of his family stories. The girls have never heard of the Beaker Folk. In fact Dinah has no idea that they could have been an ancient people who got their name from making clay beakers, so she assumes it's spelt 'Bica-Folk' – but the story makes them giggle all the same, because everybody knows that you're supposed to put 'European' in those boxes where it says 'Race', even if you're a white American. Or if you aren't a white person, then you have to put 'Native', 'Coloured' or 'Asiatic'.

Sometimes when their Dad takes them shopping in West Street, where all the glossy department stores are, he deliberately speaks to them loudly in Afrikaans. Lisa and Dinah are always terrified that people might think they are Afrikaners. They try frantically to shush him, but he only says, 'What's the matter?' He says it really loud and still in Afrikaans. The only Afrikaners Lisa and Dinah ever see in Durban, other than the smattering of Port Natal schoolboys on the bus, are semi-rehabilitated poor whites, their skins orangey and weather-beaten, who do repair work on the railways. Or during the July holidays they see huge up-country farmers with fists like hams along with their very un-citified wives: overweight, plebby types with frizzy perms and strings of barefoot blond children. They've all piled into a beat-up Chev and driven the four hundred miles to the coast to take up temporary residence in the cheap, concrete self-catering apartments on Addington Beach near the hospital.

And new police recruits are nearly always Afrikaners. Young and rural, they are usually from impoverished white sharecropper families who've been thrown off the land by big corporate English landowners. They've wandered, dispossessed and often shoeless, into the towns in search of work and the police force is fast becoming their personal system of outdoor relief. Having acquired drivers' licences, they then roar around Durban in squad cars, joyriding, catcalling women and hassling blacks. It's because the Afrikaner policemen are always so horrid to black people that Lisa and Dinah find it hard to see how much their anti-Afrikaner feelings contain large dollops of class prejudice – and they don't quite see that it's this that their dad is getting at when he does his Afrikaner-speak in public. He's trying to make them hate the sin and not the sinner.

But the sinner, right now, is making himself very easy to hate. Afrikaner community leaders are, at this moment, very busy constructing the cultural heritage of the *Volk*. They are binding together the disparate strands of white Afrikanerdom into a mono-lithic fighting force by banging away at all the potent symbols. They are preparing to raise up their own poor whites at the further expense of poor blacks. And, since all the imagery of this effort has to do with the Great Trek, Lisa and Dinah find it impossible to empathise with it. They find it alienating. Afrikaners, unlike the frontier folk of the American West, don't have a film industry to carry the imagery of their pioneering effort to an audience beyond themselves. So theirs is an exercise in navel gazing.

So Lisa and Dinah think of Afrikaners as people who, for reasons beyond their understanding, are forever sculpting life-size ox wagons in bronze, or donning goofy poke bonnets and ankle-length petticoats, or growing Rip Van Winkle beards, in order to under-take pious torchlight processions from A to B in full regalia. Along the way, they ritually enact the umpteen battles they fought during their push north from the Cape Colony into the interior of Natal and on, beyond the Vaal and the Orange Rivers. During these battles they have invariably put to rout various parties of black pastoralists. They are powerful believers in their own manifest destiny and praise God, ad infinitum, for his support through every skirmish. As a result, the rituals are always accompanied by the bullish drone of unison hymn-singing, though they are often followed up, at evening, by a form of socialising that involves massive campfire cook-outs and a form of country dancing known as *Volkspiele*. The *Volkspiele* are undertaken in full pioneer costume, to the accompaniment of a lone squeeze box, or to a sort of hillbilly band known as a *boere orkes*. As cultural revivalism goes, the *Volkspiele* look more fun than Morris dancing, because the participants don't have that look of sissies in anklets on the village green. Instead they have an earthy Brueghel-peasant quality, an innuendo of slap, tickle and incest behind the ox wagons.

For a people in bondage to religious zealots and racist fanatics, there are times when these precious strands of smut seem all that can save the *Volk* from themselves – and Afrikaners have the best dirty jokes in the world, along with a repertoire of filthy and suggestive rhymes; a creative wellspring that lodges in the *Weltanschauung* of Cape Coloured Afrikaners, from whom the new white monolith is busy cutting itself loose. The smut is not what Lisa and Dinah learn about in school when the syllabus dictates that they draw ox-wagon laagers and make voortrekker hats out of crinkle paper – and it is certainly not what comes out of the mouths of those dour Afrikaner thought-police on the radio, the innumerable clerics and *Broederbonders* – but the girls' dad has retained a small repertoire of smut from his sojourn at the University of Stellenbosch and he knows quite a few of the songs.

The Great Trek begins in the 1830s, when the poorer Eastern Cape farmers find that the Cape's British administration no longer suits them. It no longer suits them because the British, along with the more established, wealthier Boer landowners, have by now done all their own land-grabbing, cattle-rustling and coercing of indigenous peoples into pressed labour. They are into the more urbane demands of a new sort of economy, largely to do with merino sheep and free trade. They are keen to free up Hottentot labour to meet the demands of a developing urban economy and they begin to pass laws to this effect. But the poorer Boers on the frontier are, naturally, way behind; still busting a gut to assert their God-given right to undertake unregulated, armed cattle raids across the Colony's borders, and to kidnap the 'orphan' children of any indigenous persons they happen to despoil in these attempts. So, in dribs and drabs, the farmers give up and pack their stuff into covered ox wagons and – with much praying, covenanting and rhetorical reference to Moses and the Egyptian Exodus – they travel north in smallish, straggling convoys, into the unknown.

Naturally, their progress, while often characterised by feats of personal heroism and endurance, is utterly devastating to the indigenous peoples whom they encounter along the way. Desperate black chieftains, faced for the first time with oddly hirsute white strangers armed with guns, buy time for themselves by selling off areas of grazing land that aren't theirs to sell. Or, alternatively, they can wait to be starved out and killed when the Boers lay siege to their villages and co-opt their children as bondsmen. Finally, though the casualty rate among the ox-wagon convoys is not insignificant and some go missing without trace – last seen heading out towards Delagoa Bay, et cetera – the Boers triumphantly establish their two agrarian, God-fearing theocratic republics north of the Vaal and the Orange Rivers – only to find that the worst possible thing soon befalls them. The Transvaal Republic is found to be sitting on a great pile of gold.

The gold means that within no time at all every French and German fortune-hunter, every desperate Polish crook and brothel-keeper, every East European Jewish pimp and gun-runner is in there, jostling to make a quick pile. Plus the British government, which has bigger eyes for the gold than anybody else, is suddenly finding every excuse in the book for why the Boers are not capable of managing the territory, which, for its own good, needs immediate annexing for Empire. The British are also concerned for the rights of their own and other expatriates at the hands of the Boers, they say – and for the rights of indigenous black persons.

Once the British have provoked the Boer War, they find to their great surprise that, after years of pouring in something like six hundred thousand troops from all over the Empire, they have still not managed to rout the Boers, who have transformed themselves into tenacious and highly effective guerrilla fighters. So they resort, instead, to a wholesale scorched-earth policy. They herd all the Boer women and children, along with all their black servants, into the world's first concentration camps and lay waste to Boer fields and farmsteads. In the camps the conditions are appalling and the figures leaking out for deaths from epidemic disease and malnutrition transform Britain into the pariah of Europe. Europe is at this time, admittedly, committing an ingenious variety of atrocities all over Africa – the Belgians are hacking off people's limbs in the Congo; the Germans are practising their genocide techniques on the Herero peoples of South West Africa – but the British are doing something unique. They are practising war crimes on white people.

Eventually, when the Boer leaders realise that the war is giving blacks the strength to move into the gap and swipe back some of the farmland that the Boers have previously swiped off them, they decide to surrender to the British. They surrender to a crowd of obscenely young and brainy Oxbridge graduates, who are bristling with class arrogance and specialise in waxed handlebar moustaches of almost unbelievable length. The precocious youth are known collectively as Milner's Kindergarten and they are arguably more intensely racist than the Boers, since the Boers carry their racism with large dollops of pragmatism, where the Kindergarten's racism is both purist and visionary. Between them they cobble up the Act of Union and shake hands by selling the blacks down the river in perpetuity. End of story.

The only hitch is that it's not the end of the story after all, because Britain's conduct during the war has made wholesale martyrs of Boer women and children. And this has given rise to a powerful victim culture among Afrikaners which now feeds into their particular form of racist nationalism. For all that they are often anti-Semitic, Afrikaners now see themselves as the Chosen People of the Old Testament. The Promised Land is round the corner, the Boer Republics will rise again and all those rough soap-box coffins that trundled out of the camps bearing the bodies of Boer children will at last be avenged. That is what all the bronzed ox wagons and the tuneless hymn-singing is about. And while the richer, more cityfied English settlers of Lisa and Dinah's childhood are dismissing this carry-on as redneck hick, they will soon be laughing on the other sides of their faces. Because there, at the grass roots, in the rural hinterland, in every Blikkiesdorp and Pampoenvlei, the Afrikaners are staging a comeback.

The Ox Wagon Exodus is even now being commemorated in bas-relief sculpture all over the walls of the newly erected Voortrekker Monument which has become the major focus of Afrikaner pilgrimage. It stands on a hill outside Pretoria and looks just like a cross between a Mormon temple and a giant art deco radiogram.

All its sculpture is the work of imported foreigners, but then the same can be said of Henry VIII – another nationalist leader who purged his *Volk* of its creative element. So Anton Van Wouw is the Afrikaners' Hans Holbein and he's done a pretty good job. The Voortrekker Monument looks impressive. Plus it's the world's only art deco building that can boast baboons among its bas-reliefs.

FIVE

P ORT NATAL IS THE ONLY Afrikaans-language school in Durban and all the boys, even the sixth formers, get made to wear shorts as part of the uniform. They have to wear the shorts with blazers, shirts and ties – and with black lace-up shoes and socks. This makes them look exactly like grown-up men who've forgotten to put their trousers on – especially as, at this time in South Africa, shorts always come so short that they're never any longer than your knickers. Both English- and Afrikaans-speaking whites are agreed that long shorts are a badge of sissies. They are associated with pith-helmeted, skinny-legged joke-Englishmen – the sort that end up in those cartoon stew pots beloved of cartoon savages. Even though they are passionately loyal to the mother country, white Durbanites know that they are more vigorous and manly than the *English*-English back in England. Everyone in Durban has heard that the *English*-English wear tennis shoes into the sea which is a clear indication of sissiness, especially as nobody in South Africa has experienced pebble beaches. On Durban beaches the only thing that hurts your feet is the baking temperature of the sand. The obvious rightness of shorter-than-short shorts is only challenged, four decades on, by the encroaching dominance of Australian beach-boy culture with its attendant floral Bermudas.

Nobody in Dinah's school will sit next to the Port Natal boys on the bus going home, because those brawny naked thighs spreading out on the seats make them feel much too squeamish. Sometimes Dinah speculates that all this muscle-bound, sun-blasted pinko-white flesh must be utterly repellent to blacks, because blacks, when they aren't in their workman's overalls and kitchen-boy suits, wear snazzy, Chicago-gangster get-ups: zoot suits and rakishly

81

angled felt hats and perforated two-tone shoes. This is in stark contrast to the style of local white English-speaking males who generally dress like Jehovah's Witnesses. Most have bought into the post-war Sta-prest trouser look, which comes complete with Y-front pantie-line and sleeveless Airtex vest. Perma-crease synthetic 'slax' are worn with a short-sleeved nylon shirt – the latter always rigorously tucked in and belted, because a hanging-out shirt is considered slovenly and it's too much associated with kitchen-boy suits. These, by contrast, are made of undyed calico and consist of baggy long shorts worn with a loose overhanging short-sleeved top and no underpants. The suits have red braid on the shirt and trouser hems and are usually worn with bare feet.

The flash off-duty clothes that blacks wear can be bought on tick in the Indian-owned emporiums like Moosa's at the upper end of downtown Durban where the legless beggars hang out. That's the end furthest from the beachfront, so to get to the white department stores, or to the beach, you have to pass through this commercial area, where Indians ply their trade from pretty, rickety old buildings with New Orleans-style balconies and shady covered walks. The walkways have baskets full of brass bangles and cheap sandals and bales of sari cloth that spill out on to the pavements. Then there's also the Indian Market which has covered stalls bursting with flowers and aubergines and pawpaws and spices. It has drapery stalls and the odd Zulu *sangoma* selling potions of medicinal monkey gland and ground-up rhino horn. The Indian market is where the girls' mum always goes when she wants to buy cut flowers.

The reason Lisa and Dinah like to go shopping with their mum is not only because she doesn't speak Afrikaans to them in West Street or buy them Knockabouts. It's because she doesn't make them hurry past those displays in toy departments where people are demonstrating wind-up dogs and dolls that can say '*Mamma*' in little kitten voices. It's because she takes them in and out of all sorts of shops where they buy Horrocks print fabrics and gingham for Mrs van der Walt to make into dresses, and rick-rack braid and cards of press studs, and novelty buttons for little girls' cardis with teddybears and ladybirds on them, and ribbons for Dinah's hair, and Coty face powder for herself from the *parfumerie* in Payne Brothers department store. And one day she lets Dinah have her photograph taken bottle-feeding a baby lion cub in Greenacre's during a game-park promotion week.

Sometimes she goes into the Anglo-Swiss Bakery to buy Viennese Whirls; and sometimes they go upstairs to the Maypole Tearoom opposite the Cenotaph that has two yellow-and-blue ceramic angels dragging a yellow-and-blue dead soldier up the side of a yellow-and-blue stone slab. Along the bottom it says, 'At the going down of the sun and in the morning we will remember them,' and behind it, surrounded by palms and spiky aloes, is a puff-eyed bronze Queen Victoria with mynah birds squabbling on her head. There's an especially delicious cake you can get at the Maypole Tearoom that has six thin layers of biscuit stuck together with green icing. And each layer of icing is sprinkled with desiccated coconut and crushed nuts. Because the Maypole Tearoom is upstairs you can also look straight out on to the top of the Cenotaph with your eyes on a level with its yellow ceramic sunrays.

Sometimes their mother's friend, Frau Architekt Liesl Mainz, is in the tearoom and – because she's a woman of position, with a bigger house than Dinah's parents and a husband in the business community – she's often in there playing host to visiting Austrian musicians and other Teutonic ethnics who have come by bearing culture. So one day she'll be in there dispensing cakes to the Vienna Boys' Choir in their sailor suits and, another time, she'll have a whole troupe of Tyrolean yodellers. The yodellers are all wearing little hats with feathers and so is Liesl Mainz. Dinah prays that she won't notice them because the yodellers are so embarrassing and one of them is even pausing to have a little yodel over the cakes.

Liesl Mainz has a son called Peter who is Dinah's age, but his mother has declared him a prodigy which, by implication, puts him out of Dinah's league, though she and Lisa get asked to Peter's birthday parties. Even at his own parties, Peter is always encouraged to play his violin for the visitors and he also plays the piano. For a while Dinah can do little duets with him because her mother is sending her to a piano teacher, but she never practises except for in the frantic half-hour before the weekly lesson, so she soon falls behind and begs to stop. What's especially embarrassing about the piano lessons is that sometimes the teacher gets her star pupil to take Dinah's lesson instead and the star pupil is a boy. He's a

Durban Boys' High School pupil called Bobby Mills, who wears his uniform for the lessons.

Then, on New Year's Eve, when Dinah's family have gone to the Mainz's house for dinner, Lisa and Dinah decide they want to sleep over, so Mrs Mainz makes up two beds for them while Mr Mainz drives Dinah's parents home. This is necessary because they don't yet have their own car and it's ages before they get one. As soon as they're tucked up in bed on their own in the dark, Lisa starts saying she's scared.

'Let's go and say you've got asthma,' she says. 'Then they'll have to drive us home.'

Dinah isn't scared but she's much too drowsy not to go along with the plan, so Lisa tiptoes into the Mainz's bedroom at one o'clock in the morning and wakes them up.

'We've got to go home because Dinah's got asthma,' she says.

Mrs Mainz is wearing a copious nightie and Mr Mainz is as grumpy as anything because he's been pulled out of his sleep to drive them home. All the way, he's in a filthy temper and he's getting more and more sarcastic. Mrs Mainz has a face that's all twisted to one side because she's had to have half her jawbone removed on account of a tumour in the bone. She tells the girls' mum that she was going to have plastic surgery but, when he was four, Peter told her not to because he loved her just the way she was. And Peter's word holds great sway with his mother.

The classy shops in West Street are Payne Brothers, Greenacre's, John Orr's and Stuttaford's, but there are also the Hub and the Bon Marché, which are much more penny-bazaar and they never get air-conditioning. They have old-fashioned bentwood chairs and walls of cupboards with a multitude of little wooden drawers, and counters with brass yardsticks fitted to their edges with the inches and half-inches marked out. And they still have those pneumatic overhead brass tubes into which the shop assistants have to put the customers' money along with a handwritten invoice called a docket.

The shop assistant puts these into an oval capsule that twists shut in the middle and she sends the capsule whizzing along inside the brass tube. It makes a whoosh like pumping up bicycle tyres and you can see it winding along all round the shop ceiling until it reaches the cashier who sits in a cubicle high up near the roof. The cashier counts out the change and sends it whizzing back to the shop assistant who untwists the capsule and gives the customer her change. The whizzing brass tubes are really exciting, because they connect you with someone who ought to be unreachable. Lisa and Dinah have never used a telephone and don't have one at home, but the tubes give them the same tingly feeling that they get when they speak into those home-made telephones they make from *The Wonder Book of Things to Do*, with two tin cans joined with a long piece of string.

All the *Wonder* books have been handed on to them in a batch by their dad's professor who is a mild Jewish elderly called Prof Stein. They never learn his first name, but his wife always calls him Daddy, even though their children are all grown up. One is a doctor and one is a journalist who edits *Drum* magazine. If ever Prof Stein tries to sneak out of his house in his comfy shoes, then his wife pounces on him.

'*Daddy?*' she says. 'You don't think you're going out like *that*, do you? Go and change into your decent shoes at once!'

Prof Stein just pretends he's been absent-minded and he shuffles back into the bedroom to change, looking meek and sheepish.

Then his wife will say to Lisa and Dinah, just as if they were the grown-ups, 'He always tries to get away with it, you know.'

Prof Stein is very absent-minded and he once gave a lift to a hitch-hiker, but along the way he forgot that the car was his, so when he got to where he was going, he stopped and got out and thanked the hitch-hiker for the ride. Then he walked off, leaving the hitch-hiker with his car. Maths people are supposed to be absent-minded, but the girls' dad never is.

His colleague, René van den Borcht from Belgium, is, because one day when his wife Griet has gone back to Antwerp to visit her parents, he has to excuse himself from a lecture because he's suddenly remembered that he's left the electric kettle on for a cup of coffee. He dashes home, but when he gets there he's relieved to find that he must not have got round to switching it on after all. Then, having dashed home in the Durban heat, he decides that he really does need that cup of coffee before he can go back, so this time he switches on the kettle and sits down to wait for it to boil. He waits and waits until there's a really nasty smell and then he finds that the kettle is burnt out, because he's forgotten to put in any water.

The main thing Dinah remembers about René van den Borcht is that he has an obscene party song that involves rotating a beer glass three times round his crotch. The girls know about the obscene party song because once, when their parents are having a party, and they're supposed to be in bed, they're both too excited to go to sleep because their favourite person, Peter Bullen, has brought his younger brother along and his brother is called Paul. This revelation means the girls can't help but keep darting down the passage in their pyjamas to chant 'Two Little Dicky Birds' with bits of paper stuck to their finger ends:

> Two little dicky birds
> Sitting on a wall
> One named Peter
> One named Paul –

Their parents keep trying to shush them but they're too wound up to pay any attention, so they continue with their birdie theme by taking turns to run down the passage and shout 'Cuckoo!' and then run back again in fits of giggles. Finally their mum just lets them come in and run their fingers round all the cut-glass bowls with the remains of the Charlotte Russe and the Apple Snow that she's made for her buffet supper. That's when someone starts banging on her piano and René van den Borcht is singing along in Flemish whilst doing all that rude stuff around his crotch with a beer glass in his hand.

Saying 'the Hub' out loud is never a problem, but knowing how to say 'the Bon Marché' is always a headache. For all the girls at school it's simple. It's just called 'the Bonn March', as in the month that comes after February. Dinah knows this isn't right and she feels too silly to say it. But she can't pronounce it French-wise either, because that would sound even worse. So she tries not to say the shop's name at all, but that doesn't mean there isn't a problem, because Lisa and Dinah's mum is much too foreign to understand these things, so she always shames the girls in front of their schoolfriends by saying 'Bon Marché' all French-wise, without even noticing that it's making everyone snigger.

One of Lisa's best schoolfriends is a girl called Elizabeth Lazarus whose mum is German as well, except that Mrs Lazarus is Jewish.

The whole Lazarus family is proper Jewish. Mrs Lazarus always insists to Lisa that the girls' mum is Jewish as well, even though Lisa tries to make her understand that this is not the case. Lisa explains to Mrs Lazarus that their dad is sort of half Jewish, but their mother isn't Jewish at all and that, because of this, she and Dinah each have one Jewish earlobe. This is what their dad has once told them, but Mrs Lazarus is unshakeable.

'No, dear,' she says. 'Your mother is Jewish.'

This is a bit of a puzzle for Lisa because she doesn't realise that Elizabeth's mother has to believe Lisa's mum is Jewish, because she thinks that she's a nice lady and there's no such thing as a nice German. If you come from Germany, then you have to be a Nazi or a Jew. That's all there is to it.

At school, just before the 1948 general election, there are lots more jokes than usual to show how stupid Afrikaners are. Most of the jokes are about a stock character called van de Merwe who is nearly always in the police. In one of the jokes, Sergeant van de Merwe has won a trip to America to take part in a radio quiz show, but he loses the prize because he can't answer his first question in which he has to guess what item of clothing it could possibly be that is made out of canvas and has a rubber sole, plus eight eyelet holes and a lace and a tongue. Everyone at school can tell that the answer is a sneaker. But van der Merwe doesn't get it. And then, for his next question, he can't even answer what has *two* rubber soles, *sixteen* eyelet holes, *two* laces and *two* tongues. In South Africa a sneaker is called a tackie. Often it's Enid who's telling the jokes, because she's good at jokes. Enid likes to laugh a lot, but she never makes any sound. You can only tell that she's laughing because her eyes are watering and she wobbles.

Yet in spite of Sergeant van de Merwe, the Afrikaner Nationalists are not so stupid that they lose the general election. They win by a narrow margin and all the English are stunned. It's like waking up next morning to find you are walking through an alien landscape. The UP vote looks strong in the beginning because all the city votes come in first, but all through the night, while Lisa and Dinah are asleep, the votes start dribbling in from the rural areas where each constituency has three white men along with several hundred sheep and umpteen hectares of maize. So the Nats have won, with a narrow margin, on a third fewer votes than the UP have got. This is a big surprise for the English, especially as the way both parties have touted for votes is by proving that they are more racist than the other party, and General Smuts has so recently proved his credentials in this respect by ordering the suppression of a peaceful black miners' strike that has left twelve dead, a thousand injured and all the leaders in jail.

Once the Nats have won the general election – and after they've finished riding round the streets in beat-up Chevs blowing continuously on their horns for three days and nights – they set about fixing the electoral system to ensure that they will stay in power for ever. Plus they begin to pass a series of acts that continue throughout the rest of Dinah's childhood. While most are no more than intense, more lunatic versions of the racist legislation that the British have already put in place, their horrible, drawing-board ruthlessness is enough to make a person reel, especially if that person has the bad luck to be black. Some of the acts mean exactly the opposite of what they sound like, so that the Abolition of Passes Act means that blacks must now carry new improved passes consisting of ninety pages and more, and be ready to produce them at any time, on demand. And the Bantu Education Act means that all the independent black schools have to shut down, including the very good mission schools. The state takes over the running of all black schools – and, as one of the new cabinet ministers remarks, 'What is the use of teaching a Bantu child mathematics?'

The Extension of University Education Act means that the Bantu can't any longer go to 'our' universities, because instead they'll go to various tribally segregated colleges. Bantu is the new favourite word. It's favoured above native, not only because to the untutored ear it sounds more bongo-bongo, while to the educated it sounds more ethnographic, but also because white people are waking up to the idea that native doesn't have to mean a black person; it has implications of belonging to the land which they are anxious to claim for themselves. The Registration of Separate Amenities Act means that we do not need to provide much in the way of amenities for the Bantu, because we will provide these 'according to their standard of civilisation' and 'according to their need' – and, as we all know, the Bantu's needs are simple. Since this act defines everything racially, down to who's allowed to sit at every park bench and bus stop, it does, at least, necessitate a welter of new signs – and, for a while, putting up all the signs is making work for those who are in the process of being dispossessed.

Then there's the Mixed Marriages Act that says you can't marry across colour, and the Immorality Act that says you can't have cross-colour sex. This act arms policemen with field-glasses and requires them to become Peeping Toms, as they climb trees, or shin up drain-pipes and washing poles to peek through bedroom windows and sniff at post-coital bedlinen.

'It was noted that the pillow beside the accused's head was disturbed, your honour. Exhibit number one, it has been noted, is a black hair recovered from the pillow, your honour. The hair, it has been noted, is of the Bantu type, your honour.'

The only satisfaction to be got from this act is when a stiff-necked Dutch Reformed clergyman is caught doing sex with his house-maid. The Population Registration Act – with the assistance of the pencil test and the half-moon fingernail theory – is there to help decide upon your racial category. Children can be ripped away from white families because they look too black. There's a case that Dinah's heard of, because it's been in all the papers. It's about a girl called Sandra Laing who gets reclassified because the teachers at her junior school report her. At first her family fights like anything to stop the reclassification, but, when they can't, they change sides and refuse to have anything more to do with her. Even after she's a grown-up and married with two little children of her own, they keep on refusing to see her – though her brothers, who never get sent away, look just the same as she does.

While both Dinah's parents think the government is raving mad, it's her dad who takes the matter more to heart. So the most direct effect of the Nationalist election victory upon Lisa and Dinah is that they wake up every morning to the sound of their dad shouting back at Foreign Minister Eric Louw on the early morning radio. Eric Louw, wartime Nazi enthusiast and our new liaison person at the UN, is doing his regular broadcast. It's his brief to enlighten the UN as to the beneficial nature of apartheid, especially for the black man, and to explain how we, in South Africa, are single-handedly carrying the torch for Western civilisation. Eric Louw's big friend at the UN is Eamon de Valera who, thanks to the Boer War, still thinks of the Afrikaner Nationalists, not as our newest and most ghoulish racist oppressors, but as fellow republican victims of British Imperialism. Eric and Eamon sort of wear the same hat – and not only metaphorically – because it's from the Boer leader, General de Wet, that Michael Collins and the Irish rebels got their photogenic hats: those fetching leather hats with the poppers on one side. The IRA call these de Wet hats and they wear them in a spirit of brotherhood. Meanwhile, Eric and Eamon are bonded. Eric and Eamon are friends.

After their dad has woken the household ranting back at Eric Louw on the radio, he gets up and goes stamping through the house in sandals, venting his rage on all the venetian blinds, which he wrenches up with such force that their mum's family of ebony elephants regularly bounces off the living-room pelmet and bangs him on the head. The pelmet is one of several which are of his own making and they are the only item of woodwork that Dinah has ever seen him undertake. The pelmets are like three-sided wooden window boxes made of plywood that get screwed upside-down over the curtain rail to obscure the rufflette tape and the hooks. They are so much de rigueur at the time that even Dinah's dad, who is prodigiously non-DIY, is required to succumb to necessity and take up his tool kit in the cause of their construction.

While its main business is to make the lives of blacks even more of a waking nightmare than it was before the election, the new government is at the same time dealing with smaller swathes of English-speaking whites. It starts by pitching out numbers of high-profile top honchos in the armed services, the police and the civil service, especially those who might possibly have dossiers on the pro-Nazi activities undertaken during the Second World War by certain members of the present cabinet. It also puts the screws on any Afrikaner public servants that it suspects of having the wrong leanings. It sheds any English-speaking civil servants whose Afrikaans won't quite pass muster, in order that right-thinking Afrikaners can be moved into their jobs. Very soon the civil service and the armed forces are effectively the exclusive preserve of the *Volk*.

One of the government's main undertakings is to swipe the jobs off blacks and give them to poor white Afrikaners. This is what the Job Reservation Act is for, because it redefines whole categories of job as being for white people only. When Dinah and her mum go shopping in Stuttaford's, Dinah always likes the lift man whose name is Ephraim. He wears a smart khaki uniform with an epauletted drill-cloth shirt and matching trousers with very ironed creases and turn-ups. Ephraim has to move a shiny brass lever in a groove across a big brass disc to make the lift go up and down and to open and close the doors. All the shop assistants who get into the lift always start talking to Ephraim right away, because he's such a good listener.

One of the shop women will get in and say, 'You better make sure this lift doesn't break down today, Ephraim, because my feet is killing me this morning, honest-to-God. I'm telling you that, so help me.'

Then Ephraim will say, '*Hau*, madam, too much the foot is hurting today?'

'You can say that again,' the shop lady says. 'I went dancing last night, you know, Ephraim, and as true's God's my witness, my shoes was killing me all night long. Now I swear to God I've got bunions like I don't know what. Like nobody's business and that's for sure, I'm telling you.'

'*Hau*, madam,' Ephraim says again, after several sympathetic clicks. 'Too much the foot is hurting. Too much.'

Then, when that shop assistant gets out, another one will get in and she'll start right away as well.

'Well, I hope you aren't going to take so long to come when it's five o'clock, Ephraim. Because you might as well know that I'll have to be out of here like a bat out of hell tonight, as true's God's my witness,' she says.

'*Hau*, madam, too much busy tonight?' Ephraim will say.

'You not far wrong there, Ephraim, I swear to God,' the shop lady will say. 'Because I've *only* got my Ma and my fiancé's Ma and my Gran and my Auntie Hettie coming over – well, she's not *really* my auntie, but I call her my auntie – and anyway I've still got all my cooking to do and my greens to prepare and everything. And God only knows what there's going to be for dessert, so help me, plus I don't exactly want to look like I've been pulled through a bush backwards when they come, now do I, Ephraim?'

'*Hau*, madam,' Ephraim says. 'Too much busy tonight. Too much.'

'Well, I reckon it's lucky for you people that you just eat *mielie pap* and that's it, hey, Ephraim? I swear to God I'd eat it myself, so help me.'

All the shop ladies love talking to Ephraim, except for once when Dinah hears one of them say to another one, 'It really jives on my G-string the way that boy talks back all the time like that, you know? So help me, they not so cheeky where I come from on the farm. I'm not used to it.'

Then one day when Dinah and her mum get into the lift, Ephraim isn't there and a pinched-looking white girl with so-what body language is working Ephraim's brass lever. She's chewing gum while she's gabbling off her newly rote-learned lift patter and she's sniffing loudly in the pauses.

hardware-kitchenware-linenware-crockery
Go-wing-UP
lingerie-hoserie-ladies'fashions-tearoom-powder-room-
    accessories
Go-wing-UP

Dinah never sees Ephraim again, but when blacks disappear like that it's called going back to the farm. It means that the person has been sent back to the native reserve which is where the golf-ball oranges grow.

As experiment in social engineering, it's amazing to see how successfully apartheid is working. Week by week, year by year, the white poor are getting richer and more skilled; the blacks are getting more invisible. Sanlam, the ever-expanding Afrikaner insurance company, has now taken over the building in the city square that housed the Maypole Tearoom and, at some point in the future, as repression creates defiance and its suppression creates an underground, the Special Branch ensconces itself there in brightly lit offices across the whole top floor. The offices are brightly lit because the Special Branch likes its enemies to see that their guys are keeping busy.

The university people on the Butcher Estate respond in different ways to the Nationalist election victory. There are those who shudder and leave at once, taking jobs in Toronto, Los Angeles,

Glasgow, Salisbury and New South Wales. Harry Stent goes, the Pecks go, the Frankels and their three children go, Dr Lieberman goes, but of all those who go it's Peter Bullen whose departure is the hardest to accept – though he's left the girls with all his hardback children's books, including his Cautionary Tales and his childhood A.A. Milne collection. And over the next few years, Lisa and Dinah fight a war of possession over these precious relics until the flyleaves are covered with their alternately written and scratched out names:

> Lisa Sophia de Bondt
> Dinah Louisa de Bondt

The handwriting gets gradually more and more mature and it goes on until there's no more space on which to write.

There are those among the Butcher residents who assert that the Nats can't possibly stay in power for more than one term. They say that we're in it for five years and that's it. *Finito*. The whole show will be over and all we need do is to fix our minds on damage limitation. These are the people who drain away later, because, come 1953, when Dinah and her sister are twelve and thirteen, the Nats romp home with a massively increased majority, not only because gerrymandering is paying handsome dividends, not only because most wavering Afrikaners have by now been brought into the fold. It's also because lots of the English business people have discovered that they like the government's new laws, which make it even easier for them to regulate and control their black workers.

Anyway, in that same year, the English are focused on a happening which is vastly more exciting in their hierarchy of public goings-on than a general election, and the teachers and pupils at the Berea Road Government School for Girls are no exception. They are all preparing to celebrate the Coronation of Queen Elizabeth II. This is a very big occasion, but it's one that is not without its down side for Lisa and Dinah, much as they are enchanted by their free Coronation mugs. For weeks beforehand, the up-coming Coronation has ushered in a fever pitch of Durbanite royalism among the staff, and the girls' headmistress employs a non-stop three-line whip in the matter of peddling her stock of British flags. Every child is required to bring half a crown to school for the purpose of buying a small Union Jack on a stick. The flags are about the size of a standard school exercise book and they're selling at a brisk pace.

The problem for Lisa and Dinah is that their dad has a theory about flags and he says they're not to have them. Flags represent nationalism, he says, and nationalism is a Bad Thing. Nationalism, along with religion, is the root of all evil.

'Look what happened in Germany,' he says. 'Look at what's happening right here.'

Lisa and Dinah are unimpressed. They're sick of always being deviants at school and they're longing to wave their Union Jacks along with the rest of the herd.

'Oh plee-*eez*,' they whinge, but their dad is adamant.

'You go and tell Miss Marshall that I'd just as soon you waved the flag of the Transvaal Republic,' he says. 'Why not?' He is starting to get quite exercised about the flags and they can tell that he's really enjoying himself. 'Go on,' he says. 'Tell her. You go and tell her that you'll be happy to wave the *Vierkleur*.' The *Vierkleur* is the flag of the Transvaal's defunct Boer Republic.

Each day in the morning assembly, the head interrogates the children, who are seated before her in rows, cross-legged on the woodblock floor.

'Stand up all those girls who have not yet purchased their flags,' she says.

At first it's lots of children who stand up, because, even for normally coping little girls, it takes time to remember your half a crown. But each day, as the group of non-purchasers is smaller, it gets more and more embarrassing. It's especially awful for Lisa who is a prefect and in the top class. One day it's only Lisa and Dinah, plus the tiny smattering of neglected children whose parents can never get anything much together, let alone find half a crown. Then, finally, it's that terrible day when it's only Lisa and Dinah.

The girls are utterly mortified but the two possible options open to them have simply never crossed their minds. One would be to stop standing up in the assembly hall and the other would be to explain. Instead they carry their shame through the whole day and go home, where Lisa, thank goodness, breaks down over their mum and cries. Their mum promises to slip them each half a crown next morning and whispers that they're not to tell their dad. But the Coronation isn't over yet because, in addition to the flag waving, there's to be all-day feasting, singing, English country dancing and a fancy-dress parade. Your mum has got to make you a costume and she's also got to bake a cake for you to take to school for the party.

Dinah's mum throws herself into the fancy-dress project with enthusiasm. Lisa, who is now nearly as tall as a grown-up, has shed most of her puppy fat and can fit into her mother's clothes. Plus, she's newly besotted with Italian opera because the girls have recently been taken to a touring production of Verdi's *La Traviata*. For this reason, their mum conceives the idea that Lisa shall go as Violetta. She rakes through the *Klappkasten*, pulling out various numbers that date from her pre-marital dressy phase in Cape Town, and she settles on an ankle-length frilled white muslin garment which she has modified, complete with Born Arm sleeve, by Mrs van der Walt. With a camellia stuck in her auburn hair and a fan in her hand and a crewel-work scarf with a silk fringe, Lisa probably looks a lot more like Carmen than Violetta, but she certainly looks very nice. Dinah, thanks to her long blonde hair, is to go as Alice in Wonderland.

Among their fairly regular family book readings, the *Alice* books have always been big favourites of their dad's. He likes all the maths-y jokes and, since he's invariably the reader, he also gets to choose all the books. This means that until Peter comes along with his Hilaire Belloc Cautionary Tales, the girls are frequently subjected to the *Struwwelpeter* stories, which are read to them in German. Their parents think these stories are funny – though poor Lisa, the family's one-handed thumbsucker, is never much amused by the Dreaded Scissor Man who leaps on to the page in full colour, brandishing his giant's shears, and hacks off the small boy's thumbs. Lisa finds this upsetting, particularly as the picture shows his two copiously bleeding stumps in accurate close-up.

And Dinah, in turn, is wholly uncaptivated by the Fat Boy who suddenly becomes a non-eater and who – with repeated cries of '*Ich esse keine Suppe nein!*' – dwindles swiftly from Fat Boy to Matchstick Boy and then to Deceased Boy, over five graphic illustrations. The second to last picture shows the Fat Boy relegated, thread-like, to the sick bed with a futile clutter of medicine bottles alongside him on the bedside cabinet. The only thing Dinah likes about this picture is the carefully drawn chamber pot that is sitting underneath the Fat Boy's bed. The last picture is of the Fat Boy's tombstone which is planted on a sad little grassy knoll. The *Struwwelpeter* readings tend to be rotated with *Huckleberry Finn* and *Tom Sawyer*, both of which Lisa and Dinah think of as boys' books, and with the *Alice* books which tend to go way above their heads, but it's true that the books make a store of mental furniture which both girls come to relish later on.

In Sir John Tenniel's illustrations Alice has Dinah-length hair which exhibits the same kind of undulating crimp that Dinah gets when she unravels her school plaits. And Alice is wearing a full-skirted, puff-sleeved dress that happens to look very like Dinah's favourite party dress. So all Dinah needs for her fancy-dress costume is an Alice band and an apron which are both easily acquired. Then, Dinah's mum decides, she must have a flamingo: a full-sized model flamingo which is to be carried upside-down, just as Alice does in the croquet scene, when she uses the bird as a mallet. Dinah's mum has a lot of fun with the flamingo, because it's the first item of sculpture she's ever tried to make and it's also one of the few really challenging projects that's come her way in years. She starts by moulding a fine chicken-wire frame and covering it with strips of old blanket. Then she covers the whole thing with shades of flamingo-pink felt, detailing the creature's wings, beak and webbed feet with subtle artifice. The completed flamingo is a triumph and stands as tall as Dinah on wonderful spindly legs. And the crimped, loose Alice hair is rather enhancing. The girls' mum has just this once added a little blush of rouge to each daughter's cheeks, so they feel very satisfied with the way they look. There is a spring in their step as Violetta and Alice set out for school on Coronation Day.

At first they are merely slightly shaken when they meet five London Bobbies, two Beefeaters and one Grenadier Guard along the way, but by the time they are assembled in the playground for the parade, Lisa and Dinah have found themselves to be oddballs once again, in the company of two dozen crowned Lillibets and a dozen Dukes of Edinburgh. There are several more Beefeaters and a pair of Robin Hoods, four Admirals Lord Nelson, each with a cardboard telescope clamped to his blind eye, a smattering of square-mile City gents in bowler hats carrying rolled umbrellas and faked-up copies of the London *Times*, twenty-five redcoats, half a dozen khaki-clad British Tommies, three Sir Walter Raleighs and two ornately dressed Virgin Queens. One proud little girl is head to foot in yards of Union Jack. She has a Union Jack hat, a Union Jack dress and Union Jack ballet shoes with pompoms. But probably the most envied girl of all is a bronzed and tridented Britannia encircled by an ingenious, coin-like bronze hoop that miraculously says 'ONE PENNY' in apparently free-standing but discreetly wired bronze letters. The costume is a marvel and is shouting First Prize Winner before the procession so much as gets off the ground. In addition, there are a pair of Punch and Judys and one blue-painted Boadicea.

Nobody except for Lisa is dressed as a loose-living foreign consumptive and nobody, except for Dinah, is unaccountably wearing a pinny over her best party dress while carrying a large pink bird the wrong way up. Even before the parade has begun Dinah has heard poor Lisa try to explain herself twenty times.

'I'm Violetta. She's in *La Traviata*. No, it's a op'ra. I said *op'ra*.'

The listening children gawp and shrug. The nearest anyone in Lisa's class has got to knowing what an opera is comes from early evening Springbok Radio, where the Firestone Strings play excerpts from the overture to *The Flying Dutchman*. The excerpts are interrupted, roughly every fifty seconds, by the ad breaks which repeatedly remind listeners that the Firestone Strings come courtesy of the Firestone Rubber Company.

Through the gauntlet of the fancy-dress parade, Dinah's ordeal is punctuated by the onlookers' repeating refrain: 'Who's she?' 'Who's she?' 'Who's *she*?'

Only occasionally there's a variation as the more protective members of the crowd move forward to pluck her by the sleeve.

'Excuse me,' they whisper discreetly. 'Excuse me, lovey, but you're carrying that bird upside-down.'

So Dinah, succumbing to the consensus, starts to carry her flamingo the right way up.

After the procession is over, she and her bosom friend Angela Trevean abandon their accessories under a tree and run off to find the stash of home-made cakes that have been cut up and arranged on enormous platters.

'Look at that cake,' Angela says. 'Look at *that* one. Look at *those*.'

'Look at *that* one,' Dinah says.

They giggle as they point out what they take to be the funnier-looking cakes, though none of them is really that funny. It's just that everything makes them giggle and giggle-stoking has become a sort of etiquette between them. Meanwhile they are loading their plates with slices of chocolate Swiss roll and wedges of Victoria sponge. Some people's mothers have been so intensely patriotic they've done their cakes in three layers, red, white and blue.

'Look at *that* one,' Angela says.

'*Ugh*,' Dinah says, and she giggles and groans extra hard, because it's a slice of two-tone loaf cake, chocolate and plain.

It's been cut from her own mother's German marble cake and she's not at all keen to have Angela find this out. She knows that cakes should be Victoria sponge. They should be two rounds stuck together with jam. Angela's mother knows this because she comes from Cornwall. It's because she comes from Cornwall that she has a pixie on her door knocker. Angela can't remember being a baby in St Austell, but she knows that pixies are her heritage. Dinah's mum's marble loaf cake is called *Karierte Affe*, which means chequered monkey.

After the second Nationalist general election victory, Dinah's mum is in denial. She copes with it by talking up the burlesque aspects of the system and shutting out all its horrors. She pretends to herself that the whole ghoulish process is no more than a ridiculous pantomime in which blacks and whites are made to enter the central post office through different doors, merely so that they can rejoin each other in the same queue once they're both inside. And the queue, let's face it, is long enough regardless of your skin colour, because the Post Office is yet another institution that is providing jobs for poor Afrikaners. And a lot of the poor Afrikaners are learning basic skills on the job.

The girls' dad responds by joining the Liberal Party – a new party with a non-racial membership which sees itself as a free-market alternative to the now banned Communist Party. Hitherto the Communists have been the only party in South Africa to endorse the idea of a non-racial franchise, but their dad hasn't trusted Communists since the defection of the Brainy Rebel.

The Liberal Party never quite manages to enlist the kind of mass black support that it has in mind, though it gains the odd black intellectual. Alan Paton is its most high-profile member and it succeeds in acquiring the membership of a flamboyant new heart-throb on the Durban scene, a tall, curly-haired Old Etonian, who has recently taken up a lecturing post in the politics department. The public school heart-throb ends his days as one of P.W. Botha's men in the apartheid state's last-ditch President's Council, but in Dinah's childhood he is much admired, not only for needling Special Branch policemen who have a time of it trying to spell his mile-long, Norman Conquest name, but also for having the liveliest quips in answer to racist repartee while engaged upon the futile task of canvassing for the Liberal Party. The girls' dad has also been trying to canvass for the Party, but he finds it hard to make any headway and, after a whole morning's doorstopping, he has got only one promise of support. It comes from a stone-deaf and aged anti-Semite, who doesn't like the United Party candidate because he's half a Jew. Dinah's dad feels obliged to belabour what the Liberal Party stands for, but he finally gives up gratefully when the old boy's hearing aid begins to whistle at a piercing frequency.

Mainly what Dinah remembers about the Liberal Party is that her mum once agrees to billet two delegates during the annual Party conference. The house being rather small and possessed of only two bedrooms, the delegates' beds will be Lisa's and Dinah's, while the girls, for the duration, are to have sleeping bags on their parents' floor. The delegates are two unknown Cape Town academics called Dr Liebmann and Dr Manheim.

'I hope these delegates are not too big,' their mum says doubtfully, as she plumps up the pillows on the narrow, girlie little beds.

But she has hardly spoken before the delegates are standing in the doorway. Then they are bending their heads in order to effect an entry. They cast their eyes around the living room, seeking out any chairs that might possibly withstand their weight, because the Doctors Liebmann and Manheim are both almost seven foot tall and both are unambiguously fat.

Dinah's mum never ceases to find this episode hilarious and, from time to time, she'll recall it and then she'll suddenly say, '*Gott-ach-Gott! Diese dikke Liebmann und Manheim! Ach-Gott-ach-Gott-noch-mal!*' And her eyes will fill with tears of joy.

Angela Trevean has been Dinah's best friend ever since Class Three. Bossy Sally is history and it's all down to kind Miss Vaizey and her brilliant matchmaking skills.

'Sally and Dinah,' she says one day, early on in Class Three's second term. 'I'm going to have to separate you.'

'Aaw, Miss Vaiz-*eey*,' say the girls.

'There's far too much talking and distracting going on,' she says. 'Sally, I want you to change places with Angela.'

It doesn't cross Dinah's mind that Miss Vaizey might have noticed that Sally is a bully and that nice little Angela Trevean hasn't yet found anyone to team up with, but the arrangement induces love at first sight and the moment Angela is in place beside her, the chattering and giggling begin. Angela and Dinah chatter and giggle their way almost non-stop through the next four years, yet nobody makes them separate. They giggle their way through to the top class and on into the first year of high school, where the friendship abruptly stops. But, for the moment, they do their best giggling in cookery and sewing because Mrs Stewart is not only ferocious but she's eccentric, so that it's all the more exciting to court the dangers of her wrath.

Mrs Stewart is eccentric because she comes from England and she often says 'weather permitting', which always makes everyone giggle. The cake sale will take place, 'weather permitting', she says. The craft show will be worth a visit, 'weather permitting'. In Durban the weather is always permitting, so the girls see no reason on this earth for her to say it. Durban is that place where you can always plan a beach picnic five weeks in advance. Angela and Dinah giggle because Mrs Stewart makes them scrub the cookery-room tables after each session and while they're doing it she'll take hold of somebody's elbow and work it back and forth.

'A little more elbow grease, girlie,' she'll say. 'A little more elbow grease, that's the way.'

They giggle because she praises ammonia. She says it's got a 'nice clean smell'. Mrs Stewart will uncork the bottle and give it a hearty sniff before pushing it forcefully under everyone's nose and making them have a sniff. The bottle is aptly brandnamed Scrubb's Ammonia.

'Ah,' she says. 'That's a good clean smell! *Isn't* that a good clean smell?'

She says it as the class is reeling and swooning, but substance abuse is not yet a concept on the international youth agenda.

Angela and Dinah giggle in sewing because Mrs Stewart makes

all the girls allow for growth, so everything they make is always completely unwearable. Plus she always makes you sew every seam three times over, no matter how fine your stitches may be on the first two attempts. The routine is that you have to take your completed seam up for inspection before you're allowed to proceed. Everything from gym shorts to pyjamas is stitched by hand, as though the sewing machine has not yet been invented. Mrs Stewart will then take the garment off you and start wrenching violently at your seam while you're trying not to explode into giggles. She's built like a battleship and she has huge, asbestos hands which – as she has previously demonstrated in cookery – are immune to boiling water. Once she has ripped your seam in two, she'll fling the garment back at you for you to catch on the wing.

'Cobbling, I call that,' she says, though Angela's stitches are always exquisite and microscopic. And even Dinah's running stitches are moderately all right. 'That's not sewing, that's cobbling,' she says. 'GO and get a job cobbling mailbags at one of Her Majesty's prisons!'

The giggle potential with Mrs Stewart usually has to do with these predictable repeating refrains, but one day, having ripped open Angela's centre seam, she says, unexpectedly, 'I want you to run round that again.' And Angela, seizing her moment, carefully lays out the two halves of her giant's pyjama bottoms on the floor, right in front of Mrs Stewart's table, and she proceeds to run around them. She circumnavigates the pyjamas fully three times before Mrs Stewart orders her sharply to sit down.

Cookery is always the best fun, not only because of the ammonia and the elbow grease, but because Mrs Stewart makes them cook such foul, inedible things. They do 'convalescent diets' for months on end and, even when they're cooking for healthy people, everything has to be boiled, simmered, stewed and steamed. They do barley broth and stewed prunes with custard. They do lots of lumpy puddings using tapioca and sago and suet and arrowroot and cornflour. Nearly everything they cook is tasteless and gluey, but especially when it's steamed fish. This is because steamed fish always comes with an extra gluey and tasteless white sauce.

One day, after the girls have done steamed fish in white sauce, Angela forgets hers on the classroom window-sill at home time, so it stays there right through the long weekend because there's a state holiday coming up. They have lots of state holidays at Dinah's school, because, as well as all the Empire Days and Union Days, there are the ever-increasing numbers of Afrikaner Nationalist heroes to be honoured, and voortrekker battles to be commemorated. There is Kruger Day and van Riebeck day and Dingaan's Day which has recently been re-named 'The Day of the Covenant'. That's because we can't have a day named after a Zulu king and, anyway, it marks the defeat of Dingaan at the Battle of Blood River, when the voortrekkers made a covenant always to mark the day of the battle if only God would help them to win. Then, once God had done so, they promptly forgot all about the covenant for something like forty years. But now it's been resurrected as a centrepiece of Nationalist triumphalism.

Dinah's school, along with all the other schools, has just been celebrating van Riebeck Day in style, because that year it's the three hundredth anniversary of Jan van Riebeck's landing at the Cape in 1652. Dinah and Angela can now draw ground plans in their sleep of the Cape Town Castle which the founder erected, complete with moat, in the shape of a five-pointed star. And they can rattle off the names of the star's five points:

> Orange
> Nassau
> Leerdam
> Buuren
> Katzenellenbogen

Dinah's dad is inclined to welcome these patriotic holidays, because there's always more classical music than usual on the radio, since it's thought to have more gravitas. Whenever there's a bout of unscheduled classical music and it's not on a patriotic holiday, Dinah's dad will hazard that there's been a significant death.

'Prime Minister's been shot,' he'll say.

He says it more with hope than with conviction, but, eventually, on one distant day – after prolonged but unexplained extracts from the B Minor Mass – Dinah's dad turns out, at last, to be right. Someone has shot at Dr Verwoerd during the Rand Easter Show, but the bullets have just bounced off him, thus proving his demigod status.

102

Meanwhile, all through van Riebeck Day, Angela's fish is steadily rotting and stinking on the classroom window-sill and, when the girls return to school, the white sauce has grown green hairs. The smell is so prodigious when the lid of the tin food caddy is lifted that Angela and Dinah become almost ecstatic with delight. Spontaneous pilgrimages to the window-sill take place throughout the day, as the girls' admiring classmates tiptoe up to the holy site and gingerly lift the lid. Finally it's Mrs Gordon who gets wise to the proceedings and makes Angela throw it away.

Mrs Stewart has a female cousin who lives in Manor Gardens and she's got her own vegetable patch. She supplies Mrs Stewart with cabbages for the school menus, and Angela and Dinah are dispatched once a week to collect the cousin's crop. This is another ecstatic experience, because the cousin is a born-again muck and mulch person and her particular repeating refrains have all to do with the hearts of cabbages.

'Feel the heart on that one, dear,' the cousin will say to the girls.

She exhorts each girl in turn to bend down and fondle the cabbages' hearts, so that the effort of suppressing their giggles as they crouch to squeeze the cabbages is almost more than Angela and Dinah can bear. Having finally made their escape from the cousin, they howl and chortle the length of the street with a cardboard box full of cabbages bouncing between them as they run.

Angela, too, has an older sister and she's very good at thinking up sister-goading schemes. Her own sister is now in high school and, as such, is beyond their reach, but Lisa, with her new prefect's dignity, is a very rewarding target. At first the scheme is merely to cut out all the pictures they can find in the newspaper of particularly hideous men, and to ambush Lisa in the school corridors with these and flash them at her while chanting as loudly as they can.

'He's your fiancé – he's your fiancé,' the younger sisters chant and because Lisa gets so furious about it, they find it too much fun to stop.

As time passes, the game is modified and corrupted, first to a system of multiple cut-out fiancés which the two girls simply hurl at Lisa, before running off uttering their chant. 'Fiancé, fiancé, fiancé . . .' Then it becomes a system of multiple fiancés who are ripped up into a fine confetti and rained down upon Lisa as she's trying to go home. Finally, the girls simply hurl great handfuls of ripped-up newsprint at Lisa, while their chant has become so corrupted that it isn't any longer intelligible to anyone but themselves.

'Vombay-vombay-vombay –' But it still puts Lisa into a rage.

'Shuddup-shuddup-shud-UP-SHUDD*UP*!!' she says. 'I'm telling on you.'

Angela's presence is a real pain for Lisa, but it's very good for Dinah, who is transformed from weed, cry-baby and shrinking violet into swanky slouch with street cred. And Angela is the best antidote against Dinah's mother's morbid anxieties.

'Careful with a sewing needle,' is one of Dinah's mum's favourite maxims. 'Careful, Dee, that you don't lose it.'

She herself is terrifically careful and she does her lumpish sock darning with a needle she's been using since before the Second World War. If Dinah ever so much as thinks of losing a needle, she has her mum's story of Tante Berthe to stop her. Tante Berthe, Dinah's mum says, once lost a needle while sewing as a girl. It penetrated her buttock and, finally, after the aunt had suffered decades of respiratory and digestive complaints along with violent and spasmodic shooting pains, the needle emerged between her shoulder blades, having travelled at its leisure through all Tante Berthe's inner organs.

'My sister's forever losing needles,' Angela says to Dinah. 'And it's usually in her bed.'

She herself has just managed to mislay the third needle of the afternoon and is having a little scrabble on the maize mat at her feet.

'What happens to her?' Dinah says in some alarm, but Angela just laughs.

'She gets pricked,' she says and she gives a casual shrug before she gets up from the floor. 'Can't find it,' she says.

For Dinah this is a landmark moment, a moment of liberation. Every morning on the bus to school, Angela greets Dinah with unpredictable salutations, because she likes the sounds of words.

'Hello, *Mong-Cherree*,' she says. 'I didn't make that up. I think it's French.'

Or one day she'll have made up a long and complicated new

salutation which Dinah and she both internalise instantly, while nobody else can ever manage to take its sequence on board.

'Hello, *Waghoggiwempshonist*,' she'll say. And to this it's obvious that there's only one reply.

'Hello, *Waghoggiwempshonist-Ishnessishness*,' Dinah says.

Their final severance at high school is painful, like divorce.

SIX

D INAH'S MUM'S PARENTS, having emigrated to Cape Town in 1933, then returned briefly to Berlin, thinking to come back soon. But the timing of their return was such that they were very shortly caught there by the war. And afterwards – once hostilities were over – they couldn't be reunited with their children. The pro-British United Party government of General Smuts would not allow Germans into South Africa. So it was thanks to the Afrikaner Nationalist election victory of 1948 that Lisa and Dinah finally got to meet their maternal grandparents the following year. By then the girls were eight and nine.

On the day that the two foreign grandparents appeared in the Durban bungalow, they stayed for only three hours before being whisked off to Johannesburg to be billeted with one of their sons. So Dinah thereafter always felt that she knew them – knew the idea of them, anyway – not from that brief lunchtime visit, but through her mum's family stories about her early life in pre-war Berlin.

Comfortably settled in Lindenstrasse, *circa* 1928, the Jacobsens were clearly not a political family. But they knew that Hitler was common; a common little man and grubby. For Dinah's mum, 'common' survives as a frequent and defining moral quality. So Dinah's mum and her brothers were all prone to mimicking Hitler's accent, while they amused each other with anecdotes about the eggie breakfasts and other food debris which the demagogue was reputed to slop down the front of his shirts. The family was liberal-bourgeois and politically apathetic, inclined at first to view the movement not so much with alarm as with distaste – the more so, because its visual aesthetic was so predominantly kitsch.

The Nazis, unlike Mussolini's *fascisti*, could not, at this point, boast a vanguard of talented art workers with which to woo the Berlin intelligentsia. There was no Giuseppe Terragni, no Mario Sironi lending weight to the glorious cause. The city's artistic elite, its distinguished painters and architects, had placed themselves in opposition. The tone of Berlin was progressive and antipathetic and, as the Nazi machine rolled on and into power, its artists were not so much honoured and incorporated as picked off, banned and vilified – hounded and driven out into exile.

Lindenstrasse 1928 and – given that the Jacobsen children had all been doing their growing up in a context of hyper-inflation, massive unemployment, worker riots, political marches, political murders and whispered rumours of coup – they were still managing lives of sweet and gentle privilege. The family could still rise to a housemaid, a gardener and a cook. Plus there was little Duttie who, though there was no longer any need for her as nanny, had somehow managed to attach herself to the household.

When in town, they lived a few minutes' walk from Unter den Linden in a house that had its own orchard and stables, along with a well-stocked wine cellar. The Bechstein still stood in the upstairs drawing room, which was big enough for the young people to throw parties and balls for their friends. At a time when Käthe Kollwitz was making her harrowing sketches of Berlin's hollow-eyed poor cradling their dead children in bleak upstairs rooms, the Jacobsens' larder could always rise to whole sides of bacon and baskets of seasonal produce brought in from the countryside: asparagus, wild strawberries and tender little green peas.

When the family was not in town, it was wintering in the Harz Mountains or relaxing on the Wannsee or taking the motor launch past turreted castles along the Rhine. For these enjoyable nautical interludes, the Jacobsen young all had sailor suits and took snap-shots of each other in staged, larky poses: 'Man Overboard', 'Look, Pa, No Hands'. Their dad was an established and respected architect – ace dad and excellent provider.

Lindenstrasse 1930, and Herr Jacobsen's mind was gradually, increasingly, becoming infused with unease. The German electo-rate had just increased the National Socialist share of the vote and he was coming to see that, not only was Hitler inexorably on the way up, but that the man was a sure-fire warmonger, bent on territorial expansion. Along with Marianne, the Jacobsens had

107

three healthy male children, all of an age to make cannon fodder, and he was keen to keep his boys alive.

'Hitler will make war,' he said. 'Germany will once again make war.'

The young ones got easily bored by such talk. They had never been much interested in current affairs. Though they were theoretically young adults, they still played tig in the passageways and teased the maids and hid each other's shoes. They dressed up for parties and failed to notice that their father was beginning to pore over maps of outlandish and far-flung places.

Of the three boys, the oldest was Otto, though Marianne was the oldest child. Otto was bold, sure-footed and a daredevil. He was the bossy one; the brainy one, always head of the pack. By the time the Nazis had colonised Berlin and staged their book-burning photo-opportunity directly opposite the university, Otto had spent two years there as a geology student. Heinrich was the next one down: the bookworm, the quiet one, a little crushed by his forceful older brother. He had just left school and had started work in a Berlin publishing house, though the timing for book production was perhaps not particularly propitious.

Heinrich, by then, had already been devoted to Irmi for three years – his studious schoolgirl sweetheart and Marianne's classmate, to whom he was secretly engaged. The engagement was being kept secret, because Irmi's father, a self-important and stern old tyrant, wanted his only daughter to remain unmarried. He wanted her wholly committed to the needs of his own old age. For this reason, whenever the Jacobsen young had their parties, it was Herr Jacobsen's job to divert the tyrant by plying him with brandy and cigars. That way poor Irmi could have a little fun – though fun was not an attribute Lisa and Dinah ever came to associate with their prematurely faded and sad-eyed aunt.

Jurgen, tall, baby-blond and beautiful, was sweet sixteen and still at school. He and Marianne not only looked just like each other, but they were soulmates and best friends. Both had prominent cheekbones and large, widely spaced blue eyes. Both were shy, artistic, unpushy and day-dreaming. But their survival strategies began to vary once things took a downward turn.

When the Jacobsens sailed into Table Bay and stepped out into the bright sunshine of Adderley Street under the shadow of Table

Mountain, they found it all *entzückend*. Cape Town – with its plastered eighteenth-century cottages, its reassuringly urbanised 'black' population that came in varying shades of palish brown, its touches of Islamic culture, thanks to the numerous descendants of Malay slaves – it all seemed to them not so much Heart of Darkness as Eastern Mediterranean.

They had carried with them their habitual air of Old World confidence and expectation, their total lack of unease. This, though not one of the Jacobsen family had mastered English. They were, after all, Herr Architekt, Jacob Bahne Jacobsen, late of Berlin, home of Mies van der Rohe and the Bauhaus. Was not Walter Gropius a family friend? Had not Otto Klemperer more than once been a guest in their house? Frau Architekt, Sophie Jacobsen, was, as always, an imposing figure whose bosom could do credit to her discreet displays of heirloom jewellery. Otto Jacobsen was a fine and handsome young man, determined, at once, to continue with his studies in geology. And Heinrich? Well, Heinrich wanted to publish books. There were, *natürlich*, book publishers in the country? The only thing that irked the Jacobsens was the inexplicable absence of decent coffee.

Jurgen, the family envisaged, would first go to school and make his *Abitur*. Then he would study to become an architect, just like his father. And Marianne? Well, Marianne was both beautiful and accomplished. She could play Mozart and Scarlatti so charmingly on the piano. Also Schubert and Brahms. Marianne could speak a prettily hesitant French. She painted water-colour landscapes and still lifes. She painted with glazes on Rosenthal china. Marianne, once she had got over that silly infatuation with her boy cousin, would undoubtedly make an advantageous marriage.

Herr Jacobsen was, by this time, coming up to sixty, and his wife was two years younger. They addressed all the people they met in German and, when this failed, they tried French. Frau Jacobsen could not begin to envisage a world in which people did not speak German – or at least a little French. French was the international language, was it not? Why on earth should a person speak English?

Dinah's mother and her brothers had none of them enjoyed the most rigorous of high-school educations. The boys had been taught in small private establishments by gammy-legged and shell-shocked rejects from the First World War, men whose brains had been damaged by nerve gas. The older boys had got quite used to dissuading their geography master from committing suicide via an upstairs classroom window. They had taken it in their stride whenever the science master was gripped by seizure or by panic attack. One of the masters had paranoid delusions; another was a minor pyromaniac whom they needed, occasionally, to divest of his matchbox. Only then could a lesson proceed.

Dinah's mum, having been taught by women, had avoided this particular dimension. Her teachers had never tried setting her alight – neither metaphorically nor literally. History had been a dreary business of rattling off endless dates, and she was instantly sabotaged in her attempts to learn English by an aged English pedagogue, a trousered *fin-de-siècle* Bohemian – more at home in a London salon than in a 1920s Berlin classroom – a woman who chain-smoked through an ebony cigarette holder and announced herself as a one-time bed-fellow of Oscar Wilde. She was not one to tolerate a teenage German sweetie-pie who couldn't pronounce the English 'th'.

Each time Dinah's mum struggled and failed, so the trousered Bohemian simply ordered her out of the classroom to stand in disgrace outside the door. After a while it became her habit to order Marianne out of the room before the lesson had got off the ground. 'She srew me alvays outside ze class because I could not pronounce ziss foolish "th",' Dinah's mum later told Lisa and Dinah – and she always asserted that the 'th' sound could only be accomplished by a person's sticking his tongue right out of the mouth, clamping it firmly between the teeth and risking the embarrassment of showering his neighbour with spittle. The English 'th', Dinah's mum thought, was nothing short of 'common'.

One day, when Marianne was just sixteen, she decided that she was tired of standing outside the classroom door, so she went off to get her hat and coat from the cloakroom. Then she walked herself straight home.

'I'm never going back,' she told her father, and he was completely on her side. After all, for what should his daughter need more schooling? For what should she require a few vulgar certificates? Pieces of paper, testifying to various humdrum skills, as if she were destined to become some workplace drone. Some office filing clerk.

Once she began to feel a little hang-loose around the house, Marianne was enrolled by her father in a Berlin art school, where she learned to paint rosebuds on bone-china teacups and, after that, he permitted her to take employment at a fashion house designing ballgowns. This is why, among the small collection of youthful *memorabilia* that fascinated her younger daughter, Marianne could count a slim parchment portfolio of 1920s fashion sketches with little silk swatches still pinned to their edges. The drawings were roughly concurrent with the work of George Grosz, Max Beckmann and Otto Dix, but the men's minds and talents were otherwise engaged at the time. They were busy chronicling the Apocalypse. They were documenting the violent and sleazy end of Weimar Germany.

It was in the context of the art school that Marianne and Wilhelm fell in love. Wilhelm was the ski-jump champion, Marianne's own first cousin, grown by then into a curly-haired, square-jawed young man, with a jutting, deeply cleft chin. Wilhelm was also a student at the art school and the two of them had soon become inseparable. That was, of course, until Marianne's mother had pulled the plug on her daughter's career. Then it rankled a lot with Marianne as her own time hung heavy, that Wilhelm should be busy with his artist friends, bonding in the painting studios, while she was suffering under the eye of her ever-present mother who constantly found fault.

Sophie Jacobsen had never been one of her daughter's greatest admirers. She preferred the company of her sons. She considered Marianne skinny and lacking in proper womanly allure. Dinah's mum could boast none of those attributes with which Frau Jacobsen herself had been so generously endowed: dainty feet, an ample bosom, a voluptuous hour-glass figure and thick wavy hair. Frau Jacobsen could not appreciate that her daughter's looks were, in fact, happily spot-on for the time. So she was driven to expend futile energy upon hopeless attempts at reform. 'Marianne,' she would say repeatedly, 'sit up straight! Marianne, look at your hair!' She couldn't believe that her daughter's short, wafty blonde hair could ever count as a woman's Crowning Glory.

Because Marianne could no longer bear to stay at home where she felt herself on the margins of real life, that real life she had so briefly and tantalisingly glimpsed, she took to visiting the great

Berlin railway stations where she listened over and over to the litany of destinations and she watched the clouds of steam. She lingered to observe the barges from the bridges over the River Spree and she started to build castles in the air. She fantasised about travelling to exotic faraway places, having no idea how soon these fantasies would become a harsh reality and how effectively they would sever her from Wilhelm.

In Cape Town, Dinah's grandfather was soon to discover that his architectural qualifications were not recognised by the local rubber-stamping bureaucracy – a circumstance that came as the first blow to his comfortable sense of self. In order for him to practise his profession he would need to do so by devious means and he was duly persuaded into a partnership with a building contractor who presented himself conveniently for that purpose. Herr Jacobsen at once committed more than half his liquid assets to the partnership and he designed one beautiful house which was promptly erected in the elegant suburb of Oranjesicht – at which point the police caught up with the building contractor and unmasked him as a bankrupt and serial con-man. And when the law impounded the partnership's assets to pay off the bankrupt's creditors, naturally, it was Herr Architekt's money that vanished into the pit.

Once the family had stopped reeling from this misfortune, the elder Jacobsens emerged feeling the beginnings of their old age. They had also begun to feel a little unpleasantly foreign and humble. They set their sights a bit lower, then, and decided to sink what remained of their liquid assets into a market-gardening venture which beckoned with all the charm of a peaceful retirement plan. What they knew about the rural life was limited to Herr Jacobsen's childhood on a Friesian Island dairy farm, but the Cape's benign Mediterranean climate, its little wine valleys, its profusion of white arum lilies that grew wild over vacant lots, its mass and variety of bright exotic flowers that Malay stallholders offered in the market-place – all these things seduced the Jacobsens into believing that the Cape was, after all, the Garden of Eden, and that a market garden was precisely the downsizing idyll to meet their particular case. The plan was to grow flowers and to produce high-quality honey and preserves. Meanwhile, because many hands were required to get the venture afloat, Otto and Heinrich's career plans were temporarily placed on hold.

Dinah's mum, unlike her three brothers, was not a part of the project. Since her separation from Wilhelm and the experience of watching her father embark upon what looked like inescapable decline, she had become much more introspective. Throughout his financial tribulations she had struggled, more than the rest of her siblings, to play interpreter for him and she had found herself ludicrously inadequate. She knew that she would have to improve her English as quickly as possible, and, in the face of her mother's stern disapproval, she had arranged to live in with a pair of elderly English sisters as a sort of au pair and companion: 'a servant', as her mother so kindly put it.

The elderly sisters instructed Dinah's mum to address them as Miss Connie and Miss Louisa. They had soon become very fond of Marianne and they felt sorry for her misfortune in being so patently un-English. In consequence, they were rigorous in training her up towards English standards of behaviour. They liked to feel they were guiding their protégée in proper English ways.

One day, when Miss Connie had sent Marianne to the post office with a parcel, the clerk had handed her so many stamps that she couldn't fit them on to the front of Miss Connie's parcel without obscuring the address.

'Shall I shtick some of zese shtamps on to ze backside?' Marianne asked the clerk.

The clerk, a young man, giggled suggestively and made a saucy remark which Marianne, while she understood it in spirit, couldn't really grasp. She promptly returned, with cheeks aflame, to the house of Miss Connie and Miss Louisa, where she described to the ladies what had occurred and asked what she'd said to provoke it.

The two English ladies, having grown up without recourse to a word for the WC, were quite disproportionately shocked. Marianne had disgraced herself. There was no question about it. She had spoken the unmentionable out loud. They at once began to speculate whether Marianne would ever again be fit for polite society. And Dinah's mum, having not much idea that her hosts' manners were out of tune with the times, was more baffled than ever, more mortified by the enormity of her *faux pas* than she had been before she had sought her hosts' guidance.

The Misses Connie and Louisa, while much given to amplifying Marianne's small transgressions, did so always for her edification and moral growth. And, though she found the steady drip of correction lowering to the spirit, she only once lost her temper. This happened on the morning that her mentors accused her of stealing from the cooler. Marianne, they hinted, had stolen the cream.

The English ladies had what Dinah's mum considered one truly disgusting habit. Each day, they saved the wrinkled skin that had formed on the surface of boiled milk and they kept these pickings in the cooler on a saucer until the Sunday morning. Then, for a special treat, they would spread the accumulated wrinklings on their porridge. Dinah's mum had always thought that these little gobs of flayed milk looked repellent, like sweat-soaked rags, but the English ladies referred to them as 'the cream' and considered them, most mercifully, a delicacy too precious to be shared with those of lower rank in the household.

Then came that Sunday morning when Marianne was sternly summoned from bed and ushered into the drawing room. Miss Connie, as the elder, addressed her first.

'A certain something beginning with "c" is missing from the larder,' she said. 'I think you will know what I mean.'

Marianne made no reply as she stared at the sisters in puzzlement. Then Miss Louisa spoke in her turn.

'You must be honest with us, Marianne,' she said kindly. 'We do this for your own good. Only be honest with us, my dear, and we're prepared to forgive and forget.'

It was quite a while before Marianne began to catch the sisters' drift, but once she did, she was furious. She was more incensed by the aspersions cast upon her good taste than by those cast upon her sense of honesty.

'*I?*' she said. '*I?*! Eat zees filsy old rags? *Gott ach Gott! Ich ekel mich!* Never in my life!' She shuddered involuntarily and writhed with disgust.

Displacement and loneliness had by now begun to drive Marianne to a contemplation of the spiritual and this was being helped by the fact that Wilhelm's letters were now few and far between. She began to pore in solitude over The Gospel According to St Luke and, that same Sunday – the Sunday of the cream – she took herself all on her own to Cape Town's cathedral where, sixty-five years later, Archbishop Desmond Tutu, in a spirit of ecumenical tolerance, addressed the nation at the memorial service of Joe Slovo, Communist, atheist and liberation hero.

As she entered, the congregation rose and immediately began to sing what Marianne thought of as the German national anthem. For an instant her spirit soared as she contemplated the marvel of the congregation's bursting into song like that – and all just for her.

It was 'Praise the Lord, ye heavens adore Him', being sung to the tune of '*Gott erhalte Franz den Kaiser*', an anthem Josef Haydn wrote after hearing a rendering of 'God Save the King' during his visit to London in 1797. And it was hardly Haydn's fault that his effort should have turned out so much better than its English model; nor that, at that particular historical moment, the tune should have been highjacked to serve the purposes of Hitler's Third Reich.

When Marianne decided to pay Wilhelm a visit, she docked in Hamburg in the rain. Her first impression, after the balmy climate of the Cape, was of grey winter washing hanging in the grey back yards of even greyer tenement houses. Her second impression was of the ever-present tramp of soldiers' boots. Wilhelm, when she met up with him, was inexplicably edgy and sometimes openly hostile. The occasions on which he agreed to see her were almost invariably *à trois*, since he was frequently accompanied by a female person whom Marianne, in later years, always referred to as a mannequin.

The mannequin was given to expensive dress – a fact that Wilhelm saw fit to use as the opportunity to find fault with Marianne's clothes. Marianne was hurt by this, hurt and bruised by such a change in the man she had assumed that she would one day marry. But Wilhelm was not only punishing her for having left him and gone away. What she couldn't then know – because his pride would not allow him to admit to it – was that his family had fallen on hard times. His father the judge had been dismissed from his post for refusing to join the Nazi Party and had taken to heavy drinking. His mother, Tante Berthe, with her two boys to educate, had begun selling hen's eggs, door to door, in a basket strapped to her back. When the time came for Marianne to return to Cape Town, she and Wilhelm didn't even say goodbye.

And just before she made that ignominious escape, Marianne

paid a pre-arranged visit to the Berlin offices of the accountant 'friend' who had been appointed to deal with the disposal of the Jacobsens' remaining property. The interview there was dispiriting. The accountant had sent her his assistant who was oddly shifty and uninformed. The ledgers were not to hand. The kitty appeared to be empty for reasons that didn't make sense. In short, the news was not good. The weeks on the boat were hard for Marianne and, though a pleasant young doctor took her up and pleaded with her to marry him, she was too much a girl with a broken heart to be disposed towards romance.

Back in Cape Town, she found fresh disasters. The market garden had collapsed in total failure. The flowers were lovely but none of the Jacobsens had the first clue about techniques of selling. They couldn't communicate with middlemen and the flowers were left rotting by the roadside. And not only did they get stung by their own bees, but Frau Jacobsen had discovered an allergy she never knew she had. She had almost died of bee-stings. None of them had ever known what it felt like not to have money – and, by now, in addition, they had debts.

Jurgen and Heinrich were no longer in Cape Town. The former, having suddenly turned his back on school, had gone off, in his sister's absence, to work in a Transvaal mine. Heinrich, meanwhile, having given up thoughts of publishing, had got himself employment as an export clerk for an electrical goods manufacturer in Johannesburg. So two of Marianne's three brothers had already become what they were destined to remain for all of their working lives: a blue- and a white-collar worker.

Only Otto had been strong enough to keep his eye on the ball.

'I'm sick of all this,' he told his sister. 'It's pathetic. It's a mess. I'm going back to Germany to finish my degree.'

'Don't,' his sister said. 'Please, Otto, don't.'

'I'll come back, don't you worry,' he said. 'I'm beginning to like it here. But when I do I'll be qualified. I'll be good for a decent job.'

Otto had made enquiries about taking up his studies locally, but had been floored by the same bone-headed bureaucracy that had already done for his father. 'Have you got a Matric?' had always been the pertinent refrain. Matric meant Matriculation Certificate, which was the local school-leavers' exam. The *Abitur* plus two years at the university in Berlin evidently counted for nothing. Albert

Einstein without a Matric would have been sent to the back of the class.

All the same, Marianne tried begging her brother not to go.

'You'll walk right into a war,' she said. 'The streets are full of soldiers.'

'Oh blah,' Otto said. 'You're just like the old ones. War-war-war and look at them now. I'm telling you, there'll never be a war.'

Otto, it seemed, had already made his plans and had booked his return passage. In fact, he had booked two. As a person who was never reticent with women, Otto, in his sister's absence, had fixed on the girl whom he meant to marry. The marriage date has been fixed for four weeks' time and the girl was already learning German in readiness for the adventure.

Now that there were only three of them, the remaining Cape Town Jacobsens took modest lodgings in town and began to think the unthinkable. Marianne would have to go out to work – Marianne who was qualified for nothing except possibly to give piano lessons, but the family no longer had a piano. That night, Marianne tossed and turned. Then she hit upon a plan. She would approach the German Consulate for advice on employment opportunities for foreign nationals with nice-girl manners, no certificates and distinctly so-so English. Her clothes, she could see without Wilhelm's assistance, were beginning to look a little tired, but, next day, she made the best of her appearance and entered the building bravely.

The Consul himself was courteous and attentive, and he was generous with his time. He offered her a cigarette and got her to talk expansively about herself. His coffee was the best she'd tasted in years and his kindness loosened her tongue. By the time Marianne was ready to leave, he had heard all about the Friesian Island flood and the rosebuds that she used to paint on white Rosenthal china. He'd heard about the Oranjesicht house and the market garden and about Otto's return to Berlin. His response was to offer her a job.

'I'd like you to be my secretary,' he said. 'Can you start tomorrow?'

'I?' she said. 'But I can't type. Forgive me, but I've never touched a typewriter.' Ditto, drafted a memo. Ditto, filed a document. Ditto, taken a letter.

117

The Consul was undeterred. 'A girl like you,' he said. 'You will learn. Of course you will, my dear.'

So Marianne landed a job for which her evident genetic attributes had made her highly suitable. To be sure it had had little to do with her secretarial skills. She became personal secretary to the German Consul, a somewhat half-hearted career Nazi who loved her in a fatherly way, and called her by a pet name. Jacobina. He was wholly indifferent to her political views, which he understood to be vaguely formulated and divergent from the current orthodoxy of the Reich. But this was Cape Town, after all. It wasn't Berlin or Munich – and the tramp of soldiers' boots was still very far away. Jacobina was always an asset at the Consulate cocktail parties, even if her punctuation left much to be desired.

'Jacobina,' he would say indulgently. 'You scatter always ze commas in my letters just like ze salt, *nicht wahr?*'

Meanwhile, Jacobina had learned to drive a car and she'd designed herself some wonderful clothes, because she went to all the Consulate parties. Yet during office hours she found herself not only typing the Consul's letters – always with two fingers as she scattered her somewhat random commas and stops. She soon found herself dealing with more and more supplicant German-Jewish families who were beginning to appear off boats.

By coincidence, at just this time, Marianne's ageing father had been in receipt of a letter. It had come from the Reich and was offering him, in fulsome terms, a well-paid job back in Berlin as a designer of aeroplane hangars. And if it was immediately clear to him why the Reich, at that moment, should be needing quite so many new aeroplane hangars, he no longer allowed himself to dwell on the matter, nor to express his misgivings.

'It will be for a few months only,' he said to his wife. 'Just these few months and I'll come back to you. *Liebling*, you will once again have money. This will be necessary, *nicht wahr?*'

Now that there were just two of them, the remaining Cape Town Jacobsens were able to live like gentlewomen. Marianne and her mother moved into a pleasant residential hotel on one of Cape Town's many charming white beaches, where Frau Jacobsen, at last, adjusted happily to Cape Town life and set about training the servants to take her tea-time orders in German. She resisted, at first, when her lonely husband wrote and pleaded with her to come and join him – 'Just for a visit,' he said. But then, being a woman of her time, however reluctantly, she complied.

'It's just for a visit, Marianne,' she said. 'Don't worry. I will soon be back.'

So the emigration scheme was in ruins and the family that had left Germany to see the last of Hitler's Reich was once again in pocket – though Herr Jacobsen had become a migrant worker for the *Luftwaffe* and his daughter was working for a career diplomat who was signed up with the Party. The Party flag hung over the desk in the Consul's office. The Party newspapers appeared with regularity in the post. But Dinah's mum never looked at them. She threw them straight in the wastepaper basket. Why should she have to look at them, she said, when she already knew that they were common?

Meanwhile, the house in Oranjesicht, sold for peanuts by the con-man's repossessors at a time of worldwide slump – sold '*für einen Apfel und ein Butterbrod*', as Dinah's mum always put it, 'for an apple and a slice of buttered bread' – continued to stand on its corner, on its airy ridge, and would presumably go on standing there; its simple curved lines giving it the look of a Cunard liner, a hint of romantic journeys to exotic faraway places. Dinah, in later years, would hazard that it was probably the only one of Herr Architekt Jacob Bahne Jacobsen's buildings to have escaped the fall of bombs.

Now that there was only one of them, the remaining Cape Town Jacobsen began to have a seriously good time. She took the rent on a flat with a view over Bantry Bay and felt herself to be an independent, confident, stylish young woman with money to dispose of as she pleased. Her indelibly accented English was by then as fluent as it would ever become and she was learning, day by day, to put Berlin and Wilhelm behind her. In a gesture of commitment to her adopted country, she determined, now, to teach herself South Africa's second official language. She set out to learn Afrikaans.

Marianne began the project by borrowing books from the Afrikaans section of the public library, but she couldn't find anything to suit her. All the fiction she lit upon was too folksy, too down-on-the-farm. She couldn't relate to the heart-warming stories about loyal and knockabout *klonkies,* nor to the bushveld dramas for boys. The one Gothic-historical romance she had embarked upon had been set in a Rhineland castle and – perhaps irrationally – she had found it disturbing that the court's medieval intrigues were all being conducted in colloquial Afrikaans. Having twice re-read the only book that gripped her, on the elephants of the Cape's Knysna Forest, she didn't know where to turn next. The language was simply too new, too recently severed from Netherlandish Dutch, too long regarded by white Dutch-speaking settlers as the downmarket dialect-vernacular of their brown kitchen servants. Now, conversely, it was suddenly too dense with its recent transformation into a weapon in the struggle for white Afrikaner supremacy to support a decent body of literature. In short, all the books she tried were dire.

So Marianne revised her plan and sought out a specialist foreign-language bookshop that someone had told her about. She reasoned that, since Afrikaans was a Dutch-derived language, with a mere handful of Malay and Huguenot French words thrown in, she'd simply read Dutch books instead – and from there it would be a very small step to mastering the langauge itself.

What happened then was that Marianne was immediately swept off her feet by the exquisite male Hollander who ran the specialist bookshop. His name was Willem Klopper – Willem/Wilhelm – the irony couldn't escape her, though this William, also tall and blond, was leaner and more delicately made. He began at once to carry her off to his pretty old beach house at weekends. The house was along the meandering Atlantic coast and, in it, he had collected a sort of home-boy salon of arty young Hollanders: painters, poets and intellectuals. They were all of them recent arrivals at the Cape and not one of them could yet believe his luck that he should have suddenly found himself able to live like this, in a sunshine paradise where figs, apricots and nectarines were there to be plucked from trees, where wine flowed cheap and plentiful, while all over Europe the lights were going out.

The company was almost exclusively male, which suited Marianne, who had no sisters and had always been more comfortable with men. She enjoyed it all the more, because the men so patently loved her. She became their trophy, their female find. So her Afrikaans was straightaway doomed and, in any attempt she ever made to speak the language thereafter, it always emerged sounding more like Dutch. This was a thing that, later on, made Lisa and Dinah giggle.

'She says "neigh" for *no*,' they'd mock. 'She doesn't know how to say "knee-uh".' Though they themselves would not utter a word in Afrikaans out loud – not outside of school lesson time – they knew, from Mrs van Heynigen's *uitspraak* instruction, that the word for *no* was not 'neigh'. 'Horses neigh, twice a day,' they'd chant.

For Marianne there was a larger problem looming, because Willem, though for three years he took her to the theatre and to the ballet and to the opera; though he took her to every private view; though the two of them hosted lunch parties together and walked together in Kirstenbosch with Willem's lean and loping Irish setter; though he was entirely proprietorial with her, he never suggested marriage. He also never made a single advance upon her body, though for a woman of Marianne's upbringing this last didn't strike her as odd.

Then, one Saturday morning, just a week before her thirty-second birthday, she found herself sitting alone on Willem's beach. She had, earlier, been scrutinising her face and she'd decided that, yes, she'd got crow's feet.

I've got wrinkles, she thought. I'll be losing my looks.

She was suddenly alarmed to think that her bloom was on the wane and that Willem was consuming the last of her youth. When one of the beach-house guests came to join her, she noted that he had goggle specs and so many freckles that they covered all of his eyelids and his earlobes. It was the mathematician from The Hague, who was very new to the beach house. And then, to her embarrassment, she found that she was crying.

'What's the matter?' he said and he sat down.

Then she surprised herself by telling him all about her wrinkles and her fading looks. She told him it was her birthday later that week and that she was about to turn twenty-nine, because Dinah's mum was always the sort of woman who felt the need to tell lies about her age. Please, she said to the freckly mathematician, could he possibly try and explain to her why Willem had not proposed marriage. What was the matter with her?

The mathematician was seven years her junior, though he thought that the difference was only four. He was astonished by what she was telling him, because he'd thought from the moment he'd entered the beach house that Marianne was gorgeous. She looked just like Marlene Dietrich, he thought, but without the pencilled eyebrows. And here she was, crying all over him about her age and her fading looks. But most of all she was displaying a degree of mind-boggling ignorance about Willem Klopper's sexual orientation.

When he explained to her, as delicately as he could, why Willem would not marry her, it was Marianne's turn to be astonished because, even with three brothers in the house, she had managed to reach the age of thirty-two without ever encountering a reference to boy-on-boy sex.

And then the mathematician caught a glimpse of her feet. She was always so careful to keep them covered but, just then, she had had to expose them to get the sand out of her shoes. She had once had slim long elegant feet with toes to match her long fingers, but by then each big toe was distorting inwards at an angle of sixty degrees and each was glowing with an angry red bunion. The four lesser toes on both feet were very badly deformed. They all pushed sideways; all were buckled and twisted into hillocks that folded over one another in a septic-looking, angular tangle. Each toe's nail was jabbing into the flesh of its neighbour and each had a raised red corn with an oozy yellow surround glowing on its summit. He had never in his life seen such terrible feet. It made him wonder how on earth she could walk – and how she managed to do so without showing signs of pain. It made him feel suddenly protective of her and he was just as suddenly furious with Willem.

'What's happened to your feet?' he said and then she started to cry all over again.

Soon after Marianne had turned thirteen, a gang of schoolboys had started pelting her with snowballs on her way home from school. Or, mostly, it was snowballs with stones in them, but sometimes it was just stones. They called her 'Banana Feet' and 'Lanky Lottie' and 'Freak' – and they waited for her, day after day. Much as she tried to avoid the boys by walking the long way home, they always managed to find her. And it never crossed her newly adolescent mind that her beautiful face had begun to glow with something that went beyond childhood, or that her height and her hips and her small high breasts could be disturbing to a bunch of rough fifteen-year-old boys whose hormones were on the rampage. She couldn't see that their only devices for attracting her attention were inarticulate and counter-productive acts of oafish bullying.

Instead, Marianne came to the conclusion that her body was becoming deformed. She was much too tall and her feet were probably destined to be as long as boats. Her solution was to return in secret to the shoe shop with her newly purchased size seven winter boots and to trade them in for an identical pair one size down. She did this, of course, without saying a word to her parents. What followed was a winter spent in unconfessed agony, as the bones of her toes began to knit themselves together and violent shooting pains ran in spasms up and down her legs.

Of course, she knew as well as anyone that there was no way she could now change her mind and get new boots. She was growing up in the wake of Germany's First World War defeat, when clothing coupons were rationed and no one was entitled to the purchase of a second pair of boots. So, by the time she'd realised the seriousness of what she'd done, she'd accepted that her fate was sealed. All she could do was suffer in silence and try her best to bear the pain.

It was her father who finally noticed her agony and he made her take off her boots. Then he made her peel off her stockings. Dinah's mum never forgot how it felt to stand there in front of him and watch him start to cry. Marianne was his favourite child, his absolute pride and joy.

'My poor, poor, stupid girl,' he said. 'For this, my Marianne, you will suffer for the rest of your life.'

And, of course, she did. Sometimes Dinah used to watch her mum attacking her corns with a double-edged razor blade that she kept in the sewing basket. She would put wads of cotton wool over the gouts of blood and she'd interlace strips of cotton lint between the tangle of her overlapping toes. She would try not to wince as she'd push her feet back into her shoes. Dinah's mum never allowed herself to go barefoot. Not ever. Not even in her own house.

Meanwhile, there on Willem's beach, Marianne began to re-cover herself – by which time she and the freckly mathematician had begun to draw quite close. They went back into the beach house, talking and laughing like old friends, and they volunteered to wash up. He washed, she dried. This was the pattern that maintained itself throughout their subsequent marriage. And very soon it was obvious to the inhabitants of the beach house that Marianne and Fred were an item.

Willem was furious and began to raise Cain. For both men it was antlers locked. And the end result was that poor Marianne was cast out from the beach house, cut off from paradise for ever.

'And if you *must* marry him,' Willem spat, 'then promise me that you'll never have his children.'

He sent her a wedding present signed in bitterness, a set of leather-bound Shakespeares in which various pertinent passages had been meaningfully underscored – and she never saw him again. Willem Klopper sold up the bookshop and removed himself from the beach house. Then he moved to Johannesburg, leaving no address.

And, sixty years later, when her mum had just died, Dinah, who was passing through Johannesburg, remembered this story of her mother's golden time and she suddenly thought, Good Lord. She looked up Willem Klopper in the Johannesburg telephone directory and she found a bookshop listed under his name. It was in Braamfontein, just across the road from the Wits University campus. So with a sudden, ridiculous urgency, she jumped into a taxi. But she found the bookshop cleared of its stock and the door just recently padlocked. There was a newish notice fixed to the door, addressed to the bookshop's customers. Willem Klopper had ceased trading, it said, just a month before Dinah's arrival.

Dinah repaired, frustrated, to the university's staff canteen where everyone knew about the bookshop.

'Old Dutch guy,' they said. 'Great bookseller. Always knew everything. Could get you any book you wanted.'

Willem Klopper had closed his doors and gone off to enjoy his retirement, his well-earned place in the sun. So the meeting was clearly not meant to be and, after some sober reflection, Dinah felt relieved. Because what was she going to say to him? And what would he have said to her? I never wanted you to be born? I can see that you've inherited the freckles? Your eyesight's clearly not up to much – does that mean you're very good at maths? Dinah hoped that the place to which he'd gone was nothing short of a pretty old beach house somewhere on the Cape's Atlantic coast.

Marianne and Fred got married on the day before South Africa entered the war. The marriage was a hasty move – a lunch-hour registry affair. The intention was to stop Marianne being declared an enemy alien – and the date of the country's going to war was fairly easy to get right. Britain had already declared war on Germany two days before. And, since then, the South African parliament had been delaying and prevaricating, its MPs swinging both ways, the margin between the pros and the antis always too close to call. So, for the first days of September, the two party leaders, the generals Smuts and Herzog, were slogging it out, back and forth.

For quite a few Afrikaner MPs, the issue was fairly straight-forward. Britain was still the enemy and, as such, it could not be one's ally. Many were merely anti-British, but some were actively pro-German. And there were those at the far end who, in the near future, would become members of undercover pro-Nazi organisations, hell-bent on undertaking acts of sabotage to undermine the Allied war effort. In debate, it was Herzog who finally lost the argument by overplaying his hand. He was getting close to praising Hitler and this was a lapse that lost him just enough of his more moderate support. It allowed the Smuts camp narrowly to win. So on 6 September 1939, South Africa entered the war.

Just a few days earlier, Fred had persuaded Marianne to give up her job at the Consulate. He'd been appalled and astonished in the first place to find her working there.

'Are you completely out of your raving mind,' he'd said, 'to be working for a crowd like that?'

Marianne immediately did as he said, though she was full of conflicting emotions, because the Consul had always been good to her and she found it hard to see him as the villain Fred took him for. But now she was married, and there was the war and the Consulate had ceased to exist.

Since Marianne's flat was so much nicer than Fred's, that was where they decided to start their married life. And when he brought round all his stuff, Marianne found it impossible to believe that it could fit, like that, into one smallish backpack and a medium-sized cardboard box. But Fred liked travelling light. He'd always thought of 'things' as existing merely for collecting dust. In the year before taking up his South African graduate scholarship, he had set off on his bicycle from The Hague, with the very same small backpack, to make his way through France and Spain. By the time he had reached the Pyrenees, the Spanish Civil War had forced him back. But all along the way through southern France, whenever he stopped at farmhouses to fill his water bottle, the French farmers would blink at him and go to call their friends.

'Here's a crazy boy from *les Pays-Bas*,' they said. 'He wants to drink water. Tell him water is bad for the health. People don't drink water.'

They'd filled his bottle with rough red wine and given him things to eat. Cold duck glazed with black cherries; pieces of preserved goose; globe artichokes; runny cheeses and crusty loaves of bread; things that he'd never dreamed of.

'How's that, crazy boy?' they said. 'Better than water, *n'est-ce pas*? Better than salt herrings, no?'

Two of Marianne's three brothers were interned as enemy aliens on the day after her wedding. And when they emerged, six years later, Jurgen was more handsome than ever, though his cheekbones were threatening to push through his skin, and, thereafter, he never gained weight. His pretty, curly, blonde teenage bride, his young man's pre-war passion, had, two years earlier, run off into the hinterland with someone he never got to meet and he never saw the girl again. Heinrich no longer had a hair on his head and he'd acquired a whole range of nervous tics. The tics occurred in little sequences of mutters, blinks and snorts, and he was to have them for the rest of his life.

Irmi, Heinrich's Berlin fiancée, his devoted schoolgirl sweetheart, had been required to stay behind in Germany when the Jacobsens set sail for Cape Town. This was to nurse her dying mother; but her mother was a long time over her dying and she lasted until the war had broken out. After that, Irmi nursed her father, who was speedier in his dying. Her two brothers accomplished their dying without her assistance. They were both killed on the Eastern Front. Meanwhile Otto, back in Berlin, had managed, concurrently with his studies, to become the father of two small boys. He completed his degree in geology just in time for the Reich's advance upon Russia – and thereby became the only one of Marianne's brothers to end up at Stalingrad.

Dinah's mum's job at the Consulate turned out to be her last. After that, she was a stay-at-home wife. It may have been the norm in the post-war world, but all the same she was always aware that its effect was to ensure she lacked clout. Dinah noticed how reticent her mum was, especially in the company of graduate women; how she would always preface her opinions with a much-used humbling refrain: 'I am not a clever woman and I have not studied, but . . .' Only once she had uttered these protective, qualifying words would she venture a point of view.

Marianne urged her daughters to pass exams and make themselves employable.

'Zese stupid pieces of paper,' she would say, quite bitterly at times.

She meant those certificates awarded for levels of achievement in this and in that.

'All my life,' she'd say on a sigh, 'I never had zese stupid pieces of paper.'

Later, when Dinah had hit adolescence, she began to despise her mother for these insistent pragmatic urgings. She liked to think that any studious pursuit should be undertaken for itself alone, for the white heat of knowledge and for the excitement of pure reason. To embark on any such mental adventure merely for pieces of paper – this struck her as shaming and crass.

The rest of her mum's maternal advice had mostly to do with feet, but Dinah could not focus on these things. Pieces of paper and feet. Instead she took to slouching her way through high school and, before going out, would always cram her feet into four-inch, stiletto-heeled winkle-pickers.

The day that the grandparents appear in the bungalow is also the day on which Dinah's family loses possession of the two oak thrones. Because the grandparents have Heinrich's Irmi with them – bespectacled, pale and middle-aged Irmi – to whom the chairs were apparently promised as a wedding present, sixteen years before. To Lisa and Dinah, the grandparents are two remote old foreigners, persons who are more unreachable than the man who the two of them once believed inhabited their dad's radiogram.

Their dress is incongruously formal in the land of the Sta-prest shirt. Grandmother is wearing a sprigged crêpe dress with starched detachable collar and a black straw hat with pearl hatpin. The hat is set on the impressive cloud of her thick wavy white hair.

Grandfather is wearing a long-sleeved Old World linen shirt of exquisite, unfamiliar cut, which is sporting double cuffs and cuff links. His head is bald, his eyes are pale-blue and his moustache makes him look like Bismarck. Both have shiny, well-kept shoes, quality shoes left over from the days before the war. They are shoes from another world.

What Dinah remembers most about that day, beyond the gaps on the floor that are left behind by the disappearance of the Gieseke thrones; beyond her mother's flush of expectation through the morning; beyond the fine spread of cold meats and salads on the family's best plates throughout that awkward lunch – awkward mainly because *Grossmutter* is so patently affronted that the girls will only speak English and don't dare to speak to her at all – is that *Grossmutter* embraces Wendy Jones upon first entering the bungalow. She does this because she evidently thinks that Wendy must be Lisa.

Wendy is the only other redhead among the Butcher Estate's child commune and, although she is paler and more sandy-haired than Lisa, a more Celtic sort of redhead, the girls are inevitably bracketed together as 'the two little gingernuts'. Wendy, along with Lisa and Dinah, is playing in the living room that day, when the aged foreigners make their entrance, so Dinah is able to watch from her corner how *Grossmutter* – having first embraced her daughter and been introduced to her son-in-law – then makes a bee-line for Wendy Jones, as the red-headed child who has two hands.

Dinah remembers her own sense of shock in that split second, in that instant freeze-frame. Because it's immediately apparent to her that, while her mum has told about Lisa's red hair, she hasn't told about Lisa's funny arm. And Sophie Jacobsen, auburn-haired queen of the Wiesbaden obelisk, of 1900, has naturally made the assumption that her granddaughter, her namesake – Lisa Sophia de Bondt – is the redhead with two proper hands.

Then, suddenly, the grandparents are gone – gone off to be billeted with Jurgen's family in Johannesburg. It's what they do till the end. And, though Dinah's parents take their turn, the old man, by then, has already died and Dinah has left the country. So, unlike her sister, Dinah does not witness the slow decline of Sophie Jacobsen, who survives ten bouts of viral pneumonia and lives to be a hundred and four. She lives a life in which, right up to the end, she demands of alien shop assistants – and always, of course, in German – that they proffer brand-name lingerie and brand-name laxatives, items that have been obsolete since 1943.

So Dinah never really gets to know them – never thinks of her mother's parents as real. Never properly gets to know any of the Jacobsens, to speak true. She's aware of them as the long-ago players in a version of her dear mother's life. They are no longer a close-knit family. There's been too much water under the bridge. Jurgen marries an Afrikaner nurse and connects with up-country families, so that Marianne, his one-time close sister, is occasionally in receipt of the odd surprisingly rural present.

'Am sending sheep,' Jurgen's telegram will say. And the carcass of a whole dead sheep will be delivered off a goods train. 'Am sending turkey,' it says another time – but the turkey isn't dead. It's delivered, live and squawking, in a crate the size of a telephone box, which must sit out on the bungalow verandah, awaiting the countdown to Christmas. Night after night, Dinah's thoroughly urban dad will creep out at the first glimmer of dawn and throw a blanket over the telephone box to keep the poor creature quiet.

In the daytime, Dinah chats to the bird, with its strange winged dinosaur look, its scaly legs, its sparse red-and-black vulture's plumage. And the glazed brown orb on the Christmas platter bears no relation to her feathered friend, so she needs no sweet-talking adult lies to make her think that her turkey has flown away and that *this* sort of turkey – this golden orb, served with roast potatoes and with legs no longer than pencils – this is another sort of substance altogether, another category of organic matter.

Jurgen and his family live mostly in Johannesburg, in a modest white neighbourhood. Their house is one that, decades later, will be eagerly sought out as 'heritage', as an architectural jewel: a colonial workman's cottage with wooden tracery and rickety shutters and a corrugated-iron roof with ornamental coping that runs along its ridge. At the time of Jurgen's occupation, it exists merely as a statement that its occupier cannot stretch to a suburban dream-home upgrade. Because construction work is everywhere and the aspirant householder will surely desire a more salubrious location. A suburb where the hacienda style will sit side by side with the half-timbered manor house – where 'ultramodern' will co-exist with the neighbouring Tyrolean chalet.

Jurgen, Dinah believes, is father to four blond children, but she doesn't know their names. It startles her to realise that she couldn't pick them out in a photograph. She would probably recognise the elder of Otto's two adult sons. He's a geologist, like his father, whose successful sideline in playing the stockmarket has caused him to retire as a gentleman farmer, a man of means. He has two daughters, Lisa says, and Dinah believes that both of them are currently living abroad. One, Lisa's told her, is a fashion designer who lives and works in Geneva. But Dinah doesn't know these women, doesn't know their names.

Sad-eyed Irmi, no blood relation, is the one whom Dinah fixes on; the one whom she chooses to befriend. And it's the imagery of Irmi's wartime stories that sometimes bestrides her own more troubled dreams. Strange, perhaps, because all the Berlin Jacobsens have their rarely told, whispered stories, their brief and only half-intelligible stories about the last days of the war. Stories of jumping off slow-moving trains; of losing one's infant children in fleeing crowds; of legging it across farmers' fields; of running, always running and out of breath – their small, final suitcases gratefully thrown away in ditches – running from the Russian advance.

For Irmi and Heinrich, their reunion in South Africa is sixteen years on since the day they parted in pre-war Berlin. They are thirty-five going on sixty. They make a staid, childless couple and both go out to work. Irmi works as a secretary. Her typing and shorthand skills she has, thanks to her dying mother, because, one day near the end, Irmi's mother reached under her sickbed and handed her daughter a purse. She directed her secretly to the secretarial college while the tyrant was out of the house.

'Irmi, the world is changing,' she said. 'Make sure you can earn your own living.'

This meant that, once Berlin was under siege, and Irmi was an orphan with two dead brothers, and the family's assets had gone up in smoke, she was able to get herself decent employment as a qualified shorthand typist. She worked as secretary to an elderly professor at the university in Berlin. When bombs fell on the university, the faculty moved into a cellar and then into another. When her family house was bombed, Irmi moved in with the professor and his wife, whose own sons by then were both dead, and

130

she became their surrogate daughter. Irmi's house fell in what was soon to become the Russian Zone. And once, after it had already been bombed, its shell caught fire and the house was burned to the ground. Irmi then rashly crept back to it and combed through the ashes and the bits of broken wash-basin in the hope of finding something, some relic of her past, some item of value that she could possibly use for barter.

But the professor's wife ran mad with terror when Irmi returned with her story of where she'd been and what she'd done. Then and there, she fetched her work box and she sewed a makeshift backpack for Irmi that she fashioned from her only remaining tablecloth.

'There's a train,' she said. 'It leaves at midnight for Hamburg. Take it, Irmi. It will be the last. Go to Hamburg. Go to the island where your young man's family have people. The Russians will be at our door in the morning. If they find you, they will rape you. Go, Irmi. Go now!'

Irmi's story is that the train she was on was end-to-end with maimed German soldiers wrapped in newspaper and rags. They groaned and screamed through the night. Half the train's upper body had been blown away. A woman had lost her baby on the train and was wailing and pulling at her hair. There was talk that the Russians were taking up the tracks behind them as they went. And when she made it to Hamburg, the city, Irmi says, 'wasn't there'. Hamburg, as Dinah appreciates only much later, from aerial photographs, looked at the time like an early Flemish horror painting of the world after Armageddon.

The island was crowded with fleeing German civilians and there was no room in anybody's house. Irmi was lucky to get part shares in a cowshed. This was something that she did for months. She slept, shivering, on straw. When the war was over, the British authorities moved in and processed her, but everything took time. Dinah is not at all clear about what became of Irmi between her billet in the cowshed and her coming to claim the oak thrones, but at some point she must have hooked up with her in-laws and she'd learned to speak good English. Or it might have been, Dinah thinks, that, since the English 'th' had clearly never given Irmi a problem, she had long ago been the better able to benefit from the instruction of the *fin-de-siècle* Bohemian. Or perhaps the British were on the island for longer than Dinah thinks.

Not that Irmi's English was much of a help to her on the boat which, for unexplained reasons, she had boarded in Southampton – a Union Castle liner stuffed with post-war British immigrants – and none of them willing to exchange a single word with the daughter of the enemy. Poor bereaved Irmi who, thanks to the man with the egg stains down his shirt, had lost everything she ever possessed, except for Heinrich – bald Heinrich, with his little mutters, shuffles and sniffs.

Irmi and Heinrich set up house in Hillbrow, Johannesburg's inner-city flatland, overhung with the smell of ageing gas cookers. In time, it became a pioneering mixed-race area: the first place in the country where young, dreadlocked black men would neck openly with white girls in the street, the first white area in which blacks began, illegally, to rent cheap high-rise 'bachelor' flats. Hillbrow could boast South Africa's first and only all-night book-shop. It was full of elderly, concert-going, transplanted German Jews. It was the only place to get good rye bread and salt beef. It was the place where, in 1963, Barney Simon, director of Johannesburg's Market Theatre, bumped into the Rivonia Trial's two most rigorously hunted political escapees.

'Hide us,' they said – Harold Wolpe and Arthur Goldreich – 'our pick-up car didn't show.'

And he hid them in his flat, taking them up in the service lift, risking imprisonment himself – a secret good deed that needed to remain a secret for the next thirty years.

Then gradually the old German Jews got too scared to leave their flats at night and the concert audiences declined. Likewise the theatre's audiences, which got scared of the inner-city flick-knives and the muggings and the shoot-outs. Hillbrow became the terrain of drug barons and then, with the opening of South Africa's borders, the local drug barons were effectively seen off by bigger and scarier drug barons, who entered the country from the north.

By this time, Heinrich and Irmi had retired. They'd packed up and gone back to Berlin, taking the oak thrones with them. They had neither of them ever quite shuffled off that air of being displaced persons. Then Heinrich died within weeks of their re-entry, and Irmi, finding that Berlin wasn't home any more without him, returned on the rebound to Johannesburg. She placed herself in the German Old People's Home, a hang-out full of aged ghastlies who'd done time in South West Africa. *Sudwest*, as they said. Dinah, when she visits her aunt there, in her small, functional room with shower and kitchenette, doesn't like to ask Irmi why the two oak thrones are not a feature of her living space. She fancies that they'll have gone under the hammer in an auction house somewhere in Berlin.

SEVEN

Lisa and Dinah go to high school in the same year. It's the year in which Dr Malan, the Prime Minister, retires. He's replaced by Mr J.G. Strijdom who is rabid to achieve what Dr Malan has tried to do and failed. That is to get rid of the Cape's Coloured franchise. Mr Strijdom does this by increasing the number of Appeal Court judges and Nat-supporting senators until he's got enough to push the business through. This is called the Separate Representation of Voters Act. Then he makes 'mixed' trade unions illegal, so that black and white workers won't make common cause. This is called the Industrial Reconciliation Act. In Durban, most of the English are less bothered by these measures than by Mr Strijdom's determination to make South Africa a republic. And when he declares that 'God Save the Queen' is no longer the national anthem, white Durbanites are bristling. There's an English translation on offer for them, of the droney, slow-motion Afrikaans national anthem, but nobody Dinah's come across ever bothers to learn the words.

Dinah can't help noticing that Communist is now coming top among the government's favourite buzz words. There's been Dr Malan's Suppression of Communism Act, but now it's Communist this and Communist that pouring out of the radio. This is mainly because of the Defiance Campaign. Thousands of black South Africans have right then got the government shaking in its shoes, simply by organising a nation-wide sit-down in station waiting rooms, train carriages and public libraries marked 'Europeans Only/*Slegs Blankes*'. Everything has now been labelled in the two official white languages, so that even the school buses say 'No Spitting/*Moenie Spoeg Nie*', and persons visiting from abroad will often wonder why public lavatories, having announced 'Gents/ *Here*', will then go on to say 'Ladies/*Dames*'. It's confusing if you don't realise that *here* is Afrikaans for gents. It's like the plural of *Herr*. Some foreigners are also a bit freaked by the signs in butchers' shop windows that say 'Boys' Meat Two Shillings', because they don't like its cannibalistic ring. And sometimes you can still see those butchers' signs that say 'Boys' Meat Two Shillings. Dogs' Meat Two and Sixpence'.

The government has managed to arrest eight thousand of the Defiance Campaigners and is using the Suppression of Communism Act as a catchall to nobble its leaders. Dinah hasn't the first clue about what a Communist is, except that the runaway Brainy Rebel used to be one before the recent arrival of the black-edged telegram announcing his demise. So, along with most South Africans, she now thinks it's Communism for a black person to sit in a white person's waiting room, or for a black person to enter the public library. The list of banned persons is getting so long that to think about it is a bit like looking at the Roll of Honour on the Cenotaph.

Meanwhile, the Nats are pretty pleased about the firm hand that Mr Strijdom is taking and Parliament has been proudly referring to its own 'reign of terror' against the passive-resistance campaigners. Agitator is another of the government's favourite words. Agitators must be eliminated, root and branch, because it's a long-term conviction of the apartheid state that, without agitators, no black person would feel himself to have any grievance. Soon the state is rounding up five hundred Treason Trial accused – Communists and agitators from all ethnic groups – though the court whittles the number down to a mere one hundred and fifty. Even so, it's a lot of people to have in the dock all at once and the trial drags on for four years, taking on an atmosphere of macabre fairground gaiety as the accused suddenly have the world's media at their feet and the prosecution is repeatedly outwitted.

While it's impossible for the accused to earn a living during this time, the good news is that the trial provides a rare opportunity for resistance leaders to liaise across ethnic boundaries – a thing which the state has by now rendered strictly illegal in real life. This is the high point of resistance success: a triumphant farce to be remembered in the dark and brutal days to come. When the last trialist is acquitted, there's nothing much the state can do, except raid the house in which the celebrations take place in the hopes of nailing a few 'mixed' drinkers, because serving alcohol to a black person is also against the law.

As the politics gets more intense, Dinah's dad has to spend more and more of his early morning time shouting back at the radio, so this is the girls' regular daily wake-up sound – that's before he's blocked his rage by blasting them out with items from his ever-increasing record collection. Among recent early morning favourites are Benjamin Britten and Peter Pears promising doom and brimstone.

> From Brig' o' Dread when thou may'st pass,
> Ev-ery nighte and alle
> To Purgatory fire thou comest at last
> And Christe receive thy saule

Meanwhile Lisa and Dinah are getting on with their ordinary little white schoolgirl lives.

Lisa has been looking forward to the pleasure of going to high school because that way she'll get away from Dinah and Angela and the daily shower of newspaper fiancés. She's really pleased that she's going to be the only one with a hockey stick and a regulation Girls' High navy swimsuit. She anticipates that Dinah will be looking enviously at her new school atlas and her new *Concise Oxford English Dictionary*. She's already got her blue-and-silver tin box of mathematical instruments. In the event, Lisa is cheated out of this pleasure, because the school system changes that year. There's a pilot scheme in which girls from Dinah's school and Dinah's year will move up early and spend five years, not four, in secondary education. So Lisa is stuck with Dinah and Angela after all.

By this time Dinah and Lisa are no longer each other's best friend. Dinah has begun to position herself as a bit of a dissenter and she thinks of Lisa as a goody-goody. She knows that, unlike Lisa, she'll never be a prefect and she doesn't want to be one. She thinks that prefects are scabs. This instinct probably comes in part from not being the first-born, but also it comes from the government. For Dinah merely to think about the government is enough to make her believe that authority is by its nature suspect. Plus she's messy and creative. She's constantly cutting, gluing, painting and sewing which means a litter of paper clippings, dried paintbrushes, crushed pastels and glitter all over the floor of the shared bedroom. The shared bedroom rankles with both of them and with Lisa especially, who can't stand disorder and is longing to have more privacy. From time to time she draws a chalk line down the middle of the room between the beds and screams at Dinah that she's throwing away anything, *anything* that crosses the line.

Lisa, unbeknown to Dinah, has entered adolescence. She gets into huddles with their mum in a new and unaccustomed form of female bonding that Dinah finds a bit threatening. She has no idea that this has something to do with menstruation and, when she eventually finds out, over a year later, Lisa's orderliness in the matter of female monthlies is quite astonishing to her. All that business with the horrible lumpy crotch pads that you have to wear hooked on to a saggy elastic waist belt that's forever twisting and tweaking and spiralling. Oh yuk. Then there's the business of soaking and laundering your inconveniently bouffant school knickers in those useless 1950s soap flakes. Plus there's the matter of discreet disposal. How has Lisa managed this when there isn't even a pedal bin in the lavatory?

Dinah hasn't noticed any of it. She only notices that Lisa is always cross with her. She says 'Shut up' and 'I hate you' and 'Anyway, everyone in my class thinks you're goofy'. Lisa goes in for angry fits of physical intimidation so that Dinah has to fetch and carry for her at home. 'Get me a banana,' Lisa says, and if Dinah says she won't, then Lisa will always thump her. Sometimes Dinah feels so angry that she retaliates in sneaky little-sisterish ways. She cuts up Lisa's favourite shorts or she hides Lisa's charm bracelet. She knows that a charm bracelet is a prized possession, because she's got one too. And every time either sister has a birthday, people will give them more and more little silver charms, so that every link in the chain is heavy, now, with double-hung trinkets.

Dinah crouches, quaking with fear, for what seems like hours in the earthy, anti-termite zone under the floorboards of the house, clutching Lisa's things, while above her head Lisa is stamping and raging and bursting into tears.

'I *know* Dinah's hidden it,' she'll be saying. 'I *know* she has. And this time I'm really going to kill her. Just wait.'

The trouble with Dinah's strategy is that it wrong-foots her with her parents, because Lisa is very good at inspiring confidence in adults. It leaves Dinah no option but to get herself cast in the role of the bad daughter. And once you're the bad daughter, you might as well go for broke.

The move to high school coincides almost exactly with the move from the Butcher Estate. Almost, but not quite. The university's lease on the estate is up within a few weeks. For the first days, Lisa and Dinah are conveyed the extra distance to their new school alongside the undergraduates, in canvas-covered army trucks left over from the war. Since the undergraduates are all male and nearly all engineers, the testosterone levels in the truck make the girls feel so uncomfortable that they demand the right to go by bus.

In Durban all the green buses are for blacks so these roar and judder past the groups of white schoolchildren in their variously banded panama hats and blazers. There are so many different school blazers in Durban that home-time on the Berea can look like the Henley Regatta, especially as some of the boys get made to wear straw boaters as well. The white kids call the blacks' buses Green Mambas. The green buses are always on their last legs, belching out streams of black smoke and overloaded with downtown workers coming in from the black locations.

In the Transvaal, buses for blacks are right now political dynamite, because the companies who run them have tried to put up the fares. Black commuters have been boycotting the buses and walking, en masse, thirty kilometres a day, in and out of work. They picket the buses and sometimes burn them and stone them and even throw themselves in front of them. Then the bus companies hire the poorest township migrant workers to beat up the protesters. The Liberal Party has tried organising a lift system of volunteers with private cars, but all this does is give the police a chance to nail more agitators and Communists, since all they have to do is stand about taking down the numbers on the white drivers' licence plates. What's happened is that the sight of all those blacks walking in their thousands into white town centres singing protest songs has been enough to make the municipality hammer out a compromise.

Most of the white schoolkids with whom Lisa and Dinah take the bus don't know about the bus boycotts. For them the Green Mambas are a fun way to tease their friends. Because, whenever there's a Green Mamba coming, you can pretend it's the bus your friend is waiting for.

'Here comes your bus, Denise,' you say and everyone will fall about laughing. Denise will pretend to be very indignant. Then she'll take a turn.

'Look, it's yours,' she'll say. 'Stop, stop, Green Mamba! Here's a passenger for you.'

Angela gets on the bus two-thirds of the way along the route to high school, so Dinah always tries to save her a seat. She catches it in Nicholson Road outside a small semi-detached house that has Snow White and all Seven Dwarfs cast in concrete in the front garden. Plus there are several concrete toadstools and concrete butterflies. The figures are all about eighteen inches high, except for Snow White who is much bigger, and all of them are brightly painted.

Then the bus journey comes to an end for Lisa and Dinah because they vacate the Butcher Estate to make way for its new tenant, the South African Police. Dinah's mum cries when the pergola is cut down and coils of barbed wire are erected on top of the tall green hedges all the way from Ridge Road above to Vause Road below. Soon the Butcher Estate has 'Keep Out' signs in two languages, with pictures of salivating Alsatians. Dinah never enters it again, though she passes it all the time. She remembers it as a magic place, big enough to get lost in, with its giant bamboo clumps and vervet monkeys and the carpets of jacaranda flowers outside the back door. With its passing she appears to lose all interest in the outdoors. The bullying, triumphalist tone of the police force means that to look at the Butcher Estate from the perimeter fence is like looking in at an enemy occupation.

The campus families have been leaving gradually. Dinah's family are the last to go and Wendy Jones's the first. Wendy goes without saying goodbye, because there's a distance that's developed between the children. Wendy Jones, Lisa's fellow gingernut, has long ago stopped coming round to play and has closed ranks against the whole child commune. This has happened, shortly after the girls' impromptu tea party, with the arrival of the family's third child. Pregnant Mrs Jones, who sat on the grass all those years before, has given birth to baby Roddy whose head is much too big for him and who never learns to speak or to leave his pushchair. Instead his pushchair keeps on getting bigger.

Wendy has never said anything to the other children about Roddy being not quite right. The fact of his evident and serious disability isn't admitted or aired. But Wendy stops playing and becomes Roddy's obsessive second mother. She always walks alongside her mum and her little brother Owen eyeing the other children with suspicion. They are the wild, running, shrieking child-people from whom Roddy needs protection. Wendy smothers Roddy with out-loud baby talk as she passes the girls' bungalow. Meanwhile Roddy lolls lifeless in his pushchair, his sad giant head topped with orange curls, like a sad Hallowe'en pumpkin thinking sad pumpkin thoughts.

Somewhere in Roddy's yearning moon face is an echo of his pleasant, orange-haired dad; plump freckly Dr Vernon Jones from Wales with his little damp hands, who lectures in history and always wears his sandals with socks. Meanwhile Mrs Jones has doubled in size with Roddy's birth and has become a person to be scared of. When the rift becomes a feud, Lisa and Dinah know in their hearts that it's all really their fault, because, home alone for an hour one day, they spy little Owen Jones from the window and he's playing with Lisa's ball. They know that it's Lisa's because of the pattern on the rubber. From the house, the sisters swoop on Owen, two against one, like bullies. They grab the ball and dash indoors, slamming the door behind them. Victory! Then they watch Owen run whimpering home to tell his mother.

'Quick!' Lisa says. 'Quick! Lock the back door. Shut all the windows. Draw the curtains. Quick! Hide! Hide! Mrs Jones is coming!'

Within minutes, Mrs Jones is thundering on the front door. 'I know you're in there,' she says. 'Come out!' Then she raps on the windows. Then she goes round the back. 'Come out!' she cries. 'Come out! Give that ball back to Owen at once!'

The girls don't respond. They hardly dare to breathe. They crouch, scared but excited, under Lisa's iron bed.

'You've not heard the end of this!' Mrs Jones says.

Eventually, she stomps off. Yet she doesn't follow through. Dinah's mum never finds out. And then, three weeks later, Lisa

140

discovers her own ball. It's lying at the bottom of the *Klappkasten*. Dinah and Lisa look at each other. Lisa is biting her lip. They look at both balls side by side. The balls are identical twins. After that, they have no option but to make their victim into their enemy. They can't not hate Owen now, just as they hate his sister. It's no speaks with either of them until the Joneses leave the Estate.

Dinah's family moves for six months into some temporary campus housing alongside the university, while their own house is being built. The temporary house is a brick cottage, one of six, built into the indigenous woodland of Pigeon Valley, and so close to the high school that the girls are always in danger of being late for assembly. Their dad, for the first time ever, starts switching on Springbok Radio, because that way they can pace themselves by the commercials. They know that they have to be out of the house before the last line of the Zoomo Cough Sweet commercial. First they hear the forced, fake coughing fit and then the voice that says, 'Stop that cough with ZOOMO!' The word ZOOMO! must reach their ears just as they hit the main road.

The new house is being built with money left to Dinah's mum by the Misses Connie and Louisa. It's a thousand pounds and it's completely unexpected. Dinah's mum likes houses, so with thoughts of the legacy dancing in her head, she sets out to prowl the older residential areas of Durban, looking for her ideal home. She walks all the gracious, shaded streets between the Overport shops and Mitchell Park. One place is called the Elephant House, because the last elephant in Durban was seen right there, in the garden. Sub-tropical vegetation has grown up around these older houses, lush and dense, making a green shade around colonial verandahs, white-plastered walls, and wide French windows. She loves the way the climate encourages a blurring of inside and outside, and one house she looks at has a tree growing right up through the roof. The gardens end in small, scrubby orchards of pawpaw trees and banana palms. Front gardens are full of azaleas and aloes and red-hot pokers. The houses have fixtures dating from a time when ships docked in Durban Harbour carrying stained-glass door panels from England, fan lights, balustrades, whole pressed ceilings complete with borders of acanthus leaves, scalloped brick-roof copings and porcelain sanitary ware bearing the names of Messrs Shanks and Twyford.

But then there's Ta, who refuses to engage with any of her housing schemes and, having grown up in small rented flats, has no experience of gambling money on property. Having left the Old World behind him, he now dislikes anything that reminds him of Old World domestic interiors. Brass door handles, mantelshelves, wallpaper, washboards, ornamental cast iron, chandeliers and sash windows – all these bring back to him the things that he'd rather forget. He dislikes mouldings and panelled doors. He knows without having to look that old houses are about decrepitude and that any house not built to 1950s local authority planning-office specifications will mean rust, damp, termites, rot, cockroaches, subsidence and probably flood. Plus it will smell of mothballs and old ladies' fur coats.

So the nest egg is used to buy a plot of red earth on a hill behind the university where bushland is fast becoming new urban sprawl and the balance becomes a down payment on one of the municipality's approved range of bungalows. The choice is between plans A, B and C. A building contractor is employed but now there's a hitch, because the house is taking for ever. The builder, being a recent immigrant from Europe, has gone heady on the opportunities available for white-skinned entrepreneurs in the new apartheid South Africa. He has quickly realised that all he needs is an underpaid black craftsperson with no labour rights and no electoral voice who will do all the work for him. So, Dinah's parents' builder is a full-time absentee. He's keen to develop his angling skills while the house is built, start to finish, by a single Zulu labourer who has three words of English in answer to Dinah's dad's questions, whenever he visits the site. 'Boss gone fishing.'

Finally, the little house is built – a tribute to the Zulu labourer's industry and skill. Lisa and Dinah share one of the three small bedrooms so that their dad can have a study, but there's nowhere for Dinah's mum to set up a weaving loom or mess about with paints. The house has a front door that leads straight into an L-shaped sitting room with the dining table and Dinah's mum's piano fitted into the smaller part of the L. It has galvanised-steel windows equipped with basic-range burglar bars.

All the same, it's exciting to have a house and Ta is delighted with it. He's especially delighted with the plywood flush doors that smell of new glue and with the flecked Emelux finish which has been sprayed on to the walls of the kitchen, bathroom and WC in place of the more expensive ceramic-tile option. He's delighted with the corrugated asbestos roof and the asbestos drain-pipes which will never rust or crack. He is full of enthusiasm for the septic tank, an ecologically laudable sewage-disposal system which dictates that the family would be ill advised to use soft-tissue toilet roll, and ought to stick with the interleaved sheets of scratchy Jeyes. There's even a special holder for the scratchy Jeyes that's been thoughtfully recessed into the wall of the Emelux.

The house has only one lavatory since there isn't one in the bathroom and this is a source of daily concern for Dinah's mum who suffers with temperamental bowels. Dinah's mum needs the loo each morning within five minutes of her first sip of breakfast coffee, or else the day is lost, but this is almost always the time when Dinah's dad is in there working on the crossword puzzle. Dinah's mum keeps remedies called Chocolax, Brook-lax, Liquid Paraffin and California Syrup of Figs. She keeps these in her knicker drawers along with the Lux flakes and Nescafé and Swiss chocolate. She also keeps an enamel enema jug with a length of nasty rubber hose in a canvas drawstring bag. This is a thing Dinah uncovers one day while snooping but she has no idea what it's for and, naturally, she cannot ask. Dinah's dad always emerges from the lavatory looking pleased.

'The clue's "Half-moon",' he'll say. 'Look. Two letters. The answer's "Mo". How about that?'

What Dinah's parents haven't taken into account is how expensive the new house will be. Because nobody has lived in it before them, nobody has supplemented the gaps in its basic structure. So Dinah's house has no garden path, no paved terrace for afternoon tea, no pulley rigged up for a washing line, no lawn, no letter box at the gate, no gate, no fence, no coat hook behind the bathroom door, no bookshelves, no curtain rails. There are no plants in the garden and there's precious little topsoil. Dinah's mum's new garden has three steep terraces of red Durban earth, which erode into mudslides with the first heavy rains. So with no money to call her own and the weekly account book to confront, Dinah's mum sets out for the botanical gardens to teach herself about plants. And it's while she's leaning over the various specimens and taking down their names that she meets one of the people who becomes a part of the family's life. Francis-the-Gardener is an Indian employee of the parks and gardens department.

'I'm Francis-the-Gardener,' he says into her ear. 'I'll get you some of these. Cheap, madam. Very cheap. You come back later. Five o'clock. You come back.'

And from that day on, Francis-the-Gardener supplements his meagre council wages by selling Dinah's mum, lovingly wrapped in damp newspaper, all the odd corms, buds, cuttings and bedding plants that he's garnered during his days in the flowerbeds. Francis-the-Gardener's knowledge is extensive, although he's unable to read. He's stick thin and suffers from bronchial complaints, which gives them a common bond. For a while he tells her what to do with all the cuttings and the corms, but soon he's working in the garden with her in every spare minute he has. Francis is always in need of money and soon they are talking trees.

Dinah's house, as it turns out, is not far from where the gardener lives in a hovel made of corrugated iron, with his wife and his five children. This is because the Cato Manor location starts just below the road that bounds the bottom of Dinah's family's garden. Several of the poorest Indian families are living there in makeshift shacks, having been burnt out of their homes during the anti-Indian riots of 1949. Most Durban Indians like Francis-the-Gardener are the sons and daughters of indentured Hindu labourers, the indigent of the subcontinent, who were shipped in to work in the sugar-cane fields of Natal, since the Natal cane fields, unlike those of the Caribbean or Mauritius, post-date the abolition of slavery and local Zulu labour isn't all that keen. Cutting cane is very hard work and, as Dinah's junior-school history teacher has already explained, 'A Zulu's idea of hard work is to lie in the sun with his hat over his eyes.'

Most of the Indians are still dirt poor, though some, against the odds, have managed to become small market gardeners, or door-to-door vegetable traders with one second-hand van. Some have got their sons and daughters through high school and a few families can even boast a doctor or a lawyer on board. Then there are the other Indians, the free Muslims from Gujarat, who have come with a little money and established themselves as more significant traders and also as shack landlords in the black townships where they, too, are obliged, by law, to live. These are the Indians that both blacks and whites hate most. Squeezed into the Shylock role by racist laws and vicious licensing acts, property-owning Indians are always under threat and are often on the squeeze themselves. Then, in the months following the assault and trauma of the 1948 election, Natal's more impoverished, underdog Zulus turn, not on whites, but on Indians, who are more visibly in the line of fire. There's wholesale burning of Indian property and brutal mob attacks that end in a hundred and forty dead. And a mob is not disposed to discriminate between rich Muslims and poor Hindus. Any Indians will do.

Dinah's mum is at the Grey Street Indian Market when the anti-Indian riots break out. She's buying flowers for a neighbour who's in the maternity hospital. Then suddenly she's in the middle of a roaring crowd and she hears herself being yelled at.

'Hey, crazy lady, come out of there!' the policeman shouts, but the mob simply parts around her. She and her flowers are un-touched.

Given the high-speed growth rate of any plant in Durban, Dinah's mum's garden soon becomes a thing of wonder. The bald terraces of red mud are covered with coarse, un-English grass through which black millipedes crawl. There are avocado trees and pawpaw trees and a tree out front with a nobbly trunk and pendant red flowers, like fuchsias. Passion-fruit vines gallop along the verandah and along the mud wall of the side passage to the kitchen door. There are cobbles around the base of the avocado tree and there's a little bench in its shade. Some of her trees become protected species, which means that, for ever after, they must be left to loom picturesquely over the little house, threatening the eaves and the guttering.

Dinah's parents don't fence their garden. And, since theirs is the only unfenced house, their sideway path becomes a corridor for the black pedestrians of Cato Manor, which enrages the woman next door. Dinah's parents deliberately don't fence the garden, partly because they like the open aspect, but also because they're aware that, with the relentless extension of white suburbia, miles of fencing makes rings of steel around what were yesterday's public rights of way, and this means black pedestrians, often with heavy loads, are required sometimes to walk mile-long detours, just in order to get back home. And it's not only the black pedestrians, because these days, there's Evalina, who's become a fixture in the bungalow's native *kia*.

All houses in Durban are built with a routine hutch for a black domestic at the bottom of the garden. The hutch is something that Dinah's dad has no choice about. It comes along as part of the package with plans A, B and C. And the family hasn't been in residence five minutes before Charley, the Vice-Chancellor's swashbuckling, densely black Moçambiquan chauffeur, has twisted Ta's arm to ensconce his new girlfriend in the hutch as domestic servant. That way Evalina will be conveniently accessible to him.

Evalina is fabulous and she's great to have in the house. A big woman with a big personality, Evalina explodes with charm. She bangs about with duster and broom, listening each morning to the catchy sound of 1950s Radio Bantu, the SABC's ghetto radio station which is right then pouring out the cream of the townships' Golden Age black music. She has enormous boobs and a huge throaty laugh and all the phone calls that come to the house are for her. This means that, when Evalina is having her afternoon break, Dinah's parents are her constant messengers. They're forever running down to the edge of the lawn and calling down to the hutch. 'Telephone, Evalina!' Then Evalina, her headscarf awry and her person divested of its undergarments, will come chortling and bouncing up the garden path, clutching at her unbuttoned overall.

'*Hau*, master – no bodice,' she'll say and she'll sometimes have a super-quick flash to prove her point about this.

There's lots of partying and visitors in the hutch, which causes the neighbour almost to fall into an apoplexy – more especially so because she's somehow found out that Dinah's dad is paying wages over the odds. This is considered a caddish practice and is commonly referred to as 'spoiling the native girl'.

'I never know who's coming or going,' she says.

Because most white South African householders observe a strictly-no-visitors rule, the neighbour thinks it's outrageous that Evalina should be allowed visitors. Yet Dinah's house is the only one in the street that absolutely never gets burgled. And, mercifully, by the time Evalina is finally unmasked as the long-term receiver of stolen goods for a thriving burglary syndicate it's decades later, and the neighbour has been long under the sod.

Dinah's mother is pleased with her garden, but she's still quite exercised about the little strip of muddy verge that constitutes the pavement beyond her unfenced garden and she decides to distance herself from the mud by marking her property's boundary with a row of aloes in large tubs. Francis gets the tubs for her. Cheap, madam. Very cheap. So twelve handsome metal tubs appear, which the two of them paint a nice dark-green. The tubs are a source of pleasure to her, until Ta one day watches a small troop of skinny Indian schoolkids pointing and giggling at the tubs. Very soon they are marching up and down, arms swinging, and chanting as they cross and re-cross the garden. Dinah's dad cocks an ear and listens to the drift of their chant. They are keeping in step and singing lustily.

> One, two, three, four,
> Five, six, seven, eight,
> Nine, ten, eleven, twelve –
> TWELVE green shit buckets
> Outside of a YELL-ow house!

While the white areas of Durban all have water-borne sewage, the black locations don't, so Dinah's mum's plant tubs, so stylish to her white neighbours, are of course instantly recognisable to a troop of Indian schoolkids. And the revelation that his wife's plant tubs are knock-off from the location sewage works is vastly amusing to Dinah's dad, but her mum is mortified and insists that the buckets must go.

Now she's back to the undemarcated muddy verge and she doesn't have the money to have it paved. Plus it belongs to the council, doesn't it?

'Write to the council for me, Dee,' she says one day. 'Tell them to do something about it.'

'Me?' Dinah says. 'They won't do anything.'

'They will if you say that your father's a professor,' she says.

Dinah laughs at her, because she knows that her mum is daft, old-fashioned daft, foreign daft – that her pre-war German hierarchical

Weltanschauung will be a matter for derision. She knows that her mum's a bit taken with the fact that Ta has recently been made Professor of Maths, and that she probably really *does* think a strip of mud outside his garden is no longer in keeping with his status.

'Only think,' Dinah's mum says. 'His colleagues and his visitors having to walk always through all this mud.'

So Dinah writes what she considers to be a completely spoofy, hammed-up letter. She paints a vivid picture of the great man's distinguished guests – a line of Professor Brainstorms in gowns and mortar boards – all ruining their shoes on rainy nights as they wade through the seas of mud. But, incredibly, her mum seems happy with the letter and posts it right away. Five days later, there's a team of workmen jumping off the back of a lorry. They pass batches of quarry tiles to each other, hand over hand, and by the end of the day Dinah's house is the only one in the street to have twenty square metres of classy-looking terracotta paving all along the front.

Ta is astonished when he comes home but he's immediately suspicious.

'What did you do?' he says.

'Nothing,' Dinah's mum says, but she's a lousy actor. 'Dee wrote a letter for me, that's all.'

'What about?' he says.

'About the mud,' Dinah's mum says.

But soon he's plucked it out of them and for a while he's furious. All his egalitarian sentiments are affronted by the way his wife has gone and pulled rank like this. But he doesn't mind for all that long, because his new second-hand Vespa is much happier standing on the paving. The Vespa's previous owner has seen fit to adorn the scooter with diaphanous girlie transfers, but Ta considers them an irrelevance, given that the scooter runs so well. And he's completely unbothered when the girlie transfers get the odd mention, as they do from time to time, in student publications.

To reach Dinah's road from South Ridge Road, you turn right at the Manor House which is now a block of expensive two-storey maisonettes. Then you pass the overgrown corrugated tin house that penniless, brainy Eva lives in with her refugee Hungarian dad. A tin house is not really suitable for a white person for all that it has pretty Edwardian fretwork and a balustraded verandah. Tin houses everywhere are going under the bulldozer and there are lots and lots of bulldozers in Manor Gardens right now. It's a suburb that's expanding fast, even though no one has yet thought to develop the wooded green valley full of mango trees where white children go to build tree houses and Indian children go to pick the fruit for their parents to sell. This makes occasional brief opportunities for cross-race interaction, even if it's mainly name-calling.

'*Arrah-charrah-vrot-banana*,' the white children chant.

And Dinah has an abortive friendship with a girl her own age from the Indian Girls' High. She has long, looped black plaits and her uniform is always snowy-white. They chat all the way on the journey from the bus stop round the valley and always part at the turn-off for the lower road. Yet Dinah can't remember what they talked about and she doesn't even know the girl's name. All she can remember is her own embarrassment when the girl one day uses the word mis-CHEEV-ious. She can remember being ashamed of her embarrassment.

There's a steep, hairpin bend at Nunhead Road just below where the Professor of Afrikaans-Nederlands lives, with his dapper little beard and his white safari suit. Dinah's road starts with the Cleggs' grocery shop which is called a Tearoom and General Store, but it doesn't serve tea. Most corner shops are run by Greek immigrants, but the Cleggs are immigrants from Shoreditch. Mr Clegg was a Barnado's boy and he likes to regale his customers with the story of his early life. He's a small, wiry man with blackened teeth, several of which are missing. Mr Clegg has been in the Merchant Navy and, since he's often stripped to the waist, but for his sleeveless vest, his nautical tattoos are much in evidence. He has an anchor on one bicep and a crucifix wound around with what looks like barbed wire on the other. Mr Clegg has a cockney accent. He drops his 'h' sounds and says 'v' instead of 'th', but he always tells his customers that he once had an Oxford accent – that's before he lost it in the Navy.

'I once had an Oxford accent,' he says, 'and *vat's* the honest troof. Lost it in the Navy then, didn't I?'

Everyone knows that an Oxford accent is a combination of squashed, ultra-posh vowels and a tendency to pronounce one's 'r' sounds as 'w'. Dinah's dad once got sold a cheese dish in a department store by a man with an Oxford accent, so he can do an

Oxford accent to a tee – that's if ever he's called upon to do so.

Mrs Clegg is also from London. She's plump and sweaty with cropped pale-red hair and a bosom that she leans on the shop counter. The Cleggs have one grown-up son called Bobby. He's a fairly gormless young man who's supposed to be a helper in the shop, but most of the time he just lolls about with a stupid grin on his face. He has a very white beer belly and a mop of pale-ginger curls. So when Bobby gets a beautiful girlfriend with nice manners, everyone is surprised. The girlfriend is called Maria and she soon becomes Bobby's fiancée. She works in her future in-laws' shop, dealing efficiently with customers, while Mr Clegg hangs about smoking Capstans and Bobby occasionally pinches her bum or makes forays from the storeroom at the back to play practical jokes on her. Maria is a trim size ten and has the look of a young Jean Simmonds. She has dark hair and green eyes and she always wears a neat white blouse, topped with a cameo brooch. She wears a slim black pencil skirt with sheer nylons and size four black court shoes with little kitten heels.

The engagement is quite a long one, but finally the wedding day dawns and the shop is to be closed all day. Yet by midday its doors are open and it's business as usual, except that Mr Clegg is pacing up and down, smoking savagely, while Mrs Clegg is red-eyed and snivelling. The magistrate has turned up irregularities in Maria's papers. The beautiful fiancée is Coloured. Mrs Clegg is in shock and Mr Clegg is enraged. Only Bobby seems fairly unaffected. He's loping about grinning foolishly, just as if nothing has happened. Meanwhile, Maria is nowhere and she's never seen again: the charming, classy Jean Simmonds lookalike, who almost succeeded in appending herself to a family of deadbeat slobs in the cause of trying for white.

'*Piccaninnies*,' Mr Clegg is saying viciously between puffs. 'Blee-din' *piccaninnies*. Vat's what I could've 'ad for grandchildren!'

Dinah's street is like a building site because quite a few plots have recently been sold. Two identical houses are going up directly across the road and, as they take shape, it's clear that they'll be a little bit more deluxe than Dinah's house and a little bit more traditional. They are more like the houses Dinah used to build with her Bayco building blocks and they have pyramidal brick-tiled roofs and casement windows made of wood. But inside they're much darker because they don't have a picture window on to the verandah like Dinah's house and they have a lot more interior walls. The left-hand house gets dark-green drapes at all the windows and lampshades made out of sections of antiqued crackle parchment shaped like the skirts of a crinoline lady but with dangly green bobbles along the lower edges. Dinah knows this because she and Lisa are soon acquainted with the girl who lives in the left-hand house.

Catherine Cleary's living room has a dark cottage suite with flowered seats and two extra easy chairs covered in moss-green moquette with more green-bobble trim. There's a glass-fronted display cabinet made of Imbuya wood with claw-and-ball feet that has a row of Toby Jugs and a china thimble collection. Catherine's mum has three framed artworks on the wall and some framed family photographs on the occasional table. The artworks are reproductions of Gainsborough's *Blue Boy* and Sir Joshua Reynolds's *Boy with the Rabbit*, along with the new Annigoni portrait of HM Queen Elizabeth II. Catherine's mum's tastes are more traditional than those of Dinah's mum who likes Japanese prints and the French Impressionists, so that when Catherine and Dinah leaf through art books together, it's like a small skirmish in which each girl is nailing her colours to a family aesthetic. Catherine will say 'Ugh' or 'Yum', depending on whether the picture is by Cézanne or Lord Leighton and Dinah will do the same, depending on whether it's Raeburn or Renoir. Dinah thinks that Catherine's taste in pictures is chocolate box, because the French Impressionists haven't yet made it big on chocolate boxes.

Catherine's mother is a war widow whose husband died at Tobruk in North Africa, aged twenty-three, when Catherine was two months old. Sometimes, when Mrs Cleary is out, Catherine will lead Dinah down the dark passage into her mother's green candlewick and ruched satin bedroom where, in the bottom drawer of the wardrobe, Mrs Cleary keeps her husband's relics. There are his army uniform and badges wrapped in old brown paper and the letter from the Army saying that he's dead. But what Catherine homes in on is a small drawstring bag containing her father's toenails. These are Donald 'Bunny' Cleary's only earthly remains. Her father, she explains, used always to take part in the annual

Comrades' Marathon – a fifty-mile run between Durban and Pietermaritzburg. Catherine explains to Dinah that all the running in canvas gym shoes makes a person's toenails turn black and fall off because of the constant pressure. And every year Catherine's dad saved the dead black toenails as trophies. Catherine loves nothing better than to get the toenails out of the bag. She spreads the shrivelled particles all over the floral half-moon rug, but she knows that her mum will have an absolute fit if she ever finds this out.

Catherine's mum is more naggy and whining than anyone Dinah has ever met, but the mercy is that she goes out to work as a dentist's receptionist, so there's an hour after school most days and all of Saturdays before she gets in. The girls rustle up high-speed trays of fudge in Catherine's kitchen and batches of pink-and-white coconut ice. And sometimes they make rock cakes with so much soda that their teeth go all on edge. Then they have a final high-speed scuffle of dishwashing before the Moaning Minnie returns. To Dinah and Lisa, Catherine is quite amazingly disobedient, and Lisa usually bows out of Catherine's schemes because they don't suit her temperament, but Catherine has learnt that she might as well be disobedient because her mum will always find something about her to pick on, no matter what. Mrs Cleary is like a person who's in a chronic state of PMT and she's got a special down-in-the-mouth grumbling voice that she saves for talking to Catherine. If Dinah ever overhears her talking in a friendly voice, then she knows that Mrs Cleary is talking to Tinker the Corgi, or to Dingle the little black chihuahua.

'He may be as black as the Ace of Spades,' Mrs Cleary quips to Dinah's parents, 'but there aren't any racialists in *this* house.'

Mrs Cleary is as much of a 'racialist' as anyone else in Durban, but she says this because she's respectful of Dinah's dad's professorial status and because she knows that Dinah's parents are liberals. In Dinah's childhood a liberal is a person who doesn't recoil at the thought of a black person drinking out of his teacups.

Mrs Cleary has frizzed mouse hair and a passion for the Royal Family. She combines being a royalist with being terrifically snobbish. She's the only person Dinah's met who's got a way of winking meaningfully and whispering 'Top drawer' about certain categories of person. Her constant boast is that she goes out to work so that Catherine can attend a fee-paying school.

'All of my life, I've scrimped and saved,' she says, 'so that Catherine can say she's been to Wykeham.'

Wykeham is the most upper crust of South Africa's girls' boarding schools and it sets its girls apart by requiring them to wear unbelievably large black hats, huge, conical witches' hats like the ones in Ronald Searle drawings. Catherine is no longer at Wykeham, but, nonetheless, her time there means Mrs Cleary can now make reference to her daughter's close acquaintance with the granddaughters of Senator Heaton-Nicholls. This doesn't hold much cop for Lisa and Dinah, who wouldn't know who the Senator was, were he not right then at the top of their dad's morning rant list. The Senator is a dyed-in-the-wool segregationist and the UP's native expert. He's been urging Parliament to vote for Mr Strijdom's abolition of the Cape's Coloured franchise. For the Cape to have a Coloured franchise, he says, is 'holding back the natives' progress'.

These days Catherine is a day girl at a local convent school, although her mother, along with the royalism and the racism, is passionately anti-Catholic. Dinah has never come across anti-Catholicism before. There's always been her dad's dimissiveness about religions in general – though he does have a jokey little rhyme that suggests an unexpected preference:

> Of all religions I profess
> I much prefer the Methodess.

But she's never encountered the kind of sectarian paranoia that Catherine and her mother exhibit. When it comes to Catholics, mother and daughter are united, both in sentiment and in syntax.

'The priests in Ireland are living off the fat of the land,' they say. 'Meanwhile the peasants are scratching about for potatoes.'

They'll say this while their own illiterate, under-age Zulu houseboy is polishing their front steps for a full-time monthly salary of three pounds ten shillings and sixpence plus two bags of maize meal. Catholics worship idols and gabble prayers like sheep. Catholics go to Mass, only because they're terrified of the priests. The priests are always standing behind them with pitchforks, prodding them into church. The Pope is the Scarlet Whore of Rome. The Pope is Jezebel and de Valera is Beelzebub.

Dinah is completely baffled by this. She can't relate to the imagery, because she's never heard of Jezebel, or Beelzebub, and she's never seen a pitchfork in real life – only in her ancient kiddies' board book version of 'Old Macdonald'. The source for this curious, grafted-on bigotry is Mrs Cleary's long-dead husband, Donald 'Bunny' Cleary, who – though he never in his short life set foot in Northern Ireland – had his small-town childhood in Mafeking illuminated by the passionate sectarian hatreds of his Ulster Protestant parents. Then, in the few happy months he had with Catherine's mother, he was able to hand on the baton of his Loyalist inheritance.

Mrs Cleary met her husband at one of Mafeking's Saturday-night dances and she fell for him at once. This was her one brief happy time, dancing with the daredevil young Irishman, the wild one in the pack, the joker, the wag. Just occasionally, she will regale Catherine and Dinah with references to these occasions.

'Just a bit of Pond's Vanishing Cream and a touch of Johnson's Baby Powder on the nose,' she'll say.

She says it with an unaccustomed glint, and sometimes a little pointedly, as she watches Catherine and Dinah begin to dolly-up and experiment with Maybelline blue mascara and Max Factor Pan-Stick. Mrs Cleary likes to emphasise a woman's modesty and decorum, so she tells the story of the Bold Young Woman at one of the Mafeking dances. The Bold Young Woman was wearing a backless evening dress and one of the young men, before he planted his hand on her back in order to dance the quickstep, pointedly unfolded his handkerchief and placed it over the patch of bare flesh. Naturally, the Bold Young Woman was mortified and blushed scarlet with embarrassment.

Sometimes Mrs Cleary will joke about having to dance with one of the local Afrikaner farmers. They always danced 'the pot handle', as she says. She means that the farmers danced, hillbilly hick, with their right arm held straight out, pumping vigorously in time to the music.

Catherine has a fine skin and a small delicate nose but she has almost no eyebrows or eyelashes, and she has small recessed blue eyes. Her bum is flat and wide and she runs easily to fat. Dinah has more visible eyes and eyebrows and proper curvy buttocks, but she hates her nose and starts to steam her coarsening skin over a pudding basin of boiling water with a bath towel over her head. The coarsening skin has to do with biological maturity, which has come to her as a complete shock one recent Saturday morning.

I'm dying, she thinks. I'm bleeding to death. It can't be that nobody's told her about menstruation. She's surely been told and she's suppressed it. But because she knows that she's dying, rather than that she's afflicted with a routine female condition, she doesn't whisper it secretly to her mum. She announces it out loud in front of both her parents, so there's a general family to-do over it, with her mum running for sanitary towels and her dad saying, 'Well, I suppose she ought to pay full fare on the buses from now on.' Until then, Dinah has always got by on the under-twelve rate.

And given the public nature of its onset, it's pretty weird that nobody seems to notice what Dinah's going through, that what's happening to her every month isn't exactly normal, that for twelve days out of thirty she's soaking through a packet of Kotex pads in a day, and often wearing two of them at once, that every time she stands up there'll be a rush of accumulated blood, just like turning on a tap – a gush that always contains dark, jellified clots. Since the Girls' High School summer uniform is a revealing pale-cream cotton, Dinah longs for the navy serge of winter, even though Durban doesn't have a winter, just hot and very hot. That way the kindly senior girls aren't forever coming up to her and whispering that she's 'come on' – just as if she doesn't know that she's got huge stains on the back of her dress.

Every month Dinah chafes two weeping raw patches at the tops of her inside thighs from all the friction caused by the hardened, dry edges of the Kotex pads. She puts Vaseline and Elastoplast over the raw patches and tries not to wince with every step as she walks from the bus stop home from school. This routine agony goes on until, at seventeen, with the collusion of a clued-up new girl, Dinah discovers the unbelievable, the paradisal joys of Tampax and wonders why the Nobel Prize for Science hasn't been awarded to the inventor.

Catherine Cleary is Dinah's conduit to the fine detail of boy–girl street mores. Catherine knows that if a man wants to buy what she calls a rubber johnny, then he'll go into a chemist shop and spin half a crown on the counter without saying a word and the assistant will know what he wants. She knows that if a boy writes 'Father

Uncle Cousin King' on a note that he passes to you on the school bus, then it means that he wants to F-U-C-K you, though for the moment Dinah doesn't know what fuck means, either. That's until Catherine explains it to her. Catherine knows that when a boy writes 'SWANK' on the back of a letter it means 'Sealed with a naughty kiss', which is a way of saying he wants to snog you. She knows about bulges in boys' school trousers and she knows that boys pant when they're sexually aroused. Catherine giggles at the sight of Dinah's mum's sewing machine shuttle flying up and down and she likes to pull the caps off tubes of lipstick and shunt the waxy red sticks up and down in their holders.

'What does this remind you of?' she says, but Dinah is either too ignorant or too repressed to be reminded of anything. All she knows is that Catherine is being rude.

Catherine explains the Virgin Birth to Dinah by telling her how the Holy Ghost 'came upon' the Mother of God.

'The Holy Ghost did this to her,' Catherine says, and she makes a fist of her right hand with the thumb jutting saucily between her index and middle fingers. Then she waggles the fist in Dinah's face. It is not a gesture Dinah's seen before but she begins to get the point. The Virgin Mary has become pregnant by the Holy Ghost, as a result of receiving a schoolboy's note while sitting on the bus. Father Uncle Cousin King.

All through junior school Dinah and her friends have kept autograph books – little hard-covered books with pastel-coloured pages on which classmates, teachers and best friends signed their names. Or sometimes people would write verses or draw a picture with a snappy caption. If somebody wrote something witty or clever, then one could save it and use it oneself to write in someone else's autograph book:

> When God gave out legs
> I thought he said kegs.
> I asked for two fat ones.
> When God gave out noses
> I thought he said roses.
> I asked for a big red one.

This is what Enid once wrote in Dinah's book, except Enid's rhyming couplets went on and on. Another classmate's rhyme is lost on Dinah, because she's never heard the expression 'fellow feeling':

> Fellow feeling is wondrous kind
> But I wonder just how a fellow would feel
> If he felt a fellow feeling
> In his pocket behind.

Best of all is Angela's page that shows a pot-bellied Marmite jar with its label at the top – 'MARMITE'. Underneath the jar, Angela has written, 'But Pa won't.'

Autograph books have pretty well disappeared with high school, but Catherine still has one and she asks Dinah to sign it, so Dinah borrows Angela's Marmite pun and sketches it into Catherine's book. Underneath she writes, 'With love from Dinah'. Then one day soon afterwards, Catherine's all fired up with excitement.

'I got into such trouble from my mum,' Catherine says. 'She read my autograph book, you see, and she's seen what you wrote. God, she had *three fits*.'

'Why?' Dinah says, but Catherine ignores her.

'It's all right,' she says. 'Well, I think it's all right. Just about. I managed to persuade her it was another Dinah. Somebody at school. So I've saved your bacon for now. God, if she *really* thought it was you, you'd *never be allowed to come to my house again*.'

'Why?' Dinah says again.

'She's forbidden me to ever have anything to do with that person – so for heaven's sake, pretend you know absolutely nothing about it. That's if she ever asks.'

'All right,' Dinah says, thinking that maybe one day – *one* day – she'll be a little bit less green and she'll understand why the Marmite pun is so smutty and unacceptable but, as time passes, Dinah never does get to understand. Instead, it comes to her that, underneath the pursed-up exterior and the social climbing and the would-be vowels, Catherine's mother is just about as vulgar as her own winking Toby Jugs. She has a one-track mind, like her daughter.

'You've got a one-track mind,' Dinah's peers at school have

started saying to each other. 'Honestly, Michelle, you've got a one-track mind. And it's a dirt track.'

Every Sunday Catherine goes to St Paul's Anglican Church in the town centre to attend the Sunday school where the ethical issue of sitting beside the small smattering of not-white children is a big one for Catherine and all the other white attendants. Barney, whose hobby is knocking out street lights, says that it's disgusting, but Catherine says, piously, 'It's all right in the House of God, Barney. It's only outside church that He doesn't want us to mix. It's got to be whites on top.'

Blood and water don't mix. Catherine quite often employs this maxim, but Dinah has never managed to work out if it's whites who've got blood and blacks who've got water, or whether it's the other way round. It reminds her of the lines in one of the morning hymns at school:

> Let the water and the blood
> From Thy riven soul which flowed,
> Be of sin the double cure,
> Save me from its guilt and power.

Because Dinah still harbours her religious passions, she confides these to Catherine who has a plan. She's talked a lot about a handsome, dark-haired young curate at St Paul's whose name is Andrew Dalkeith. She arranges a meeting between Dinah and the Revd Dalkeith who, as Dinah understands, has agreed to baptise her without involving her parents. So Dinah, after several sessions at matins and evensong, where she soon knows the Common Prayer liturgy by heart and can point all the psalms to perfection, conquers her shyness and meets the Revd Andrew Dalkeith in a small, curtained ante-room off the sacristy. Revd Dalkeith is just as handsome as Catherine has told her, but it's soon perfectly obvious that he's not intending to baptise her and risk her father's wrath. He doesn't have the decency to say this to Dinah, so, instead, he tells her that it wouldn't be enough for him to save just her soul. He needs her father's soul as well. What he needs is for her to do him a favour and convert her father first. This is clearly God's purpose for her.

So the Revd Andrew Dalkeith sends Dinah away with a bunch of tacky tracts and a copy of *The Screwtape Letters* by C.S. Lewis which she's to leave in her father's path. Dinah obediently does what he asks, knowing that it can't possibly work and that all it'll do is make her feel an idiot, because her father will think it a great joke. Her dad duly piss-takes over the pamphlets and picks several holes in *The Screwtape Letters* before settling down to pick more holes in the moral fibre of the current Archdeacon of St Paul's Church, whom he considers to be as mealy-mouthed on the race issue as most of the local Anglican clergy. That's with a few honourable and sometimes heroic exceptions. Archdeacon Eustace H. Wade of St Paul's, soon to be better known as the father of Virginia Wade, future Wimbledon champion and right now the crowning glory of Dinah's high-school tennis team, is not one of Ta's heroic exceptions and is rewarded by Dinah's dad with the title of Archdeacon Useless H. Wade whenever he comes on the radio to conduct the morning service.

In spite of the Revd Dalkeith's let-down response, Dinah loyally goes along, year in, year out, to matins and evensong, until the rhythms of Thomas Cranmer's prose have burned their way into her mind. She endures three hours of Good Friday devotions although the dust in the hassocks always gives her hay fever and she's never brought along enough tissues. She does this, although she and the Revd Dalkeith never exchange a glance. Then one day she suddenly stops going and it's hard, thinking back, to know why. The baptismal business really bugs her. She's too shy to re-ignite the issue and she's demoralised by always feeling marginal. It's sort of like the Brownies business all over again. Before you got your Brownie uniform, you were called a Tweenie. These days Dinah feels that she's been a C of E Tweenie for far too long to be comfortable.

Catherine Cleary's mother decides to take in a lodger to help make ends meet. The lodger is a balding engineering student who is one of Ta's more hopeless serial repeats. The repeat has re-taken each year of the degree course because he keeps on failing maths. Ta, who has the art of teaching maths to almost anybody, is nonetheless always in jaunty mood when confronted by a truly hopeless failure. While marking exam scripts, he mutters triumphantly out loud as he strikes errors through with red ink.

'Ah-ha! So you're a fool!' he'll say and he'll pause to chortle over the unfortunate's algebraic *faux pas*. 'Give up. It's wrong from beginning to end!' he'll say. 'Zero for you, my boy. Ha!'

Sometimes Dinah's mum will intervene, because she always feels sorry for the students.

'*Ach, Tächenherz*,' she'll say. 'But he has such beautiful handwriting.'

Dinah's dad always takes especial pleasure in marking down a fool with beautiful handwriting, though just sometimes he'll say, in response to her interventions, 'Oh all right. We'll give him three. Three per cent. Much good may *that* do him!'

Mrs Cleary's repeat is so prematurely aged and so painfully polite that Catherine and Dinah can't help but giggle in his presence. Catherine's mother is contracted to give the repeat an evening meal and his perfect conduct at mealtimes makes Catherine play up really badly. Catherine tells Dinah that the repeat is so polite that he bends his head almost under the table in order to blow his nose. Catherine copies him at once, getting right under the cloth and blowing a few rousing fake blasts that make her mother send her out of the room. Catherine's mum is always sending her out of the room at mealtimes.

Mrs Cleary, though she never has dinner parties, does occasionally have her much younger sister Nan and brother-in-law to supper, who live in the twin house next door. Once Catherine reports to Dinah that she has been sent out when her Uncle Philip has made a remark which is not altogether in keeping with Mrs Cleary's sense of propriety. Philip Herbert is a handsome young man, slightly touched with a hint of blue-collar – because clever, competent sister Nan is thought to have married down. Philip goes to work on a push bike which is definitely not quite the thing in a place where bicycles are a mode of transport only for black delivery persons. Or else they are white children's toys.

'Somebody's farted,' Philip says, possibly to wind up Catherine's mother. Or it could be that the culprit is Tinker who is given to inopportune venting.

'A fox smells his own hole first,' Catherine quips.

She's sent to her room, but climbs out of the unbarred bathroom window to report the matter at once, though Dinah is not quite sure, from Catherine's account, if Mrs Cleary is shocked because

Catherine has insulted her uncle by the use of a foxy metaphor, or if there's a connection in Mrs Cleary's mind between the words hole and anus. Does Mrs Cleary think that Catherine was saying her uncle could smell his own anus?

When Mrs Cleary gets a gentleman caller, Catherine's behaviour reaches heights of vulgarity. The gentleman caller has come to canvass for the newly constituted Federal Party which has in mind, in the event of Mr Strijdom's declaring a republic, for royalist Natal to secede from the Union of South Africa. The airing of the republican idea has been causing one of Durban's periodic flurries of Union Jack planting in suburban flowerbeds and Mrs Cleary now has one, thanks to the help of the gentleman caller. But after planting Mrs Cleary's flag, the canvasser just keeps on calling. Mrs Cleary obviously welcomes his visits. She wears lipstick and smarter clothes and she smiles more often and asks the canvasser to stay for meals. But Catherine behaves so offensively that she drives the canvasser from the house. Her incessant fake burps at table finally do the trick and the battle is won.

Poor Mrs Cleary is miserable. She can clearly no longer stand the sight of Catherine who has wrecked the only second chance for happiness that has managed to come her way. She rises to heights of nagging and nitpicking until, some months later, she dispatches Catherine to an up-country convent boarding school. And it's at the school that Catherine, possibly in an act of revenge, or merely while falling under the influence of her namesake, Sister Catherine, the art teacher – an emotionally, morally and intellectually more impressive woman than her own mother – converts to Catholicism, a faith which she practises devoutly and conscientiously for the rest of her life.

EIGHT

GHS IS TRYING TO BE like an English girls' grammar school, but the time-warp factor plus the colonial cringe are making it very different. While the school's original building looks quite English – a little brick schoolhouse in the town centre, with low sash windows and a tarmac playground and its motto carved into the stone lintel over the front door – the current building, Dinah's building, stands, gleaming-white, in six acres of landscaped grounds, high on Durban's airy south ridge, with panoramic views over the bay. Inside the building, several past headmistresses are staring down at you from the walls and most of them are Scottish. This is because the British Imperial project in South Africa has ensured that education is dominated by Scots. When the British swiped the Cape off the Dutch in 1795, it seemed to them like a good idea to anglicise Dutch Calvinists. So they introduced British Calvinists to do all the preaching and the teaching. This means that, in addition to the predominance of Scottish headmistresses, there are lots of Afrikaners called Murray.

Girls' High still has the motto and there's also a school song. The motto is 'Time Lost is Never Regained'. Dinah can't really relate to this because she knows that time goes on for ever and, however much of it she wastes, there always seems to be more of it. The school song was composed by one of the dead Scottish headmistresses and it's all about dead male war heroes. That's except for Joan of Arc. The school song is all about Nelson and Napoleon and Coeur de Lion. Plus there's a line about 'stout courageous Wellington', which is why Dinah knows that the Duke of Wellington was a fat man. Cortez, she knows, was fat as well, because it says so in the Keats poem: 'like stout Cortez when with eagle eyes he star'd at the Pacific'. Cortez was a fat man with pop eyes. She's recently found Keats and the Romantics for herself, because the syllabus keeps the junior girls on 'suitable narrative verse'.

Dinah likes the assembly hall which has a proper stage with wings and a proscenium arch and thick velvet curtains with gold tassels. There are sets of French windows to right and left that give on to shady loggias, beyond which are gardens with frangipani trees and there's an exciting upstairs gallery as well. Theatrical productions at GHS always have the taller girls dressed up in buckled shoes and cravats and wigs pretending to be men. There's a production of *She Stoops to Conquer* and one of *The Dueña* and a play about Robert Browning and Elizabeth Barrett falling in love. Shakespeare doesn't happen on stage, because he's kept for reading round the class over periods of roughly nine months per play. Dinah's first Shakespeare is *Twelfth Night* which takes from January to September. So come September, the play has lost any shape. Plus she's got no idea why the characters keep on saying 'Marry' and 'Sblood' to each other.

Miss Bardsey puts on Gilbert & Sullivan operas and Miss Byrd, the art teacher, does Living Art which is a series of tableaux in which she recreates Old Master paintings on stage with pupils in costume. She gets the art girls to help with the painted backdrops and she finds suitable props and does artful lighting effects. Dinah has a part in Rembrandt's *The Night Watch* and another in Poussin's *Dance to the Music of Time*, but everybody envies beautiful Pat Slavin because she's Queen Nefertiti. Quite often the audience doesn't recognise the art works on which the tableaux are based, but Pat gets a lot of applause, because the recent, much photographed London exhibition of artefacts from Tutankhamun's tomb means that she's a well-known celebrity icon in her necklace of Plasticine lapis lazuli.

Mostly the stage is used, day-to-day, for seating the staff during assembly. The teachers sit in a wide arc with Miss Maidment always dead centre, a bit like Christ in Glory. Then there's a sort of age-before-beauty arrangement that falls away from her to left and right. When Miss Maidment gets up to address the girls it's always from the lectern. She exhorts them to heights of achievement and good behaviour with certain favourite repeating refrains.

'You gels are the mothers of the future,' she says.

Her point is that GHS girls must excel in order to make

163

themselves capable of producing the right sort of daughters who will then become pupils at GHS and go on to produce yet another generation of suitable GHS girls. This is pretty well the beginning and end of the GHS careers advisory service, but somehow, the brainy Jewish girls don't need a careers advisory service to know that it's important to take Latin as one of your subjects, because then you can go on to become a doctor or a lawyer. The glossy airhead Jewish girls never bother with Latin. They have nose jobs and do flirting on Durban's North Beach. They have beautiful tans and they spend the breaks comparing gold neck chains with Star of David pendants. They hide these under their school shirts, because at GHS it's strictly no-jewellery-allowed.

Dinah's family dentist is called Dr Goldman and his daughter is one of the tanned airhead glamour girls. Dr Goldman is always grumbling about his son who, by all accounts, is a bit of an airhead as well. He grumbles while he's injecting your gums with what feels like a large rusty nail grinding through bone and gristle, but Dinah's mum won't let the girls switch to young Dr Weiss, the junior partner, who gives injections that you can't even feel, just in case Dr Goldman gets offended. Dr Goldman is always so busy touching up his female assistants that he never finishes your fillings in one session. He does temporary fillings over and over and he tells you to keep on coming back.

The dentist has always loomed large for Dinah, who's got useless, hazard-prone teeth in spite of all the nutritious force feeding in childhood and the gollops of cod liver oil and malt from the big elliptical brown glass jar. Being premature and anaemic and sub-standard has meant that she's forever in there with Dr Goldman and his rusty-nail routine. Dr Goldman has even started to flirt with *her*, in a half-hearted sort of way, though she never gets a nice golden tan like his daughter. Dinah will lie in the sun for hours until her balance has gone all wonky and those swirly optical distur-bances start invading the backs of her eyelids, yet she always stays lily-white. She doesn't know that her copious daily hay-fever drugs are sabotaging her efforts: antihistamine is the active ingredient in all the sun-block pills.

During assembly, Miss Maidment likes to find moral uplift in all the music that Miss Bardsey chooses for filing in and out. So, whether it's 'The Royal Fireworks' or 'The Harmonious Black-smith', she always says the same thing.

'That *invigorating* piece of music,' she says, 'serves to remind us of the energetic, yet *orderly* way in which we go about our tasks at GHS. School dismiss.'

Each morning there are two hymns which the girls sing from their little hardback copies of *The Public School Hymn Book*, compiled by the Headmasters' Conference and published in 1949 by Novello and Co. in Wardour Street, London W1. From this address it has clearly made its way around the globe from Greenland's Icy Mountains to Afric's Coral Strand. At the front of the hymn book it says, 'Verses marked with an asterisk may be omitted if it is desired to shorten a hymn', but at Dinah's school they nearly always sing all the verses. Dinah loves the hymns and she especially likes the names of some of the people who wrote them, like Nahum Tate and Percy Dearmer, which she reads as 'Percy Dreamer'. She thinks it's exciting that some of them were written very long ago, by the Venerable Bede, or by the twelfth-century Bishop of Cluny. The hymns are her first introduction to the metaphysical poetry of George Herbert and Henry Vaughan, because the poetry lessons in class are always taken up with the 'suitable narrative verse'.

> I sprang to the stirrup and Joris and he.
> I galloped, Dirck galloped, we galloped all three.

Every time she reads this poem, Dinah wonders if she's got it right that 'he', in line one, is 'Dirck' in line two. The most memorable thing about the 'suitable narrative verse' is that, thanks to the Caledonian factor, all the most fabulous and bone-curdling Scottish ballads have sneaked on to the syllabus, full to the brim with drownings, hangings, poisonings, infanticides and eye-pecking mutilations.

The girls go lisle-stockinged in winter and wear cotton ankle socks in summer, but the teachers have to wear nylon stockings all year round. Then there's the academic gown. Miss Maidment wears her gown every morning, but the rest of the staff wear theirs only on Speech Days and on special occasions. That's all except Mrs Keithley who doesn't have a gown because she's come from the non-graduate Afrikaans-language teachers-training college in

Bloemfontein. This is clearly why Mrs Keithley is always stuck up in the gallery on special occasions, with the job of looking after Dinah's class of junior girls. And once the girls have realised this, Mrs Keithley gets no peace.

'Why aren't you on the stage, Mrs Keithley?' they say. 'We think it's *not fair*.'

Mrs Keithley tries a brave smile. 'Because I'm up here in the gallery, looking after you, my girlies,' she says.

On Speech Day a visiting dignitary will come and he'll speak almost for ever. Then he'll have to hand out all the prizes and cups and shields. These always go to the same five girls, who already have their blazers decked out with gold grosgrain ribbon and rows of silver badges. Standard GHS blazers are plain navy with a green-and-white badge on the pocket – except for dumbo Marjorie's. Marjorie is in Dinah's class and one day her mum spots a brace of the high-achieving gold-braid girls on the bus, so she thinks to herself, Now that's a nice way to brighten up a blazer. When Marjorie comes to school next day with bunting all over her blazer, she gets sent straight home in disgrace to have it removed.

Dinah's dad once gets asked to present the prizes on Speech Day but he manages to wriggle out of it. He's only ever turned up once on Speech Day and he carries on about it afterwards as if it were a re-run of Dinah's Brownie Show Day. He's got a story he likes to tell about interminable speeches that he's heard from a colleague who's come from Yale. It's about a celebrity speaker who decides to take all the letters of the name Yale and expand, one by one, on a particular virtue that each of the letters represents. So after he's gone on and on about 'Youth', 'Ambition', 'Learning' and 'Education', he finally winds up by telling the assembled shining youth how fortunate they are to be at Yale. Then the chairman rises to give his thanks.

'We are indeed fortunate to be at Yale,' he says. 'Because we could have been at the Massachusetts Institute of Technology.'

Occasionally, the girls are gathered in the hall to hear Distinguished Visiting Persons on the lecture circuit – people like Helen Keller and Sir Vivian Fuchs. Once there's a phoney 'explorer' who is making everything up as he goes along. At the end of any particularly unlikely adventure, he stretches out his left arm and runs the palm of his right hand along it.

'Now *that's* a long one,' he says. 'You can believe that if you like.'

He tells the girls that he's got a mileometer strapped to his hip which he'll show them, if they come up and see him afterwards, and some of his stories begin to border on the risqué. In the background, Miss Maidment, slightly flapping the batwing sleeves of her academic gown, is trying to decide on a strategy of damage limitation – whether to keep on miming normality or whether to arrange for the explorer's premature ejection.

Then there's the Afrikaner intellectual who prematurely ejects himself. He's been a distinguished academic but he's fallen foul of the *Volk* and he's been hounded out of his job. There's only one place to be an Afrikaner at this time and that's inside the laager of religious-racist authoritarianism. Defy the thought police and you're out. Naturally, the professor's banishment has enhanced his reputation among the English community, because any chink in the monolith is always met with relish. So he's soon on the English lecture circuit. Nobody has foreseen that the poor old professor will have found his isolation sufficiently troubling to have led him into alcohol addiction, or towards a penchant for low life. His speech from the platform is thick and slurred and he has the yellowing vestiges of a black eye. Plus he keeps on looking sideways out of the window. Then he dismisses himself after only fifteen minutes.

'Excuse me,' he says politely, 'but I can't stay any longer. I've got Poppy waiting for me in a taxi.'

This is Dinah's best exit line, ever. Better than 'Exit pursued by a bear'.

GHS is a state school, but it's one in the context of a state that spends three-quarters of its education budget on one-tenth of its children. White children. There's no entrance exam, so you go there because your parents choose it – which is what they do, on the whole, if they're middle class. If you don't go to GHS, then you go to Mitchell High School. 'Going to Mitchell' is seen as slightly downmarket at this time, because it's what you do if you're going to leave school at sixteen and do shorthand and typing at the Tech. In this way, Dinah loses touch with half her junior-school class, including the two serious brain-boxes, Jennifer Wilson and Janet Camperdown. Those two most frequent recipients of the A1 ice-cream Top Girl rosette are both of them 'going to Mitchell'.

Throughout Dinah's first year at GHS, it's fairly clear that the staff don't quite know what to do with them, so they're dealt with as if they were still in junior school. Normal procedure at GHS is for girls to be grouped in forms according to their Matric subjects, after which they move, on the hour, to the classrooms of their allotted subject teachers. But Dinah's year of under-age new-bugs is kept all day in one or other of the four new form-rooms under the eye of a class teacher who takes them for nearly everything. Dinah is separated from Angela who's in a different form, though they still come together in all the breaks. They are still each other's Best Friend, even though they can't perform their primary Best-Friend function of whispering and giggling together in the back row of every classroom. So they long for the second year when they can be reunited through judicious choice of Matric subjects.

'You're still my Best Friend,' Dinah says.

'You'll always be my Best Friend,' Angela says. 'I've never had such a friend.'

Dinah is lucky in her form teacher because she gets Miss Barnes who's an Old World beauty with pearl earrings and Celia Johnson hair. Miss Barnes wears sprigged crêpe dresses with shoulder pads and she's got a charming retro look. Dinah can't remember anything much they do in class, except that at the end of every day Miss Barnes chooses a book and reads it aloud. She remembers this because one day the book is *Pride and Prejudice* and it's like nothing she's ever come across before. The language is like watching a flying kite. It's like being lifted off the ground. For Dinah – her dad's read-aloud Boys' Book sessions excepted – fiction has always been a matter of finding one's own easy-option page-turners unaided in the city library, which has meant a steady diet of Enid Blyton school stories and the *Bobbsey Twins* followed by *Sue Barton Staff Nurse*, and the mysteries of Nancy Drew. These have been punctuated by occasional accidental highs such as *Anne of Green Gables*, *Little Women* and *Ballet Shoes*. Then there's Anya Seton and Georgette Heyer. Just recently Dinah has discovered Lorna Hill, whose slightly wacky 1950s characters, with their highbrow musical and balletic ambitions, have supplanted the hearty, lacrosse-playing heroines of Enid Blyton's *Mallory Towers*.

Lorna Hill's combination of North Country pony-trekking, combined with the lure of the Sadler's Wells ballet school, has managed to echo Dinah's unfulfilled longings for riding and ballet lessons. Plus Lorna Hill's books have boys: brainy, sexy boys for Dinah to fall in love with. The boys are sexy *because* they're brainy, not because they're smoochy. This is the bliss of them. They provide Dinah with a blueprint for the desirable male other which effectively renders ineligible most of the groping, real-life local boys. Lorna Hill provides the establishment brainy boys like hunky Northumbrian Guy who's going to be a vet. Then there are the anti-establishment brainy boys like orphaned, stroppy Sebastian, the threadbare musical genius and rightful heir to the Hall, who's one day going to be a famous conductor, because nearly everyone is going to be famous and special.

'You only read those books because you're in love with Guy,' Lisa says one day at the supper table.

It doesn't cross Dinah's mind that Lisa can only be making this observation because she's been reading the books herself and she too has fallen for Guy. She feels the blush rising, neck to hairline, like cherry lemonade being poured into a glass.

'You've gone all red,' Lisa says.

'No I haven't,' Dinah says.

'You *have*,' Lisa says. 'Even your ears are bright red.'

Most of Dinah's 'cultured' reading – *The Arabian Nights* and the Brothers Grimm, William Blake and the Shakespeare songs, Robert Louis Stevenson and John Bunyan, St Paul and the Psalms – it's all come to her in little bite-sized chunks, courtesy of her junior school Beacon Readers.

– in the time of the caliph Haroun al-Rashid, there lived in the city of Baghdad –
– now it happened that the king loved gold above all things –
– o Rose, thou art sick –
– come unto these yellow sands and then take hands –
– I should like to rise and go, where the golden apples grow –
– and from him came fire and smoke –
– though I speak with the tongues of men and of angels –
– for I have eaten ashes like bread and mingled my drink with weeping –

With school reading she's had to take in every word and do comprehension exercises on it afterwards. But with her own easy-option reading for pleasure, she's often just skipped all the 'description' and homed in on the dialogue. The dialogue is where all the characters are – and it's the characters who become your special friends.

'For two pins I'd put you in my rucksack,' says Guy when he rescues fragile balletic Jane who is lost in a mountain mist in highly unsuitable shoes. Dinah likes to replay this scene over and over in her mind. She plays it with herself as Jane, yet at the same time she's longing to be the one who says 'For two pins' out loud. It always sounds weird when she plays it out with her everyday speech – that's the trouble. She's tried for a while to change the way she speaks, just as she's recently tried telling people her name is Beatrice, but none of it will stick. She *has* managed to change her writing recently. She's given up on the looped cursive she's been taught in junior school and has mastered a spiky, non-looped italic that she's learned by herself from a book.

Many of Lorna Hill's ballet types are foreigners, so they do humorous foreign speak with long 'e's and lots of 'z's, while the kindly working classes all drop their 'h's and say 'Lawks-a-mercy'. Not one of the books quite throws at Dinah, as *Pride and Prejudice* does, how dialogue can lift and dance on points, how sentences can shine and crackle with a concentrated energy and a sharp crystal intelligence. So listening to Miss Barnes read it is like falling in love. It's like walking on air. It fills Dinah's mind with a new kind of music. Language is all the music she's never learned to play. Language is all the ballet steps she's never learned to dance. And maybe what she loves best of all is the book's disregard for any 'description'. 'Description' isn't there. It's expendable. It's burned away. All that's left is dexterity and concentration. *Pride and Prejudice* is real life, but all transfigured, and dancing in a box.

At the end of that year, Miss Barnes leaves to get married and her photograph is on the social page of the Durban *Daily News*. She's in white lace, standing next to a tall man with a moustache and Brylcreemed hair. She looks really pretty and smiley, even though the photographs make most of the brides look dumpy and weird. They have triangles of harsh Durban sunlight distorting their smiles and sometimes they look extra silly, with rows of bridesmaids who are grown-up women all wearing identical little girls' party dresses made out of matching pastel taffeta. Plus the grooms often look like warthogs in scratchy hired suits.

In December, each of the first-year girls has to bring along her parents and have a meeting with Miss Maidment in her office. This is to decide on her subject choices for Matric. Miss Maidment spends the whole interview ignoring Dinah and her mum. She's focused exclusively on Dinah's dad and she's talking about Dinah in the third person, so it's all 'she' and 'her'. She's shaking her head over Dinah's long list of 'could-do-better' and 'disappointing' subject reports, because the days of Dinah's A1 ice-cream-row achievements are now well behind her. They have been ever since the moment that she and Angela teamed up to make school into their favourite social club. So nowadays Dinah is either giggling or daydreaming, or she's reading the wrong sort of book under the desk. Moreover, she's completely incapable of ever focusing on homework. She's resolved this by never doing any, so there's never any work for her to hand in.

In this transformation from A1 rosette girl to dreamy slouch, no one, including Dinah, has taken into account the fact of her altered body chemistry. With adolescence, Dinah has suddenly shed her asthma. It's been replaced by chronic, violent hay fever for which she's kept on round-the-clock maintenance doses of timed-release antihistamines. Big capsules full of hundreds-and-thousands to be taken always at bedtime and then supplemented as necessary by instant-effect alternatives. And while asthma drugs will shock you awake, will keep you buzzing and have your heart racing with palpitations, hay-fever drugs will turn you into Lewis Carroll's dormouse. They have the effect of putting you to sleep. Then Miss Maidment passes judgement.

'I suggest that Dinah takes the domestic science route,' she says.

Dinah's response is to feel a sudden, stabbing shock. She knows she'd rather die than spend her life in Miss Broughton's gigantic kitchen with all the pots and pans. Plus the needlework room is even worse. She's all too aware that Miss Maidment isn't making a positive statement about the quality of her apple turnovers or the finesse of her slip-stitch hems. What Miss Maidment is saying is that Dinah isn't academic. She's committing Dinah to the domestic science graveyard. And then, just as the graveyard is yawning, Dinah witnesses a miracle. She hears that her dad is paying her the only compliment of his life.

'Granted she's a pain in the neck,' he's saying, 'but she's strong on abstract reasoning. I think you're making a mistake.'

Angela's parents, on the other hand, are thoroughly deferential and they're happy with Miss Maidment's advice. The girls get together and talk about their meetings the moment they're released into the hall for orange squash and custard creams.

'But I want to do domestic science,' Angela says.

Dinah merely stares at her friend as though she's somehow desecrating the memory of that tin caddy of stinking fish in white sauce – as if she were betraying the genius of all those bouncing cabbages with hearts. True, Angela has always turned out super-light shortcrust pastry and her buttonhole stitch is past compare. She's even recently turned the heels on a pair of lacy white socks. What neither of them will dare to mention is that they'll never again share a classroom, never again sit side by side in a double desk at the back. It's something that Dinah is thinking about all the way home.

She's still thinking about Angela when her mum notices Punch who is lying curled up in the gutter about twenty yards from the house. His wiry black broken coat is ever more streaked with grey, but now it's unusually matt in texture. He looks as if he's asleep, except that he isn't doing his usual sleepy-dog breathing and, when Dinah touches him, she can feel that he's gone stiff. Punch hasn't been run over. He's just died of old age. He wasn't all that young when he came, though he's always been young at heart. Time Lost Is Never Regained. Punch is dead and he'll never come back. Dinah and Lisa spend the evening in tears – and all the more so, because Punch, lovely Punch, has tried so hard to do his dying nicely, by crawling away from the house.

Big school proper means a reshuffle of existing first-year forms so that Dinah's is made up of lots of girls taking French and those few, like Dinah, who are taking fine art with art history. Miss Byrd is always picky about which girls she'll have in her class, but she's agreed to have Dinah after giving her a stern pep-talk. Pep-talks turn out to be quite out of character for Miss Byrd, who materialises as one of those rare and wonderful teachers who never needs to raise her voice. She treats her pupils as if they were adults and the girls simply rise to meet her expectations.

Lots of the girls in Dinah's form are new entrants from other schools. There are the two new Cornelias from Holland who quickly become each other's best friend and are known as Corrie and Cornie. There's dainty blonde Lynn with close-together eyes and immaculate levitating handwriting. Not only is Lynn's handwriting of such improbable and microscopic regularity that it looks as if it comes off one of those typewriters that prints cursive, but it proceeds along an imaginary line exactly two millimetres above all the lines upon which normal people write.

There's jaunty Adele with chestnut hair and matching freckles who thinks it's a big laugh that her dad was going to call her Adolf, after Hitler, but then she was born a girl. There's grating, impossible Bernice, who does ballet out of school and carries all her school stuff in a vanity case. Bernice always stands with her feet at ten to two and she's fixed the winsome expression on her face so that it looks permanently like that of a calendar pin-up. Bernice is drenched in protective affectations which are always counter-productive. She's afflicted with an unerring instinct to make her classmates loathe her.

'I'm not *bragging* or anything,' she'll say, while making Bambi eyes into the mirror on the inside lid of the vanity case, 'but don't you think I look just a *little* bit like Audrey Hepburn?'

There's something about Bernice's body language that's begging people to abuse her. Something Blanche Dubois. And on parents' day Bernice is performing a sort of grown-up buddy-buddy act, arm in arm with her dad who's got an Austrian accent and silver maestro hair. None of the girls ever gets to clap eyes on Bernice's mother.

Boy-mad Beattie Blain is a girl oozing street-cred whose challenging blue eyes make all the teachers take one look at her and think trouble. They all make Beattie sit at the front of the class but sometimes this can misfire. Miss Cornbury has cartoon-book spinster's features and a lingering sibilant S. So Beattie reacts promptly to the S, not only by maintaining a sort of Grandmother's Footsteps of almost undetectable snake-like hissing which stops the moment Miss Cornbury pauses in her speech, but also by spreading it about as fact that Miss Cornbury showers the front-row girls with spittle. Beattie brings packs of paper-cocktail umbrellas to school which she holds up over her face whenever Miss Cornbury starts to speak, so that very soon she's established a ritual to cause general delight. One glimpse of Beattie's little umbrellas waiting in readiness on the desk top and the class is tittering and nudging. Though Miss Cornbury never makes the connection, she knows that the class is behaving badly and she embarks on a strategy. She brings in ready-to-use handwritten notes which she holds up at the start of every lesson. On the notes, the names of prospective offenders have been omitted, but she announces her intention of filling them in, should the need arise:

—— has been a constant nuisance throughout the arithmetic lesson . . .

'One peep out of *you*,' Miss Cornbury says. 'One peep out of *any* of you, and you will take this – thisss – note straight – ssstraight – to Miss – Misss – Maidment. Under-ssss-tood?'

Beattie has a supply of tiny plastic clothes-pegs that come in a range of colours. She wears one or other of these clipped to her blazer lapel to show what stage she's at with whoever is her current boyfriend. Dinah can't remember the details of the colour coding, except that a green peg means French kissing and a red peg means going steady. Most of the girls don't have boyfriends yet, but Beattie is never without.

Bet Ramsgate's got a sweet smiley moon face and faint traces of her parents' strong Yorkshire speak which, to Dinah and her classmates, counts as exotic. It's the kind of accent they've only ever heard done badly during occasional recitations of 'Yoong Albert'. Bet's dad has brought a whiff of Yorkshire to the shores of the Indian Ocean by fitting out the family home with new-style, wall-to-wall patterned carpeting. So when Bet takes her friends home to practise rock 'n' roll in her bedroom, Mr Ramsgate will roar up the stairs and utter a line so blissful to the girls' ears, so perfect in its delivery, that they'll return again and again in the hope of provoking a repetition.

'An WOT'S alt'thoomp – thoomp – THOOMPIN' on't'OON-DRED an – twent – eh – pound CARpet?!' he bawls, promptly causing the rocking 'n' rolling girls a spasm of giggles so intense that they almost choke in ecstasy.

Rock 'n' roll is the big thing, so, while Elvis records are being ceremonially burned in the Afrikaner heartlands and parents everywhere are thanking God for the squeaky-clean option of Pat Boone, apartheid is keeping Dinah and her classmates from the sound sensation on their doorstep. Miriam Makeba and The Skylarks, Kippie Moeletsi, Hugh Masakela and The Manhattan Brothers are performing at black weddings in Sophiatown. They're playing in black cinemas and in illegal black shebeens. So when Sophiatown gets bulldozed, it's one of the first urban 'black spots' to go – because although unscrambling the Cape's racial mix is giving the government its biggest headache, Sophiatown is really getting to them. For one, it's right there in Johannesburg and its residents have freehold title. Black families bought the land, way back, off a speculator. He'd wanted whites to buy it, but then came the sewage works bang next door, so he sold it to blacks instead.

Now the government hates everything Sophiatown stands for. It's multi-ethnic and densely populated. It's very urban and very wised-up. Every freehold backyard has sheds full of illegal tenants. It's full of artists, journalists, musicians, bohemians, shebeen queens, gangsters and protection racketeers. It's got Father Trevor Huddleston fighting hard for its survival: Father Huddleston, the Anglican priest whose high school is where generations of bright black kids have learned how to feel as good as anybody. It's Father Huddleston who has arranged for Hugh Masakela to get his first trumpet, a trumpet from Louis Armstrong.

So it doesn't matter now if you're part of a great swing band when the big trucks come for you. What matters is, are you a 'Bantu' or a Coloured, or an Indian, or sometimes even a Jew? This is what will decide where you go when you get removed – on that day when you wake to hear the verandah posts that your grand-father built being smashed up by police sledge hammers. If you're lucky you get time to grab your baby's laundry and bundle your pots on to the back of the revving truck. If you're lucky, you'll have rights to stay in the urban area under the terms of Section 10 of the Black Urban Areas Act. If so, then you'll get removed to Meadow-lands – that core of what is Soweto-to-be – Meadowlands, which is waiting for you bleakly in the gleam of the cold dawn. If not, then your number's up. Suddenly, all over the country, Pass Raids are being stepped up.

For blacks they've become the nightly terror. Because if your pass shows you don't qualify under Section 10 to live and seek work in the urban area, then you're out. A husband might qualify, a wife not. So you go one way, she goes another. Back to the native reserve which hasn't quite yet been re-named the Homeland. You're lucky if you're Coloured, because you may not have the vote any more, but you have rights of residence in the urban area. Blacks are another kettle of fish. This is because the black man in his natural state is not meant to be a city animal. The Secretary of State for Native Affairs has declared him 'innocent and trustworthy'. But that's in his natural habitat. The Bantu must at all costs be protected from the corrupting effects of exposure to 'city tricks'.

Meanwhile Dinah has joined the all-white beginners' class at the Dudley Andrews School of Ballroom Dancing where, uniformly togged up in stiff petticoats and gingham circular skirts with wide elastic belts, hair in swingy blonde ponytails, the class is learning to jive, quickstep, waltz and rumba. Girls sit along one side of the room, boys along the other. And then, whenever one of the unfavoured boys starts to cross the room towards you, there'll be a shameful shrieky stampede of girls all heading for the Ladies. Mrs Dudley Andrews issues periodic stern lectures on the etiquette of the ballroom. If a boy asks a girl to dance, then it's rude not to say yes. For Dinah this is somehow analogous with the etiquette of the marriage proposal. If a boy asks you to marry him, then it's rude not to say yes.

Mrs Dudley Andrews makes you dance the quickstep very close together, so that you and your partner will move as one gliding body, joined at the pelvis, to the strains of Victor Sylvester. When she does a try-out with you, she's so close to you that her high, conical breasts are poking into your chest and they feel like giant versions of those steel studs bull terriers have on their collars. All breasts have to be high and conical, so you've got to have a bra, even if your chest size is thirty treble A, but Dinah's dad has a theory that bras are just for saggy old ladies. So Lisa has had proper breasts for a while before the girls' mum manages to sneak her into the Stuttaford's lingerie department and buy her a couple of schoolgirl bras by 'fiddling on ze greens'.

Dinah has also got a bra, but she hates it because it's so uncomfortable. She's bought it cheap and all by herself, in the

OK Bazaars without even trying it on – because anything is better than having to put up with what Lisa's just gone through. In Stuttaford's, Lisa has had this hyper-genteel lingerie lady with a penetrating voice. The lingerie lady has stationed herself just outside the curtained cubicle and she's kept on trilling out instructions to Lisa in between taking peeks.

'Shake yourself into it, dear!' she trills. 'Have you shaken yourself into it properly?'

Lisa is certain that everyone in the five-floored department store is listening.

'That's the way, dear,' the lingerie lady trills. 'You have a good shake in there!'

Another of the new girls is not so much new as recycled, because she's the teacher's pet from Mrs Vaughan-Jones's Class Two. The teacher's pet lives quite far away, but she's come to GHS because of the art. Art is one of the three subjects that the teacher's pet is keen to be best at and the other two are English and drama. The teacher's pet still looks the same, with the same short mouse-brown hair and the same slightly down-in-the-mouth expression. The difference is that now, instead of having to be Teacher's Best Little Duster Cleaner and Message Monitor, she's more preoccupied with claiming the class monopoly on intellect. That's except for in maths and music. And any sporty stuff doesn't count, because – even more so than Dinah – the teacher's pet can't do games. Not to save her life. Plus she's got three left feet when it comes to country dancing, so in the end Miss Bowen has to tell her just to hop from one foot to the other during the Scottish Reel display. Even then she can't seem to hop in the right direction, so she's forever crashing into other people.

The teacher's pet is the only person Dinah has met, except for Catherine Cleary, who's completely and utterly tone deaf. It's not that she's a bit off key, or that she hits too many flat notes. The sound that she makes in singing lessons bears no relation to the music whatsoever. When it comes to maths, the teacher's pet has found a suitable quotation in D.H. Lawrence's letters that suits her particular mathematical stance. 'Having a relationship with *them*,' it goes, 'is like trying to have a relationship with the letter "x" in algebra.' The teacher's pet likes to quote this out loud as a way of needling any person who is a little bit interested in maths. The teacher's pet does lots of drama and elocution out of school, so she often gets chosen to read the lessons in assembly when it's Dinah's class's turn. Whenever she reads out loud or does her poetical recitations, the teacher's pet will do these in a special elocution voice in which her accent is quite different from the one she uses for her normal speech.

These days the teacher's pet will quite often demonstrate her intellectual ascendancy by taking issue with the quality of the work set. So if Miss Byrd has got the class busy with still-life painting then the teacher's pet will assert her right to make a composition of writhing nudes. And if Miss Yale is busy with Rider Haggard, then the teacher's pet, instead of reading *The Devil's Disciple* under the desk, will cast public doubt on the school's ability to distinguish good literature from bad. But poor Miss Yale has to do whatever's on the syllabus, so it's not really her fault that most of the books are boys' adventure stories.

Dinah's class has to read *Stalky and Co* and *Prester John* and *Barlasch of the Guard* and *My Early Life* by Winston Churchill. And Miss Yale is trying so hard to help the girls understand what's going on in *Prester John* that she even falls off the rostrum one day, whilst re-enacting Richard Hannay's reconnoitre round the evil black leader's cave. In the story John Buchan has been explaining that Prester John, the charismatic but misguided black preacher who's 'gone native', is destined, not for leadership, but for perpetual subjugation. This is because in the Bible, Noah's son Ham has accidentally seen his father naked. So he gets sent to Africa as a punishment and he turns into a black man. This is why it's always got to be blacks at the bottom and white people on top. Dinah thinks that bloke-ish Empire racism is always at its most mind-crushingly boring when it comes together, as in *Prester John*, with lots of boy stuff about terrain. Any reference to scarp, scree or sedimentary rock will make her brain go fuzzy.

Right now the best thing about school – the best thing about life for Dinah – is the posh-voiced new girl with widely spaced blue eyes, whose name is Maud McDonald. The new girl has half-inch-long black eyelashes and a thick rope-like blonde plait that comes halfway down her back. Shock waves pass around the class when she first speaks, because her accent is proper RP, which is a thing only heard of in the movies and on long-wave radio. Plus Maud is an automatic giggle name. Everyone knows that.

'It's from Tennyson,' says the new girl and she promptly starts reciting – a thing that she does in the same voice as she uses for her normal speech.

Yet she hasn't come from England. She's come from the Maris Stella Convent, just down the road. And, like the teacher's pet, she's come to join Miss Byrd's art class. The posh-voiced new girl hasn't been in the class five minutes, before she's established that she'll take no part in games.

'Sinus trouble, Miss Chase,' she says.

Miss Chase is wearing her jaunty little netball skirt with Airtex shirt and pendant whistle and she's blinking at the new girl in amazement. The accent has left her momentarily disempowered.

'Tennis?' she says. 'Hockey? Netball?'

'Sorry,' says the new girl. 'Doctor's orders. Not until I've had my sinuses drained.'

'Swimming?' says Miss Chase. 'PT?'

The new girl is sorrowfully shaking her head. 'All out of bounds for me,' she says. 'I only wish I could.'

Miss Chase ventures that the new girl will need to bring in a doctor's certificate.

'But of *course*,' she says. 'Of *course*.'

The new girl has learned lots of Latin at the Convent. Plus her art work is very good.

In the shuffle of moving to the morning's first lesson, the new girl seats herself alongside Dinah. Both have headed for the back row. Within minutes Maud has won Dinah's heart by passing over a spot-on cartoon of the Girls' High School's most aged and boring pedagogical fixture – Miss Legge, who is right then taking the class for history. By the end of the week, by the end of the day, Dinah and Maud are firm friends. And they've soon become so transfixed by each other's company that they can't ever go home straight after school.

Instead they slope around the town centre for hours, trying on all the clothes in Truworth's and playing with the rows of little pots at the make-up counter in Payne Brothers. They ride the escalators up and down in John Orr's and spend hours over the *Vogue* Paris Original patterns in the big books at the Sewing Notions counter.

Between them they become completely obsessed with clothes and, on weekend occasions at Dinah's house, they put her dad into a rage by spending several hours at a stretch doing literary criticism on a single month's issue of *Vogue* magazine. They do this on the lawn just below his study window, so he can't block it out.

'When I was your age,' he yells out of the window, 'I saved up all my pocket money to buy a microscope!'

The girls sit tight, biting down their giggles and waiting in hope that he'll elaborate. They want chapter and verse on his meagre fiscal allotment in childhood, but he just retreats back through the window. Once he's gone they whisper some verse to each other:

> And sometimes if I have been *gud*
> I get an orange after *fud*.

This is one of their best giggle poems, a thing which they relish along with 'Say not the struggle naught availeth' and certain Wordsworthian lapses. Soon they are running up clothes together on Dinah's mum's ancient Singer and Dinah is nagging for a clothes allowance which she promptly spends, when she gets it, on a powder-blue wool overcoat in a climate that has no winter. She says goodbye to her flat buckled shoes and buys torturing stilettos with four-inch heels and vicious winkle-picker toes. She chooses an 'auburn' hair tint in the chemist that makes her blonde hair go neon-orange, especially in bright sunlight. Then she settles, after a month, for a more permanent, sophisticated silver. The silver happens in the nick of time because the 'auburn' has provoked Lisa's wrath and Mrs Clegg hasn't exactly helped.

'I see you've dyed your hair to match your sister's,' Mrs Clegg says to Lisa when she goes in to the Tearoom and General Store to get some flour.

Lisa returns, incandescent.

'When *my* hair,' she spits, 'is normal. And *yours* makes you look like a walking Belisha Beacon!'

Maud has had her hair cut, Grace Kelly-wise, to the shoulder and both girls have begun to sleep in huge steel rollers every night, which gives them permanent cranial corrugations.

And then there's Angela. Sweet, curly-haired Angela with her rosy cheeks and sparkly eyes, who can now do *mille-feuille* pastry and a rough-puff that melts in your mouth. For weeks, every breaktime, the girls come together in an awkward threesome, though usually it's with their respective, uninvited hangers-on. Then one day Dinah does the deed. I divorce thee. I cast thee out. Maud is my best friend now. Angela walks away in silence, accompanied by her attendants who are muttering *sotto voce* and casting backward glances.

After that the girls never speak again. They make no eye contact. Not once in four years. Yes, once. By mistake. Angela and Dinah are alone in a long school corridor. They are walking towards each other. They come face to face. They look into each other's eyes. They smile. Then each girl remembers. Oh my God. This is the person I do not acknowledge. This is the person whose existence I deny. They erase the smiles and walk on.

In the history class, the aged Miss Legge never leaves her teacher's chair and she seldom looks up from her notes. She rules by virtue of her powerful toxic aura and manages to catch every whisper. She sits four square with her knees wide apart in a mannish navy pinstripe suit which she wears with a collar and tie. Her stockings are rolled to the knee just above the level of the pinstriped skirt and she wears black unisex lace-ups. Her straight, snow-white hair is cut severe and short. Miss Legge has small darting eyes and a flickering silvery tongue. She has infallible, rigid classroom control, even though her teaching method can bore almost to death. It consists of her gabbling out the Gestetner-ed history notes non-stop for the whole hour. Then she'll instruct the girls to go home and learn that section by heart. So every alternate history lesson is spent in total silence, as the girls write out the previous day's notes from memory while Miss Legge keeps an eagle eye open for signs of conferring or copying.

Miss Legge requires the notes to be repeated word for word. No synonyms allowed. So that if, for example, a pupil writes that at the Boston Tea Party, colonists were angered by the tax imposed on 'certain listed commodities' Miss Legge will cross it out and write, ' "Certain enumerated commodities" – see notes.' Then she'll write, 'Minus ½% – see me.'

Even given Miss Legge's regime of reptilian terror, Dinah and Maud find it almost impossible to focus on their homework, except for when it's one of the half-yearly exams, where you have to pass or else you get kept down at the end of the year. So it's thanks to Miss Legge's brain-rotting history exams that Dinah suddenly discovers her own prodigious short-term memory. She's found that she can sit down at night with a flask of strong black coffee and five hard-covered foolscap notebooks and by sunrise she'll be able to recite the whole lot off by heart. She does this through a system she's evolved which depends on memorising paragraph headings that cue her into the detail. It's a futile skill – except that it ensures she can always pass exams on last-minute cramming – because Dinah's brain will only hold the information for a certain limited time. After a fortnight the contents of the notebooks will have gone – erased as if they had never been. And it has the advantage of driving Miss Legge completely up the wall with rage, because it confounds all her direst and most malicious predictions.

'You will fail your exams, Dinah de Bondt,' she says. 'You will fail most miserably, mark my words.'

And then, two days later, Dinah will sail smugly through the history exam without a synonym in sight. Miss Legge is absolutely certain that Dinah has to be cheating. She begins to make a habit of positioning herself behind Dinah's left shoulder for the duration of any exam. Over the next four years she becomes Dinah's personal one-on-one invigilator, but Dinah doesn't mind. She's usually too busy regurgitating. 'Certain enumerated commodities, blah, blah and blah.'

In the four years of Miss Legge's brain-rotting history lessons, there's only ever been one single out-loud challenge, only one proper interruption. And that's when, suddenly, in the middle of Miss Legge's reading out loud, she utters the word Fascist.

'Excuse me, Miss Legge,' Adele calls out, 'but who exactly were the Fascists?'

Miss Legge pauses in shock. The darting eyes look up and finally fix their poison rays on the speaker. 'They were a rival party to the Communists,' she snaps. 'Don't interrupt.'

Then she reads on. Gibble-gabble, gibble-gabble, gab-gab-blah.

'Excuse me, Miss Legge,' Adele says, again, 'but what I mean is, what did the Fascists actually believe in?'

Miss Legge stops to flick her silvery snake-like tongue. 'They were a rival party to the Communists,' she says. 'I've already told you once and that's enough. One more peep out of you, Adele –'

'Ask Yael,' drawls bad-girl Beattie pointedly. She's showing her insubordinate side in history for the very first time, though she's admittedly been busy behind the scenes, stoking the idea that Miss Legge doesn't wear a bra. 'Yael will know what a Fascist is,' she says. 'Ask *her*.'

Miss Legge promptly dispatches Beattie to stand outside the classroom door, whilst shy, myopic Yael is hanging her head and trying not to smile. Yael is an Israeli brainbox with highbrow parents on sabbatical. She's been billeted so temporarily upon GHS that the teacher's pet has not yet bothered to regard her as serious competition. The moment passes. Miss Legge proceeds. Gibble-gabble, gibble-gabble, gab-gab-blah.

The notes are not of Miss Legge's own composition. They've been written by Miss Norris, the long-ago head of history, a spellbinding teacher, by all accounts, and a dyed-in-the-wool Durban racist, whose notes on the coming of Indian indentured labour Dinah will for ever hold by heart.

'The first shipload of coolies arrived in November 1860. Although the first few cargoes were unsatisfactory and had to be repatriated as unfit for work, later importations were more satisfactory . . .'

These notes cause Dinah and Maud to roll about on the lawn and shriek with laughter until the tears are streaming from their eyes and their clothes are full of grass. They enact absurd burlesques with each other, miming to chisel open wooden shipping crates.

'Another rotten crate of curry balls!' Maud says, in her customs-officer voice. 'Nail it up again and throw it into the sea! Next!'

'Curry ball' is an expression that Maud has overheard recently during the course of her first date and she's told Dinah all about it. She's gone in a foursome to the Cuban Hat Drive-in Restaurant on North Beach, where her date's best friend's date has used the expression on one of the Indian waiters.

'Hey, Curry ball!' the best friend's date has yelled. 'Hey, Curry ball? Aren't you going to serve us?'

At the Cuban Hat a waiter will clip your hamburger and Coke to your motor-car window on a special custom-built tray.

Maud and Dinah are fond of Miss Bardsey who teaches music. She has one thin polio leg and wears support stockings with orthopaedic sandals. Once a week she does music appreciation with Dinah's class in her quarters beyond the corridor where the cycle racks are housed. Miss Bardsey behaves as if she's got a soft spot for the two girls, possibly because, along with Yael, they're the only ones in the class who've ever heard of Khachaturian. Or perhaps it's merely because she wants to redeem them from the slouchy reputation they've acquired with most of the staff. Perhaps she's disempowering the girls with kindness. She lets them take her records home and she chooses them for the choir.

On one occasion, she picks them for sending off to a residential music school which takes place in a mock-Gothic boys' public school in the country near Henrietta's farm. The music school is all Sir Hubert Parry in the chapel and High Anglican ritual. The girls are enchanted by the whole thing and the music master is fab. They make friends with a trio of pitch-perfect counter tenors who are all pupils at the school. Two of them are currently being tormented by their gender leanings and the third is keen on Maud. Their talk is a constant unfamiliar innuendo of buggery and cold showers and ritual beatings by prefects, though just sometimes they'll talk to the girls about music.

'Never heard of Bax?' they say. 'Arnold Bax? Master of the Queen's Music?'

But neither Dinah nor Maud has ever heard of Arnold Bax.

On the fourth night Maud has arranged to meet one of the boys in the dead of night by escaping out of the window. Dinah helps her knot bedsheets together once everyone else is asleep. Dinah is leaning anxiously over the sill, hoping to clock Maud's progress, but the country darkness is absolute and she can't see a thing. Then she hears a thud and a feeble groan, because Maud, instead of descending hand over hand, has proceeded by sliding down at speed until her hands reach the first knot – at which point they spring apart. She's fallen into the courtyard from a height of something like ten feet. And all the doors are locked. Just as Dinah is about to swing her leg over the sill in rescue, a light snaps on in Matron's bedroom and all hope is lost.

Once Maud has been sent packing in disgrace, the music school stops being fun. And what's puzzling to Dinah is that she's the only person who ever seems to understand why Maud felt she had to do it. The knotted sheet escape was nothing to do with wanting to commit sex in the small hours with a schoolboy. It had to do with the school's Gothic setting. It required a Gothic response, a Gothic school-story response.

Maud and Dinah especially love Miss Bardsey's tolerant coexistence with the bicycles which are stacked in overlapping formation, right outside her domain. Just one nudge of the first bicycle in the row and the whole lot will come down.

Then Miss Bardsey will always rush out, waving her stick-thin arms and calling out, entirely without recrimination, 'Crisis girls, crisis! All hands to the pump!'

It means that Maud and Dinah feel impelled to send the bicycles crashing at the rate of once a fortnight. And dear Miss Bardsey is always equally obliging over Maud's missing bus fare.

'I've lost it, Miss Bardsey,' Maud will say.

Unlike Dinah, whose parents regularly fill in the scholar's season-ticket form and get it rubber-stamped at the depot, Maud never has a season ticket and her bus money's usually nowhere. Some days she'll start out with the money, but it falls through the holes in her blazer pockets or – if ever her mother has given her the whole week's money in advance – she and Dinah will have spent it before the time is out. At such times Miss Bardsey will invariably act as Maud's personal loan facility, though Maud, who always means to pay her back, merely goes around feeling guilty. That's until the Cherubino song, which causes her feelings of guilt to rise uncomfortably.

Miss Bardsey likes to provide the choir with her own eccentric translations of Italian or German arias, and one day she's translated Cherubino's *Voi Che Sapete*. She's rendered this as 'Say Ye Who Borrow'.

> Say ye who borrow
> Love's witching spell,
> What is this sorrow
> None can dispel?

'Oh God, I can't bear to look at her,' Maud says. 'I'm so ashamed, Dinah. I'm so ashamed. It's all about my bus fare, don't you see?'

'No it isn't,' Dinah says. 'It's just to rhyme with sorrow. That's all. Borrow – sorrow.'

'Oh God. Now I'll have to give up choir,' Maud says. 'It's so unfair, but I will. I'll have to.'

The irony is that Maud's actually got her bus fare that day, plus exactly a penny to spare, so after choir practice the girls dawdle to the bus stop via the chip shop where, the day before, they have watched a group of Zulu schoolchildren asking for penny scraps.

'Penny scraps, please,' Maud says, having never tried this before. The chip-shop lady gives her a whole bag full of those delicious little dripping-soaked crunchy bits that have fallen through the basket into the fryer. The penny scraps are a marvel, a taste sensation to delight the palate, so Maud keeps on asking for them day after day. But on the fourth day the chip-shop lady has suddenly turned unwilling.

'Penny scraps is just for the native kiddies,' she says. 'The natives has only got pennies. You kids has got to buy proper chips, or else you can get out of my shop. Go on. Scram, the both of you!'

Maud and Dinah slink away, mortified in the knowledge that, for four days running, they've been stealing from the poor.

'Eating in uniform' is a very bad crime and one Miss Maidment periodically lectures against in assembly. It's easily as bad as 'leaving litter' and Dinah can remember one occasion when an unclaimed apple core on the window-sill of the assembly hall caused the whole school to be kept in for three days running because nobody would own up. 'Disrespect for school uniform' is another very bad crime, so Maud and Dinah are forever being hauled before the prefects. 'Wearing an indoor garment outdoors' means you've got your cardigan on in the street instead of your blazer. Or there's 'winter uniform in summer' which means you're wearing your navy beret instead of your panama hat. These things seems totally irrelevant to the two girls and quite peripheral to the educational process. But the prefects will never agree to engage them in honest debate.

'When you're in the sixth form, then *you* can tell the juniors to wear proper uniform,' they say.

This is all the prefects will ever venture.

'*Pathetic*,' Maud says. 'You people are *pathetic*. As if we'd ever want to do such a puerile thing.'

They admire and envy Yael who, being protected by cultural difference as well as by star quality in maths, has managed, without appearing dissident, to carve out a niche for herself as the class-room's licensed eccentric. Yael has the best solution to the periodic GHS hat blitz – a surprise event known as the hat parade. She keeps her panama, folded and firmly compressed, right at the bottom of her desk, so that, whenever the summary hat parade is announced, Yael is never without headgear, albeit somewhat misshapen. There'll be a long line of girls looking like the AGM of the Women's Bowling Confederation, and then there'll be Yael, myopically sporting a topknot that looks like an inverted zig-zag ice-cream cone, a fluted scarecrow's hat spitting bits of straw. Yael has also pointed Maud and Dinah to an unlocked storeroom beyond the music room where, inexplicably, along with old rakes and theatrical costumes, there's a large fish-moth trunk of aban-doned property – an endless lucky dip of mouse-nibbled replace-ment berets and cardigans and ties.

While Lisa's Afrikaans teacher is the gorgeous, glammed-up Mrs Prinsloo, Maud and Dinah are blessed with Mrs Keithley. Mrs Prinsloo wears figure-hugging sheath dresses with broad gold belts and gold hoop earrings. Her DNA is sexily shouting its evidence of early racial mixing with green-eyed Cape Malay slaves. Mrs Keithley, on the other hand, is a tired-looking grey-haired Afri-kaner woman who is rumoured to have been abandoned by an abusive Scottish husband. Unlike the triumphant Mrs Prinsloo who has no problem with negotiating the enemy minefield of an English-language girls' school, Mrs Keithley lacks her advantages and misreads every cue. Whenever the girls have completed their classwork, for example, Mrs Keithley will let them read Afrikaans women's magazines for a special treat – magazines about which they are openly and gleefully snobbish.

So now Dinah and Maud, having learned their Afrikaans poem off by heart, and having recited it to Mrs Keithley's satisfaction, are given an issue of *Die Huisgenoot* to share, which they find particu-larly rewarding. Because not only has *Die Huisgenoot*, on this occasion, got a haunchy peroxide blonde in pink tutu on the cover, who is striking a pirouette pose in what appears to be the middle of a maize field, but there's a double page, full-colour centre spread of the entire Springbok rugby team. The magazine is issued on the sort of cheap newsprint paper which causes the colour reproductions to give everyone two sets of eyebrows. Plus the Springbok rugby team, even without double eyebrows, represents everything that the girls most hold in contempt.

The South African rugby team is both ethnically and ideologically dominated by white-supremacist Afrikaners. It represents the government's triumphalist racist Nationalism, rampant and brutal, on the playing field. And then there's the fact of the players' physiognomy. The rugby men are like a species on their own. They all have incredibly thick necks and massive shoulders and cabbage ears and close-cropped bullet heads. These are features that are wholly out of kilter with the girls' current heart-throb material which runs much more to a precious, faggoty English public schoolboy look, complete with washboard chest and Rupert Brooke profile. So cricketers are sometimes OK heart-throb material. Rugby players, never.

Just recently, during one of their malingering sessions in town, Dinah and Maud have encountered two members of the touring MCC and have followed these demi-gods into a record shop in West Street, where they eye them up as the men are waiting at the counter to be served.

'Quick!' Maud says and she dives into the display racks. 'Let's have this one.'

Dinah can see that she's holding up a record of the choir of King's College, Cambridge. Both girls know that one of the two earmarked cricketers is a King's and Cambridge man. At the counter, they stand and stare meaningfully at the two men just ahead of them in line, while flashing the record sleeve with conspicuous intent.

'I DO think the King's College Choir is WON-derful,' Maud is saying in loud slow-motion speak. 'Don't you, Dinah?'

Then it's the cricketers' turn to get served. 'Have you got Bill Haley and the Comets?' one of them says.

It's the Cambridge man himself. The men pay for the record as quickly as they can and hurry out of the shop, clearly hoping to give their stalkers the slip.

'Damn!' Maud says. 'Bill Haley and the Comets. Of course!'

'Would you like to buy that record?' says the shop assistant.

'Er, no actually,' Maud says. 'No thanks. Not today.'

'I thought not,' says the assistant.

Meanwhile, back in *Die Huisgenoot*, some of the full-colour rugby players are sporting double sets of Hitler moustaches as well as the routine sets of multiple eyebrows. Their names are printed, left to right, in rows under the photograph. All of them have Afrikaans nicknames, like 'Baasie' van Wyk and 'Tiny' du Preez and 'Skoppie' van der Westhuizen and 'Mannetjie' Joubert. They have huge, bulging thighs and the shortest of very short shorts. Dinah and Maud have worked themselves into a state of bliss over the photograph. They giggle until their stomach muscles are aching almost unbearably. They are feigning swoony passion and picking the worst of the bull-necked sports persons to be each other's fantasy husbands. They're in full swing, kissing the newsprint and clutching at their hearts, when they become aware that Mrs Keithley is advancing up the aisle. Then she's standing over them with a kindly conspiratorial air. She bends to undo the centre staples with care.

'There you are,' she says. 'You can take the picture home, my girlies. You can take turns to pin it up in your bedroom.'

The girls are halfway dead with the joy of it.

'It's mine!' Dinah says at once, play-acting to clutch the newsprint to her bosom.

'It's mine!' Maud says, snatching it from her.

'Control yourself,' Dinah says. 'We'll have to take turns. That's what Mrs Keithley said.'

'Never!' Maud says. 'It's not fair. I saw it first. Mrs Keithley, tell her I saw it first. Now look what you've gone and done!' She says this because, in the tussle, 'Baasie' van Wyk has lost a section of his left cabbage ear and 'Skoppie' van der Westhuizen has parted company with his right thigh.

When Mrs Keithley gets the girls to write letters to the newspaper, it's to practise writing business letters in Afrikaans. They are set to write about the matter of unwrapped bread, because this is one big hygiene issue that keeps on rearing its head. Dinah and Maud write their address and the date on the right-hand side in their exercise books. For the address they have to write 'Durban Girls' High School', only they write it in Afrikaans. After that, Maud enters into the spirit of her letter, assuming the role of concerned white housewife and mother and waxing indignant about the health hazard to her children.

'Dirty black hands are crawling all over the crusts that our children love,' she writes.

'Hey, Dinah. What are crusts in Afrikaans?' she says.

Dinah looks it up for her in the dictionary and passes it over.

'Right,' Maud says. 'I've finished.'

Both girls are working at high speed, with slipshod results, in the hope of becoming eligible for another issue of *Die Huisgenoot*. When Mrs Keithley returns the books, she's not best pleased, but it's nothing to do with the letters' contents. Rather, she feels the need to point out a grave mistake to the whole class.

'High School' in Afrikaans is '*Hoërskool*,' but Maud has left out the two little dots over the e – an omission which, apparently, has turned 'High School' into 'Whore School'. Mrs Keithley is bent upon explanation, but she can't say the word whore out loud, so this is making her struggle increasingly rewarding.

'The examiners,' she says, 'are good, upright, clean-living men. They don't want to see such filthy words.'

By now the whole class is feigning persistent incomprehension, but Mrs Keithley has finally hit upon an explanation.

'My girlies,' she says, and she lowers her voice to a gruff whisper. 'My girlies, it means – it means – a *street woman*.'

Everyone knows what a street woman is, because the Durban docks are pretty well right there in the town centre and Point Road is full of one-night cheap hotels. But when Maud gets round to scanning the small print of her corrected exercise book she's aware of another mistake.

'Hey, Dinah,' she says. 'That word you gave me for crusts. Well, look here. Mrs Keithley says it means scabs. I've put, "Dirty black hands are crawling all over the scabs that our children love."'

Maud's mastery of sports avoidance is good for Dinah's self-esteem. Dinah's always been useless at games, yet she's always felt the need to try. So during her first ever GHS hockey practice – and just when she's giving it all she's got – Dinah hears Miss Chase saying sarcastically, 'The object is to *advance* upon the ball, Dinah, not to retreat from it. Understood?' Miss Chase also has a low opinion of Dinah's tennis hand. That's ever since the day that Dinah's passed out unconscious on the court. Something about the excessive summer heat and the dazzling sunlight and the uncorrected astigmatism, along with the routine menstrual excess and the hay-fever suppressants. They've all left Dinah charging use-lessly from one side of the court to the other, always too late to scoop the ball, until her brain has sensibly made the decision to take a little holiday. At sixteen, Dinah is possibly the only white South African in the country who can't swim a decent front crawl. Yet she always sits in the stands during swimming galas, lustily cheering for her house, or her school, or her team, just like everyone else.

Now, thanks entirely to Maud, Dinah has learned to wear her sporting incompetence with pride. She's learned that there's an alternative to that perpetual floundering in the shallow end as the butt of Miss Chase's contempt. She's learned to malinger in the school library where the kindly librarian, who has fallen under Maud's spell, will always agree to let them hide. And the librarian confesses, shyly, during one of their occasional conversations, to a parallel career as the author of several hardback historical novels with somewhat lurid dust jackets. Maud writes a series of spoofy, hockey-mad poems as parodies of John Masefield and gets them published in the school magazine. So after that Miss Chase gives up on the pair of them and stops even trying to make them do PT. They're licensed to sit out all the physical jerks on the bench, alongside the usual rotating assortment of shirkers.

'I've got my periods, Miss Chase,' says Michelle Blumhoff, who is one of the North Beach airhead set, but she's very good at drawing. She says it week in, week out, until Miss Chase finally loses her rag.

'PERIOD, Michelle. PERIOD!' she screams. 'Have them ONE AT A TIME, if you please!'

Michelle's dad has once revealed to Beattie Blain that his swirl-patterned kipper tie has a nudie pin-up on the underside.

The only teacher whom Maud and Dinah admire and respect unreservedly, the only one they never send up, the only one in whose classes they never whisper, or giggle, or pass notes, the only teacher whose homework they always do, is the fifty-something Miss Byrd, whose art history classes are their perpetual inspiration. Miss Byrd and her sister are two shy professional spinsters who are rumoured to be living at home with a domineering mother. Yet in the classroom Miss Byrd is a colossus. Miss Byrd is always spell-binding. She takes her girls through a rigorous, high-speed chron-ology of Western art, along with some concessionary forays into the arts of India, Africa, Japan and China, so that within two years their files are bulging with hand-sketched details of Doric, Ionic and Corinthian columns along with several kinds of architrave plus the façades and ground plans of something like fifty classical buildings.

Then they do Romanesque churches, both in Europe and Asia Minor. After that, they launch into the Gothic. They can sketch the sequence of the Parthenon frieze. They can write essays on the Charioteer of Delphi and on the Praxiteles Hermes. They know the sequence of the bas-reliefs on Trajan's Column. They know the Pantheon, niche by niche. They know barrel vaulting and flying buttresses. They can draw the columns of the Córdoba Mosque and the fan-vaulted ceiling of the Divinity School in Oxford. They can draw, from memory, the various side elevations of Notre Dame and Chartres Cathedral and of Wells Cathedral and Westminster Abbey. They can make drawings of Ghiberti's baptistry doors and of Brunelleschi's dome.

They know, cell by cell, all the paintings in Fra Angelico's monastery and all the Masaccios in the Brancacci Chapel in Florence. They can write about the influence of Bellini on Mantegna and about the influence of Duccio on Giotto. They can tell, at a glance, what makes Giovanni da Fabriano different from Benozzo Gozzoli. They can write about the Dutch School and the Flemish School and the paintings of post-Reformation England and the influence of Constable on the French Impressionists. They can sketch each of the figures of Rodin's *Burghers of Calais*.

Because Miss Byrd's teaching has uses beyond its own field, the art girls know about Balzac because of Rodin; they know about Platonism because of Raphael; they know about *commedia dell'arte* because of Watteau. And Dinah knows more about the enclosure movement from looking at Thomas Gainsborough than she's ever learned from listening to Miss Legge. Miss Byrd is never afraid of the present, which means that the girls know Sickert and Stanley Spencer and Francis Bacon and Diego Rivera. They know Rothko and Jacob Epstein.

Perhaps because her Protestant soul has difficulty in taking it on board, Miss Byrd simply leaves out the artists of the counter-Reformation, so that the baroque, except for Rubens, is one big blank. Seventeenth-century Italy has suddenly gone very quiet and, though Dinah knows de la Tour and Honthorst, she's never heard of Caravaggio: the man himself, the founding father. Dinah also believes that Spain has 'three great painters', all of whom were 'accidents of genius'. Velázquez, El Greco and Goya have no context in Miss Byrd's book. There is no Ribera, no Zurbarán, no Murillo. They emerge, luminous, from a strange and barbarous nothing.

Miss Byrd is, in all sorts of ways, a woman limited by her time and her context, but Maud and Dinah don't see this, because her brilliant extraordinary teaching is somehow coming from the other side of her head. Then, one day, after she's given a lesson on prehistoric cave painting, Miss Byrd lets drop a cheery, unreviewed anecdote about having once seen South African Bushmen on display in a cage at Johannesburg's Rand Easter Show. Maud and Dinah are staring at her, trying not to believe that she's saying this without seeing that it's appalling. They are trying hard themselves not to see the sad, violated rump of South Africa's hunter-gatherers, the straggling survivors of persecution and genocide, in a cage alongside the prize bulls and the innovative tractors and the hot-dog stalls and *boeremusiek*. People as exhibits at an agricultural show. Yet it's clear from Miss Byrd's tinkling laughter in response to their squeamish expressions that she thinks Maud and Dinah are just being silly.

In their perpetual hanging out in the town centre, Maud and Dinah don't always stick to dress shops. Sometimes Maud is having new jodhpurs fitted, which means, for Dinah, hours of waiting in the tailor's shop, among all the bales of cavalry twill. Maud is unbelievably fussy about the jodhpurs and about all her riding gear. Horsemanship is an important part of what she does when Dinah isn't with her, though Dinah knows that she's an instructor at the riding school, as well as one of the school's star performers. So she likes to nit-pick for ever. Sometimes Maud and Dinah hang out near the Cenotaph where they watch the impassioned Bible-thumpers going hammer and tongs at the queues of tired white commuters who are waiting for their buses to carry them home.

One day they have a try at being Bible-thumpers themselves, but their voices just get lost on the air and the hymn they try and sing peters out on them. Plus the school uniforms, they feel, are undermining their credibility.

'That was terrible,' Maud says, as they retreat behind the Cenotaph. 'Nobody was taking any notice of us. Did you see that? They couldn't even tell that we were *preaching*.'

Baptist evangelism is big right now and Billy Graham has recently gone global. So Maud and Dinah are not too surprised when one day, while dawdling alongside the vacant lots behind the beachfront hotels, they see that the Green Tent has risen up in the night, huge as that of Boswell's Circus.

'Let's go in,' Maud says. 'Come on. Let's.'

Inside, the tent has a green grass floor and rows of stacking chairs that have been arranged leaving a wide central aisle. There's a long table at the altar end and an invisible Würlitzer is playing religious choruses, sort of quietly, under its breath. The tent is filling up fast as Maud and Dinah take their seats three rows from the front. Some of the women are wearing hats and gloves. Everyone in the tent is white, but maybe there's a parallel tent somewhere for blacks. The Würlitzer gets louder and everyone sings 'I met Jesus at the Crossroads' and one or two other choruses before the preacher starts his harangue.

Just when they think he's starting to wind down, he runs his eyes menacingly over the assembled worshippers and pauses to stare at particular individuals in the congregation. He's making some very determined eye contact. Dinah is thinking, 'Please let it not be me.'

'Whoever will offer his life to the Lord?' he says. 'Who will be saved on this day? Who will repent him of his sins and be washed as white as snow? Come forward! Yes, *you*, sir! Come forward. *You*, madam! Come forward and give yourself to the Lord!'

People in ones and twos start shuffling timidly towards the front where the preacher lays his hands on them and directs them through a canvas doorway into an invisible place beyond the altar.

'Come on,' Maud says. 'Let's go. Let's be saved.'

The girls join the line of people shuffling forward more boldly now, as the Würlitzer is stepping up the volume. Though they're motivated by no more than a desire to see what goes on beyond the canvas doorway, they're feeling little tremors of excitement.

Once through the doorway, all they can see is more tent, though this time it's been subdivided into lots of little canvas cubicles. Each cubicle has got a row of three stacking chairs, along with one on its own for the saving monitor. All the saving monitors are wearing green tabards with enamelled badges that say 'Jesus Saves'. Maud and Dinah's monitor is a young woman, probably no older than seventeen. And she's so sincere in her desire to see them saved that the girls right away start to feel like heels. They sit side-by-side on the stacking chairs and stare fixedly at the tent's grassy floor, not daring to glance at each other. Yet soon the inevitable vibrations, the portents of giggles about to burst forth, are beginning to give them away.

'You just came in for a laugh,' says the monitor. 'Didn't you?'

They nod in silent shame.

'Well, that's not very nice, is it?' she says.

They shake their heads, no, but the giggles keep rising to the surface.

'It's not very clever either,' she says. 'I think you'd better go, don't you?'

They nod. They still can't stop giggling. Then they retreat, ignominiously, back up the aisle in haste, pushing through the crush of people still lining up to be saved. They make their way out into the sunlight.

'Phew,' Dinah says. 'I feel terrible.'

'Me too,' says Maud. 'But I wish we could have got the badges. What shall we do now?'

Just occasionally, Maud has money. Lots of money. Like once every six months. Maud calls this money her divvy.

'My divvy's come,' she'll say. 'Let's go and spend it.'

This is when she buys new riding boots and when they both buy clothes in Truworth's with her money. Maud buys them each a thing called a waist cincher which is a stiff elastic item like a twelve-inch deep belt that goes around your waist, underneath your clothes. It has whalebone struts at four-inch intervals and it looks like the middle bit of a merry widow, with no boob sections and no suspenders. It makes their twenty-inch waists go one and a half inches narrower, which they find very satisfactory.

Then they go and get their hair expensively dyed. Maud has found a tall Swedish hairdresser who proceeds along radical lines with startling effect. She starts by bleaching all the colour out of the hair so that their tresses look as white as those of Miss Legge. They sit side-by-side staring into the mirrors, two sixteen-year-olds, each with a white-string floor mop fixed to her head. After that, the Swede paints on a kind of mink blond paste, section by section, laboriously wrapping each strand in a little square of tin foil until their heads are nothing but overlapping silver scales. When they emerge from the foil they look fabulous. Their hair is an identical, exquisite mix of silver and palest sand. All their natural yellow is gone. They are the glamour twins of GHS. The only annoyance is the regulation black Alice band, which must be worn at all times 'to keep the hair off the brow'. But Dinah and Maud don't want their hair to be kept off the brow. They want it tousled and hanging in their eyes, just as the Swede has left it.

Maud's divvy is lots of fun, though for a long time Dinah has no idea what it is or where it comes from. Then one day – but only after ages – Maud takes her home. It's a big surprise for Dinah, because Maud's family is working class. Maud's is the only white working-class family that Dinah's ever met.

NINE

MAUD'S MOTHER IS SHIPPED out from Aberdeen to the coal mining regions of northern Natal, as a mail-order bride for a Scottish migrant coal miner. She's seventeen and he's twice her age. For her family this makes one less mouth to feed at a time when the workhouse is looming, because Maud's maternal grandfather – another long-distance Scottish migrant worker – has recently stopped writing letters home and his postal orders have dried up. The biggest coal towns in Natal are called Newcastle and Dundee, but Maud's mother and her stranger husband live in a one-horse town called Danhauser where their daughter Lilian is born. But then, five years on, something happens. It happens because Maud's mother and a woman friend are treating themselves to a winter holiday in Durban and they decide to go to the races.

The Durban July Handicap is the social occasion of the year. It's terrifically dressy and some of the more extrovert women wear hats with whole nests of blackbirds on the crown, or entire banana plantations, in order to get their pictures on the social pages of the South African *Sunday Times*. Maud's mother doesn't have the wherewithal to dress up and she isn't wearing a hat, but all the same she catches the eye of a racehorse owner who leaps social boundaries to become her long-term lover and he longs to be her husband. The lover is a man of means. He belongs to one of the landed families of the Natal sugar plantation elite, a group who are locally known as the Sugar Barons. And then, when podgy little dark-haired Lilian is eleven, the lover gets Maud's mother pregnant.

The little blonde fairy girl is duly registered as the coal miner's daughter but her arrival has made the lover all the more determined to become Maud's mother's husband. The problem is that the coal miner's lungs are already showing signs of trouble and Maud's mother will not desert him, because two wrongs don't make a right. Plus there's her crosspatch displaced daughter to consider, who's on the edge of adolescence: Daddy's girl Lilian, whose loathing for the new baby never abates. The Sugar Baron nonetheless pursues a policy of biding his time. He begins by making over a sum of money for his daughter which Maud's mother invests, deciding to spend the bulk of it on sending the child, as soon as it's possible, as a boarder to the Maris Stella Convent School in Durban. She's full of secret pride at how bright the little girl is proving, though she dares not let her pleasure show in front of the coal miner or her elder daughter – given that the little brainbox is already no big favourite with either of the above.

At the convent five-year-old Maud soon learns to cry without making a single sound while the nuns comb the knots out of her long blonde hair and smack her on the head with the back of a hairbrush. Most of the nuns are Irish immigrant and killjoy. They have a grim northern mindset which is distinctly pre-Vatican II. And being acquainted with the circumstances of the little fairy girl's origins, they are more than ever anxious not to be sparing with the rod. Meanwhile, Maud, who is missing her mum like mad, is certain that she must keep on striving to do her very best and then she'll earn a reconciliation and be allowed to go back home. So the little fairy girl comes top in all her subjects and waits in hope for her mum to come and reclaim her. She isn't remotely ready to understand that the more she shines at everything the more her big sister will resent her, or that it's her own very presence in the house that is stoking all the anger and sense of grievance.

By the time Maud has been at the convent for five years, the coal miner's lungs are sufficiently wrecked for him to be invalided out of the mine service on a small occupational pension – an ill wind which doesn't blow everyone ill, since it provides the Sugar Baron with a chance to gain greater access. He buys Maud's mother and her family a pretty little town house in Durban on the landward side of South Ridge, so the little fairy girl can now become a day girl at the convent and have riding lessons and a pedigree cocker spaniel puppy with wavy ginger ears. He visits the little house almost every day, especially now that poor old grumpy Lilian has seized the first opportunity to escape into a teenage marriage and establish a place of her own.

So these are good times for Maud and her mother, but the idyll doesn't last, because, within two years of the purchase of the house, Lilian's marriage has fallen apart and she's back under her mother's roof feeling ever more short-changed. And she's filling up all available space, given that she's already managed to produce two children. So now there's little Darren and Debbie. The pretty little house is now dominated by the forceful if lowering presence of Lilian – an overweight, embittered young battleaxe who hates her pampered sister and longs to murder the dog. She hates Maud's brains and her private-school accent and all the rosettes in Maud's bedroom pertaining to successes at sundry gymkhanas. She hates the accident of Maud's Botticelli face with the wide blue eyes and blonde braids.

So this is the toxic atmosphere into which Dinah walks one Friday afternoon when she finally goes home after school with her best bosom friend. Lilian is playing the role of Mrs Joe Gargery, bullying and biffing to left and right. She's abusing the cocker spaniel in a querulous parrot voice and staring daggers at her half-sister's friend.

'And look what the cat dragged in,' she says. 'Who's *she*?' – but nobody dares to risk a reply.

The poor old coal miner, with his toast-rack chest and ravelled lungs, is sitting in the corner, his knees under a green plaid rug. He's flicking through back numbers of the *Daily Mirror* – the first English tabloid newspapers Dinah's ever seen.

Maud's slip of a mouse-quiet mother doesn't look like a person to make a conquest at the races. She looks like everybody's favourite dinner lady; the one who'll always sneak you an extra helping of treacle tart and never make you finish up your greens. She makes tea and sandwiches for everyone, puffing end-to-end on ciggies and talking in a voice that's almost a whisper. Her job is to practise appeasement within her household's warring walls. Her mouth is fixed into a sweet, conciliatory smile that gives her face a pleasant, somewhat pussy-cat appearance.

With Lilian's return to the little house, the Sugar Baron has finally, and very decisively, cut his losses. He's backed off and quickly made a marriage to somebody else. Then, almost at once, he's produced two daughters, legitimate daughters, Maud's younger half-sisters, but there's a stipulation that the girls should never meet. All contact with the Sugar Baron must cease. All patronage is understood to be at an end. It's as if he never was. Maud's the coal miner's daughter and that's that. From the time she enters Dinah's class at GHS, Maud is never in her father's company again, though she can't help coming upon his picture from time to time, because he's often in the newspapers initiating worthy civic projects. Nor can she stop herself from speculating about the two half-sisters who – kitted out in their bottle-green uniforms and regulation Quality Street straw bonnets – will be pupils by now at Durban's prestigious girls' private school. The College on Marriott Road. All that's left is Maud's half-yearly divvy which her mother allows her to spend.

None of the girls at GHS knows anything about Maud's family life. Only Dinah. Because Maud confides in her that same afternoon as they escape the house and walk down the hill till they reach the corner by the Marist Brothers' Roman Catholic Boys' School.

'He's not my real father,' she says. 'And I don't mind. I'm glad.'

She's been embarrassed by the coal miner's racism in front of Dinah, whose family's wider, more sophisticated take on ethnic matters has had an instant conversion effect upon Maud's own racial preconceptions. She resorts there and then to a mode of reference for the coal miner which sees her through in their conversations from then on. 'Me mam's 'usband,' she says.

'Me mam's 'usband was once had up in court,' Maud says. 'He rammed a black man into a brick wall, because the black man was trying to have a pee.' The black man was permanently maimed, Maud says, but the coal miner got off with a smallish fine. 'A man like *that*,' Maud says.

She's shredding grass blades between her fingers as she speaks, picking them one by one from the Marist Brothers' verge.

There aren't any public conveniences for blacks. Not in the white urban areas. Public toilets are always labelled 'Europeans Only/ *Slegs Blankes*'.

Two months after Dinah's visit and Maud, her mother and the coal miner have given up on the little house. They've ceded it to Lilian, along with the cocker spaniel. They've moved into a tied flat on the top floor of a factory in Umbilo Road because the coal miner has got himself a little part-time job as the factory's night-time caretaker. Maud misses her dog and she hates her new address in the smoky industrial end of town. She embarks on a charade of always getting off the bus two stops early and walking up the hill first before doubling back. Dinah colludes with her in this, but Catherine Cleary, nose to the ground as always, has managed to root it out. And Catherine sees it as her duty to spread the fact as widely as possible.

'It's a sin to be ashamed of your family,' she tells Dinah. 'Maud needs to be taught a lesson.'

Dinah finds this position repellent as well as incomprehensible, because she takes it as normal by now for people to be ashamed of their families. Isn't that why everyone would rather die than have their mum or their dad turn up at school? Wrong hair; wrong shoes; wrong bag; wrong accent; wrong body language; wrong laugh. Wouldn't all the girls in her class rather starve all day than have their mum appear at the classroom door, eagerly waving their packed lunch?

And Dinah knows that she isn't unique in having discovered adolescence as a time when you can hardly bear being in the same room as your parents for more than five short seconds. For herself she has to look away these days, rather than watch the angle of her mother's hand as she lifts a cup of tea. She must block her ears rather than bear witness to her mother's every little sigh or sniff – a cruel but necessary revulsion if one is ever to sever from one's parents and learn to live on one's own – especially, that is, if one's mum has been as close as Dinah's has been to her.

'It's for her own good,' Catherine is saying, who is these days wearing a small gold crucifix on a neck chain and alternating her routine smut with a range of pious convent homilies derived from her mentor, Sister Catherine. But her outing of Maud is a parting shot, a final arrow from the bow, because Catherine, who has screwed up on her Matric, has now left school and is about to head out for England and a nurse's training in Hove. As Mrs Cleary has put it, Catherine is to have a spell 'at home'.

When the coal miner is carted off for long-term hospital care in a ward for the dying near to his old mine in northern Natal, Maud and her mother have to move out of the tied flat. Her mum gets a job looking after the linen in a small residential hotel which comes with a room on the premises that mother and daughter share. Maud's territory is more comfortable to Dinah once the poor raddled invalid is gone, so that Dinah will now stay over in the hotel, just as Maud often stays over with her. In both venues the girls always manage the soundest sleep while sharing a two-foot-six-inch single bed. And tidy long-suffering Lisa now puts up with two muddly little sisters throwing their knickers around in her space.

Dinah enjoys the novelty of the hotel where, in the dining room, there's always a typed menu, even at breakfast time. Tinned grapefruit and stewed prunes; All Bran and oatmeal porridge; eggs, poached, scrambled or fried. At lunch on Saturdays there'll be a starter choice of mulligatawny or cock-a-leekie, followed by macaroni cheese, or the cod mornay option, both served with marrowfat peas. One weekend there's a Sunday dinner of roast pork and Yorkshire pudding, but the typewriter's 'r' has gone peculiar, so it's 'Roast ponk and Yonkshire pudding'. Dinah and Maud are delighted. Yonxie-ponxie-pudding-and-pie.

Maud's mum, as well as checking the linen, has to see that the tables in the dining room are properly set because the native servants don't always appreciate the vital importance of nickel-plated fish forks. Sometimes, when Maud and Dinah are helping, she'll tick them off as well.

'Side plates, Maud,' she says.

'Dinah's family don't have side plates,' Maud says. 'Dinah's dad just puts his bread on the tablecloth.'

Maud's mum pauses to polish the diplomacy of her reply. 'That's because they're foreign, dear,' she says.

Once the coal miner is into the last phase of his dying, Maud's mum is summoned in haste and she leaves her daughter behind in the hotel. But the coal miner's dying extends to a period of four months during which time Maud's extraordinary lack of parental constraint strikes Dinah as the enviable height of sophistication. Maud's unsupervised night life is expanding in adventurous directions and she's going off on mid-week dates with senior students from the architectural school – students who habitually stay awake all night. Then, in between, there are the short-term liaisons with birds of passage in the hotel.

Maud sometimes arranges dates for Dinah but Dinah finds that these occasions, though they provide an excuse for running up a range of boned and strapless brocade evening dresses, fall wholly outside her range of management skills and leave her feeling all thumbs. It's like being expected to dance in public when no one has taught you the steps. She's aware that a modicum of touching and groping is part of the etiquette of the venture but, because she's unschooled in the know-how of courtship and feels her skills to be roughly equivalent to those she's displayed for Miss Chase on the netball field, she always sits, off-puttingly ramrod straight, giving off unintended ice-maiden messages and throwing her partners into confusion. She sits, waiting for the elegant mating dance of literary-verbal interplay, where her partner's intent will merely be to deposit saliva inside her mouth. Or to get his hand in her bra. The verbal dimension, such as it is, will exist in her partner's crooning Pat Boone lyrics into her ear and there's one particular favourite here that comes up all the time. Pat Boone has crooned it as follows, but it's always being locally amended:

> The less you caress them,
> The more they like your technique

'It isn't "the *more* you caress them",' Dinah says. 'It's "less",' but the dates will never believe her.

Dinah and Maud, who talk about nearly everything, but most especially about clothes, will never talk about sexual practices so Dinah has no idea what it is that Maud gets up to when she's not watching. And Dinah's sole snippet of sexual guidance is a one-line utterance offered months earlier by her mother, who then, immediately afterwards, clams up in sudden embarrassment, refusing further elaboration or even a moment's eye contact. Dinah must not allow men to 'fumble' with her, she says – especially not with dirty fingers. For Dinah this advice, with its maternal emphasis on hygiene, has more the tone of the Home Doctor than any entrée into the secret world of sex, so that by the time one of the dates has accomplished a fumble inside Dinah's swimsuit on one of Durban's more deserted beaches, it's no surprise when the upshot is a vaginal itch brought on by sand grains up her crotch. And, though she's haunted by the idea that she'll have to take her itch to Dr Schaeffer at the surgery, she manages to cure it herself, with an all-purpose cream that her mother always keeps in the bathroom cabinet. The cream is made by May & Baker whose initials are M and B. These, her mother asserts, stand in for the words Much Better. Dinah's mum has gone on from here to evolve the phrase 'Much MB'. 'Tächenherz is much MB,' she'll say, when one of Dinah's dad's three-day migraines has at last begun to abate. '*Ach*, today he is much MB. Much, *much* MB.'

Because Maud is such a glamorous figure for Dinah, it doesn't dawn on her that life at fifteen alone in a hotel isn't altogether satisfactory. But it's more or less from this time on that Maud becomes devoted to Dinah's parents. And Dinah's parents love her back, allowing her all sorts of liberties that they wouldn't allow Lisa and Dinah. There's no disapproval, for example, when Maud, rising at midday in nylon shorty pyjamas, sidles mock-sexily on to Dinah's dad's knee and puts on her Marlene Dietrich voice. She does this as a way of helping him to eject a party of Jehovah's Witnesses who have managed to effect an entry.

'Vhy don't ve show ze gentlemen out *und* have some vine, my darlink, huh?' she says and she runs her fingers through his hair.

Then – just as she's got the Jehovahs on retreat at the front door, and Dinah's dad is pulling out his wallet to pay them off with a compensating purchase of *The Watchtower* magazine – Maud embarrasses him deliberately by changing tack. Transforming herself into an infant spoilt brat, she grabs his wallet and hugs it to her person. She's stamping her foot and yelling loudly.

'DON'T give them our ice-cream money, Daddy! I SAID, don't you DARE give them our ice-cream money!'

It's fun to watch Dinah's dad's ears going pink as the Jehovahs are making a hurried getaway. And Dinah, who never really minds about it, is perfectly aware of the relish with which her dad always likes to point out that Maud's drawing homework is so much better than her own. Maud's drawing is that much faster and more deft, so that while Dinah is still laboriously cross-hatching their assigned arrangement of watering can, pot plant and trowel, Maud will have already accomplished hers and is adding spoofy speech bubbles for the amusement of Dinah's dad. 'I am a watering can,' the speech bubbles say. 'I am a trowel.'

Thanks to Maud's increasingly hectic night life, she's now as close to falling asleep in class as Dinah is from the hay-fever pills. For this reason it makes a lot of sense for the girls to spend more of their school-time socialising from inside the medical room. The problem here is that, while Dinah's chronic allergies mean that the teachers will always believe her, Maud's professions of illness often fall on sceptical ears. The girls have already devised a system whereby they stagger their requests for sick leave, in order to ensure that Maud will always plead incapacity, either in Miss Bardsey's or Mrs Keithley's lessons. Then Dinah will follow her in the next, by gaining permission from a different teacher. But even then it isn't always easy.

'You look very well to me, my girlie,' Mrs Keithley says one day. 'You must go right back to your place and get on with your work.'

Maud is filled with such righteous indignation at having her word placed in doubt that she's at once bent on proving Mrs Keithley wrong. If she takes a swig from the ink well, she says, it will make her lips turn blue and that will prove her case.

The effect of drinking the school ink is, unfortunately, rather more dramatic. One small swig and Maud's teeth have begun to chatter. Within minutes she's turned a ghastly white.

'M-my eyeb-balls f-feel like b-b-b-boiled eggs,' she whispers. 'D-d-d-dinah, I'm n-n-not j-joking.'

Both of them are transfixed. When the bell goes for break, they eventually manage to stagger outside, both convinced that Maud is fading out. Yet neither will dream of summoning a teacher. They sit in the shade of a jacaranda tree, half paralysed with fear. Then, thank goodness, after several swigs of water, the fit begins to pass. And by halfway through the next lesson Maud is still sufficiently pale and shaky, not only to earn herself an open-ended place in the medical room for the day, but also to have company, because Dinah is allowed to go along with her to check that she's all right.

In the medical room you have to write in the record book what's the matter with you that day, so Dinah always writes 'hay fever'. Maud usually writes 'sinus trouble', but now she writes 'chattering teeth'. Quite often in the medical room they'll meet Carmen

Shapiro who is older than they are and wilder. Carmen is very beautiful: a dark, glossy beauty who lives up to her name. She intermittently intersects with the North Beach airhead set but in truth she's far too eccentric and far too original for the herd. Carmen always writes whatever she likes in the medical-record book. She writes 'hypochondrial diffusions' and 'period pains'. She writes 'septicaemia' and 'gangrene' and 'scurvy'. One day she writes 'sweaty feet' and another day she writes 'labour pains'. Thanks to Carmen it becomes perfectly obvious to Maud and Dinah that the staff never consult the medical-record book and that you don't really need to fill it in at all. Carmen is brilliantly gymnastical and she does handstands, or she turns cartwheels round and round the medical room. She and her friends are expert truants and she has funny stories about their various close escapes. They hide in the lavatories during assemblies and during lesson cross-over times.

'Always stand on the lavatory seat,' Carmen advises the younger girls. 'Then the prefects can't see your feet under the door.'

Carmen is in Lisa's class and Lisa has now become a prefect. Once Carmen's caught red-handed in the medical room while Maud and Dinah are watching from neighbouring beds. She's doing a headstand against the opposite wall when the head of maths pays an unexpected visit.

'I'm anaemic, Miss Unwin,' Carmen says, having hastily turned the right way up. 'My doctor's told me it's vital to get blood to the brain every hour.'

It's a mystery to Maud and Dinah why Carmen hasn't been expelled, especially as they've repeatedly teetered on the brink of it themselves for several much more innocuous and minor transgressions. Most recently it's been because of what they've done while sitting out the swimming lesson on the tiered stands one morning. Maud believes that she and Dinah can rescue the class from an impending follow-on maths test. They can do this, she says, by prolonging the class's changing time at the end.

'We'll muddle up all the bras,' she says. 'That'll take for ever to sort out.'

So the two girls leave the sunny stands while Miss Chase is busy in the pool. They spend a few brief, happy minutes in the changing room, transferring Fern Levy's size 36D to the cubicle of Pat

Mayer's 32AA. They switch Adele's 34C with Lynette's 34A and Bet's 34B with Marjorie's 36C. Then they return unnoticed to the stands and wait for the shrieks and confusion. The scheme is highly successful since the class takes for ever to sort out its undies and the maths test is well and truly missed.

And Miss Maidment, subtle creature that she is, then takes three days to summon them to her office. Plus, because she does this one by one, both girls are caught off guard. Maud is summoned first and Dinah has no idea that she's to follow. They don't even know what it's about.

'Godalmighty, but look at me,' Maud says. She casts an eye over her routinely desecrated uniform. 'Swap me your blazer, Dee,' she says. 'Swap me your tie. Swap me your shoes.'

With the uncanny knack of best friends the two girls not only share a shoe size but they can fit into all of each other's clothes. Maud has spent her mother's school shoe money on lots of Helena Rubenstein and on a pair of pink party pumps. Her current school shoes, a clapped-out pair of Grey Street cheapos from the Indian bazaar, are dusty with age and gaping at the toes. Her tie is twisted and very un-ironed. Her Alice band is nowhere. Her blazer is shouting its origins from Yael's fish-moth trunk. So Dinah hands over all her clothes in a lightning swap before Maud proceeds to the Head. Then, ten minutes later, when Dinah is summoned as well, it's hard not to catch Maud's eye and explode with giggles as Miss Maidment is lecturing her on the state of her derelict blazer and tie, on her gaping, dusty shoes and missing Alice band. Dinah does what she always does at such times. She stares fixedly at Miss Maidment's floor, trying in vain, this way and that, to make her size six feet fit exactly into the chevron wood blocks which are always half an inch too short.

Then, when Maud's mum and Dinah's dad are summoned from the ante-room, the girls know that things are getting serious. They watch in silence as Maud's mum expresses genuine wide-eyed surprise in her little whispery voice, because she cannot possibly believe that the little fairy girl is capable of transgression.

'Och, but she's always such a gud wee gerril,' she says. 'There's surely been a mistake?'

Meanwhile Dinah's dad keeps on looking at his watch and tapping his feet impatiently on the floor.

'Chuck her out,' he says. 'She's a waste of your time. Search me why you've kept her all this time.'

In the event, both girls are allowed to stay, though the reprieve is not of great significance for Maud who, with the coal miner dead and her mother returned to the hotel, has just confided to Dinah that she's leaving school come Christmas. Dinah's own feelings of shock and loss aside, she naturally understands this move as having to do with Maud's much greater sophistication and general grown-upness. Maud will get a job and have real money and even more boyfriends and fabulous clothes and a bank account. Most glamorous of all, Maud and her mother will first take a Union Castle boat to Southampton and proceed by train via King's Cross Station to Aberdeen where Maud's mum after an absence of nearly three decades will reconnect with the siblings she left behind at seventeen.

'Now the teacher's pet will try to be your friend,' Maud says.

'Rubb – ISH,' Dinah says. 'She hates me.'

'Correction,' Maud says. 'She hates me. And that's because I'm your friend. Can't you tell by the way she looks at you? Anyway she thinks you're the only person who's cultured enough to be her friend. So just you mark my words.'

They giggle their way through a final assembly, and get especial satisfaction from the line in 'Lord Dismiss Us' that exhorts the Almighty to keep them free from 'sloth and sensual snare'.

Maud has brought a blanket to school into which she shovels her heap of possessions and they carry it between them like a hammock down the long hill. On the way Maud stuffs her panama hat into a letter box and throws her blazer into a hedge. Then, four days later, Dinah is watching the *Warwick Castle* being tugged out from Durban harbour. It's carrying Maud and her mother out, out into the open sea.

School is different without Maud. Without Maud, there's no option but to sink yourself in the work. So Dinah becomes, once again, a sort of modified A1 rosette girl. This for all that she's been all at sea in maths for the last three years. She's always done well in Miss Byrd's art history classes and now she really starts to shine. Plus she's found favour with the senior English teacher who regards her as one of the elite: one of the girls she'll always call upon to deconstruct 'Sailing to Byzantium' in class and whose essays she'll read out loud. And the bliss, now, of the poetry lessons is that the suitable narrative verse has finally transmogrified into *Palgrave's Golden Treasury* which provides a feast of Robert Herrick and Ben Jonson; of Byron and Shelley; of Yeats and Hopkins and Auden. Dinah learns a lot of the poetry by heart, just for the pleasure of having it as furniture in her head, but mostly it just sticks in there without her making any effort. If you can recite 'Felix Randal the Farrier' to yourself, inside your own head, she's discovered, then standing alone at the school bus stop – standing there without Maud – well, it helps you not to get bored. It helps you not to feel alone. But Dinah is not alone for long.

It's being chosen to read the lesson in assembly that brings the teacher's pet to her side.

'I've been talking to Miss McAllister,' she says. Miss McAllister is the drama teacher. 'And both of us agree,' she says, 'that your voice production's all wrong. Miss McAllister says that you'll probably *have* no voice by the time you're thirty-five.'

The warning has little effect on Dinah, who can't envisage ever being thirty-five, though the put-down is slightly bruising to her confidence about public performance. And she hasn't failed to notice that the teacher's pet, even as she speaks, is moving her chair alongside Dinah's for the start of the day's English lesson. By the end of the day she's sitting beside Dinah for all the lessons they share. The teacher's pet is alongside Dinah in all the breaks as well. And it's during the breaks that she's always clutching the small vocabulary notebook in which she composes poetry. She writes it very fast, on the wing. The teacher's pet sits very close to Dinah and sometimes she likes to hold hands.

Yet she continues to be as put-down as possible at every opportunity. Dinah's performance in the title role of Miss Bardsey's production of *The Mikado* has the teacher's pet observing that her stage movement is 'embarrassing'. And her part in the chorus of T.S. Eliot's 'Coriolanus' elicits the observation that her facial expression is 'dopey'. The teacher's pet, in her friendship with Dinah, is pretty well analogous with a 1950s husband. In all the women's magazine stories Dinah reads at this time, a husband, or a would-be husband – because all passion must needs lead on to marriage – will require the female object of his love to be an endearing, frothy creature, a pretty thing who pines for frippery in the form of shoes and jewels and trinkets. And then, once her sparkly magpie hoard is outed, Mr Masterful can play the benign custodian and guide.

'Oh you adorable little fool,' he'll say. 'How I *dote* on you, dearest silly-billy. A week's wages on a pair of shoes! What next?'

And then Mr Masterful will embrace Miss Frothy and offer his hand in marriage. Of course, Miss Frothy mustn't really be a fool or she wouldn't be a credit to Mr Masterful – and she has to be able, in her role as wife, to advance Mr Masterful's career. She has to be like the female spouse in the cartoon-strip Horlicks advertisements that Dinah reads in the newspaper. Mrs Horlicks, who is always experiencing a period of inexplicable lethargy at the beginning of the strip, is reneging on her household chores and causing Mr Horlicks to think, in several worried thought bubbles, that She's not the girl I married.

She then goes on to take tea in a café with a wise woman friend. Both Mrs Horlicks and her wise friend are always depicted taking tea in their gloves and smart little head-hugging 1950s hats. The friend recommends a regular nightly mug of Horlicks which rescues Mrs Horlicks from the perils of 'night starvation'. The time leap in the story is then indicated by a square box that says, 'HORLICKS EVERY NIGHT UNTIL . . .'

Once the night starvation's been dispatched, Mrs Horlicks is completely revived and she can once again exhibit the guile, wit and prettiness to charm her husband's boss at the works Christmas party and to give his promotion a helping hand. And naturally, he's very proud to be the envy of his colleagues for having the most enchanting wife in the firm. A female consort, all the messages read, is required to be both a career leg-up and a trophy to carry on one's arm.

This is more or less what the teacher's pet seems to have in mind for Dinah, though neither girl, at the age of sixteen, is able to see these matters quite as clearly and straightforwardly as this.

On the first Saturday that the teacher's pet asks Dinah home to tea, she doesn't wear a hat and gloves but, because she's addictively dressy, she's as dolled up as usual for a day out of school uniform. She's wearing her newly made apple-green lawn shirtdress with high waist and full skirt and little amber buttons. She's wearing it with her new T-bar shoes, the shoes that – hopelessly Miss Frothy-wise – she loves with such a degree of passion that she's still taking them to bed in their box filled with crumpled tissue paper. Plus her hair is newly silvered and rolled into an acceptable state of studied, bouffant touslement. Dinah's teenage love affair with clothes is far more necessary to her and far more sensually rewarding than anything she might hope, right then, to get going with a boy. And, unlike the boy thing, it's a love affair in which she feels the joy of getting it right.

She takes two buses to the teacher's pet's house: one to the town centre and one from there to the north of the city. As she steps off the first bus into the bustle of the Saturday crowd, a photographer swoops and starts to take her picture. 'Do this, do that,' he says. Click click. Then he picks her up, shoulder high, and carries her ten yards down the road where he plants her on top of a silver Buick with a shiny wide chrome grin. 'Do this, do that,' he says. Click click. Everybody is turning and looking at her. Click click. 'Lovely,' he says. Click click. 'Terrific.' Click click. 'Superb.' Dinah doesn't think to ask him what he means to do with the pictures. She's too busy walking on air. And when she gets to the teacher's pet's house, she's still sufficiently upbeat about it to tell her story there.

The teacher's pet rolls her eyes to denote the degree of Dinah's witlessness and she's making a pull-down mouth. 'God how can you be so *stupid*?' she says. 'Don't you know that he does that to *every*body?'

The teacher's pet doesn't do clothes much, but she's got a high-school boyfriend whose picture's in a frame beside her bed.

Next time Dinah visits the teacher's pet she's wearing the bottle-green plaid wool suit which is the first thing she's ever made with linings. The suit has a short wide swagger jacket and a skin-tight skirt with a long kick-pleat which makes it just about possible to walk – even in the four-inch-heeled black winkle-pickers whose current torture of Dinah's toes is worth every moment measured in agony.

'*Chelsea*!' says the Payne Brothers make-up lady where Dinah has dropped in to buy herself a lip brush. She claps her hands in the rarefied atmosphere of pinkish fluorescent light and dry-ice air-conditioning. Then she's emerged from behind her mirrored counter to give Dinah a girlie little twirl.

'My *dear*,' she says, sounding utterly ex-pat. 'You look as if you've stepped *straight out of Chelsea*!'

Dinah has naturally never been to Chelsea, but, in her own personal version of Mrs Cleary's cultural cringe, she knows for certain that it's exactly where she most wants to be in this life. She knows all the names of places in London – the ones she's just been reading about in Iris Murdoch's first novel – names like Vauxhall and Pimlico and the Embankment – and she knows that one day she and Maud will be Chelsea girls, sharing a flat and going to the Billingsgate Fish Market to buy mackerel heads for the cat that they're going to keep for sure – a detail they've added to their London-life fantasy ever since T.S. Eliot's *Old Possum* has provoked in them a passion for the feline species.

In general English landscapes are more familiar to her, via J.M.W. Turner and John Constable and John Piper, than anything she sees – or does not see – in her own backyard. Something about the menace inherent in the local white agrarian class; in the patent horrors of local notions of manifest destiny; in the too recent expropriation of land – all newly compounded for her by the coming to office as Prime Minister of mad, blond, perpetually grinning Dr Verwoerd, the man who believes he's the black man's best friend, the man who, like Joseph Stalin, looks as though he's awaiting those garlands from smiling black schoolchildren even as he's signing the death warrant for the same children's education, downgrading a graduate black teacher's pay to the sum of two pounds per week; 'Thank you for my happy childhood'; 'Ninety-eight per cent of South Africa's Bantu approve of our policy of apartheid' – these things have made Dinah shut down on the terrain which she ought to feel is her own. So she doesn't see the beauty of the banana palms and the flame trees and the spiky orange aloes that grow wild on the vacant lots with their two-tone, razor-edged leaves. In fact she doesn't see them at all. Nature isn't her thing. Yet she's capable of getting quite swoony on reading *A Shropshire Lad*, or on the opening lines of *The Prelude*. Or on Hopkins's thrush's eggs, those ooh-aah 'little low heavens'; 'that English thrush who, through the echoing timber, does so rinse and wring the ear, it strikes like lightnings to hear him sing'. And yet, and yet, there are no lightnings anywhere that strike like the lightnings of coastal Natal.

She says nothing to the teacher's pet that Saturday – nothing about the Payne Brothers lady dancing her round the floor. Instead Dinah sits stiffly on the edge of the teacher's pet's bed and watches as she removes the boyfriend's photograph from the frame. Then she inserts a photograph of Dinah instead. In the picture Dinah is wearing lilac gingham of the sort just then made fashionable by the fabulous Brigitte Bardot. She's sitting alone on a garden bench in a shaft of dappled sunlight. On the bed beside her Dinah notes that the small vocabulary notebook is filling up and filling up with poems.

Dinah's relationship with the teacher's pet reaches its pitch of killjoy claustrophobia when they go together, just the two of them, to undertake that ultimate English-language schoolchild's night-mare: the language-learning sojourn on the Afrikaner farm. The teacher's pet has arranged it all and has presented the scheme to Dinah's parents as an efficiently organised project. She has Afri-kaner relations via her maternal line. Her mother, a pretty blonde Afrikaner woman who goes about the house in fluffy pink mules, has given Dinah the strong impression that she feels somewhat exiled in Durban, with her brisk English-speaking husband who looks exactly like his daughter. He does the books in a downtown office and makes unpleasant jokes at table. Jokes about having to take his wife off the shelf and dust her; jokes about having to buy a 'mole bomb' for his daughter who has a small, unobtrusive facial mark. The teacher's pet's mother likes to collar Dinah for the odd stolen moment of furtive girl-talk. So they whisper about lacy knickers and bras.

The farm is located in the furthest outpost of the Orange Free State. It's on land that's been carved out of what is rightfully Basutoland: high green mountain country where the indigenous Basuto wear wide conical hats and ride horses while wrapped in blanket cloaks against the cold, blankets made in Witney for the far-flung native trade. And for all that nothing awful happens during the language-learning fortnight, Dinah, doubtless through her own feebleness and inadequacy, remembers the weeks as a horror experience in Rip Van Winkle land, a fortnight of endlessly visiting neighbouring farms and sitting down to those prolonged afternoon teas in huge time-warped dining rooms with *riempie-*

seated chairs and white lace tablecloths and ticking clocks. Glass-fronted bookcases carry whole runs of Walter Scott and Charles Dickens along with brass-edged family Bibles. Bearded patriarchs glare in sepia from the walls.

Tea-times are when she sits in an idiotic cold sweat of terror lest someone, addressing her in Afrikaans, should expect a reply in kind. Dinah sits listening to the cut and thrust of humorous racist anecdotes being swapped between huge white farming men with hairy arms like joints of meat and those faces on which horn-rimmed glasses sit as if permanently wedged in tightness there, like youthful wedding rings on old swollen fingers. She watches the to and fro of the barefoot Basuto housemaids, the gaunt and gap-toothed female serfs who shuffle silently back and forth with platters of tea bread on doilies and custard tarts and *koeksusters* – those especially horrible plaited doughnuts that get soaked in Lyle's Golden Syrup.

Meanwhile the teacher's pet is revealing herself as a grand master of the bilingual interface – a tea-time star who clearly has no need of intensive immersion. But the *boereplaas* experience is providing exclusive and uninterrupted access to Dinah. Dinah who is now both audience and recipient of the ever-burgeoning contents of the small vocabulary notebook. So the fortnight drags unbear-ably as the teacher's pet is sunk in gloom because she's in the grip of an emotion she can't yet begin to understand. And Dinah's head is about to explode because she finds herself in no position to tolerate or to fathom the weight of the teacher's pet's constant presence, the presence of a person who thrives on wrong-footing her at each and every opportunity and yet is always there.

Yet the horror farm yields a keepsake in the form of a six-week-old marmalade kitten. Dinah claims it and calls it Muschka and carries it home, hoping that a small orange puffball will tug at her parents' heartstrings and fill the hole that's been left by the death of Punch. She cuddles the kitten through the night on the endless, rackety train journey that carries her back to Durban. Modder-poort – Ficksburg – Fouriesburg – Bethlehem – Harrismith – Van Reenen – Ladysmith – Colenso – Estcourt – Mooirivier – Notting-ham Road – Howick – Pietermaritzburg – Nelsrus – Cato Ridge – Drummond – Kloof – Pinetown – and then she's home! And then it's the new term. And then, exactly four days late, Jenny Stern walks into Dinah's classroom and her life, once again, turns around.

Jenny's family has relocated from Johannesburg, her mother, her stepfather and her younger brother Sylvester. And the reason why Jenny's four days late is because of Carmen Shapiro. Jenny's mum, on the eve of the move, has thought to reacquaint herself with a girlhood friend, because three decades earlier, she and Edie Shapiro, née Klingmann, were the only little Jewish girls at the Transvaal's Rosetta Convent, preparatory branch. Struck, as they were, by the convent's awesome religious rituals from which they were exempt, Jenny's mum and her friend Edie conceived the idea that God was manifest in the gold silk tassels of the school hall curtains, around which they invented their own ingenious rites.

'Edie,' says Jenny's mother into the telephone. 'Long time no see.'

'But, Pansy, dear,' says Carmen Shapiro's mother. 'What a lovely surprise. And if your Jenny's starting at GHS – why my little girl's there as well. My Carmen can fetch her and take her to school.'

So, for the first three days of term, as Jenny tells her new friend Dinah, Carmen Shapiro has fetched her from her family's maisonette at the top of South Ridge Road and taken her off to the amusement arcade on the beachfront near the burger bar. There they disport themselves in the Hall of Mirrors and eat candyfloss and hot dogs and play on the pinball machines.

'Achtpenny-achtpenny-achtpenny-see-yourself-in-the-hall-of-mirrors-scream-of-your-life,' screeches the poor white crone with the varicose veins who's hired to lure people in.

But Jenny is not by inclination a rebel and by the fourth day she's decided to make her own way to school. It's two days before her seventeenth birthday and one of the things that impresses Dinah, along with Jenny's lovely looks, is the fact that she's straightaway pinned a notice to the classroom newsboard listing all the gifts that she'd like to receive. As an icebreaker this has worked wonders and Jenny is popular and integrated at once. So it's flattering for Dinah that Jenny has chosen her. Plus Jenny isn't a wimp like Dinah, so for her to usurp the teacher's pet's chair is simply not a problem.

'I'm being your friend because I like your silver hair,' Jenny says. 'And because I'm planning to copy all your essays.'

Jenny is not as intellectual as Maud, but she's directed and she's oozing charm and flair. Jenny has independence of mind and she likes to do her best. She's always eager to answer questions in class, so sometimes she'll shoot up her hand before she's thought of any answer. Then she'll utter a sort of highbrow jabberwocky that sounds like abstract poetry.

'Sorry?' the head of English will say. 'Can you say all that again?'

'I think what Jenny is saying,' Dinah says, 'is that she thinks as follows –'

'Well, yes,' Jenny says. 'Yes, *exactly*. In fact, that's exactly what I've just said.'

All the teachers love Jenny, even though she'll speak her mind most forcefully on the subject of some of their sacred cows.

'Frankly, *Lycidas* is boring,' Jenny says. 'So I've brought you a much better elegy. See, if Milton could've only written like e.e. cummings, Miss Holdsworth. Listen.'

And then she recites that poem about the defunct Buffalo Bill, death's blue-eyed boy and paramount pigeon-slayer.

Jenny's an older sister and she's older-sister-ish with Dinah. It's Jenny who swiftly introduces Dinah to Tampax, instructing her from outside the cubicle in the school lavatories at break.

'Left leg on the lav seat and keep your right knee bent,' she says. 'Just keep thinking gorilla. And make sure the string's hanging out.' And then, half an hour later, when Dinah says, 'I feel sick,' Jenny says, 'Well, go to the bathroom and pull out the plug, you feeble creature. You'll get used to it. You've got to. Because you can't walk around with a hammock between your legs. Jesus, where do you *come* from?'

And it's Jenny who pushes Dinah into the optician's. 'You're as blind as a bat, you fool,' she says. 'And not having glasses is just helping to make you look goofy. Christ, if I was a gorgeous leggy blonde like you, d'you think I'd go around looking goofy?'

'No,' Dinah says. 'No, you wouldn't.'

'Well, don't you know that you always screw up one of your eyes?' Jenny says.

This is true. Dinah screws up her much less myopic right eye for close work and her much more myopic left eye for distance viewing.

If she doesn't use just one eye at a time, then she always sees everything double. In the optician's Jenny and Dinah choose her a pair of gigantic men's horn-rims in defiance of the current fashion for up-turned pastel glitter wings. They do this though the glasses keep sliding down Dinah's nose and the optician thinks they're both insane. Dinah imagines Gregory Peck taking the horn-rims off her face and saying, 'Oh, but, Dinah, you're so beautiful. For two pins I'd put you in my rucksack.' Gregory Peck is her number one male turn-on. Gregory Peck and Lord Byron. And maybe Rupert Brooke.

Jenny is small. Her feet are size four and she's only five foot two. She's a pale but luscious beauty with curvy hips and proper bosoms. Jenny has a perfect, straight nose like something from a Greek vase painting and beautifully incised heavy eyelids. She has a fine pearly skin and fine small pearly teeth and the pearliest of sweet-girl smiles. A mass of dark-brown corkscrews grows on her head, which she can bundle up with one hand and hold in place with a single gigantic hair clip, or with a twisted pipe cleaner. Dinah loves the hair but Jenny's often cross about it because the humidity in Durban makes it much more curly than it ever was in Johannesburg, so she gets her hair straightened all the time and she stretches it after every wash over enormous steel rollers that tug at her roots. Jenny never totters about on winkle-pickers, but has good-quality, well-polished court shoes with two-inch kitten heels. There's no way Jenny and Dinah could ever share their clothes, but Jenny wouldn't want to because she's much too fastidious for that.

In her bedroom Dinah is amazed to find that the drawers are lined with tissue paper and that everything is folded – knickers, bras, stockings and cashmere jumpers (cashmere!), along with scarves and gloves (scarves and gloves!). Where Maud and Dinah have always rushed their garments to completion on Saturday afternoons, always ignored the need to finish the inside edges of seams, always stitched each other, at every emergency, into tight-bodiced party dresses with a quick snatch of green or black tacking thread – that's when time has run out on them and a zip would take too long – Jenny teaches the merits of neatly bound seams and self-covered buttons and silk linings and tailor's tacks. Inside neatness will make for outside confidence, she says. You can't feel good if you're a slob. And Jenny has the perfect minimal wardrobe. Not a teenager's wardrobe at all. She has three good-quality basic garments in black, navy and cream which she dresses up with Hermes scarves and shoes and different lipsticks.

Dinah knows that Maud and she and Jenny will love each other and be a threesome of best friends. She knows that Jenny will join them in the flat in London and they'll be a trio, not a duo, of Chelsea girls. To this end she already has Jenny writing postscripts to her long regular letters to Maud and Maud writes back to the girl she's never met. Maud's letters have started out full of descriptions of the Aberdeen aunties and their high-stodge high teas, all arranged on high, three-tiered serving plates: baps, buns and bannocks galore along with several scarcely credible follow-ups like cloutie dumplings and cullen skink. But now her letters are full of London life: London, where she's got herself locked inside Hyde Park all night by mistake, in the company of an adoring young police constable; London, where she sits for an hour in Lyon's Corner House in Charing Cross Road and writes her letters on a two-yard scroll of scratchy lav paper, stamped at all the perforations 'London County Council – Now Wash Your Hands'. Maud and Dinah have a project for Jenny who is phobic about using escalators. She can't use the London Underground without conquering this phobia, Maud writes, so she's to practise every day. Every day Dinah's to take her up the John Orr's escalators. Up and down. Up and down.

But Jenny's not one for mooching round the town and besides she has other calls on her time. Dinah understands that Jenny, just like Carmen Shapiro, is required to make periodic forays into the North Beach airhead set as an ethnically specific form of courting ritual. Without this her mother will fear that Jenny is becoming a blue stocking and won't learn how to flirt.

Dinah soon gets to meet Jenny's mother because visiting Jenny is so easy. Her family lives just round the corner, in one of the classy two-storey maisonettes made out of the converted old Manor House. So the girls always walk to school together. Jenny collects and is always punctual. Dinah dawdles and threatens to make them late. On all their outings Jenny will set off, always in front, her buttocks ball-bearing along, her whole person bristling with energy and purpose – yet just sometimes she'll stop and turn round.

'So where are we going?' she says.

'Don't know,' Dinah says. 'I was following you.'

'Well, don't!' Jenny says.

Jenny has no time for Dinah's sub-standard health, so she'll phone over weekends and say, 'Please come to my house, Didi. But not if you've got that boring hay fever. If you're snotting and sneezing, then you can bloody well stay at home.'

En route to school the girls always pass a big corner house covered in bougainvillea where there's a sports car in the drive owned by a dark, smouldering student with craggy facial bones like a man on a Mills & Boon cover. The girls entertain themselves with fantasies about him and then in no time Jenny's got a date.

'His name's Richard Mason and he's a drip,' she says next morning. 'No, I assure you. He's the drippiest drip alive.' Jenny, who has the art of attracting men with every turn of her head, will nearly always find them wanting unless they're old and pompous, or else if they're unattainable.

Jenny's parents are a little bit scary because they've got money and worldly wisdom. And they're the first people Dinah's met who have 'drinks'. She knows that all her own parents ever drink is Nederburg Stein for a special treat at Christmas. The drinks live in a special glass-fronted cupboard: whole rows of coloured liquids, some in bottles, some in decanters wearing pewter necklaces with labels. Until she meets Jenny's parents, Dinah has never seen a soda syphon and she has no idea that bourbon can be anything other than a dynasty of French royals. Sometimes Jenny's stepfather will refer to a drink as a snifter, or a snorter – or that's what Dinah thinks she hears him say. Jenny's parents have drinks before dinner, and drinks after dinner, and then they go rosy and shiny-eyed and they get flirty with each other.

Jenny's stepfather is not a big favourite with either of the children. He's dark-haired and plummy-voiced and he's got a coal-black RAF moustache of fairly monster proportions. He sometimes does anecdotes about the war, because he was de-mobbed in London, so he's got a story about how the Queen Mum bore down on him with one of her radiant smiles, when he and his two comrades were almost too drunk to stand up. So they all held on to each other and swayed mightily to left and right. Yes, Ma'am, and No, Ma'am, they said to her, before they collapsed in a threesome at her feet.

'Old trout was so thick with make-up, she looked like a freshly plastered wall,' Harold says.

He has anecdotes about lovable cockney tarts in bars plus lots of local anecdotes, because Harold is a raconteur. He knows how to mix any kind of drink and how to be attentive to a lady's needs. He's always ready with the flick of his silver cigarette lighter, or to offer an arm into dinner. He knows how to arrange a fur wrap around a lady's bare shoulders. Harold is very comfortable in the company of comfortable widows and Jenny's mother adores him.

Pansy Kaufmann is a gorgeous creature who's a lot younger than Dinah's mum. She has dark hair and scarlet lipstick and scarlet nails and she's never not looking glamorous. Even when she's just washed her hair she'll have on a purpose-built terry-cloth turban and a slinky Hollywood dressing gown and all her rings will be in place. She's got a dazzling wide smile and, more than anything, she likes to have a good time. Pansy's impatient with motherhood, so she talks to Jenny and her friends just as though they were a clutch of wised-up girl pals out on the pull together. She's the only mother Dinah knows who's always on at her daughter to wear sexier shoes and plunging necklines. She wants Jenny to walk with a more come-on swagger. She thinks Jenny's clothes are too severe and if Jenny's ever wearing flat shoes then she'll never let it go by.

'What's with the orthopaedic shoes today, Jen?' she says. 'Aren't those shoes for a person who's got a sickness?'

Or she'll come home from the shops with handy new seduction ideas.

'Jenny, I want you to go without your bra,' she'll say one day. 'I've just seen a young girl in town today. Luscious bosoms, just like yours. She was bouncing all down West Street admiring herself in the shop windows. Try it, Jenny. Don't be boring. What do you think, Didi? Should my Jenny take off her bra?'

Dinah spends most of her time with Jenny's mother trying hard not to blush. And mealtimes are the most dangerous because Harold will suddenly pounce.

'Got any boyfriends, then?' he'll say, while you mumble and try to look suave. 'More than old Jenny here, I hope?' Or he'll say, 'Tell me. What do you put on your pimples? Anything good? You girls know all the tricks.'

Harold is especially horrid to Jenny's brother Sylvester, who is thirteen and bulging with the beginnings of awkward adolescence.

A small skinny boy with new black down on his upper lip and a new, unreliable breaking voice, Sylvester has a huge new Adam's apple and a clump of new, fuzzy underarm hair in each of his small-boy armpits. The hair is revealed whenever Sylvester does his Tarzan swings from the bars of the open staircase that rises up from the dining room.

'*Armpits*, Sylvester,' Harold says, delicately sniffing the air. 'Armpits . . . armpits . . . Not in front of the ladies.' He likes it when Sylvester gets embarrassed and lets go and crumples to the floor.

Harold is like a new tomcat on the block, putting his smell on Pansy's things. So Sylvester escapes to his soapbox cart and zooms down the steeply gradiented pavements of South Ridge Road, while Jenny escapes to her friends. Jenny and Sylvester are children who've been displaced by their mother's passion for Harold – and there's damn all that they can do about it, though Jenny's poise has provided her with better coping strategies. She's always motherly towards Sylvester who has the air of a wounded bird.

Sometimes Jenny's mum will press Dinah to sit beside her on one of the gilded bergère sofas and she'll grow expansive on her life story.

'– and then my father lost all his money,' she says. 'So I was forced to go and work in Ackerman's.'

Pansy worked as a shop assistant in Ackerman's – a large downmarket chain store that's never got a foothold in Durban. But she wasn't there for very long because she caught the eye of Jenny's dad, who was an older man with means. Jenny's dad is dead, but Jenny has lots of pictures of him that she's stashed away in her bedroom: precious pictures of the two of them together, pictures of a solid, bald, imposing man, like a handsome version of Alfred Hitchcock. And alongside him, locking eyes with him, is an adorable smiley moppet, a dainty doted-on Jenny Wren in expensive little smocked frocks and shiny patent-leather shoes. Jenny says that she always helped her dad to choose his ties for the office. She'd stand on a stool in his dressing room and pick out the one for that day.

Some of the pictures are of Jenny and Sylvester with that almost unheard of local status symbol, a white English nanny. In the pictures, when Sylvester is in his going-out clothes, he's dressed up in a white suit like Richie Rich, but without the dollar signs in his eyes. Some of the pictures are of Jenny's dad with Pansy on foreign cruises, or on shopping trips in Manhattan. Pansy looks like a film star in the pictures, a gorgeous rich man's wife in Dior costume and lots of jewellery, holding on to striped cardboard hat boxes. Whenever Dinah thinks about Pansy, she thinks about Cunard Liners.

Pansy has a lot of sayings and one of them's about her late husband who died when Jenny was nine. 'He came from Russia with a piece of string,' she says.

It takes Dinah a while to understand what Pansy means, but she uses this expression about Jews who left Eastern Europe with no money in their pockets. She means that they were part of the vast migration of penniless early twentieth-century Jews to the Rand where the streets were – of course – paved with gold. If Pansy talks about immigrant Jews who, unlike her late husband, have failed to acquire bourgeois finesse, then – for reasons Dinah doesn't understand – she calls such persons Peruvians. So Pansy is having a dinner party one day and she says to the early arrivals at the event, 'I must tell you that the Pikaskis are coming. They're dreadful Peruvians, I'm afraid.' And then, of course, the Pikaskis turn up and one of the earlier guests is disposed to try a little conversation.

'Mrs Kaufmann tells me you come from Peru,' he says. 'Is that from Lima?'

'No, no,' says Mr Pikaski. 'Not Lima. Fanny and me, we come from Riga.'

Pansy does lots of entertaining but she never enters her own kitchen and she doesn't know how to cook. She's never heard of washing-up liquid, so her maid is still grating bars of blue mottled soap every time she's got a sink of dirty dishes. Pansy has a large black woman in the kitchen whom she refers to as 'the slave'. The slave has a limited culinary repertoire, so it's nearly always shepherd's pie and orange jelly for pudding with sliced bananas set into the mould. Jenny and Dinah have noticed that the grande dame in the next-door maisonette has a variation in servant terminology. She calls her maid 'the savage'.

'Oh my *dears*,' she says one day to the girls. 'Have you set eyes on my new savage? Her name's Aurelia.'

Blacks often have the nicest names, Dinah thinks – elegant, Old World names like Seraphina and Theodora, or long biblical names like Ezekiel and Hepzibah. Whites are called Lynn and Terry and Barry and Eileen. The grande dame in the next-door maisonette is a striking Rubens beauty, an ample pink-and-white goddess with dangly gemstone earrings that aren't clip-ons, because she's the only bourgeois person Dinah's ever met who's got pierced ears. She's also the first person Dinah's met who likes to use daring language, so if Jenny is climbing over her gate instead of undoing the clasp, she'll say, 'Jenny will you stop *raping* my gate?! I will not stand over your marriage bed and vouch for you!'

Jenny's dad was a poor but brainy immigrant who got rich inventing something that was vital to the wheels of industry but Dinah doesn't know what it is. She knows that he took out a patent which, like bourbon, is all new to her. Jenny's family have moved from a grander house in Johannesburg to the maisonette in South Ridge Road, so lots of their stuff is really big. There are large looming oil landscapes in chunky stucco frames and all the furniture looks a bit as though it's come from a French château. Jenny tells Dinah that she hates it. She likes Dinah's mum's fixtures and fittings better because everything comes in several tasteful shades of beige. That's except for the row of black-and-white woodcuts that she's hung over the sofa, woodcuts sent by handsome Wilhelm from the Harz Mountains, the skiing champ who'd turned her down in the rain in pre-war Berlin.

Married, middle-aged and the father of teenage sons, Wilhelm has once again decided that Marianne is the only girl for him. He writes her long extravagant love letters and bombards her with cardboard rolls full of lithographs, etchings and woodcuts. Dinah's dad has got exercised about all the letters and the art works and he's made Dinah's mum tell him to stop. So Wilhelm has gone to ground once again, but Dinah's mum has kept a few of the prints for old time's sake. Some of them are in the frames on the wall and some are stashed in a cardboard box under her bed, along with all the old photographs of the young Jacobsens fooling at the Tiergarten or on the deck of the motor launch. All of them are being eaten away by Durban's ubiquitous green mould.

Jenny is the only person Dinah knows who calls her parents by their first names and Pansy insists on it with all of Jenny's friends so there's no 'Thank you for having me, Mrs Kaufmann.' It's all 'Thank you, Pansy,' and 'Thank you, Harold.' Sometimes Jenny's mother, when she sits Dinah down, will hint at bedroom talk.

'My first husband was a *good* man,' she'll say with meaning. 'But if I'm truthful with you, Dinah, I never ever *felt* for him the way I feel for that swine Harold. Tell me, Dinah. What do you think? Am I a fool for love?'

Sometimes, as they sit drinking together in the evenings, Jenny's mum, with her tinkly glass of amber liquid in hand, will make significant faces at Harold to try and coax him upstairs. But Harold always likes to hang back, like a child delaying his bedtime. It's at times like these when there's something about them – and maybe it's nothing more than the high-backed gilded chairs – but there's something about them, Dinah thinks, that causes one to call up images from Hogarth's *Marriage à la Mode*.

And then it's time for Maud to come back. And she's a grown-up, a working girl, with packets of ciggies in her handbag. Maud gets a series of crappy short-term jobs by pretending to employers that she can type. Then she meets two gay boys who are planning a café. Maud runs the coffee bar – Durban's first. It's a chic little arts café, with the first espresso coffee machine that anyone local has ever seen. The boys look after the art gallery upstairs, because one's a potter and the other one does textiles. Maud's mum gets a job in a bun shop in town and Maud soon has her own little studio flat in a central high-rise block where the girls, now a threesome of best friends, can do their sewing and practise keeping house. Jenny likes to make cheese soufflés a lot, while Maud and Dinah do chilli con carne and shortcut casserole things from the *I Hate to Cook Book* using onion-soup mix and tinned pineapple chunks. And they do those deadly post-war risottos where you mix pre-cooked long-grain rice with pre-cooked chicken and frozen peas.

People always talk to Maud, especially intense, creative people, and one day she's got a new playwright in her flat. He's a small, wiry man with too-big trousers and a beard and, to look at him, you'd take him for a poor white railway worker. His name's Athol Fugard and he's worked as a clerk in the Native Commissioner's Court, watching the endless parade of black South Africans getting done for Pass Law offences. He's right away seen that the real drama is in the lives of urban blacks and suddenly, thanks to him, theatre is transformed from *The Barretts of Wimpole Street* and *No No, Nanette* into *No Good Friday* and *Nongogo* and *The Blood Knot* – electrifying plays that come like a passionate scream, out of the Bantu Men's Social Centre and the African Theatre Workshop.

All the while Jenny and Dinah are swotting for the final exams that will take them on to the university, they hope, the place where Lisa has already done the first year of a degree in geography. Durban is always so hot around exam time that sometimes they fill Dinah's bath with cold water and immerse themselves in it naked with their notes on a plank across the tub. 'The first shipload of coolies arrived in November 1860 . . .' Dinah's mum takes pity on them and brings them grapes and cold-sausage sandwiches and iced orange juice that she's squeezed with her new Estrella citrus press.

Dinah's decided that she'd like to be an architect. This is because she loves shapes. She loves to make pop-up books for the neighbours' children and she unpicks cardboard boxes to copy their various intriguing groundplans. Besides, she's never stopped being seduced by the memory of her pipe-cleaner doll's house, the many-roomed margarine-box mansion with its rooms full of matchwood Chippendale and matchwood grandfather clocks. So she goes to talk to Miss Byrd.

'It's not a career for a girl,' Miss Byrd says. 'They don't want women in the profession.'

'But,' says Dinah. 'But . . . but –'

'They won't have you, my dear,' Miss Byrd says. 'They won't have women in the architectural school.'

And that's the end of that. Dinah right away gives up, collapses on the first round – and has, of course, never mentioned the idea at home, has never confided any of her affairs – and this, even though she knows that her dad greatly admires his only female engineering student, a brave girl in a boiler suit with blonde hair, called Georgette.

'I'm going to major in English,' Dinah starts to say from this time on.

The only hitch with regard to the exams is that Dinah doesn't know any maths. And without maths she can't get a Matric. This is something which slowly dawns on her once the time is almost up.

For nearly four years she's sat there daydreaming in the maths class and she's never once done the homework.

'I don't know any maths,' she says, one night at dinner, in front of her dad. It's four weeks, to the day, before she'll have to sit the exams.

'Well, you've been in the maths class for four years now,' he says. 'Come on, you must know something.'

'I know nothing,' Dinah says.

'So what's a plus b into a minus b?' he says.

'Don't know,' Dinah says.

Her dad puts down his fork. 'What's an isosceles triangle?' he says. 'What's pi? What do you understand by cosine?'

'Don't know,' Dinah says. 'I don't know. I'm telling you, I don't know.'

'Christ Almighty,' says her dad. 'You really do know nothing.'

'Told you,' Dinah says. Her brain, right then, is pure of mathematical concept, clean as a bleached-white sheet of paper.

It's in a spirit of challenge combined with a degree of withering contempt that her dad takes her on as a project. They're off school anyway, on study leave, so he sometimes teaches her all day. Then, if he's got lectures, he sets her some work to be getting on with. He gets her to work through books and books of past papers. Algebra, geometry and trig. Every day for four weeks she takes new concepts on board until the mist of four years has lifted and the high-school maths syllabus has jumped into focus before her eyes. The past papers are pretty formulaic, once you've cracked the code, so that, after three weeks, they're a cinch, a series of fun-and-games puzzle books in which Dinah knows all the tricks, is sailing through getting A's. Her dad is going through her work. Tick, tick, tick.

Yet nobody could be more delighted than her dad when Dinah comes home from the algebra paper white in the face and shaking. It's a paper that's wholly different from all the ones in the books of past papers – one which has caused her to scrabble feebly for the odd question she can understand.

'Aha,' says her dad. '*Aha*! The first intelligent Matric algebra paper in years, as far as I can see. Now this will separate the sheep from the goats.'

Dinah has never been sure about this expression. Ought one to want to be a sheep or a goat? And especially when it comes to ¯

226

algebra? And ought her own father to be quite so delighted that, in this year of all years, the algebra paper should be so unusually 'intelligent'? The only one in ten years in which all the predictable formulas have been turned around to stump the likes of his dozy daughter?

She pulls up on the geometry and the trig and – hurrah – she's got a Matric. She and Jenny are off to the uni and Dinah, in addition, has been awarded a nice little bursary that will pay for her to have a room in a hall of residence. Florence Powell Hall. Her very own room for the first time. And this isn't all, because Miss Maidment is on the phone soon after the Matric results come out.

'Dinah,' she says, sounding a little skittish. 'Now you'll be wondering why I've phoned.'

Dinah has straightaway begun to shake. She's trying to rack her brain. What now? What can it be now? Is it possible that she and Maud can be expelled, even now that they've actually both left? Are they to be the first posthumous cases of expulsion from GHS?

'You,' says Miss Maidment, 'have brought honour to the school.' She's using a curiously long 'oo' sound in the words you and school.

'Ah –' Dinah says.

'You have won the Queen Victoria Memorial Award,' Miss Maidment is saying. 'Dinah, it's a prize for the best Matric English Essay in the whole of the Union of South Africa.'

'Ah –' Dinah says. 'I see. Thank you.'

Funny thing is, it seems like no big deal to her. Not anything like as exciting as having a photographer pick you up and plant you, click click, on a silver Buick. Plus she has the usual spoiler's hunch that the prize will be specific to racial category – that the Queen Victoria Memorial Award will be one for which only white eighteen-year-olds are eligible.

So it's quite a surprise for her when, three weeks later, she meets the teacher's pet in a bookshop.

'By the way,' says the teacher's pet. 'About that essay prize of yours. I've been up to the Union Buildings in Pretoria and I've spoken to the Education Department. They gave me access to the Matric English papers – so I just happen to know that my essay got half a per cent more than yours.'

Dinah is blinking at her without comprehension. Half a per cent? What is she on about? It doesn't for a moment cross Dinah's mind that the story doesn't quite ring true. It's just that it doesn't seem in any way significant to be competing over half a per cent. And especially not when Maud has just decided to go off and live in Swaziland, because she and one of the boyfriends are planning to manage a hotel in Mbabane. Not when she and Jenny are busy on the important business of planning their student wardrobe, a project they are embarked upon with all the devotion of twin brides laying down their sisterly trousseaux.

'They decided to give you the prize,' the teacher's pet is saying, 'because my essay was much too controversial.'

Dinah doesn't remember what the subject choices were, nor which one it was that the teacher's pet had happened to choose. 'The Pen is Mightier than the Sword. Discuss'? She does remember, however, that her own was on the subject of 'Clothes'. So the effect of the teacher's pet's passing shot is to make Dinah once again feel trivial. Little Miss Frothy, the 1950s wife, with her head full of frippery and frocks. A week's wages on a pair of shoes?! What an adorable silly-billy.

Jenny and Dinah have decided on the look. It's a pale consumptive look. They plan it in opposition to the predominant tanned beachcomber look, the Surfin' Experience look. They'll have pale make-up and pale lipstick and pale crisp lawn and pale sheer stockings the colour of buttermilk. They'll be visions as pale as desert sand. For Dinah, the look is making a virtue of necessity. For Jenny it's a quiet act of defiance against her mother who longs for her to be deepening her tan in a small bikini on North Beach. And then, that month, just as they set foot on the campus, the police turn their guns on an unarmed and peaceful crowd.

The people of a black township, thirty miles from Johannesburg, have gathered in answer to a national call to protest against the Pass Laws. More and more people crowd into the square between ten in the morning and lunchtime. Men, women and children. The police start shooting without any warning, raking the crowd in a wide arc from the top of an armoured car. They shoot and shoot until there's no one left in the square – that is, no one who isn't already a corpse. Afterwards, the police try to say that the crowd was armed. There is reference to 'ferocious weapons'. But nobody at Sharpeville finds a single weapon among the dead, whose shot wounds are mostly in the back. All they find are the scattered hats and shoes. Plus there's the odd abandoned bike. It's the end of peaceful protest in South Africa for what begins to seem like for ever.

Then, twelve years later, sixty thousand black trade unionists go on strike in Durban. So, legal or not, the trade unions are once again flexing their muscles. And then, four years after that, twenty thousand Soweto schoolkids take to the streets in protest. They've had enough, they say. They'd rather not go to school at all than put up with what's on offer. And that's the beginning of the end, for all that the government spends the next fifteen years on repression and window dressing. Because it looks pretty bad on global TV when a state turns its guns on its own children. But by this time Jenny, Maud and Dinah – all three of them – are long gone.

TEN

THE SHARPEVILLE PROTEST OF 21 March 1960 is not an ANC event. It happens because the newly formed Pan-African Congress has just then broken away. It thinks the ANC is too cautious and too willing to work with whites. But the ANC is a movement with a history. It's founded in 1912 by distinguished black professionals who can be seen in old sepia photographs, wearing stiff collars and gold watch chains. They are the men who have founded black newspapers and black private schools. They've been educated at mission schools. Or some have been to English public schools. They put their faith in petitions and delegations. Steeped in Shakespeare and the Bible, they see themselves as Her Majesty's loyal subjects and as citizens of the wider world. It takes a lot to drive them to desperate measures, but the 1950s have seen their boldest and bravest strategies to date. The ANC's membership has increased hugely, thanks to the Defiance Campaign, and, right then, on the eve of the PAC breakaway, the organisation has decided on a nationwide anti-Pass Law campaign, which is planned for 31 March. So the newly formed PAC, in order to make an impact, jumps the gun and declares its own anti-Pass Law campaign for 21 March instead. That's the day that becomes the day of the Sharpeville shootings.

Robert Sobukwe is the new PAC leader. He isn't anti-white and he isn't short on brains but he has a passionate African dream. He believes the time is right for blacks to take bolder action. African states to the north have been winning their independence, and Harold Macmillan, the British Prime Minister, has just made his 'Winds of Change' speech to the all-white South African parliament. 'The Winds of Change,' he's announced dramatically, 'are blowing through the African continent.' The PAC has decided that South Africa can liberate itself by 1963 – that's if its black leaders will only grasp the nettle.

Robert Sobukwe is a tall, gentle, self-effacing man, but his speeches are fiery and effective. He's a lecturer in African Languages at the University of the Witwatersrand in Johannesburg. Wits is the most radical of South Africa's universities, just as Johannesburg is the boldest and most pacey of the cities. It's a city that's very unlike Durban. So that Dinah, on her only visit there to date, is surprised by the confident stride of its slim, stylish black women, because, in Durban, the black women she sees are nearly always domestic servants – plump, patient creatures in housemaid's overalls, their Afro hair hidden under a *doek*. That's unless they're up-country girls with mud hairstyles and bare breasts. Plus Durban's got the stupefying influence of its humidity. And then there's the lure of the beach. So Durban – white philistine Durban – is the place where repertory theatre has to cut short its runs and where the City Hall's classical music concerts have so far failed to thrive. Small sub-groups of record-collecting aficionados, like Dinah's dad, will gather in private living rooms to discuss the respective merits of Rosalyn Tureck and Glenn Gould, while Johannesburg, by contrast, is a hotbed of live performance. And there's a slogan Dinah's noticed, high up on the outside wall of the 'Whites only' Johannesburg Public Library: 'US BLACK FOLKS AIN'T READIN' YET', it says.

Sobukwe resigns his lectureship to lead the PAC's campaign. He sets out at dawn on 21 March, to begin the five-mile walk to his local police station, gathering groups of followers along the way. At the police station he's duly arrested and he's sentenced to three years in prison. But the state grants itself special powers to hold him for as long as it likes. It does so by inventing a special clause: the Robert Sobukwe Clause. So he's held for a decade in solitary confinement until his health has gone to pot.

Meanwhile, it's 21 March 1960 and black men all over the country have first destroyed their passes, then presented themselves for arrest. Mostly the crowds at police stations are dispersed by baton charges, but there's the odd fatal shooting. By the next day there's a State of Emergency along with fifteen thousand arrests. In Langa, on the Cape Flats, the police greet their new emergency

231

powers by barging into the single men's hostels and beating up the inmates. They enter the township houses and shoot at people, at random. And, in the morning, much provoked, thirty thousand black inhabitants are marching from Langa to the centre of Cape Town. They march in an orderly, peaceful way, twelve abreast, all along the wide expanse of de Waal Drive till they get to the main police station at Caledon Square. And, at their head, is a boy, a boy in shorts.

The boy is a young university student who has stepped into the leadership vacuum left by all the arrests and, though he looks more like a high-school boy, the crowd obeys him to a man. He negotiates with the police chief who tells him that passes will be suspended for a month while the law is reviewed. He's told that, if he disperses the crowd, a meeting will be arranged between him and the Minister of Justice. So the boy in shorts leads thirty thousand people back the way they came. Not a voice is raised in anger. Not a single stone is thrown. The Minister of Justice at this time is John Vorster. He's one of the dourest of the government's posse of wartime pro-Nazi saboteurs and when the boy presents himself for the appointed meeting, Mr Vorster is nowhere and the boy is thrown into prison. His name is Philip Kgosana.

So Jenny and Dinah start university under the shadow of the State of Emergency which lasts through most of their first year. Plus the army have occupied the campus, because it provides a perfect view of Cato Manor, the black township just below Dinah's house. Right then – from the vantage point of the library – Jenny and Dinah can see the men of Cato Manor surging out of the township and heading for Durban's main police station. Their aim is to demand the release of arrested leaders – and they're heading out in their thousands. Some are pouring up through Dinah's mum's unfenced garden where she's alone at home drinking coffee under her avocado tree. For a moment her heart is in her mouth at the sight of a hundred Zulu males who have armed themselves with stout sticks. But they greet her in a friendly manner, fists raised in the ANC salute, and Dinah's mum, who is shy about such gestures, gives them a girly little wave in return.

She doesn't know that, just beyond the valley, the police have gathered in armoured cars to block the protesters' routes. Nor that the police are being assisted by eager white male volunteers who have brought along their personal guns to shoot into the crowd. Even so, a thousand of the Cato Manor protesters manage to get through. And they make it all the way down West Street to the city's main police station. So sleepy Durban turns out to be the venue for the last mass black protest before the ANC and the PAC are banned.

The PAC barely manages to survive. The ANC finally changes its strategy to one of clandestine armed resistance. Its leaders are spirited away into exile, or they go underground within the country. Meanwhile, the poor old Pass Law protesters, who so confidently burnt their passes, are now standing in abject lines, waiting to be issued with new ones. And that is the year in which Cato Manor is re-zoned for whites.

So Dinah's four years at university coincide with a dramatic downturn in the texture of national life. It leaves her with ongoing feelings of moral discomfort and unease. Dinah is feeling out of tune, because the mass of the white student body is clearly hell-bent on having a good time. And it's only if you're a weirdo that you don't feel up for it. Dinah is always feeling that she's got no right to a good time. Because how can she claim any right to such a thing, when all around her most people have got no rights at all? And everything that's on offer for her is set up at their expense? Plus, right now, you can't get into the lecture halls for the Saracen armoured vehicles which are lining the university's main access. Soldier boys in heavy boots are tramping up the library stairs.

Yet Dinah loves the work. She especially loves discovering the early English poets, but not even the medieval literature man can remain immune from the soldier boys' presence – and, one day, after his Sir Gawain lecture, he's tried to take himself home, but he finds he can't. His car's been hemmed in by two armoured vehicles, so he taps on the window of the front-most contraption to ask if the driver will pull forward.

'Suddenly a creature leapt out at me,' he reports. The creature, he says, was carrying a gun with fixed bayonet. Plus he was wearing a steel helmet with wire netting on top. The netting, says the medieval literature man, was covered all over with camouflage foliage.

'YOU a SCHOOdent?' the creature asks him.

'N-no,' the medievalist quavers, 'I'm a member of staff.'

'DJOO KNOW ANYONE WHO WANTS A GOOD DANCE BAND?' the creature says to him.

The medieval literature man is now in possession of a phone number that's been scribbled on the back of a cigarette packet and he's rather proud of it. Dinah is fond of this anecdote, though she doesn't believe in the foliage. Nor in the wire netting. The Saracens, the guns and the bayonets – she's seen those for herself.

The events of March 1960 have had little impact on the white student body, which hasn't seemed to register that there's been a change in the style of racist repression. Plus Harold Macmillan's 'Winds of Change' speech has mainly seemed to have had the effect of causing comment on his teeth. White students are used to blacks having terrible teeth. And poor white Afrikaners, as well, are often missing some teeth. But a posh-voiced English Milord?! Those derelict, tobacco-brown teeth?!

'Jeez, man, have you checked out his teeth?' the students are saying to each other. 'Jeez, man, can you *credit* it? Teeth as bad as that?'

And nothing, not even the soldier boys, is interfering with the fun and games of the Freshers' Reception Committee.

On Jenny and Dinah's first day on campus, the order has come from the high command of the Freshers' Reception Committee. It's been posted up in the halls of residence and on several campus lamp-posts. All new first-year students – all Freshers and Freshettes – must assemble at three o'clock, sharp, in science lab B4. Afterwards, throughout the month of induction, all Freshers' Reception sessions will take place daily on the lawns alongside the ornamental fish ponds on King George V Avenue. All Freshers and Freshettes must be appropriately dressed. That is to say, they must all be got up like village idiots in giant green Easter Bunny bow ties for men and giant green propeller hair ribbons for women. Plus all Fresh Persons must at all times wear a cardboard disc one foot in diameter. This must be hanging round a person's neck and must state name, age, sex and subject.

Jenny and Dinah, having expended so much time on their pale-sand Voguey look, now find themselves on campus with little time and no materials with which to construct their Freshette discs. Dinah can't remember where the green ribbons came from. She can only think that they must have been issued, by some senior female commandant, in standard one-yard lengths. But grabbing such bits of cardboard as they can find stacked behind the hall-of-residence refuse bins, they proceed to Dinah's dad's maths department to locate a pair of compasses – which, as it turns out, not a single member of staff can boast among his possessions. Dinah's dad makes use of his shoelace and swings it for them, deftly, through three hundred and sixty degrees.

There are three girls by now, not two, because Jenny and Dinah have taken pity on a waif-like, lisping blonde. They've encountered her in Dinah's new hall of residence, in the throes of an asthma attack brought on by extreme anxiety in the face of the disc ordeal. Her name is Jacinta-May Fairweather and she's obviously not local. Her dad is an engineer on contract to a company in the Transvaal and she's spent something like eighteen months in Johannesburg's only progressive school. It's a school that proceeds along A.S. Neill lines and it's unique in offering its pupils access to a sexual guidance counsellor. Jacinta-May doesn't look as though she's had recourse to the services of a sexual guidance counsellor. Not yet. Her face is pure Mabel Lucie Atwell and her voice is Violet Elizabeth Bott. And, while Jenny and Dinah's cardboard discs have been contrived from two sides of a sturdy, twelve-pack soft-drinks carton, Jacinta-May has seen fit to dismantle the skimpy pink tissue box which her mum has bedded in her trunk. The tissue box is not only inadequate. It has all its bend lines in place, which means that, however much she flattens it out, it keeps on reverting to its former cuboid shape. The three of them gather round Dinah's dad's desk, taking turns with his propelling pencil until their discs are complete.

Dinah's disc is the most acceptable. Jenny's is all right except that her spacing's gone a bit eccentric, so that instead of having her full name, Jennifer Stern, on the top line and her sex on the line below, her disc has 'Jennifer' on the top line with her surname and sex alongside each other on the second line. Jacinta-May's is a hopeless non-starter, likely to fall to bits with the first puff of wind. The academic staff, as far as Dinah can see, are indifferent to these undergrad induction romps. That's except for the English professor, who earns her admiration for insisting, at the start of every lecture, that the bows and the discs come off. On the whole, the authorities seem content to let the seniors have their fun – now that the Freshers' Reception Committee is no longer actually drowning Fresh Persons in the campus fishponds. Or flushing people's heads down the lavs.

By the time the discs are finally hanging round the necks of the three girls, they are already five minutes late. Jenny and Dinah trip into the science lab, proceeding, as indicated, all the way to the front where the Committee is glaring at them, stony-faced. Jenny and Dinah are would-be sophisticates in their respectively beige and black sheath dresses with matching slingback shoes. Jacinta-May is in kiddies' sandals and a little sprigged frock with a shiny sash. They stand in a row before the eight-person Committee, Jenny smiling radiantly, showing her sweet pearly teeth. The Committee members are scrutinising their discs.

'This one's a stern female,' says one, a remark which is followed by male roars from the rest of the high command. Jenny laughs too, while still maintaining eye contact with the head honcho.

'Freshettes don't laugh,' says the head honcho grimly.

He is sitting dead centre. They are all ignoring Dinah, embarrassed by her evident connection with their own maths professor. They glare instead at Jacinta-May, who is still breathing with difficulty.

'Hey, Freshette, what's the matter with your disc?' demands the one at the centre of the Reception Committee.

'Well, you *theee*,' says Jacinta-May, wheezing and mincing at the same time, 'I wuth *obliged* to make my dithc out of my tithoo bokth. And *twy ath I may*, it will *perthitht* in returning to the shape of a tithoo bokth.'

The Committee is pretty well floored by this. They stare at her as if she's just descended from some alien planet. Then they look at each other in puzzlement.

'And if you keep on being *tho howwid* to me,' Jacinta-May is saying, 'then my athma will jutht keep getting wurth.'

The Committee clearly considers it judicious to order the trio to sit down. Two of the eight are women. There's the spinster and the tart. The first is a shrill and stick-like person with scratchy blonde straw for hair. The other is a dark-haired glossed-up creature with broad shoulders and fearsome boobs. Dinah considers the boobs a deformity, until she discovers, as time goes on, that these are perceived as a desirable extra in campus mating rituals. There's a myth abroad that busty girls are more ready to make themselves available and the female Committee Person in question has obviously bought into the myth. The rest of the panel, bar one, are white male engineering students, most of whom are wearing shorts. They're looking not unlike Mrs Keithley's *Die Huisgenoot* Springbok rugby team – only none of them has got a moustache. One of the Committee, and only one, is a final-year Jewish law student, which makes him seem like a traitor. The women both have the pathetic look of collaborators who've joined the high command in the hopes of finding favour with the half-dozen bully-boy alpha males. But, instead, right now, the alpha males are intent on eyeing up the new female intake. And, because of their front-row-position in science lab B4, Jenny and Dinah can pick up the undercurrent of *sotto voce* obscenity that the male Committee members are engaging in among themselves.

'Now *there's* a pig I'd like to stick,' says one, nodding his head towards row three. 'Jeez, but would I love to stick that pig?! I'd love to make it squeal.'

The Freshers' Reception Committee's daily follow-up sessions are referred to as Song Practice. Everything about them is repellent to a degree. Jenny, brave Jenny, turns up for just two sessions and from then on she gives them a miss. Dinah is more vulnerable for being resident on campus, so she goes along for the first week out of four. As far as she's aware, she and Jenny are the only drop-outs – that's except for beautiful Jed who looks too much of a wild man for anyone to stop him. To Dinah's amazement, the remaining Fresh Persons are giving every appearance of being eager to play along – and this, by now, includes Jacinta-May, who has quickly discovered that her lisping-moppet attributes are pleasing to the Committee's high command.

The Song Practice sessions are taken up with coercing the first-year students into memorising and belting out a range of rugger choruses which have been set to the tunes of popular songs. Some have been borrowed from America, so they make no local sense. There's 'Morphine Bill and Cocaine Sue', for example, who are 'walking down Fifth Avenue'. It has a chorus that counts as the soul of wit:

> Honey have a (sniff) have a (sniff) on me
> Honey have a (sniff) on me.

In place of the word sniff, the Fresh Persons all have to execute a vigorous, loud sniff. Some of the songs are obliquely racist, while others have racism as their *raison d'être*. There's the one, for example, that borrows the word muntu from white Southern Rhodesia and depicts black people as living in trees.

> Mamma Muntu
> And Baby Muntu too
> Climbed to the top
> Of the Big Bamboo.

Dinah can't remember the intervening stanzas. But she remembers the last line as an incitement to assassinate a local clergyman:

> Look, said Mamma Muntu
> Look who we've shot.
> We've shot the Reverend
> Michael Scott.

Michael Scott is a hate figure, because he's defended black squatters against eviction and has worked, together with Ruth First and others, to expose excessive punishment beatings among white farmers using prison labour. At this moment he's in the news again, as one of a delegation to the UN, to plead against South Africa's being granted rights to incorporate the mandated South West Africa into the apartheid state. The South African Government has effectively done so already, having, just a few months earlier, shot eleven people dead whilst imposing one of its illegal township 'forced removal' schemes.

Dinah's most un-favourite song has a repeating refrain that goes 'Roll your leg over'. Whenever this song comes round, the Freshers' Reception Committee will always pluck out a mixed pair of Fresh Persons, who are then required to come out front and mime the sex act whilst lying on the grass, one on top of the other. Dinah has noticed that the Committee members will almost always make a point of picking on the most weedy-looking and flat-chested among the girl students – the ones with the skinniest legs, or the most unworldly look. And they'll choose the most owlish and gormless of the young men – the ones with bad acne, or the ones that look as if they might have been brought up by the Plymouth Brethren. It's only when they run out of substandard specimens that they start picking on people like Jed.

In between the horrible songs, the Committee makes offensive personal remarks and propagandises for an event which is being promoted as the grand finale of the Freshers' induction. This event is called Freshers' Dinner. All Fresh Persons are to attend the dinner, which will take place in a B-rated north-coast hotel. It's in the nature of a dinner dance, so there's a promise it will get quite smoochy as the night wears on. None of the girls can go to Freshers' Dinner without being invited as someone's partner – and it's the male Fresh Persons who are being coerced into inviting the girls. That's after the male Committee members have had first pick themselves. It's at this point that Dinah decides to drop out of the Song Practice sessions, for all she knows that, at some point soon, she's going to be taking the rap. She drops out the moment she hears the head honcho utter a line that strikes like déjà vu.

'Stand up all those Freshettes,' he says, 'who haven't yet been asked to Freshers' Dinner.'

The whole increasingly ghoulish ritual is bizarrely reminiscent of the Union Jack fiasco at Berea Road Government School for Girls. Plus Dinah just knows that none of the Fresh Persons is ever going to ask her to Freshers' Dinner. And neither, thank the Lord, are any of the bully boys on the Committee. It's already perfectly clear to her that she's a freak in weirdo stockings with weirdo silver hair; a freak who thinks she's above it all; a freak who doesn't know how to simper; a freak who always walks, ramrod straight, eyes to the floor, in weirdo, snooty-girl clothes. Plus she's a freak whose dad is head of maths, so any messing with her undergarments is probably no-go. So Dinah knows that the weirdo silver-haired offspring of Prof du Bondt is not going to be snapped up with alacrity as a favoured dinner companion. And she's damned if she's going to be one of that ever-dwindling band of girls – the girls with pebble specs and overactive grease glands, the girls with callipers and funny teeth – who is going to get made to stand up, day after day, until she's forced into the arms of some reluctant male Fresh Person with unpleasant body odour.

So now, when she isn't in lectures, or hazardously crossing the campus trying to avoid the Freshers' Reception Committee, she's hiding in her tiny room, filling up on cream crackers and not daring to eat in the dining hall. She's running the gauntlet between the residence and the lecture halls, trying not to get intercepted, because the whole purpose of the bows and the discs is to announce one's status as a first-year female student and, as such, one is required to make oneself available to the entire male student body. That's the Committee's much emphasised rule. Any senior male student can bawl 'Freshette, come here!' and the rule is that you've got to stop and present yourself for inspection.

'These two will do,' says a male senior to his companion one day. He and his friend have intercepted Dinah and Jenny. And they've contrived to block the path.

'OK. We think you'll do,' he says.

Jenny's response is to look suitably withering. 'Well, sorry, guys,' she says. 'But we don't. We don't think you'll do at all.'

She grabs Dinah's arm and they skirt deftly around the two senior males. They're on their way home to Jenny's house for lunch. Jenny has just gone on two exciting dates with a handsome Rhodes Scholar architect who has recently returned from England where he's been dating the Deb-of-the-Year, as featured in *Country Life*. Both factors – the Rhodes Scholarship and the Deb-of-the-Year connection – are considered high achievements for a Jewish colonial boy.

'Jen,' Dinah is hissing urgently. 'Hey, Jen. Did you notice that one of those guys has got a *withered arm?*'

'Oh crumbs,' Jenny says. 'Oh blast. Oh well. So what? *C'est la vie.*'

Then they both start to giggle. They giggle about it all the way home to Jenny's maisonette where Pansy Kaufmann is on the patio, wearing two cucumber slices, one over each eye.

Jenny, who has a way with grown-ups, has already been getting invitations to parties by younger members of staff. The major conduit for these engagements is a glamorous older undergrad who buys her clothes in Paris and drives a silver Carmen Gia. She's currently married to a man of means to whom she refers as 'my Jewish draper', but she's showing all the signs of being about to trade him in. And it's at the salon of the glamorous older undergrad that Jenny has managed to get introduced to the Rhodes Scholar architect. Jenny, because she's still living at home, doesn't have to worry about being waylaid at the entrance to the women's hall of residence, where the all-female House Committee is, if anything, more besotted by rules than the Girls' High School prefects.

'Freshette, your bow's not right,' some senior female person will pronounce, looming the while over Dinah's carefully flattened bow – flattened to make it look as much as possible like one of Mrs Horlicks's smart little head-hugging hats – and she'll plump it into an idiotic parody of a small girl's party ribbon, or until it looks like an aircraft propeller, about to go off into spin. So, once inside, Dinah lurks in her room, working hard on her Chaucer essays, until Maddie Holmes, or Lindsay Greig, or – just occasionally – Lavinia Steadman, will come and knock on her door.

All of them are older than Dinah but, between them, they make up the sum total of the people in the hall of residence to whom she can relate. Maddie, who is still collecting first-year credits, has been in the place three years. She's one of the uni's repeats. Maddie makes no pretence of intellect and she raps her knuckles against her skull to suggest that the contents are made of wood. University is her finishing school. It's been a chance for her to meet boys and have fun, because Maddie is all extrovert. Maddie's got quite a brassy look without her having to contrive it, since her entirely natural yellow hair comes the colour of bottle blonde. Plus it's even got natural split ends. She's got a big untidy mouth and she walks, unselfconsciously, with a slightly knock-kneed gait. This, together with her hint of hollow thighs, has given Maddie a sexy, fucked-out look which, oddly enough, she manages to combine with the manner of the girl-next-door. Maddie is always kind and motherly. And it's Dinah's impression that she's probably the most sought-after girl on campus – all of which means nothing to Maddie, now that she's fixed on boring Bernie – her steady, her husband-to-be, the man for whom she's currently wearing her twinkly engagement ring.

Maddie clacks about the campus on backless stack-heel shoes. She's got a slim, trim, fabulous body and she always looks unfussed. She has easy-to-wear, pull-on stretch jersey dresses and broad elastic belts. There's no artifice in her appearance because she's too comfortable in her own skin – and Dinah can't help liking her for being the opposite of herself. Plus Maddie never behaves like one of the prefects and she couldn't give a bugger about Dinah's green bow and disc. So it's not long before Dinah's helping Maddie to put together her essays. And Maddie is offering Dinah all her worldly wisdom about condoms and oral sex and How Far a Girl Should Go.

Maddie's noticed that there's a senior male student who's begun to eye up Dinah – and she thinks that he'd be a disaster. He's been sitting on the wall across the road from the hall of residence and he's been calling out, 'Freshette, come here.' So far Dinah's been doing what she always does. She's walked straight past without stopping. But she's begun to notice that he speaks with a guttural 'r'. Plus he speaks as if he were doing the offensive routine just slightly tongue-in-cheek. Like her, he's pale as curd cheese. He has nice Slavic cheekbones that make him look like a boy in a Pasternak painting and his eyes are a startling ice-blue.

'Oh God. I wish it wasn't *him*,' Maddie says. 'You'll have to watch your step with him.' But then all she'll say is, 'He's foreign. He's a smoothie. Well, you know what Continentals can be like. Anyway, he's much too old for you. He's twenty-five, you know.'

'So what's his name?' Dinah says.

'Dieter,' Maddie says. 'But everyone calls him Didi.'

'Well, they can't do that,' Dinah says. 'Because Didi is what people call me.'

'Tough,' Maddie says. 'Because that's his name. Didi von Schweiten.'

'Von Schweiten?' Dinah says.

It's a name that rings a bell because she's recently read it on the sleeve notes of one of her dad's new records. Baron von Schweiten, patron of several German baroque musicians, including Carl Ditters von Dittersdorf, subject of the record sleeve in question.

Lavinia Steadman is a graduate student in social anthropology. She's a beautiful olive-skinned brunette who is fascinating to Dinah, because she spends all her daylight hours indoors in the hall of residence wearing a dressing gown and slippers and with her hair twiddled up in enormous rollers. Then, at nightfall, she puts on her Chinesy-looking sheath dress and her gold backless high-heels. She takes out the rollers and paints her half-inch-long eyelashes. Then, with her hair all ravishingly bouffant, she goes out with a young heart-throb maths tutor in Dinah's dad's department.

Because she doesn't have lectures any more, it's possible for Lavinia to stay in the rollers all day. Lavinia's a big favourite with the anthropology professor, the same wiry female in laced shoes and ankle socks whose lav paper Lisa and Dinah once tore askew in childhood. The anthropologist has done early pioneering work among the Venda peoples and is known on campus as the Rain Queen in recognition of this work.

Dinah's third and favourite residence-girl companion is an orphaned wild girl who gives the impression of having brought herself up. She's a final-year social-work student and she's definitely not one of the prefects. Lindsay Greig is fairly manic. She lives on Multivites and on Super Plenamin tablets. Plus she chews on caffeine pills, so that she can stay awake all night. Lindsay is right then relishing her sojourn in the women's hall of residence, because its intake is offering satirical possibilities which she finds hard to resist. The residence – Dinah's residence – is brand new. It's a supplement to the older one and it's been built on a prediction of increasing student numbers. Right now, however, it's only half full with undergraduate girls, so the authorities have decided to offer the extra bedrooms to a group of up-country Afrikaner girls who are students at Durban's newly established Afrikaans-language teacher-training college. And – given that this is the year of Dr Verwoerd's Republican Referendum – the resulting English–Afrikaner mix is predictably explosive.

Dr Verwoerd, under the shadow of Sharpeville, has just been howled down in London at the recent Commonwealth Conference. This has been the response to his wish to have South Africa remain within the Commonwealth once it's declared itself a republic. He's failed in this and been booted out – yet he comes back declaring 'victory not defeat'. He says that we're celebrating our freedom and he refers to our 'new dawn'. This in the year when the State of Emergency has swept like the Black Death through the home of anyone – black, white, Coloured or Indian – who is, or ever was, a little bit active in protest politics. The sun, Dr Verwoerd has announced, is 'breaking through the morning mist'. This is because the Boer Republic is about to come again.

So naturally, the little Afrikaner Nationalist girlies are busily pinning up their patriotic posters for the coming republican referendum, because, in the referendum, all white eighteen-year-olds will be able to cast their vote. The posters carry the 'new dawn' imagery and they're done in the style of Soviet Realism. Or, more accurately, it's Prairie Realism. They depict a Boer on horseback, beard and leather breeks in place, and complete with his fetching General de Wet hat which he's waving in the air like Andrew Jackson. The Boer is riding triumphantly into a large art deco sunrise.

'*Opsaal*!' says the poster. '*Die Republiek Kom*!'

'Saddle up!' it's telling the voters. 'The Republic is Coming!'

Lindsay likes to wind up the girlies by pasting over these posters a home-made version of her own. She dashes these off at lightning speed and they all show a fat-arsed and very small Boer, drawn cartoon-wise from behind and seated on a clapped-out donkey. He's trotting, a-hobbledy-hoy, into what looks like a kindergarten sun face with a grumpy down-turned mouth and straggly spider's-leg rays. '*Opsaal*!' says her caption. '*Die Republiek Kom*!' Her caption is emanating, in a saucy, scalloped speech bubble, from the region of the donkey's rump. Lindsay's posters are constantly to be found, ripped, crumpled and dashed to the ground. But she just keeps on pinning up more.

Lindsay isn't perceived by the campus males as girlfriend material, but she's one of a tiny handful of girls who is rumoured to have slept with blacks. On one occasion she enters Dinah's room with the news that she's just been all round the residence, interviewing the Verwoerd contingent with the help of a bogus questionnaire. She's told the leader's loyalists that the questionnaire is to do with her social-work finals and that it's essential for her degree work. As a result, she's got the girlies to describe to her their first sexual experience. Lindsay's delighted because one of her poster girls – an upcountry innocent with two flaxen pigtails and tiny pimples for breasts – has offered her a whispered confession to write down anonymously in her files.

'One day,' the girl has told her, 'I put two oranges down my blouse to make myself false bosoms.'

Dinah is just a bit squeamish about this, but Lindsay is rolling about with laughter on her floor and Lindsay's laughter is always infectious. She's the life and soul of any female gaggle, but she terrifies all the campus men. Lindsay has a raucous laugh and one of those two-fingered whistles that can carry for miles across valleys.

As to the campus at large for Dinah – well, it's easy enough to make friends, in a way, because there isn't really much choice. What happens is that she's drawn together with four aberrant first-year males – drawn into a satisfying closeness because of the uncongenial racist context which creates their togetherness. So Dinah's new friends are four weirdo men. Weirdo by campus standards. Jed Matthews is a hunk, over six foot six, a sort of beatnik before his time. That's in South Africa, anyway. He's sufficiently dark of skin colour to have the average white-girl student taking suspicious peeks at his fingernails in search of absent half-moons. But Jed has beautiful, 'u'-shaped fingernails with all his half-moons in place. He's got glinty green eyes and a craggy, villainous look, like the bad guy in a Western movie. Plus he's got two enchantingly ziggy-zaggy chipped upper incisors.

Jed exists in opposition to the Sta-Prest Jehovah's Witness look and he doesn't seem to own a shirt. Oblivious to the sweltering heat, he wears woollen jumpers next to his skin; and corduroy trousers; and sneakers without socks. Dinah has never seen him in shorts. His dress is often missing accessories, such as buttons and functioning zips. Sometimes he ties a crumpled red snuff hand-kerchief around his throat and he always smokes his own roll-ups. Jed has dimples like slashes when he smiles and these, along with his pointed teeth, his corduroys, his roll-ups – Jed and everything about him – causes Dinah to go weak at the knees.

It's taken a while to get to know Jed, because he's early on walked out of the Song Practice sessions and, after that, he's gone to ground. His whereabouts are a mystery, though he pops up in the odd lecture. Jed walks out when he's called upon to mime the sex act during 'Roll your leg over' with one of the first-year girls. He gets up and lopes to the front, just as if he's going to oblige. Then he says, 'Go to hell, you stupid bastards,' and, turning his face towards the glinting bay, he strides out towards Pigeon Valley. The Committee doesn't even try to stop him. He looks too strange and intimidating, too hard for them to fathom. So instead they practise damage-limitation and try to shrug him off.

'Listen, it's *his* loss,' they say. 'It's *his* tough, hey? If he's got no community spirit – well, that's *his* tough.'

Later on Jed tells Dinah that he's spent the week sleeping on a beach. Mostly Jed lives in a garage and he looks after himself. He comes from a British Home Counties family that's gone native in various Outposts of Empire. His dad's gone native in the Caribbean; his mum's gone off to find herself.

'But he looks just like a native boy!' Maddie says, when Dinah confesses her crush. 'Ugh! I couldn't *kiss* him. You couldn't seriously kiss him, could you?'

Jed Matthews is majoring in English, so he and Dinah are soon sitting together in most of the lectures and tutorials. The first-year English class is pretty big, so they're broken up into lots of smaller tutor groups. But, just at first, by way of introduction, the class as a whole is set an essay. Dinah and Jed get first and second top marks. They're one per cent apart.

'God, but you're such a fool!' Jenny says. 'You'll never get him if you beat him at essays!'

But Jed is already not hers, she can tell. He's been revealing a discouraging tendency to go for fragrant women; twin-set-and-pearls girls from private schools who look and behave like debutantes. They all try him briefly, as a sort of dare, before turning him down for something a whole lot safer. So Jed is her head-friend, her soulmate, her buddy – a kind of giggling companion for whom she struggles to suppress desire.

Her other men friends are Ben and Simon. And then there's Francis Cull. Ben is a precocious maths-bod with a lisp and black frizzy hair. The hair is a little bit Ouma Smuts – but then Ben says that Ouma's related. Ben is a seriously good violinist who looks like a nine-stone weakling. But in fact he's the only person Dinah knows who can lift a good-size prone tree trunk without any help from his friends. Simon is a tiny Catholic male with some sort of growth hormone problem. He's a lovely, gossipy, brainy chap who's funny as hell about the rugger-bugger engineers who've bullied him through Freshers' induction. Simon, oddly, is poised enough to 'Roll his leg over' for anyone without causing humiliation, either to himself or to his allotted partner. That's as a mime act, anyway. In real life Simon is committed to abstinence and has planned his future as a Benedictine monk in an abbey he's liaising with in Devon. Simon is always funny about the sillier flirtier girls who tart up in the Ladies before the Samuel Johnson lectures – because the classes are being given by a pretty blue-eyed young man. And the young man's tastes, Simon says, most certainly do not run to girls.

Simon always notices every garment that Dinah wears and everything she does to her hair. Simon is the one man who always knows exactly what's in the latest issue of *Vogue*.

Francis Cull is thirty-five and a Church of England priest. He's doing an arts degree along with his job and he's out of tune with the complacent body of the white church. He ministers to a congregation of impoverished Natal Indian Christians in Meerbank, which is damp and mosquito-ridden, so lots of his parishioners have chronic lung disease. He's been a priest in the East End of London and he's full of righteous fury about the obscenities of the local scene. They hang out together – Dinah and her friends – in the flash new students' union building, where, in the canteen, they can dip their chips into a range of condiments that are always on offer for free. And because Dinah still likes mayonnaise best, she always chooses that.

And then it's Rag Week. On the wide, pristine steps of the new students' union building, one of the students, in the night, has spray-painted a message. Dinah blinks at the bold red letters as she proceeds down the steps with Jed. 'KEEP KAFFIRS OUT OF OUR RAG.' Dinah's quite surprised by this, because she hasn't considered that there'd be any black students clamouring to take part in Rag Week. Dr Verwoerd wants all black students off campus by 1961 and – since Durban has the part-time degree students hived off in a place called City Buildings which sits in town near the central bus station – most black undergraduates have never been a presence on campus. But Jed tells Dinah that he's been to a meeting where one of their first-year English classmates, among others, has felt very strongly about keeping the Rag Week white.

'Why should we give *them* our Rag on a plate?' Jed is cruelly mimicking. 'Why can't *they* have their own Rag?'

' "They", "them",' Jed says. 'And I expect you've noticed who the authorities have hauled in to scrub the bloody thing off?'

'A kaffir,' Dinah says. 'Who else?'

She's referring to the crouching black skivvy in house-boy get-up who is right then on his hands and knees, going at the graffiti with scouring powder.

It's Dinah's impression that Rag Week is running on seamlessly from Freshers' induction and that it's the same quorum of white racist males who are in charge of both events. Rag is offering a preliminary night of drunken float-building and rah-rah student bonding which includes an all-night, all-white sexual orgy, strongly intimated to take place underneath the hired lorries. Then, next morning, there's the election of one pretty, hung-over Rag Queen and two pretty, hung-over Rag Princesses. There's also the sale of a Rag magazine so mind-boggling in the mediocrity of its smut that Dinah's amazed the Rag Committee doesn't fall on its own sword. Trouble with Rag Week is, although it's for charity, it's been so rigorously highjacked by racist philistines that anyone halfway literate, anyone who could rustle up a decent Rag Mag, wouldn't want to touch it with a barge pole.

· And then, once Rag Week is over, Dinah loses Jenny. Jenny who has just been dumped by the Rhodes Scholar architect. He has brought out from England his peaches-and-cream fiancée: his Oxford fellow student, his Cotswold sweetie-pie in her little green ballet pumps. She's a class act with whom Jenny – being Jenny – right away makes Best Friends. And it's because Jenny is feeling a bit low that Dinah and Jed take her along with them when they go to visit Peter Mainz. Dinah and Jed have discovered that they've got Peter in common. Jed has been friends at school with Peter, the pampered singleton of Dinah's mum's friend Frau Liesl Mainz, with the unreformed, lopsided face, the civic-minded matron who once entertained the Tyrolean yodellers in the Maypole Tearoom by the Cenotaph where the Special Branch now hang out. Jed and Peter have written plays together in the sixth form of Durban Boys' High School. The plays are written in the shadow of Samuel Beckett and require a modest cast of two – that's always Jed and Peter. They also require some predictably modest props, like stepladders and empty dustbins. Dinah finds out about the schoolboy connection because Jed, for purposes of satire and self-mockery, pulls out of his pocket one morning a copy of the Boys' High School magazine.

'But I know that boy,' Dinah says.

So Dinah and Jed, along with Jenny, set out to visit Peter. It's one weekend when he's home from his art school in Pietermaritz-burg. Dinah observes that Jed has a curious relationship with Peter. It's a relationship of genuine friendship crossed with the kind of disdain that a person who shifts for himself in a garage will have for a person who revels in the role of mother's darling. So Jed is piss-taking over the fondue that Frau Liesl Mainz has placed before them – the four Nice Young People, all twirling their bread in a copper pot of oozy cheese. But, more than Jed, Dinah can't help noticing that something is happening to Jenny. Because Jenny has taken one look at pampered Peter and the glance has changed her life. Jenny has given away her heart and this time it's for ever. And Peter is obviously charmed by her and fancies himself in love. Frau Liesl is right away over the moon, because Jenny is her idea of dreamgirl. Jenny will be the daughter-in-law; the *liebling* female companion; the comfort of her old age. So it's happily ever after as far as everyone's concerned.

By the next day Jenny has made up her mind, because Jenny is always decisive. She'll abandon her degree in modern languages. She'll give up on the volumes of Montaigne that she's been carrying about in her summer basket, up and down the steps of the library tower. And, there and then, without Matric art, she'll talk her way into the fine art BA in Pietermaritzburg. Plus she'll talk her way into the women's hall of residence alongside the male equivalent in which Peter Mainz lays his sacred head.

But Peter, within the month of Jenny's arrival, has fallen for somebody else. A chunky, dark Afrikaner girl from a farming family way up north. Solid as a figure by Juan Botero, Sandra is a country girl. She has raven hair and thick unplucked black eyebrows and thick unshaven underarm hair. Sandra has the broadest feet that Dinah's ever seen. She's a cute soap-and-water girl. So Liesl Mainz goes into mourning and cries over Dinah's mum. And Jenny does what Jenny does. She becomes Peter's girlfriend's Best Friend. Jenny is now a student of fine art, fifty miles away. And – being Jenny – she's soon being courted by one of the academic staff, a young physicist who, Dinah thinks, has much more going for him in looks, charm and courtesy than pampered Peter Mainz. But then, it isn't Dinah's life.

And, decades later, while staring out of her window on to her street off the Boulevard St Germain, Jenny – pretty, immaculate Jenny, middle-aged, childless, depilated Jenny, as always, trimly in-shape Jenny – sighs and says to her one-time schoolfriend, 'Oh Didi, if only Peter had *loved* me, my life would have been different. It would have been better.'

It's on the last day of Freshers' Induction that the head honcho of the Freshers' Reception Committee finally catches up with Dinah.

He's standing there, on his tree-trunk legs, filling the path to the women's hall of residence like Apollyon on the Bridge.

'Hey, Freshette,' he says. 'We've noticed that you haven't been coming to Song Practice.'

Dinah is stopped in her tracks. She's hoping to God that she hasn't got those instant giveaway red blotches that, in stressful circumstances, will jump forcefully into evidence all over her neck, blotches to indicate terror. There are two of the Committee standing before her, but one of them is doing all the talking. The second is the square-shouldered female person, the harridan with outsize boobs. The boobs are a disconcerting in-your-face presence, because Dinah can see that they are rising and falling with the harridan's emphatic breathing. She's evidently in a state of elation through the pleasure she's being afforded by this eleventh-hour fair cop. The show is, after all, nearly ended and the *grande finale* of Freshers' Dinner is due to take place that night.

'We'd like to know why,' the head honcho says. 'Why haven't you been showing up?'

Dinah finds that her mouth has gone dry. She longs right then to have Jenny beside her to blurt out something cocky, something to break the ice. Because it's boring, Jenny would say. Because we've got better things to do.

'I'm speaking to you,' he says.

'I –' Dinah says.

'And I suppose you think you can just *waltz* along to Freshers' Dinner?' he says, saving her the need to make reply.

'I –' Dinah says.

'Because if you *don't* come to Song Practice –' he says. His volume is increasing and he's turning puce with indignation. 'If you *don't* come to Song Practice – *If you don't come to Song Practice* – then you – you *CAN'T COME TO FRESHERS' DINNER!*'

Dinah is staring at him in astonishment. Because it's just beginning to dawn on her that he has no ultimate sanction. Absolutely no power at all. Except to ban her from Freshers' Dinner. And she doesn't want to go. The realisation leaves her so elated that she almost laughs out loud. She's suddenly feeling great.

'Well, frankly, so what?' she says.

'I told you she'd be like this,' says the harridan, getting in her sixpence worth. She's edgily tapping the painted red claws of her right hand against the painted red claws of her left. It's making a sound like a thrush cracking a snail against rockery stones. 'And who's your partner for Freshers' Dinner, Freshette?' she says. The technique is never to use a Fresh Person's name. It's always Fresher and Freshette.

Dinah doesn't answer. Instead, slowly and deliberately, she slides the bow out of her hair. Then, equally slowly, she pulls the disc off over her head. The disc, the badge of ignominy. Dinah du Bondt. Female. Eighteen Years. BA English.

Then, just as she's about to hand the items to the harridan, there's somebody standing beside her and he's putting his arm around her waist.

'It's all right, Vee,' he says soothingly to the harridan. 'Just back off a bit, OK?' It's the Continental smoothie. The man with the ice-blue eyes. 'She's coming to Freshers' Dinner with me,' he says.

'No I'm not,' Dinah says.

'Yes you are,' he says. Then he turns back to the pair on the path, talks to them, man-to-man. 'It's OK. It's all sorted out,' he says. 'Can't you see she's just very shy?'

Shy! Just shy! Can't you see she's *just very shy*! Right in the moment of her first great triumph. And now he's gone and snatched it from her.

'Well, I'm not going, as it happens,' she says. 'I'm not going to Freshers' Dinner.'

'Just listen to her,' the harridan says, heaving a martyred sigh. 'Honestly! Just like Lady Muck on toast. I told you she'd be like this.'

'Like what?' Dinah says, but now that the Continental smoothie's made his appearance, neither of the Committee Persons is paying her any attention.

'So how about the Sixty-Seven?' says the Continental smoothie. 'Will you come and have dinner with me in the Sixty-Seven instead?'

'Didi!' says the harridan, because the Sixty-Seven is Durban's only seriously classy restaurant.

That's except for the restaurants within the Edward Hotel. Durban, for all its ever-increasing Indian population, has not got a single Indian restaurant. That's because the Group Areas Act will always get in the way. Dinah has never been to the Sixty-

Seven and neither have her parents. Jenny's been there – just the once – with the Rhodes Scholar architect.

'Oh all right then,' she says.

'*Didi* – !' says the harridan once again, but then she can't proceed, because the Continental smoothie has undone her very simply, by mouthing her a kiss.

To Dinah's absolute and infinite joy, she sees the harridan blush. The only trouble is that the harridan has seen her seeing the blush and it brings out her scorpion sting.

'I'll be watching out for you, Freshette,' she says. 'No question about that. I'll be watching for you.'

The head honcho, thanks to Didi's intervention, has simply relaxed and given up.

'I'll sight you then, Didi,' he says. 'Come on, Vee.' Then he begins to walk away.

'Yep,' says the Continental smoothie. 'I'll see you guys around.'

Didi von Schweiten, second-year student of business administration, can't understand why Dinah's so menaced by the people on the Freshers' Reception Committee, because, really, it's just a bit of fun and it helps get students together. He's not allergic to what the Committee stands for, because, unlike Dinah, he's not a deviant. He's a conservative, a status quo man. They're all good blokes, he says. Or sometimes he'll call them the boys. Even the harridan's a good sort. Didi isn't quite one of the good blokes. He's a little bit set apart. He thinks of them as the children. But he's happy enough, occasionally, to hang out with the children, when there's nothing better to do. And at such times they'll defer to him in matters such as wine and menus. Didi isn't exactly *cordon bleu*, but for the good blokes, he's Escoffier. He can distinguish Merlot from red anti-freeze. Plus he knows that tinned pears can be made to taste better if you boil up the sugar syrup with arrowroot, brandy and cloves. On the race thing as well he's not quite Dinah's cup of tea, though he's not exactly in the same box as the good blokes. Didi has a kind of racial arrogance that's different from the local brand. But it's racial arrogance for all that. It's about Old World European hierarchies, rather than local ethnic phobias, but, in effect, it comes to the same. So for Didi, blacks are jazz musicians, or else they clean your shoes. Or they toil invisibly in factories. Or they live in hovels on the land, increasing the national product. That's the way the world is. That's the way it's meant to be.

Dinah's ashamed to admit to herself that his name holds glamour for her. This is because of Baron von Schweiten's aforementioned musical associations. She's shy to bring this up with Didi, but when she does he's surprisingly dismissive. He's more interested in horses than in symphonies and he considers that musical genius confers no particular social distinction.

'Yes, I have an idea there's a Haydn connection,' he says. 'And Carl Ditters, you say? I think they were probably both family servants at some point.'

Dinah is blinking at him in disbelief. 'But I'm talking about famous composers,' Dinah says. 'People who write symphonies. Composers aren't anyone's servants.'

'If you're attached to a household,' Didi says, 'that makes you one of the servants. Anyway, so what? I'm bored with this conversation.'

Didi is often bored with Dinah's conversation. Or that is what he says to her. Plus he doesn't like it if she laughs when she talks. He wants her to stop doing it. The idea is that he's grooming her, because he thinks she's worth the effort. Back home on the estate, before the war, he tells her, his father used to call all the male servants Hans and all the female servants Maria. It was a lot easier for Didi's father than learning the servants' real names. Didi is amused by this. He tells it to Dinah by way of an affectionate anecdote. It's an anecdote that's intended to cast his father in a good light. And that's because he's intending to take her home to meet his parents.

The family has relocated from Austria and has evidently known grander days. His father, once a career army officer, now manages an up-market furniture factory. His mother is the niece of the Archbishop of Heidelberg. Didi has come to university late, having spent time learning English and getting himself a Matric. Plus he's had a try-out working in an office. Now he's doing economics and accountancy with the intention of making his fortune, as befits the oldest son. Or, at any rate, he's intending to be a man of power and influence. He wants a nice life for himself. He wants to be a mover and shaker. That's in the world of business and commerce.

He's not interested in all the academic stuff. *Kultur und Klavier* are things he leaves to the girls, so for this reason he's pleased that Dinah's on the arty side. He's always liked arty women. Didi will do the bare minimum to scrape through his course assignments and he'll not ever be bothered by his resulting scrape-through grades. Dinah goes on being besotted with her subject and – especially after the mind-rotting boredom of Miss Legge and her rote-learned history notes – she's now set on fire by almost everything on her English literature course. She can't get enough of the lectures and the books, so it's back to the A1 ice-cream row. And, although she's always getting better grades than Didi, this doesn't give him a moment's grief. He's never bothered by her performance, never threatened by it.

'Women are born to be diligent,' he says. 'Good work, there, my baby.'

Didi always calls her my baby and he likes it that she can sew. He says that his mother will teach her to cook, because his mother is a marvel with food. His grades never have the effect of leaving Didi feeling diminished – not even before his tutors, because his tutors are like Josef Haydn. They are there to provide a service. So Dinah will hover and watch, incredulous, as he retrieves his slipshod essays from his tutors with whom he'll linger and chat. Man-to-man. Just a little bit *noblesse oblige*. His ego is in no way involved with academic prowess.

Didi doesn't read very much except for *The Kinsey Report*. It entertains him to know in detail exactly who's doing what to whom. Especially with regard to erogenous zones, especially in the backs of cars. Didi is ego-involved in sexual performance and – mercifully for Dinah for whom the area is panic stations – he's very relaxed and very practised. That's at feely-touchy stuff.

Even so, Dinah has bought the idea – pronounced forcefully from the rostrum in her sixth-form year by a popular and motherly biology teacher – that girls just have to be virgins until the day they get married. Break this rule and you'll find yourself the girl that nobody wants. Soiled goods. Second-hand merchandise. Left on the shelf. Oh the shame and horror of it. No decent man will ever want you.

'I'll give you this, and it's straight from the shoulder,' the biology teacher says. 'When a man is looking for a wife, he's always looking for a virgin.'

Dinah knows that Maud does sex, but then Maud is on another plane. Maud is Danger Girl. She has the right to make up the rules for herself. And then there's Maddie who's having sex all the time with boring Bernie – but she's going to marry him and she's got that fat engagement ring to prove it. Plus it's Maddie herself who's most anxious to protect Dinah from the Continental smoothie. She has higher standards for Dinah than she's ever had for herself.

'You're too good for him,' Maddie says. 'You're special. Don't, Dinah. You don't want to be like me.'

It's a stupid, time-warped maidenly stand about which Didi is remarkably good-humoured – mainly because he's so confident that she'll succumb to him in the end.

'Of course you'll sleep with me,' he says. 'My girlfriends have always slept with me.'

Dinah is at this stage unaware that Didi has other outlets. He's popular with the nurses in the residence at Addington Hospital and there's one pretty paediatric nurse in particular who's always been more than happy to offer him favours in return for the odd night out. But Dinah doesn't know about this until some two years later. That's when Catherine Cleary has returned to the local scene. She's got a nursing job in town and she soon sees fit to fill Dinah in from her fund of local nurses' gossip.

'Well, I think it's *disgraceful*,' Catherine says. 'I think you ought to know.'

But by then Dinah's first love affair is, at last, about to hit the rocks. It was never right for her from the start, but she's been too insecure to extract herself. So all through the rest of her degree course it has had the effect of separating her from friends. She no longer hangs out, after the lectures, with Jed and Simon and Ben. Nor with Father Francis Cull – or rather, she does so only rarely. That's when Didi's away on hunting trips, or he's off doing boy stuff on horseback in the company of his younger brother. Because a woman must forsake her tribe and cleave to the tribe of her man. And Didi is taking her seriously as the girl he's going to marry.

This hopelessly impractical project is the result of Didi's fatal flaw. Because he does seem to have a fatal flaw when it comes to choosing women. That's the women he's serious about, the ones he plans to marry. He always goes for off-beat girls, arty girls, highbrow girls. Girls with left-wing politics and unconventional habits.

Then he works at moulding them, but at some point the girls grow up. Dinah isn't aware of this, though she does know about his first serious flame who, once, in the Sixty-Seven restaurant, flatly refused to order anything except for beans on toast. Didi himself has told her about this. He tells it as though the girlfriend has committed a crime against humanity. And later – much later – Dinah gets the chance to hear about the episode from the first flame herself. Because later – much *much* later – Dinah gets to meet all Didi's girls.

They've all cut their teeth on him and then moved on. All of them, of course, are living abroad – in Toronto, Edinburgh and Oxford; in London, Cambridge and Adelaide – all of them part of the 1960s diaspora, part of the anti-apartheid brain drain. They discover each other at conferences and fund-raising concerts and literature festivals. And then they cackle together. Didi's highbrow harpies. That line of deviant female poets and forceful medics and vegetarian sociologists, of development economists and sculptors and Jungian psychoanalysts.

Didi's women, for some bizarre reason, have all gone on to marry Jews. Left-wing intellectual Jews, deracinated socialists who've got no time for Zion. An ageing band of Danny Cohens, Zacky Benjamins, Harry Shapiros, Sidney Steinbergs and Mannie Silbersteins. These are the men who reap the benefits of Didi's courtship routines.

And it's all because of Didi's reputation as the campus Continental smoothie that Dinah – determinedly virginal Dinah – gets expelled from the women's hall of residence. It's thanks to her, the Lady Warden says, that Florence Powell Hall is fast becoming known as Fleshpots Hall.

What's happened is that Lindsay and Dinah, revising together late at night, have decided to sleep outdoors. Because, indoors, it's quite impossibly hot. They're fanning themselves with sheafs of foolscap in Dinah's little shoebox bedroom because exam time is always high humidity time and the night isn't getting any cooler. They've both been guzzling Lindsay's caffeine pills and by now they are far too stimulated to do any more proper work. Dinah's got her first-year exams. Lindsay's got her finals.

'God, but isn't it hot,' Lindsay says. 'If only we could sleep outdoors.'

And then she's got a plan. First they throw two blankets and two pillows out of Dinah's window. Then they proceed downstairs in haste, because the doors are locked at midnight. Lindsay has got it all worked out. First, Dinah is to engage the senior House Committee person in conversation at the reception desk. This is when Lindsay will tiptoe out. Then Lindsay, from the nearby callbox, will telephone the hall of residence. That will require the senior House Committee person to enter the little ante-room. This is when Dinah will make her escape.

The scheme works to perfection and it's all the more pleasurable because the House Committee person that night is the very queen bee of the Afrikaans-language teacher-training college contingent, the most zealous of the republican-poster pasters. And the sleep-out is duly fabulous. The stars are dizzily bright, Dinah's never slept outdoors before and nothing that she can remember has felt more magical than that secret snuggling-down, rolled in a blanket under the whoosh-whoosh of the trees – and not twenty yards from the residence. Then to wake, with the early light dappling one's eyelids, to a chorus of Durban's amazing birds. It feels like being made new.

Dinah and Lindsay are so pleased to be alive that they make the mistake of shaking off their dew-damp blankets and dancing together under the tree, their sleeping tree. They take hands and skip like flower fairies, barefoot on the broad-bladed grass. Then, with their stomachs growling healthily, they sit waiting for the residents' doors to open. Because by now they're longing for breakfast. Once they're back inside, showered and dressed, they proceed to the dining hall and feast on slices of pawpaw and scrambled eggs. End of story – or so they think.

At this stage they've got no idea that the large-bosomed harridan from the Freshers' Reception Committee is an early-rising competitive swimmer with special dispensation to practise her aquatic arts outside official door-lock times. So she's up with the lark and heading out for the pool to do her daily lengths while the two girls are still out dancing under their tree. Without them being aware of it, she's immediately returned to alert the Lady Warden, who has checked their empty bedrooms.

By mid-morning, Lindsay and Dinah are both in serious trouble. They're side by side in the Lady Warden's office and it's just like school all over again, except that Maud isn't there. Plus, instead of Miss Maidment, there's Dr Maisie Horne, the stout-brogued social-work tutor who takes Lindsay for social administration. Dr Horne has a very straight, very wide parting in her very straight jaw-length hair. Lindsay has always made reference to the wide parting as Dr Horne's firebreak.

'And you,' says the Firebreak, indicating Dinah, 'and you. Given the masculine company you're keeping, I can only conclude that you'll have spent the night in the men's halls of residence.'

Dinah can somehow not reply to this. It's too massively off-beam. The remark merely causes her to wonder whether she's the only virgin left in the Florence Powell Hall of Residence – that's with the exception of Lindsay's training-college girl who put the oranges down her blouse. She knows that even Jacinta-May has recently succumbed to her boyfriend, because Jacinta-May has told her.

'Itth so *howwid* the way boyth pant when they're thekthually a-wow-zd,' she says. 'I hate it becauth itth jutht like dogth. I've alwayth hated dogth.'

'Dinah slept under a tree,' Lindsay is adamantly insisting to the Firebreak. 'We both did. She was with me.'

'Kindly be quiet!' the Firebreak says, but Lindsay can't be quiet.

'Honestly,' she says. 'She was with me. All night. I'll show you the tree, Dr Horne.'

But the Firebreak is busy with Dinah. 'Look at me!' she says, because Dinah is observing her schoolgirl practice of staring at her feet while trying to fit them into the shapes of the woodblock floor.

She makes an effort to look up into the Firebreak's eyes, but all she can manage is to raise her own eyes until she's fixed them on the wide firebreak parting.

'What is the name of this residence?' the Firebreak says, but Dinah isn't sure which one she means. Does she mean this resi-dence? *This* one? Or does she mean the men's hall of residence? The one in which Didi will be currently fast asleep?

Dinah's hesitation has given the Firebreak her chance. 'The residence which you have disgraced!' she says. 'I see that you don't have the temerity to pronounce its name.'

'Oh,' Dinah says. 'Oh sorry. Do you mean Florence Powell Hall?'

'Yes,' says the Firebreak. 'Florence Powell Hall. Fast becoming better known as Fleshpots Hall.'

Dinah is still staring hard at the Firebreak's firebreak.

'*Fleshpots Hall!*' the Lady Warden says. It's as if she likes the sound of it. 'We have you to thank for that, Dinah de Bondt.'

Though she hears Lindsay's muffled snort, Dinah doesn't dare to look sideways. She's wondering whether the Firebreak has suddenly gone mad. Is 'Fleshpots Hall' her own bizarre invention? One she's been working on since dawn? Or has the somewhat pedestrian Firebreak been liaising with her opposite number, the Lady Warden of the older women's hall of residence? The empire-building drama exponent who speaks almost entirely in catch-phrases culled from the writings of Rudolph Laban?

'You may go,' says the Firebreak suddenly. 'You will find that your rooms have both been cleared. Your effects will have been boxed. They will be waiting for you in reception.'

'Sorry?' Lindsay says. 'Excuse me?'

'GO!' says the Firebreak. 'Leave the premises! You're very lucky, both of you, that you're being permitted to continue with your studies.'

'But where are we supposed to go?' Lindsay says. 'I've got nowhere to go.'

The Firebreak ignores her. Instead she addresses her final remark to Dinah. 'Think carefully about the company you keep.'

And, with that, the girls are dismissed.

The expulsion is more dramatic for Lindsay who's got nowhere to go and her finals to write within the fortnight, but Maud comes to the rescue. She's back from Swaziland and living in a one-bedroom flat off Musgrave Road. So that's where Lindsay goes. Maud's got a job as a vet's assistant with the man who always patched up Punch. And she's also designing a range of garments for one of Jenny's older female friends. The female friend has an interior-design boutique which is funded by a wealthy husband. The idea is that she will launch Maud's collection as a small experiment on the side. But the wealthy husband pulls the plug on the project after Maud has made up all the clothes, so Maud shares them out between herself and Dinah and all of them are fab. Some are in two pieces with hipster trousers and little truncated tops that stop short of the waist, so they show five inches of your midriff every time you reach up. The clothes are made out of quality curtain fabrics. Heavy-weight calico and chintz and corded silks. Or else they're made of denim. There's a pillow-ticking jacket for drowning in that Maud has lined with flowered chintz and piped with geranium red.

Dinah's wearing the jacket to go back home in, back home to share a bedroom with her sister. Her mum has come to fetch her in the new Renault Dauphine. It's the family's first car. But Dinah's dad can't drive the car because he's too myopic. Dinah's mum says nothing to her on the short journey home. She utters repeated heavy sighs and does little disapproving sniffs. The whole family is fed up with Dinah. Dinah the Bad Daughter. Bad Sister. Always a nuisance. *Zänkisch*. Scorpio *zänkisch*. What can be the matter with her?

'And *don't* disturb your sister.' That's all her dad says to her when she walks in through the door. 'She's got exams to write.'

Dinah's got exams as well, but everyone in the family knows that Dinah doesn't mind exams. It's Lisa who hates exams, Lisa who turns into a bag of nerves at the very idea of them. Lisa gets so bad during exams that she can't concentrate for worrying about how much she can't concentrate, so it's Lisa now, not Dinah, who's the focus of their mum's anxieties. Dinah's mum is taking Lisa on lots of soothing little shopping trips and treats. She's trying to help poor Lisa to remember that there's life beyond exams.

So Dinah's mum, Dinah's special person; the mother of Poor Little Dee – frail, artistic, non-eating Little Dee – has clearly transferred her allegiance. Little Dee has been a disappointment to her. She's far more comfortable with Lisa now, because Dinah's gone off the rails. Plus Dinah's not even artistic any more. She doesn't paint and sketch. She doesn't do any of that little-girl stuff with paper and felt and clay. She talks about English poetry and English plays and English novels, books written in a language that, for her mother, will always be a not quite comfortable medium of exchange. Neither does Little Dee appear to be her usual frail and sickly self, not now that the hall of residence has provided her with nine months of utility foam pillows and cheap acrylic blankets in place of the Kaiser's feather beds. Dinah's allergies, for the moment, seem to be taking a break.

So, wrong-footed and shamefaced, Dinah has come home to find that her mother is more than ever bonded with her sister. They're two adult women together. They're the women of the house. Dinah is the kid sister who is always in the way. Plus Lisa is certainly not best pleased to be back sharing the bedroom that she's got used to considering her own.

'You're such a pain,' she says. 'God knows why you've always got to be such a pain.'

There's only one person who's really pleased about Dinah's eviction from the hall of residence and that's Didi von Schweiten. Dinah can tell that he's flattered and that he's trying not to preen.

'Fleshpots Hall, eh?' he says. 'Fleshpots Hall? Well, given your terrible reputation you might as well sleep with me now.'

And so she does. They borrow Maud's bed. And Dinah feels absolutely nothing. That's except for a certain excitement about a very significant surrender. Didi's a bit disappointed because there's no spillage of maiden blood, no virginal gasps of pain.

'You must have done this before,' he says. 'That's unless you've fallen off a horse.'

But Dinah has never been on a horse, so she knows that she's never fallen off. 'I used to climb a lot of trees,' she says. 'When I lived on the Butcher Estate.'

Naturally, she's been far too modest to gawp at Didi's body parts, so she's no idea whether he has used any form of protection. Has he or has he not spun his half a crown on the counter of the local chemist shop, as described to her so graphically by Catherine Cleary? How on earth should she know? As the days and the weeks go by, Dinah gets so anxious about the possibility of being pregnant that she misses out a whole month's period. And naturally she can't discuss this with Didi – because you can't talk periods with boys. Instead she freezes over. The ice maiden returns. And just when Didi has come to expect that, from now on, access will be assured.

Yet once she's done sex with Didi, the effect on Dinah is as dramatic as the sex is understated. Because she finds that she's lost all her power. She's over night become Didi's zombie. He is the man she's got to marry now, so she'll just have to keep on working at moulding herself until she becomes his ideal consort. She'll practise playing female back-up and second fiddle to a man who, for all his undeniable charm, is unexcited by the very things that she herself holds most dear, a man who doesn't read anything

261

except for *The Kinsey Report*. And then of course there are Didi's parents, who require quite a lot of moulding.

Mutti, the Archbishop's daughter, is an almost spherical person with yellow, bleach-blonde hair. Her major talent, as Dinah sees it, is her ability to make any edible substance absorb up to three pints of double cream by a process of slow cooking. And *Mutti* has right away sussed Didi's girlfriend as a person with too much intellect to make him a proper wife.

'A man can't live on poetry,' she says, having come upon Dinah in the garden reading 'The Love Song of J. Alfred Prufrock'. This, even though Dinah has chosen a safe and faraway spot, one from which she's not able to see the guard dog in his zoo-sized cage, who hurls himself salivating against the bars at the appearance of black service persons. It's *Mutti*'s firmly stated belief that Dinah should be learning how to darn a man's sock – but Dinah can darn a sock already. Dinah, as Didi hastens, appeasingly, to point out, is a girl who makes her own clothes.

'*Hmm*,' *Mutti* says. 'Hmm.'

Because Dinah's clothes are something else that *Mutti* and *Vati* don't care for. *Vati* is not one to bother much with 'Hmm'. He has no need of innuendo. *Vati* always claims the right to say whatever he likes – and especially to any person who is residing under his roof. *Vati* is a big man, heavy and gouty-looking. He has a huge bald head and a tongue that's too big for his mouth which makes him speak with a spattery sort of lisp and leaves foam deposits on his lips. *Vati* looks like a carousing country squire who's spent his life in the saddle. He has the look of a man who eats devilled kidneys for breakfast, followed by a brace of partridge.

'*Mahlzeit!*' he cries with boyish enthusiasm, as he sits in his outsize carver chair, napkin tucked in at the chin. He waits at the head of the table for *Mutti* to appear from the kitchen with her platters of pork loin seethed in cream, her dishes of plump, white Alsatian sausages, which she serves with sliced potatoes layered and baked in cream. *Vati* is especially affronted by the pillow-ticking jacket.

'You come out viss me in your *mornink* gown?' he likes to say, meaning to imply that the fabulous jacket looks like a dressing gown.

Vati wears his trousers belted firmly below his paunch. *Mutti* wears what looks to Dinah like a car coat of karakul lamb. *Mutti* likes Dinah to be in the kitchen, learning how to make fifteen mushrooms absorb two pounds of butter. But what Dinah remembers most about the kitchen is that Seraphina, the Zulu maid, is always in there, ironing while bent double. This is because the ironing board is made for a person three feet high and Dinah thinks that it probably pre-dates the Battle of Blood River. Yet *Mutti* and *Vati* are forking out for their daughter to be 'finished' in Switzerland. Didi's sister Lottie is currently at an educational establishment for young ladies somewhere near Lausanne.

Didi won't do sex with Dinah when he's in his parents' house, because this would be insulting to *Mutti* and *Vati*. So he beds her in the stables on a heap of hessian feed sacks. The sacks cause instant bursts of hay fever, because, by then, she's already been re-sensitised by *Mutti*'s Austrian feather beds. These are more potent than the Kaiser's dust-mite versions. Plus *Mutti*'s pillows are of so venerable an age that the duck down has crumbled into a lethal powdery dust in which the mites are having wholesale orgies. For Dinah, it's like burying her face in the contents of a well-used Hoover bag. It induces the kind of excessive seizures that she hasn't had since childhood. Through the night in Didi's house, gasping for breath and trying hard to smother her every sneeze, Dinah creeps along the squeaky corridor to grab herself hanks of lavatory paper with which to mop her nasal flow. And she's got that asthmatic's little cough. Short and dry. Non-stop. Cough-cough. Next morning *Mutti*'s in a fit of the sulks but she won't tell Dinah why.

'You kept my mother awake all night,' Didi explains reproachfully. 'With all that sneezing and coughing and your constant visits to the bathroom. Can't you try and be just a little bit more considerate?'

'Sorry,' Dinah says.

Her eyes are little pink slits. The skin around the wings of her nose is shiny red and cracked.

'Don't say sorry to *me*,' he says. 'Try saying sorry to my mother.'

When Didi deserts her in February to go off hunting somewhere, Dinah designs and executes for him twelve different Valentine cards, each with its own neat rhyming couplet written out in Chinese ink, and she posts these to his family home. She remembers this act of excessive devotion, because it's with these Hallmark greeting-card skills that she finally draws from *Mutti* her one and only sort-of compliment. Dinah is '*so künstlerisch*', she says, that she ought to be finding herself a boyfriend whose talent matches her own.

And then, once Didi has accomplished his degree in business studies, he goes off to Johannesburg and gets himself a job. And Dinah, who is suddenly being courted by three far more suitable young men, is telling them all, one by one, that though she likes them, she can't possibly take them on because she's going to marry Didi. One is a journalist and a talented batsman who plays cricket in the national team. He's one of that generation of Springbok sportsmen whose careers get aborted by the boycott. Another is an up-coming Rhodes Scholar, an ambitious academic brainbox who gives her lifts on his clapped-out red Lambretta. He weaves it perilously all over the road and crashes it so frequently that Dinah develops a theory of inverse correlation between road skills and high intelligence quotient.

The third, unbelievably, is Jed. Jed who has suddenly decided that she's the girl for him after all. He's given up on his line of twin-set girls and he's opened his heart to Dinah. And Dinah – weeping inwardly as she hears herself utter the words – tells him no, that, though she *really* likes him – as a friend, of course, not as a boyfriend – she's going to marry Didi. Jed, unlike the other two, doesn't hang about. He doesn't linger on her mother's living-room sofa, hoping to find favour with her by outstaying his rivals. He tells her she's a fool. Then he leaves at once. And, from then on, he addresses not a word to her for almost half a year.

Jed is into something political, Dinah is fairly certain, but then there are all sorts of people about whom it's become better not to ask. There'll be the person with whom you're having dinner who, all unbeknown to you, is keeping a store of dynamite underneath the divan. And nobody with half a brain will ever talk politics on the phone. Or in a public place. Or even in the garden where a neighbour might overhear. Bombs have been going off at regular intervals, mostly in government buildings, because, since its banning, the ANC has pulled off over two hundred successful acts of sabotage. There's been the unmasked 'Blonde Spy' at Wits, who has hit the Sunday papers – and spies are everywhere. Some of Dinah's small inner circle will whisper that the librarian's a spy and, to be sure, he likes to draw one aside and offer one, in confidence, his cupboard full of banned books. So any time you're after reading *The Communist Manifesto*, well, that will be no problem. You just come along to him.

John Vorster, as Minister of Justice, is looming over the security apparatus in a formidable double act with his friend Hendrick van den Bergh – his own appointee as head of the Special Branch; his wartime fellow conspirator from their *Ossewabrandwag* days. There's the Sabotage Act and the Ninety Day Act, by which the police can arrest any person and hold them, on suspicion, with no warrant and no access to a lawyer. That's for ninety days. Then it's a hundred and eighty days. And the police can always re-arrest you, the moment you've been released. Plus people in custody are suddenly beginning to manage fatal accidents – in the showers, on the stairs, taking tumbles from upstairs windows.

Things are not as bad as they'll get, but they're certainly getting worse. Dinah's response, in Didi's absence, is to join the madrigal group. Because Alfred Deller, the English counter-tenor, has caused a sudden revival of interest in early English music.

ELEVEN

When Lisa graduates, she decides to become a librarian, mainly because she's so certain that she doesn't want to be a teacher. Both girls are completely certain that they don't want to become teachers. Because who'd want to end up like Miss Legge? Plus Dinah's still convinced that nearly all teachers are mad. Teacher, librarian, secretary, nurse. These are the careers that appear to be on offer. That's if you're a girl. Lisa's got herself a place on the librarians' course in Johannesburg because Durban doesn't have one. So Lisa and her mum are up in Johannesburg, looking for the cheapest digs they can find. They're looking for a nice boarding house, preferably one that doesn't reek of boiled cabbage and Sanilav, because Lisa, like her mum, is fastidious. Both of them don't like common.

So, for the first time ever, Dinah's alone with her dad. And, because she's suddenly filling the space that her big sister's vacated, she's being trusted to take the odd turn with preparing the evening meal – and she's just accomplished her first roast chicken with roast potatoes. Then the phone rings and she's being asked out on a date by a person she only knows by sight, a person who is new on campus. The date's got tickets for a mime show, he says, and it's starting within the hour. There's a touring French mime artist in town, but Dinah's in a quandary, because her roast chicken is ready to serve.

'I'll just have to ask my dad,' she says.

This is a remark which the date later tells her he's found a bit of a turn-off. But he comes to fetch her in his VW beetle which is reeking strongly of cat pee. This is because, three days before, the date has acquired two feral cats from the animal rescue, who have spat and pissed their way home. They're not cuddly cats to look at, he says. In fact they're not cuddly at all. They're like those electrified cats that you get in children's cartoon films. They're fierce and scrawny and, when they take fright, they re-assemble themselves with zigzag outlines. So they're not like Dinah's farm cat then, the comfy and rotund Muschka, who saves all his energy for purring and smiling and for blinking his flecked yellow eyes. The date has named his cats Wyatt Earp and Jesse James. Dinah notes that the back seat of the beetle is awash with crumpled airmail editions of the *New Statesman* and with Pogo comics from the Okeyfenokey Swamp.

The mime artist is Marcel Marceau and, because Dinah hasn't thought to bring her Gregory Peck men's horn-rims, his performance is lost on her. Thanks to his black hat and trousers, however, she can tell that there's a figure on the stage and that the figure is moving about. But in the interval, because everyone else is raving about the mime artist, Dinah feels the need to fake it and she has a little rave as well. She and the date are in the bar with two of Dinah's lecturers – two newly appointed young post-grad persons who've swiftly got it together. The male young person has made his mark on Dinah's final-year tutorial group – mainly through his misreading of a line in T.S. Eliot's 'Fire Sermon'. He's come to grief over Eliot's description of a young woman's life in London bedsit land.

First he's read the line in his wide-boy Germiston accent that goes so well with his weathered black lumber jacket: ' "Her drying combinations," he reads, "touched by the sun's last rays".

'OK,' he says. 'OK. So she's got these drying combination things on her head. Sort of like this.'

He gestures, making a beehive shape in the air above his head to indicate one of those stand-up dryers found in women's hairdressing salons before the advent of the blow-dry. Then he looks quite threatened when all the students start to laugh. For Dinah and Jed it's the first time in months that they've made eye contact, so things are looking up.

'What's so funny?' says the young male party. 'Have I got egg on my face?'

'Combinations,' Jed says eventually, 'are a kind of winter underwear. They're "drying" because she's hung them up. She's laundered them, you see.'

'Oh shucks,' says the young male party. '*Underwear*? So I have got egg on my face.'

The young female party has been a lot less fun and she's got a streak of Miss Whiplash. Her first move is to give everyone really no-good essay marks and this is true for Dinah's essay on the novels of E.M. Forster.

'You didn't seem to notice,' she says, 'that Forster is a *minor* novelist.'

But, as Dinah now snipes in private to the date, once they're safely back in their seats, 'I thought it was an *essay* I was writing. I didn't think it was a league table.'

The young female party is under the sway of Dr F.R. Leavis, who has isolated the Big Five in the history of the English novel. He's cut and slashed, until only the lucky five are left. Only five are in the Great Tradition. Dinah thinks that the list has to be crap, because it doesn't include Charles Dickens.

'I mean,' she says to the date, 'I mean – if you had to make a choice – which would you be saving from the burning fiery furnace? *Sons and Lovers*, or *Bleak House*? *The Shadow Line*, or *David Copperfield*? Which would you rather burn your hands for? *Washington Square* or *Little Dorrit*?'

Then she feels a terrible drip for having mentioned her essays on a date. But it's all right, because the date has got an essay story as well. He tells her that, as a student activist, he's been probed by the Wits Blonde Spy, the spy whose taped information to the police has now been splashed all over the papers.

'Oh him,' the Blonde Spy has said about the date. 'Oh him. He never tells me anything. He just talks and talks about his history essays.'

The date's also got a story about someone he knows who, as a cocky graduate student, was once rude to E.M. Forster. Dinah has never thought of E.M. Forster as someone she could be rude to. She thinks of famous writers as being names on the spines of books.

Dinah enjoys her night out. She likes the date's curly black hair. And she likes it that he's got himself two cats. Plus she thinks he's very amusing. But still she stiffens as he parks the beetle outside her parents' house.

'I'd like to kiss you, but I won't,' he says, taking the wind out of her sails. 'I had two molars out this afternoon and the inside of my mouth is still feeling like lumps of chopped liver.'

The date's teeth are a disaster area because he's spent his years at university letting the students in the Wits dental school attend to his mouth for free. So now he's got lots of unnecessary crowns and experimental bridge work. He's got fly-overs and cantilevers all threatening to come down.

Dinah seizes the opportunity to make her little speech. 'I really like you as a friend,' she says, 'but my boyfriend's in Johannesburg and I'm going to marry him.'

'Well, that's no problem for me,' says the date, 'because I don't want to marry you. Anyway, he's in Johannesburg. And I'm right here.'

The date teaches history in the African studies department. He's recently come from Cape Town University where, like Dinah's dad several decades before, he's had a job as a junior lecturer. Now he's got a proper job in Durban, but he comes from the Transvaal. He comes from Krugersdorp, which is a West Rand mining town about twenty miles from Johannesburg. It's famous for the Sterkfontein Caves, he says, where a young Scottish doctor uncovered a very significant missing link. *Plesianthropus Transvaalensis*, otherwise known as Mrs Ples. He found a female skeleton that finally offered hard evidence of an adult humanoid that stood up and walked, using its hands like people. Krugersdorp, being thick with gold mines, has had a concentration of white English miners, often immigrant Cornish tin miners. But it's also one of the spiritual heartlands of Afrikaner Nationalism. Krugersdorp is where President Kruger's forces impounded the ramshackle English conspirators of the pre-Boer War Jameson Raid. Plus it's got the Paardekraal Monument, where people in voortrekker costumes like to gather for heritage occasions. In addition, Krugersdorp, like most Rand mining towns, has communities of Asian and Jewish small traders, of which the date's family is one.

The date has spent his only-child boyhood playing near the Sterkfontein Caves with his mongrel best-friend dog called Cheeky. Or squatting on the riverbank with his father's black assistant, a man who models hump-backed oxen for him out of river clay. This is before he has to go to school. After that, from the time he's about nine, he always gets beaten up en route, by brawny Afrikaner high-school boys, because he's Jewish and English-speaking and the year is 1942. So the date's mum arranges boxing lessons, but he still goes on getting beaten up, until one day five years later. This is when his chief tormentor appears with two little pipsqueaks. The plan is that the pipsqueaks will beat up the date, while the big boy stands by to watch. But let the date lay a finger on the pipsqueaks, and the big boy will wade in. Feeling his honour to be at stake, the date brushes aside the pipsqueaks in one swift movement and goes straight for the big boy, where, by sheer good luck, he breaks a blood vessel in the boy's nose. So blood pours over both their school shirts and wrecks their respective school ties. That's the day when the bullying stops and reputations are made and lost.

The date's mum is sent out from London to South Africa in 1928. She's sent out from the Mile End Road to go and work for one of her ten brothers with whom she's already spent a pinched and squabbly childhood in varying degrees of watchful resentment. Plus, because she's the only girl in the family, she's always been made to polish her brothers' shoes. All eleven siblings are seriously brainy, but the family can't afford school uniforms so, aged fourteen, they all go out to work, which for most of them means shipping out to the Rand, where they set about earning the passage out for the next sibling down. That's except for the youngest one who – always top of his junior-school class – is discovered by the school nurse to have an irregular heartbeat. So he's carted off, kicking and screaming, to the residential special school where, after two years of weaving baskets, he gives up the spirit and dies.

For a brief while it looks as if the date's mother might have found a way out and up. Because in the months before she leaves London, she's being courted by a clever young Zionist student at the Imperial College of Science and they have whispered plans. But this is when her mother moves in and shops her.

'If you stay in this country, you'll have the life that I've had,' she says. 'And, Ida, you've never been strong.'

Strong enough to polish all the shoes. Not strong enough for love. So Ida is shipped out to Krugersdorp to be her brother Benny's typist. And, after some years – since Krugersdorp is not the greatest spot for dating opportunities – Ida enters into a marriage with a man she considers her inferior. This is because he's got a Lithuanian accent and not a lot of money. She derives her precarious sense of status from being an Englishwoman, an Englishwoman and a Londoner who has ridden the District Line. And now she's pregnant and married to a foreigner who scratches a precarious living by buying and selling what he can.

But the date's dad is a fabulous guy – or that is what Dinah thinks – because she gets round to meeting him quite soon, sooner than she expects. The date's dad has taken a different route to Krugersdorp, because at the age of ten he's been sent out all alone from a *shtetl* in Lithuania. He docks in London speaking no English and boards a boat en route for Cape Town. A rich uncle, as he has been told, is going to educate him. Once in Cape Town he makes his way to a village somewhere in the Transkei where the rich uncle lives. But the rich uncle turns out not to be rich. He runs a small native trading store and he puts the boy to work. So the date's dad doesn't go to school. He learns English and educates himself by reading everything he can lay his hands on – most of which is what comes out of the Victor Gollancz Left Book Club.

Ever since the date can remember, his dad has had 'the business'. He's got one small van and one black assistant and he drives the van into the Transvaal hinterland to buy agricultural produce from Afrikaner farmers. Then he sells the produce to wholesalers in various towns round about. He drives the van at twenty miles an hour and, one day, having trundled the routes for something like nineteen years, he runs over a sheep, and finds that his licence, got years back in the Cape – from that place he still refers to as the Colony – has been invalid for fifteen years. Then there's serious panic in the household because he has to take another test. He's been one man with a little van right through the Second World War when news of families like his own is filtering out from occupied Europe – families herded into synagogues and burned alive, en masse. Some of the farmers he visits have got pictures of Hitler on the wall. But they still have a drink with him on the stoep, because he's got the common touch. And they always speak in Afrikaans.

'Piet,' they say, 'you're the only Jew that we will have in the house. And you're the only Communist.'

They call him Piet because his initials are P.T. even though his name is really Philip.

And he is a sort of Communist because, having left his homeland seven years before the events of 1917, he knows that the Russian Revolution was a very wonderful thing. He knows that all the stories leaking out about Stalin and the labour camps are the invention of the capitalist press. Once, way back, he heard an orator on the steps of the Johannesburg City Hall. 'If the *Rand Daily Mail* tells you it's day,' the orator said, 'then you know it's night.' So the date's dad knows that the Soviet Union never invaded Hungary. He knows that this is another conspiracy on the part of the capitalist press. The orator was one Jock Campbell of the South African Labour Party.

The date's dad anticipates that his son will grow up to join him in the business, but his mum has other ideas. Her boy is very clever, she tells all the neighbours. That's the neighbours in Blikkies, which is the modest to poorish tin-house white suburb in which the family lives. But this is way before they've made a move to more salubrious quarters.

'He's going to Oxford one day,' she says.

And the date *is* very clever, which means that after his first year at junior school he's pushed up into a class of older children, where he's terrorised by the teacher and bullied by the older boys. The school experience means that, by the time he's twelve, the date has known for many years that school is very bad news and he's become a professional truant. When he truants he hitch-hikes into Johannesburg where he sits in the basement of the Johannesburg public library and reads back numbers of the *New Statesman* and the *Observer* and the *Listener*. Which explains why he's the only person Dinah's met who knows all about Malcolm Muggeridge and Kingsley Martin and John Strachey and the Aldermaston Marches. He knows what Jacob Bronowski has been saying on the BBC. He's also the only person she knows who owns a genuine duffel coat with proper horn toggles. But the trouble with the duffel coat is that it always sets him wheezing because, like Dinah, he's asthmatic. Plus his birthday's on Bonfire Night, which is stretching credulity.

'Well, I don't believe you,' Dinah says. 'I'm sorry. I do not believe you. Nobody, except for me, has ever had a birthday on Bonfire Night.'

The date's name is Sam and he must, she thinks, have leapt from the womb as a fully fledged political animal. Or perhaps he gets it from his dad. He can't ever leave columns of newsprint alone and he's known, for longer than he can remember, that religion is the Opium of the People. As a child he's led a walk-out against the local rabbi who runs the after-school Hebrew class, and after that he doesn't go back. School is boring enough, he says, without having to spend his Saturdays sitting at the feet of an autocratic bully when he could be out playing cricket.

At school, unlike Dinah, Sam has never been grabbed by the morning hymns in assembly. He doesn't know ten verses of any hymn to speak of. In fact he knows not a single verse. Dinah finds it almost impossible to believe that he's managed not to pick up any hymns, but he's never possessed *The Public School Hymn Book*. He's never got round to buying it, so he's never heard of Nahum Tate. Nor does he know the works of Percy the Dreamer. Because he doesn't have the hymn book, he's always been among that band of school slouches who've been issued with the grudging hymn-sheet handouts on which the school secretary has typed up only the four verses of each hymn that the school body actually sings. And it's because of the hymn-sheets that Sam right away knows that his high-school headmaster is mad.

'Hymn number two hundred and three,' the head announces. 'The first two verses and the last two verses.'

But Sam's only ever got four verses printed on his hymn-sheet. He also knows that the headmaster's mad because every morning, on his way to school, the head stops and takes two bricks from the building site where the new high school's being erected. He puts them into his rucksack and carries them off to the old school, where he uses the bricks to mend a broken wall. The head says this is to improve his posture – in which case, as Sam deduces, he ought to be carrying the two bricks back. But the bricks only go one way.

It's Dinah's conviction, furthermore, that Sam is remarkably unclued-up about Jewish religious rituals, though he always likes to deny this whenever she tries him out.

'What's Yom Kippur?' she says. 'What's Rosh Hashanah?'

'Um,' Sam says. 'Urm . . . I think that's when you eat horse radish.'

'That's pathetic,' Dinah says. 'Anyway, which one is for eating horse radish?'

'Um,' Sam says. 'Urm . . .'

But he knows about Pesach, he says. That's when you have to eat matzos. As Made Under the Supervision of the Beth Din, as it says on the matzo box. He knows that his dad always grumbles about having to eat matzos for all those days on end.

'Tenks *Gott* next veek is bread,' he says as the Passover begins to wind down.

Sam's dad likes to drink cheap whisky in one or other of the working-men's clubs on Jewish religious holidays. He prefers the hangouts of old white miners and he likes to wear his cloth cap.

'So what's Hanukkah?' Dinah says.

'Um,' Sam says. 'Urm . . . I think Hanukkah must have been invented around 1958. That's to coincide with Christmas. Sort of a bit like Fathers' Day in relation to Mothers' Day. Well, we never had it in *my* day. Not when I was a boy.'

Two things really puzzle Dinah about Sam. They threaten her carefully nurtured prejudices. One is that he's a sporty person and he's been a schoolboy jock. He's run for the province in a vest with his number sewn on the front and no less a person than 'Baasie' van Wyk with the double set of eyebrows has been a member of Sam's athletics club. His schoolboy means of bringing honour to his high school has been via the rugby team. Plus he's once been touched on the shoulder by Denis Compton, the famous English cricketer. Sam also quite likes to do sports talk.

'I was at the Ellis Park Cricket Ground,' he'll say, 'when Hutton and Washbrook put on three hundred and sixty-five runs in a day.'

Dinah's never been with anyone before who'll say things to her like this. Not even her Springbok cricketing admirer. Not in front of the ladies. As a child, Sam always used to play cricket in the local park in Krugersdorp with an assembly of neighbourhood white children. Meanwhile, at the other end of town, Krugersdorp's Indian children would gather to do the same thing. So one day Sam crossed town and challenged the Indian boys to a cricket match. The boys agreed and the match was fixed for the following weekend. It was everybody's first experience of inter-racial sport.

'And the boy who captained the Indian team,' Sam now tells her, 'that boy was Yusuf Dadoo's brother.'

Dr Yusuf Dadoo is chairman of the now banned South African Communist Party.

The second puzzling thing is that Sam is really keen on South African history. In fact he's consumed by it. Dinah knows that South African history is that yawn-inducing propaganda subject she's been made to do at school. 'The first shipload of coolies arrived in November 1860.' But now it's being transformed for her, because Sam is telling her all sorts of stuff that she's never heard before. He tells her about the white miners' strike of 1922, when the miners marched under a banner that said, 'Workers of the World Unite for a White South Africa.' He knows why Pansy Kaufmann calls her Russian-Jewish visitors Peruvians. It's because the English and German Jews wouldn't let the Polish and Russian Jews into the Kimberley Club, he says. So they started their own club and they called it the Polish and Russian Union. Then, because its initials were PARU, it quickly became Peru. 'So its members became Peruvians.' This is what Sam says.

He knows that the first written Afrikaans was commentaries on the Koran. So the language that Dinah's resisted learning as the medium of white fascists is really a brown person's language. It's the language of Cape Coloured Muslims.

'An imam was summoned from the Caliphate,' he says. 'And, because the Malay population's theology had fallen into disrepair, he ordered that certain religious writings be translated into the vernacular.' The vernacular, by then, was Afrikaans. Or, as the white people called it, Kitchen Dutch.

Sam's got bizarre stories about Malay slave craftsmen who've got Irish immigrant apprentices. He knows that Britain emptied its surplus orphanage population into the Cape Colony, but the orphans quickly vanished from view by falling into the labouring classes and thereby became brown people. He knows that migrant workers from beyond South Africa's borders are classified as 'foreign natives'. He knows that Maud Gonne's husband – Yeats's 'drunken vainglorious lout' – has fathered a line of Cape Coloured politicians – a family of orators called MacBride. He knows that Nylstroom – as in 'Nile Stream' – in the Transvaal is called Nylstroom because a group of trekboers, who were searching for the Holy Land, believed the stream to be the source of the Nile. But the doubting hardliners among the party trekked on and on into Angola, where, instead of finding the source of the Nile, they became destitute and inbred poor whites. He knows the person who, some years before, painted the slogan on the Johannesburg Public Library: 'US BLACK FOLKS AIN'T READIN' YET.' The person is a member of the Transvaal Indian Congress and he paints up slogans all the time. He knows that, during the Second World War, the Italians in Abyssinia surrendered to the South African Army, because the British Army deliberately held back its Indian troops. This was so that the Italians wouldn't have to surrender to brown men.

Partly because of the truanting factor, Sam's kept on failing school maths, so his mother gets him a crammer. He's had a notion to become a mining geologist, for reasons that Dinah can't fathom. So finally he gets to university late, having earned some money in a gold mine with one black mine 'boy' to carry his pick and another to carry his lamp. Then, just when Applied Maths One is beginning to drive him up the wall, he's rescued by a history student who's spotted him in the canteen.

'There's a guy I've been watching for days,' he says to his history-student friends. 'He looks like an engineer. And he's dressed like an engineer. And he's sitting with the engineers. But he's always reading the *New Statesman*.'

So Sam becomes a history student and begins to win golden opinions. Leastways, Dinah's leafed through his books and some are presents from two of his tutors, with inscriptions on the flyleaf that indicate faith in his purpose. One of the tutors is a Balliol man and the other's from the LSE – a man who likes to see himself as the last of Laski's sons.

When Sam gives Dinah a lift to Johannesburg so that she can go and stay with Didi, he suggests that, as they drive along, she teach him the words to Blake's 'Jerusalem'. That's the words as set to music. So she spends the hours between Durban and Ladysmith giving the project a go. And, in the process, discovers not only that Sam has difficulty with learning words verbatim – he who can remember the date of every cattle-raiding skirmish between the Kei and the Kieskhama Rivers – but that he's the third person she's met in her life who has trouble holding a tune. In return he teaches her all the songs he knows from the International Brigades. Which means that, one day, decades on, when Dinah's train stops at a Spanish suburban station, she looks up and reads a railway sign that's announcing 'Manzaneres'. And instead of a suburban station, she sees a bloodstained trench, where one Hans Beimler gave his life, leading the fight to save Madrid.

> With heart and hand I pledge you
> As I load my gun again
> You will never be forgotten
> Nor the enemy forgiven
> Hans Beimler, *Kamerad*.

Dinah deduces the probable tunes from Sam's runs of slightly off-beam notes and, having transposed them into standard tunes, she accompanies him with gusto.

Ladysmith is a good halfway house on the road between Durban and Johannesburg, so this is where they stop, en route, for a mixed grill. On the road, there are always transport cafés to be found attached to the filling stations. The next town along is called Harrismith. The towns are named after Sir Harry Smith, one-time governor of the Cape Colony and final scourge of the Xhosa. Plus his Spanish wife, Lady Smith, who is famous for importing Spanish melons. Dinah and Sam are taken with a poster that's pinned to the café wall, because it's adding a new dimension to the idea of the governor's marriage:

WRESTLING!
HARRISMITH v. LADYSMITH!
NEXT SATURDAY NIGHT!

Meanwhile the filling-station lady has brought them a pot of tea.

'In Ladysmith,' she says proudly, 'you always get tea in a pot.'

Because Didi's out at work all day, Dinah spends the office hours playing hookey with Sam, who drives her to lunch at the Zoo Lake Restaurant, where the resident duck family is descended from a pair of English mallards presented by Princess Elizabeth, during her visit in 1947. Another day they go to lunch with one of Sam's old tutors. The one who is the last of Laski's sons. The tutor and his wife have a unisex look, in similar cardis and corduroys. The cardis are grey, but Dinah recalls them in sepia. The couple look like Sidney and Beatrice Webb. And Mrs Tutor is the sexual guidance counsellor at the school once attended by Jacinta-May

Fairweather. Though they are having several guests that day, the couple keep their dining table piled high with books. Both of them read throughout the lunch, stopping every now and again to fire questions at one of the guests. Among the guests is a Harvard graduate who is wearing a button-down collar. He's a man called James Dryden Richards III, to distinguish him from his grandfather and his father, who are James Dryden Richards I and James Dryden Richards II.

On the third day of playing hookey, Sam takes Dinah to his family home in Krugersdorp where his mother has laid out a lunch for them of salads and cold cuts. These are preceded by a thin consommé which is eaten with dumplings called *kneidlach*. And, because she's caught Sam swiping one of them from the kitchen before lunch begins, she's pointedly ladled twelve *kneidlach* into his bowl, while she and Dinah have three *kneidlach* each. So Sam is looking a little bit wrong-footed as he tries to wade through the mountain. Sam's mum is a sarcastic lady who can wrong-foot anyone in seconds, but she's best at wrong-footing Sam. She's nurturing her own wasted intellect in a precious crucible of unexpressed rage.

In the kitchen, Sam's mum keeps a jar of *schmalz* which is chicken fat for use instead of butter. But the *schmalz* isn't really chicken *schmalz*, because it's a kosher vegetarian alternative. On the jar there's a picture of a very happy chicken. And under the happy chicken, the label says, 'Not even the chicken can tell the difference!!' Dinah finds herself pondering the slogan for quite some time, because the logic of it is eluding her. She deduces eventually that the chicken is happy because it can't tell the difference between the taste of the vegetable substitute and the taste of its own rendered body fat. It pairs up in her mind with Sally's dad's Overport butchery where in the window was a plaster model of a smiling pig in clothes. He was wearing a dark-blue striped butcher's apron and holding up a cleaver along with a string of plaster pork sausages.

In the evenings, in Didi's tiny bathroom, Dinah washes all Didi's socks. Then, after that, they do sex. Dinah remembers that, in the bedroom, there's a white painted cupboard she can see over Didi's shoulder. It says on the doors, in nice angular black writing, 'This cupboard is Maggie's – to await collection.' Dinah decides she likes the tall black down-stroke on the white painted surface. She also likes the name, Maggie. Then, next day, Sam arrives to drive her back to Durban. During this time they have another go at the words of Blake's 'Jerusalem' and by the time they've, once again, stopped off in the Ladysmith café, Sam is quite pleased with his progress.

'I think I've got the gist of it,' he says.

Sam has been politically active all through his student days in Johannesburg, so naturally quite a few of his friends are the people who go on to become the nation's struggle-royalty. Unless, that is, they become the nation's struggle-casualties first, as quite a few of them do. He's distributed Congress leaflets and sold Congress newspapers in downtown Johannesburg and in the white suburbs and in various black eating houses and bus shelters – newspapers that have to keep changing their names because they keep getting banned. And one of his important contributions to the movement has been to bulk-buy booze for the big shots. Since black persons are banned from buying alcohol, Sam will enter the bottle store on behalf of the ANC bigwigs and he'll buy whatever they need. They tell him to say that his 'native boy' will come and collect the order on Saturday.

Now, with the new draconian bannings, Sam is full of misgivings about the ANC's capacity to convert itself into a feasible guerrilla movement. It's hard to be an underground, he thinks, with yesterday's above-ground leadership. A leadership which keeps on leeching away into jail or into exile. And, given the police's new special powers to arrest and detain indefinitely, he thinks the job of hunting people down might not be terribly difficult. Just haul in enough marginally active people and threaten them for long enough until one or two of them crack. All the state will need to do is arrest enough rank-and-file activists who can be leaned on and terrorised until they produce hypotheses which might hold a grain of accuracy. It's an open secret that the state is using torture. And, during his recent molar extraction, the dentist has happened to comment to Sam that his pain threshold is rather low.

So Sam has decided to call it a day. He's reached his cut-off point. And the move to Durban has made the perfect moment to withdraw. He's unacquainted with the local activist scene and he won't need to get involved. But, naturally, there can be little harm in responding to the hand of friendship that's being offered by a Durban colleague who is a member of the Liberal Party, a colleague who, by coincidence, is living in the very same house that once belonged to Mrs Stewart's cousin. The cousin who grew all those cabbages with hearts, which are now no longer in evidence, because the colleague has got lots of pre-school children who have turned the garden into a sandpit. The colleague is struggling to make ends meet, so the family doesn't have a car. And it seems only reasonable, therefore, that he should sometimes ask to borrow the beetle.

It's shortly after these requests begin that Dinah and Sam start getting stopped in road blocks as they come in and out of Durban. Twice, the police pull them off the road and shine torches into the car. Then eventually they're waved on. A third time, the police get quite excited and talk very fast into walkie-talkies.

'We've got the car,' they're saying in Afrikaans. 'We've got the car. We've found it.'

Suddenly everything is off to forensic; all the airmail editions of the *New Statesman* and all the runs of Pogo. They've taken Dinah's hay-fever spray and her make-up bag with her Max Factor Pan-Stick and her Apple Blossom scent. But they're especially excited by the title of a doctoral thesis that Sam has on the back seat. It's about the Anti-Convict Agitation at the Cape in 1848, but the words convict and agitation are pressing several buttons. Yet normal life is still going on, because Maud is about to get married.

Maud is marrying the beautiful mathematician for whom Lavinia Steadman of Florence Powell Hall once, nightly, took out her curlers. But now, against all expectation, he's marrying Dinah's best friend. So Sam drives Dinah to Maud's flat one evening, in order that the girls can pin and cut and tack Maud's wedding clothes. Maud has bought a *Vogue* Paris Original pattern and several yards of brocade. The garment will be a knee-length ivory two-piece, with a low-cut fitted bodice that has fifteen self-covered buttons. Sam has decided to stay with the girls and he tells them funny stories all night as he watches the effects of their exotic female skills taking shape under his eyes. Maud's vet – Punch's vet – has volunteered both his house and his wife to host Maud's wedding reception. And the vet's wife has already lined up Jenny and Dinah as her under-chefs. She's been putting them through the art of making canapés and dainty cocktail sandwiches. Dinah remembers that the vet's wife always refers to the sandwiches as sammickers. She says that the sammickers must be wrapped in clean damp muslin cloths. This is so that they won't dry out, because the plastic bag has not yet made it into general household use.

Once Maud and Dinah are finished for the evening, Sam drives Dinah back home. Then he returns to his flat, after midnight, where the two Special Branch policemen have been waiting for him all evening. Both have been drinking to pass the time and now they're reeking of brandy. Plus it's clear they're not best pleased.

'We know you did it,' they're saying in loud voices to rouse the neighbours.

They've already been through the flat quite thoroughly, but they've found nothing there except the two electrified cats who've hissed and spat at them in terror. Wyatt Earp's gone into zigzag mode and he's lit out for the territory. After that he's never seen again. Jesse James is crackling with static, but he hangs on for the next two weeks. That's until the landlord comes to treat the place for termites. The message from Wyatt and Jesse is clear. They don't want to be kitchen cats.

'We know you did it,' the Special Branch men are saying. 'What we need is the details of your movements. And we want to know who was with you.'

Someone, that evening, has managed to blow up the offices of the local Afrikaner Nationalist newspaper. And of course they know Sam did it. And they don't like his time-wasting, bullshit story about two girls and a wedding dress. So they make him keep on telling his story until the dawn starts to break.

'We'll be back,' they say.

This is a promise they like to keep and they particularly like to ring the doorbell very late at night. Sam is good at withholding information. He keeps calm and he's not a natural chatterbox. But right now, he's got not a clue in any case, because the ARM is so very new that nobody's heard of it. Not yet. The activists of the African Resistance Movement are mostly young and mostly in-experienced and they are members of the Liberal Party – though both their existence and their modus operandi come as news to the Party's leadership. Two of ARM's youthful saboteurs turn out to have been Sam's undergraduates at Cape Town University. And one has panicked and has talked out everything – everything he knows about everyone who has been involved along with him. So the police can't quite believe their luck and they're high on it for weeks.

The young man in question was once Jenny's idolised next-door neighbour. But that was long ago in the Johannesburg house in which, throughout her early childhood, Jenny always chose her father's ties. For Jenny, the neighbour was a glamorous figure, a handsome, stylish boy and just a few years older. She remembers, once, how exciting it was when he and his gang conspired to peep while she and her ten-year-old birthday-party chums were changing their clothes after swimming. And Jenny – as always, brave little Jenny – having wrapped her towel about her person, marched briskly out of the changing room and confronted the boys over the wall.

'Stop being so rude,' she said. 'Us girls think you boys should go away. Go away!'

Then she turned her back on the boys and walked just as briskly away. She was greeted by hoots and howls of laughter because, as she'd realised, once it was too late, the towel wasn't adequate to cover the cleavage of her rump. And, even at ten, her curvy little buttocks were staunchly ball-bearing along.

Now the next-door neighbour has become the state's star witness. And it's not long afterwards that the car-borrowing colleague is rounded up as well. Some weeks well before this, Sam has put a stop to his intermittent borrowing of the beetle – though he's managed not to say why and he certainly hasn't told Dinah. But Sam has opened his boot one day to find it's got traces of white powder.

'Oh shit,' he says. 'Oh Christ.'

'What?' Dinah says. 'What's the matter?'

'Never mind,' Sam says. But he's looking sort of white. 'Who do we know who owns a vacuum cleaner?' he says.

When Sam next drives up to Johannesburg, he takes Dinah along, as usual, and he drops her off with Didi. And it's when she and Didi are doing sex that she notes, once again, the white painted cupboard with the bold black italic writing. It's still evident over Didi's shoulder. 'This cupboard is Maggie's – to await collection.'

'Who's Maggie?' Dinah says, but Didi is not best pleased. He abruptly aborts his sexual performance and gets up off the bed.

'Shall I tell you what I hate about you?' he says. Then he begins to tell her. 'We're in the middle of making love, all right? And what do you say to me? "Who's Maggie?" Who's *Maggie*?! Well, how the fuck should I know? It's just a cupboard, all right?'

'Sorry,' Dinah says. 'I like the writing, that's all. I think it looks nice –'

'*Nice*?' Didi says. '*Nice*?!' By now he's aiming a kick at the cupboard. 'And another thing –' he says.

Maggie is not his new girlfriend. The new girlfriend is called Veronica. It turns out that Lisa has known about Veronica, but she's thought it best not to tell. She thinks that Didi ought to be telling Dinah; and now, of course, he has. Lisa knows, because she and Veronica and Didi all play tennis together at the same club over weekends. Lisa, unlike her sister Dinah, has always been good at tennis. The Born Arm notwithstanding, she's got an effective and powerful serve. Plus she's never passed out in bright sunlight in the face of an oncoming ball. Dinah flees from Didi's flat and spends the night with her sister, where she shares Lisa's single bed. Then Dinah wakes after a couple of hours. She tiptoes to the bathroom and locks herself inside. This is so that she can cry without waking up her sister.

Lisa is in a rosy mood because she's a girl in love. She's met a young industrial chemist who has bought her an engagement ring with lots of little diamonds around a central stone. They're planning a wedding in the Old Fort Chapel in Durban. The wedding reception is going to be in the Edward Hotel on the beachfront, because Lisa likes things done properly. Dinah's been signed up to be her bridesmaid and she knows what she's going to be wearing. A pale pistachio-green Thai silk suit with high-heeled shoes to match. But now Dinah's turned into a red-eyed heap. She can't see how she'll ever be Lisa's sweet and smiley bridesmaid. She'll be the thirteenth fairy at the feast, casting gloom and noxious mists. She's an unwanted, unhappy jilted woman. Soiled goods. Second-hand merchandise.

And right now she's feeling all at sea. She's spent three years clinging like a limpet to a man who she's known, in her heart, was all wrong. She's gone against her instincts. Yet now that he's sensibly rejected her and saved her from her own stupid, spineless self, she can't seem to feel that she's been liberated. All she can feel is fear. She's worried that she might have no idea who she is any more, because, for years now, she's been defining herself through her connection with Didi von Schweiten and now that connection's not there. At sunrise she wakes up, aching and shivering, to find that her head is crammed between the bath and the wash-basin pedestal. So she must have fallen asleep. She gets up and creeps back into Lisa's room and gropes for a cardigan. Then, once Lisa has gone off to her lectures, Dinah gets back into Lisa's bed and sleeps until midday. After that she tries phoning Sam, but he's been away from his parents' house since early morning, she's told.

Sam, having called for her at Didi's flat and got no answer, has found himself on the loose in Johannesburg and he's gone off to visit a friend. It's no longer all that easy for him to find friends whom he can visit. More and more they've fled into exile. Or they're in hiding. Or they're in prison. Or else they'll be under surveillance and he's determined to play it safe. So he's gone to visit an architect friend, an architect and man-about-town. The friend is called Arthur Goldreich and, with his wife, he's recently bought a farm-house in an affluent white suburb on the edge of Johannesburg. The suburb is called Rivonia and the farm is called Lilliesleaf.

'Come and see us,' Arthur has said the last time Sam ran into him.

At the farm Sam's greeted warmly, but in spite of this, he doesn't stay long. By mid-afternoon he's back and ready to meet up with Dinah after all. Both of them are in sombre mood, though they try a visit to the cinema where Dinah can cry in the dark. He doesn't say anything about his morning's visit. But quite a long time later – once there's really no point in keeping quiet – he talks out the unease he felt that washed over him at the time.

'Well, I knew there was something going on,' he says. 'Because Joe Slovo was visiting Arthur as well. But instead of sticking in the living room with us, he spent all his time out the back.'

And by this time the whole nation knows that 'out the back' is where the secret police have staged their triumphant coup. They've uncovered the entire ANC high command in an outhouse at Lilliesleaf Farm. That's except for Nelson Mandela, who's been arrested several months earlier, while working in disguise as a

chauffeur, for a white actor friend. The police have done their work
well. They've infiltrated a young German spy, who is currently
courting the daughter of one of the ANC's men. The national mood
is triumphalist and the state can't seem to stop crowing. Everyone
knows that the captured men will probably get the death sentence.
And, for anyone wanting change in South Africa, it's the blackest
day they can remember.

But normal life carries on. So, one day Sam is opening a parcel,
an unsolicited parcel. It's come addressed to him at the university
and a colleague is standing by his elbow alongside the pigeon-holes.
The parcel contains inflammatory leaflets of the sort that can get
you a five-year prison sentence. They've been sent by a freelance
freedom fighter from the safety of a bedsit in Kilburn, or Camden
Town, and they've come with an accompanying letter which is
asking Sam to pass the leaflets on. He's being asked to hand them
over to a high-profile human-rights activist, a person under constant surveillance. Sam reckons the human-rights activist is hardly
likely to welcome unsolicited calls from north-west London to
embark upon instant revolution. So he proceeds to the gentlemen's
toilets where he shreds the leaflets and the letter. Then, with no
small difficulty, he flushes the whole lot down the U-bend. Within
two weeks, the Special Branch have hauled Sam in for questioning.

'Did you receive a parcel from England containing leaflets?' they
say.

'Yes,' Sam says, after a moment's hesitation. 'Yes, I did.'

He has his little mantra. Never tell them what they don't know
already; never get caught telling lies.

'Well, it's good you told us that,' they say, 'because we already
know you did and we've got a warrant to search your property.'
The Special Branch man knows that Sam knows that he doesn't
any longer need a warrant. 'And what have you done with the
contents?' he says.

'I flushed it down the lavatory,' Sam says.

'Now why did you do that?' he says.

'I wanted nothing to do with it,' Sam says. 'I wanted to get rid
of it.'

'So was there a letter with the parcel?' he says.

'I didn't see any letter,' Sam says. 'I didn't stop to look. I was in
too much of a hurry.'

'Why were you in such a hurry?' says the Special Branch man.

'I wanted nothing to do with it,' Sam says again. 'That's why I flushed it away.'

'So what was the name on that letter?' says the policeman. 'You must have seen a name?'

The name is flashing inside Sam's brain. 'Sorry,' he says. 'I saw no letter.'

'You might as well tell us, because we know about it already,' the Special Branch man says.

'Sorry,' Sam says. 'I saw no letter.'

And so it goes. Round and round. For hours. Finally they believe him.

'We'll be watching you,' they say.

These days, whenever Sam's doorbell rings at night, he's never sure whether it's the Special Branch, or a person on the run saying hide me. Meanwhile, Dinah, at exactly this moment, is in the middle of writing a final-year essay on Conrad's *Under Western Eyes* – in which Razumov is having his life ruined by a late-night knock at the door. A fellow student is on the run from the Tsar's secret police. Sam's not a sleeper at the best of times, but now he's lying awake at night, waiting for the doorbell to ring. And the doctor's given him some sleeping pills that are having a curious effect. Before he drops off into dreamless sleep, Dinah's noticed that Sam flowers into a stream of verbal fluency, during which he talks out whole non-stop novels of small-town Jewish life. So Dinah knows all about Mr Lubovitz from the men's outfitter's in Krugersdorp, whose wife thinks he's tight-fisted and whose daughter has gone to the bad. She knows about the two Jewish families who jointly own the wet-fish shop that has a deli counter on the side. The families are no longer on speaking terms and rely for all communication on their go-between, their black delivery man, who by now is fluent in Yiddish. Dinah knows about the Mayor of Krugersdorp whom Sam's dad calls Transvaal. This is because he always tells lies that are as big as the Transvaal. She knows that Mr Dupe is the next-door neighbour in Blikkies and that he once threw a rock at Sam's dog Cheeky when Sam was three years old. Mr Dupe was trying to teach Cheeky not to chase after bicycles, but Sam's response was to pick up a rock and throw it at Mr Dupe. Mr Dupe is pleased about this and he tells Sam that he's plucky. His real name is Mr du Plessis. He was the South African pole-vaulting champion in 1936 and he's been to the Berlin Olympics.

Dinah is witness to Sam's new verbal flow, because she's recently moved in with him. She's had a fall-out with her dad and the cause is Liesl Mainz. Liesl has organised a twenty-first birthday party for her son and Dinah's gone along to it with Sam and Jed. But the party, having been rigorously stage-managed by Peter's mother, is full to capacity with Durban's middle-aged German business community, along with a stalwart but outnumbered smattering of Peter's various friends. Dinah's parents are there as well. Plus Liesl is parading one of her periodic itinerant protégés, a back-packing Freiburg medical student, by name, Karl-Heinz Schultz. And the protégé has brought along a squeezebox. Liesl always likes young people to do recitations in public – or virtuoso sequences of one kind or another – but while Peter's friends have dived for cover in the recesses of the garden, Karl-Heinz Schultz seems more than willing to oblige his hostess in this respect. So Liesl has clapped her hands for silence and has given her protégé the floor.

'I zing for you now, *ein* zong in zixteen lank-vitches,' the protégé says.

These fatal words are scarcely out before something clicks between Sam, Jed and Dinah. They all three start to vibrate with laughter and they are very soon uncontrollable. The party being mainly al fresco, the three are seated on a grassy bank, half hidden by the merciful darkness. The song is a constant repetition of one line: 'Everybody loves Saturday night.' The line is sung, four times over, in each of several languages. Plus the audience is being encouraged to sing along with the chorus. So it's very soon like a sort of multilingual Bouncing Ball and the middle-aged German business persons are heartily singing along.

By the time the protégé has done it in French, Spanish and Italian, the trio are whooping and snorting out loud and they're having to use their shirt-tails and skirts to wipe away tears of joy. By the time he's doing it in Afrikaans and Zulu, they have all three rolled down the grassy bank, balled up like hedgehogs. And each has a fist stuffed into his mouth. Then Sam is nudging the other two.

'Let's go,' he's hissing frantically. 'Let's disappear, for God's sake.'

So they creep around the side of the house and out through the gate into the road where the beetle is waiting for them. The strains of the protégé launching into Swahili are filling their ears as they depart. Then, gradually, their seizures die away and their stomachs cease to ache. Sam knows about a late-night café, run by the Indian comrades. It's a sort of mixed-race greasy spoon, where they'll do you some cheap curry and rice. So it's while they're eating their plates of curry that a tortoiseshell cat with lactating nipples lures them out into the yard where she's got a litter of kittens. In a cardboard box – awaiting adoption or drowning – are four kitsch greeting-card puffballs. Two are palest creamy orange and two have panda patches.

'You like to have some cats?' says the comrade.

So Sam and Dinah take the two orange ones and, by the time they've reached Sam's place, the kittens have both got names. They are called Mattie and Bart. Then Sam drives Dinah home where, having preceded her parents to the house, she goes straight to bed and sleeps.

Next morning, at breakfast, her dad is incandescent. He hauls her into his study and starts tearing a strip off her. Liesl Mainz has been on the phone and she's very hurt, he says. Dinah's offended old family friends who don't deserve to be the object of her displays of sneery contempt. And who, pray, does she think she is? Little Miss Too-Clever-By-Half? She and her duo of swaggering friends who think themselves a cut above? Liesl Mainz is a decent sort who deserves better than to have her party ruined by a silly snobby adolescent who isn't yet fit to understand that the middle class is the salt of the earth. Dinah even sort of knows that some of what he says is true. But she also knows that the song was a scream and to laugh at it was bliss. Besides, she has no techniques for meeting her dad halfway. So she opts for defiance instead.

'I thought it was supposed to be Peter's party,' she says. 'Wasn't that the whole point?'

She refuses point blank to phone and apologise, or to write a letter. Instead she flounces out in tears and runs off down the road in her little white shorts and sandals. She runs past the Cleggs' tearoom and general store; past the bus stop and past the old Manor House where Jenny's parents live. She runs past the convent hospital and all the way to Sam's doorstep. Sam knows that it's just before her final exams and he's nice about taking her in, even though it's a bit embarrassing for him, given that she's still one of the students and fraternising isn't quite done. So Dinah sleeps on a spare divan in the glassed-in sub-section of Sam's upstairs verandah, from which vantage point she watches the two orange puffballs tap dancing on the old wooden floorboards. And every night she's lulled to sleep by the complex scrabble of the pigeons' feet, who've taken up residence in Sam's steeply pitched Edwardian roof space.

Dinah loves Sam's flat. It's the whole top floor of a detached colonial house with an upstairs wooden verandah and huge, low sash windows. There's nothing much in the flat to speak of, except for Sam's clothes and papers and books which he keeps all over the floor. He got one auction-sale chaise-longue with the horsehair falling out the bottom and one capacious wing armchair with a baggy grass-green loose cover that she thinks might be made of Astro-turf. In the kitchen there's a double-fronted Queen Anne cooking stove that comes in mottled blue enamel. It's got mottled enamel cabriole legs and it gives off mild electric shocks unless you approach it sideways. The fridge makes the kind of rackety din that speaks to Dinah of goblin people hammering to get out. Then there's Sam's large unmade bed.

The bed is unmade because Sam can't make beds. He can't seem to fit a pillowcase with the corners to fit the corners, so the side seams run across the face of the pillow with the corners jutting like prick ears. He has a problem with distinguishing longways from crossways when it comes to a fitted sheet. So there's plenty of tuck-in room at each side, but the length can be missing two feet. Sam fits plugs to electrical appliances with a fine disregard for the cord grips, so the flexes work themselves loose. She's noticed that bills and necessary papers don't stay on their spikes for Sam. They like to abscond into oblivion. Inanimate objects are menacing to Sam. They always like to play lost. So one day, when Dinah comes to call for him in his room at the university, she finds him shifting his tottering piles of books in a major excavation project. The books have mostly come to him courtesy of Blackwell's overseas mailing department.

'The bloody thing was here a minute ago. I've had it this morning,' he says.

'What?' Dinah says.

'Someone's come in and taken it,' he says. 'It's Donald. He's forever swiping my stuff.'

'What?' Dinah says again.

'The *New Statesman*,' Sam says. 'Well, it only came this morning.' And he goes on shifting and excavating. 'It was here. This morning,' he says. 'Right here. He's taken it. I know. And I'll kill him. I will. Don't look at me like that, because I will.' And, as he speaks, the *New Stateman* emerges, bearing its trademark Vicky cartoon. But Sam doesn't need to blink. He doesn't need to change gear. 'Well, it isn't any of his business that he didn't take it,' he says. 'I think I'll kill him just the same.'

Something is happening to Dinah at this moment, as she's watching the sequence unfold. Because Sam's methods for getting through the day are so entirely, so excitingly new to her, so exotic, so convoluted; so wholly unlike anything that she's ever witnessed at home. So, as she stares, she feels her heart within her suddenly lift and lift. And then it's started dancing. She's thinking that there is something about the whole tottering construction which is liberating to her; it's allowing her to take wing. She's suddenly thinking, So what if no one ever marries me? So what if my life's not going to plan? For what do I need plans? All I know is I love this person. I love to be with him. Because he's nuts. Because he's best fun. Because I've never met anyone like him. All the things I do with him, each one is a little adventure, a little escapade. It's all a bit like buying penny scraps at the bus-stop chippie with Maud.

Take that visit, just yesterday, she's thinking. The one to Sam's corner shop. The shop is run by Mr Tomlinson and they've gone there to buy washing powder. But once Sam's got the box on the counter, he's decided to have the larger size.

'I've changed my mind,' he says to Mr Tomlinson. 'Hold on. I'll have the big one.'

'Good idea,' says Mr Tomlinson, feeling himself on safe ground. 'These native girls, they like to use the stuff like water.'

'Well, I wouldn't know about that,' Sam says, 'because I always do my own washing and I use it like water myself. That's why I'm going to buy the big one.'

Dinah is trying to suppress her giggles, because it's a lie that Sam does his own washing. Christine Mkise the washerwoman is coming in that day. That's why he's buying soap powder. Wednesday is Christine's day.

And Dinah hasn't been there very long before Sam's got a houseboy as well. The houseboy is Christine's younger brother and he really is a boy, because David Mkise is just fifteen. Christine wants him rescued from a bully-boy white policeman by whom he's employed as a servant. David has been working there in the hope of clocking up enough time in domestic service to become eligible for factory work within the municipal Durban area. But what's happened is that the policeman has moved house two months earlier, and now he's living just outside the city's boundary. This move has wiped out all the time that David's done so far and, unless he moves back inside the boundary, he hasn't a hope in hell of ever escaping domestic service. If you're black you must skivvy for a year before you earn the right to look for factory work. And David, being just a kid, has panicked and run away. But then he's been caught and the policeman has now impounded David's passbook. So it's vital that Sam employs David, which will require him to sweet-talk the policeman. Plus he'll have to get the passbook off him as well.

Dinah goes along with Sam in the VW beetle, because Sam has a notion that a blonde girl in pink-and-white gingham will have the effect of softening the policeman's heart. She watches him negotiate with the policeman in his Krugersdorp Afrikaans. Sam is using all the terminology he can muster to keep the policeman on his side. He's come for the *umfaan*, he says. His 'native girl' is the *umfaan*'s older sister and she wants to keep him under her thumb. Because we all know what these *umfaans* can be like and she's scared he'll go to the bad. And, finally, amazingly, David Mkise is released and he's settled in the car – a little, cowering Zulu boy whose instinct is to shrink and flinch. Plus Sam's got possession of the passbook, which the policeman has thoughtfully defaced.

And David who, for the first few weeks, cringes and hugs the walls, has soon blossomed into a swaggering adolescent who is anxious to run with the big boys. So he comes home smelling of drink. And, equally soon, Sam is spending long hours in court, rescuing David from a flick-knife frame-up and other more minor charges.

'Football,' an elderly colleague advises. 'Football is what can save him.'

So Sam is struggling to sign up his charge for a local black football club when David catches the eye of the older maidservant who works for the family next door. She and David become an item and the wild boy settles down.

By now, Dinah and Sam are also an item, thanks to Dinah's moment of revelation over the disappearing *New Statesman*. So she and Sam are sleeping together in the large unmade bed. Dinah can sleep almost anywhere, so she doesn't mind the tangled sheets. She can even sleep through the prodigious snores of Mattie and Bart who've been playing chicken on the upstairs balcony, weaving in and out of the balustrades. And then they've fallen off, so their hard palates are cracked, which will take quite a while to heal. Sam is, as usual, hardly sleeping. He's wiling away the early hours, reading Galbraith and Seymour Martin Lipset, while eating lots of rye bread liberally spread with honey. And sometimes, when he's feeling twitchy, he'll drive out in the small hours to see whether the lights are on in the building that once was host to the Maypole Tearoom.

'Special Branch were working late last night,' he'll say to Dinah in the morning. 'Watch out for new arrests.'

So he knows before the dawn breaks, before it's announced on the morning news, that something significant has happened. Two of the captured Rivonia accused have made a sensational breakout and the newspapers are very soon filled with demonising articles about Sam's friends Arthur Goldreich and Harold Wolpe, a Johannesburg lawyer who, for years, has been giving his time and his skills for free, in defence of the state's impoverished scapegoats. Dinah, not long before the arrests, has met him with Sam – a chance meeting – in a large Bavarian eating house in downtown Johannesburg. Her only contact with Arthur Goldreich has been through an exhibition of his paintings which are currently on show in the Durban Municipal Art Gallery – presumably because nobody there is quite certain about whether or not to take the pictures down. Because are you allowed to exhibit the paintings of a person whom you cannot quote? Mercifully, the mug shots look nothing like the two escapees and the text beneath makes repeated reference to Wolpe's 'prominent Jewish nose'.

These days lots of people have started sleeping away from home. And one of the two visiting Special Branch policemen keeps on popping up, like the Cheshire Cat, in Mr Tomlinson's shop. Or sometimes he's in the local chemist, where he likes to make pleasant small talk. He's living just round the corner, he says, now that he's split from the wife.

'So you've got yourself some new cats,' he says. 'Hey, sorry about the old ones!'

'That's right,' Sam says. 'New cats.'

'Do you find there's a big black tom cat around here that's always bothering them?' he says. 'I tell you, my cat is frightened to death of him. Frightened to death, I swear to God.'

Then it's not long before Bart and Mattie have also come to grief. They've both of them started to court girl cats in the flats across the street. Bart is killed outright by a car. Mattie disappears until, four days later, when Dinah thinks to crawl into the anti-termite zone under the house. And there is Mattie, unable to move, because his back legs have been run over. She and Sam have rushed him to Maud's vet, but his pelvis is hopelessly broken and that's the end of him. So everything around them is just sort of folding up. And then, that night, in the cinema, ten minutes before the film's end, Sam nudges Dinah in the darkness and whispers to her that they should leave.

'Let's go,' he says. 'Leave now.'

So they creep out under cover of dark and make for the VW beetle.

'Why?' Dinah says.

'Just someone I know in there,' Sam says. 'He's a little bit of a cowboy. He'd have asked us for a lift home. And he's into stuff, I'm pretty sure. Look. He's not discreet. He likes danger. The cops will be watching him for certain.'

Sam turns the key in the ignition, but then he turns it off.

'Oh shit,' he says. 'I really hate all this. I can't stand what it's doing to me. Dinah, for Christ's sake let's get the hell out. Let's go.'

'Go where?' Dinah says.

'London,' Sam says. 'Will you marry me, Dinah, and come with me?'

Dinah is thinking that marrying Sam might just be what she'd most like to do. For tomorrow and tomorrow and the day after that, and the month after that as well. For the future as far as she can see it. She can't get her mind round for ever any more. Not after the Didi experience. Plus she's also thinking of Chelsea and

Vauxhall Bridge and of the escalators on the Underground and of all those people she wants to meet from Iris Murdoch's first novel. She knows that by leaving the country she won't be striking any blow for freedom – that's to say – except for her own and Sam's. Because white people can go anywhere. They don't only own South Africa. They have access to the wider world. They get passports. They travel. It's not like having those useless wretched papers from the Bantu Homeland of the Ciskei. Even so, if you're Sam, you're taking no chances with your passport. Sam, for over a year now, has been keeping his passport stashed away in somebody else's house. Dinah's is simply with her mother.

'But there is one thing,' Dinah says. 'You don't want to marry me, remember?'

'Who says I don't?' Sam says.

'You,' Dinah says. 'You said.'

'What rubbish,' Sam says. 'I never said such a thing. You must be making it up.'

So Sam and Dinah get married right away and Dinah has to be Lisa's Matron of Honour because married persons can't be brides-maids. But she still gets to wear the pistachio-green suit with the narrow pencil skirt. Before that, for her own wedding, she's made herself a dress. She's made it like a Flower Fairy's dress, with wide, layered petal shapes for sleeves. And she wears it with a little white headscarf knotted under her chin.

Sam's mother has told him that she won't come to the wedding. This is because Dinah's one Jewish earlobe is not quite enough to pass muster. Yet, in the event, she comes. The party is in Dinah's parents' garden, where everything is swiftly melting on account of the Durban heat. The avocado dips and the apple pies are melting along with most of the guests.

Sam has already cashed in his pension. Then, last of all, he sells the car.

'One Volkswagen wreck,' as the dealer says, fixing the beetle with a jaundiced look.

All of it helps to buy two tickets for the smallest berth on the oldest and cheapest Union Castle boat, which will sail from Durban to Southampton Docks, via Cape Town and Las Palmas. Everyone is suddenly leaving. Going, going, gone. Maud is off to

New York soon, where the beautiful mathematician has got himself a graduate student fellowship at Columbia University. Jenny is off to the States as well, with a person whom she's recently married. Jenny has married a much older man, an eminent medical person, who likes her in tweeds and Burberry. Plus he likes to choose all her clothes.

'Now *there*'s a garment I'd like to buy for my Jennifer-Anne,' he says.

The only hitch about leaving the country is what to do with David, who is still short of completing his year in domestic service, so it has to be a condition for any new tenant that David comes with the flat. Plus the tenant must be willing, when sign-off time arrives, to airmail David's employment papers fraudulently to London, where Sam will fraudulently sign him off and fraudulently post the papers back. So it's good that everyone wants the flat so much. All their friends are lining up to cheat for David Mkise. Sam has arranged to transfer his Ph.D. registration from Cape Town to London University. And Dinah is going to teach. (Teach!) She's got a letter from the Ministry in Whitehall to say that she'll be eligible. But she's telling herself five times a day that she isn't *really* a teacher and that it won't be for very long. She couldn't possibly be a teacher, could she? Because aren't all teachers mad?

The last thing they've got to do is hitch-hike up to Krugersdorp and say goodbye to Sam's family. But Sam's mother's in a fury with him so it's four hundred miles for the privilege of being wrong-footed, big-time. She's furious with Sam because he's going off to lay claim to her native city and to travel on the District Line. Plus the return hitch-hike is not going well and they've missed out on lifts all day. Then, at twilight, they're finally picked up by a local farmer who's returning from the shooting range. It's soon very clear that he's been drinking and his rifle is disconcertingly running the length of the front seat. The farmer is suddenly inviting Sam and Dinah, with a heavy drunkard's hospitality, to spend the night at his farm. And, when they refuse, he just as suddenly goes into a tantrum. He believes them to be 'overseas foreigners', as he says, and 'the Afrikaner', he will have them know, is traditionally Very Hospitable. So if they're from England, he'd like to make them welcome on his farm. If they're from Holland, welcome to the farm! If they're from France, or Germany, welcome to the farm! Then suddenly the car is veering from side to side in the darkness. But if they're Russians, then get out of the car! If they're Communists, out of the car! Then he turns to fix Sam with a look.

'Or if you're Wolpe or Goldreich,' he says. 'Out! Out of the car!' His brakes are suddenly screaming to a halt and he's wrenching open the back door. Then he's reaching for his rifle. 'Out!' he says. 'Out! Out!'

'Jesus Christ!' Sam says, exhausted, as they collapse on the grassy verge. They're gratefully watching the dust cloud rise behind the farmer's departing car. 'So what was all that about?'

Dinah shrugs. 'Prominent Jewish nose? Now we'll never get a lift back.'

They're seated, in the pitch darkness, on a small minor road. Nobody is going to come by for hours. But yes! It's after only ten minutes that two young Indian trading brothers are pulling up in a truck; a large, ancient truck which judders heavily to a stop. And they're driving all the way back to Durban. Hurrah! Hurrah! The four of them are soon seated, wedged tightly, in a row up front and, almost as soon, the brothers have insisted that Sam take a turn to drive. Sam is fairly terrified because the thing is huge and un-familiar, but at least, in the darkness, he's unaware of the reason he's being made to drive. This is so that the two trading brothers can commit acts of sexual interference with Dinah all the way back home. And they are doing so in tandem. One has his hands inside her pants, while the other is busy down her blouse. And Dinah is spending the entire homeward route silently wrestling with two sets of wandering hands, while trying not to give offence. She's not quite daring to assert herself, just in case the day should turn ugly. Well. Uglier than it's proved to be so far.

So that is Dinah's last memory of her last day in her own country. Or of the place that, once upon time, *was* her country. Is. Was. Long ago. I go to create in the smithy of my soul. Or do I? Why, exactly? For what reason do I go? Nonetheless, I go. I went. But always at my back I hear. I see. I smell. That land where lemon trees grow. And avocados and lychees. And pawpaws. And spiky aloes. And giant bamboo. *Kennst du das Land?* Well, perhaps I do no longer. Sometimes – though not very often now – Dinah will still put on her jacaranda-pod earrings. And then people in England think that she's wearing varnished potato crisps.

AFTERWORD

Sam and Dinah dock in Southampton on a dark cold day in January. It's seven-thirty in the morning, but it could be the middle of the night. The light begins to glimmer feebly as they approach the city, via the boat train that runs along the backs of grey-brown terraced houses. It flashes past all the grey-brown yards with their grey-brown sheds and grey-brown garden fences. On the hoardings, all along the railway line, are posters that read like patriotic boasts. Or sometimes they read like exhortations. 'This is the STRONG country' one set of posters says. The other set says, 'TAKE COURAGE'.

'It's beer ads,' Sam says eventually. 'There must be a beer called Courage. Maybe there's another one called Strong?'

Though the day is cold enough to stiffen Dinah's toes, Sam is not wearing his duffel coat because he's still got asthma from the boat. Dusty blankets have appeared after the stop-off day in Las Palmas and that's what's brought it on. After Las Palmas the economy-class swimming pool is filled with bright-red spherical tomatoes. All are the size of ping-pong balls. All are exactly the same. To Dinah and Sam the spherical tomatoes are a thing of miracle and wonder. That is, until they try one of them and find that it tastes like mush. Every tomato they've eaten hitherto has come an irregular orangey-green and it's often had scallops and grooves – sometimes even cracks and scars. But it's always tasted intense and lemony; it's tasted of tomato heaven.

Their first stop is a fortnight's free lodging with a kind friend in south London, who has a very small newly built flat. In the flat it's always raining indoors. Water is pouring down the insides of the windows and black mould is growing up the frames. This is because the flats have been built without a gas supply. The building contractors have made a deal with the Electricity Board – and nobody now living in the flats can afford the electric heating. So the heating ducts have no function at all, except to slice up adventurous pet hamsters, while the residents are all using paraffin heaters, which are causing the indoor rain.

Sam and Dinah, who are given the only bedroom, are to sleep in a pretty old iron bed that the friend has bought from a second-hand stall under the Brixton railway arches. It has two ancient horsehair mattresses to compensate for its sagging wires. And the old black Valor paraffin heater is throwing a pretty rose window of light on to the ceiling. The problem is that, in addition, it's filling the room with smoke. And it could hardly be more embarrassing that, within ten minutes of going to bed, Sam has to be rushed into Dulwich Hospital, because his chest has gone into spasm. Once admitted, he's kept there for a week where he shares a room with an old Brixton white man who has had his voice box removed. The old Brixton white man has learned to speak on burps, so he's using all the burps he can muster to rant against the Caribbean immigrants who are currently moving into Brixton. Meanwhile, out in the real world, Dinah must sign up at the local police station because, ever since Dr Verwoerd has got South Africa expelled from the Commonwealth, that country's citizens count as aliens.

'It's a crying shame, nice white people like you having to register as aliens,' says the police constable. 'When these nig-nogs and all sorts, with names we can't pronounce, can come swanning in here just as they please.'

It's at times like this that Dinah feels impelled to get on her personal soapbox. She feels the same at the greengrocer's when she refuses to buy South African fruit.

'Quite right. I agree with you,' the greengrocer says. 'When you think of all those dirty black hands that go crawling all over the fruit –'

But this is London 1964. It's long before that city has become the multi-ethnic showpiece of Europe.

By now it's started snowing. It's the first snow that Dinah's ever seen. So she goes shopping in Oxford Street for some sturdy winter clothes. Her hostess has persuaded her that she'll need vests along with those passion-killing knickers that come halfway down your thighs. Dinah can never get used to the knickers and she finds that there's something peculiarly horrible about wearing a vest with a bra. It makes you feel as if you've got all your underclothes on back to front. So she never wears her purchases. Plus, because she has no idea that Oxford Street is a little bit penny bazaar, she's puzzled to find that all she wants to buy there is a set of squeaky plastic mice that are on sale alongside the Underground station.

By the time Sam's been discharged from hospital, Dinah has found them a flat. Well, in the ad it's called a flat, but in fact it's not quite self-contained. Not like a Durban bachelor flat. The flat is the top two rooms of a tall house in Highgate and it's got its own kitchenette. But the bathroom on the landing is shared. And it's very soon clear that the landlady expects them to use the Hoover every day and the bath tub once a week. Sam and Dinah want to use the bath tub every day and the Hoover once a week, so there's a conflict of lifestyle from the start. And that's before Dinah commits the faux pas of removing a pair of net curtains. The net curtains are blurring the pleasant wintry view over Highgate Woods, so Dinah takes them down. In doing so she has no idea that she's committing a major transgression and she goes tripping off to her teaching job in Hackney which has just begun that week. Meanwhile Sam is taking the rap.

'My nets!' says the landlady, accosting him on the stairs. 'My *best nets*! What on earth have you done with them? I looked up from the garden and just imagine my shock. "My *best nets*!" I said to my husband. "Where are my *very best nets*?!"'

Sam is blinking at her in confusion, because he hasn't noticed the nets in the first place, nor that Dinah has taken them down. And he's on his way to the Reading Room of the British Museum, which is why he's halfway down the stairs. So that weekend Sam and Dinah are once again scanning the lettings as they sit morosely in a coffee house in Swiss Cottage alongside the John Lewis shop. It's exactly the sort of strudel hangout that feels like German-Jewish Johannesburg, so at least they're feeling at home. And it's there that they run into Harold Wolpe who has come in to buy some cakes. He laughs at their story and doesn't believe them that it's the net curtains that have got them thrown out. He says they must have done something worse. But he nonetheless invites them to stay.

'We've got all these bedrooms,' he says.

Harold has arrived in a blaze of glory as a high-profile escape artist from the apartheid reign of terror. He's been interviewed on all the news channels and the British Home Secretary has loaned him a house on Hampstead's salubrious Heath Drive. The rooms are vast and the en suite bathrooms have black-and-white marble floor tiles. The Edwardian bath tubs have roll tops and elegant old-fashioned chrome taps with elaborate chrome shower contraptions. Only there's not much sleep to be had in Harold's house, because everyone there is playing bridge through the night. The Rivonia Trial is going on and it's hard for people to go to sleep when they're waiting to know whether their comrades are about to be sentenced to death.

Each day, Dinah takes the train to Dalston Junction, near Stoke Newington. Then she takes a bus. Her school is near the Hackney Marshes where she's in charge of a class of seven-year-olds, about whom she knows nothing. Absolutely zilch. She has no idea that seven-year-olds like lots and lots of rules. Rules about whose turn it is to hand out the milk. Rules about whose turn it is to lead the class crocodile into assembly. Rules about the gathering in of pencils before each playtime comes round. So this is why, by the end of day one, her class doesn't have any pencils. And when she sends to the secretary for more, she's told that she's had her lot. Her class has had its pencil ration until the end of the spring term. The school year, Dinah's discovered, has only three seasons in England. And, curiously, though it's freezing cold, there's never any winter. The terms are spring and summer and autumn. Then it's the Christmas Holidays. Then – hey presto! – it's back to spring.

The crisis point of her every school day comes when Dinah has to take PE. Because not only is she conspicuously useless at any form of physical activity – that's with the exception of ballroom dancing, in which art, thanks to Mrs Dudley Andrews, she's possessed of a bronze medal – but PE always takes place in the hall: the communal, old-fashioned assembly hall, on to which all the classroom doors open. So her every failure is mercilessly public; her exposure is absolute. And always, before she can blow her whistle to assemble her children into lines, every male seven-year-old in her class is halfway up the wall bars, loudly whooping out Tarzan noises that are echoing round the whole school. Even when it comes to classroom work, the noise level emanating from her corner is unacceptably high. Which is why, after three days, Mr Sparks has come in to rescue her. Mr Sparks is an old hand at teaching juniors and he's been raised in Hackney himself.

'Let me give you a little demonstration,' he says.

Then he turns to glare at Dinah's children. Dinah's class has fallen completely silent upon the moment of his entry.

'Line up!' says Mr Sparks, sounding very Fi Foe Fum. Then he says, 'Back to your places!'

He has the class do this four times over. Each time he says their lining up won't do. They're not doing it quickly enough and they'll have to do it again. Finally he changes the drill. Throughout his demonstration he's assumed a man-eating ogre's voice that comes an octave down from where his normal voice is pitched.

'Stand up!' he says. 'Hands on heads! Sit down! Stand up! Hands on heads! Sit down!'

The children are all scrabbling feverishly to do Mr Sparks's bidding, but still Mr Sparks is not pleased. He stretches out his fearsome right arm and points an accusing finger. The object of his attention is an unusually small boy. The boy's name is Jeffrey Hirschmann and his testicles haven't dropped. Jeffrey's mother has told Dinah this on the afternoon of the first day.

'You, boy!' says Mr Sparks. 'Why don't you put your hands on your head when I tell you to?'

Jeffrey has been doing exactly the same as all the others have been doing, but now he's shaking and gulping in a paroxysm of guilt.

'Sir,' he says, in a small capitulating squeak. 'Sir. Sorry, sir.'

Mr Sparks meanwhile has turned aside to Dinah and he's speaking a little skittishly, half under his breath.

'Pick on one of them,' he's saying to her. 'Preferably the smallest.'

Then he returns his attention to the class. He's picked up the hymn book from Dinah's table and he's leafing through it as he speaks.

'Take out your hymn books,' he says. He's reverted to the ogre's voice. 'Open them at page ninety-three. Copy out hymn number one hundred and two. All five verses.'

The hymn books are out, the jotters are out. Heads are bent in concentration. Then he turns again to Dinah.

'Keep them doing that for a week,' he says. 'Lining up. Sitting down. Hands on heads. Copying out hymns. You'll have them eating out of your hand.'

Then Mr Sparks leaves the room.

The classroom door has barely closed behind him when pandemonium breaks loose. All ten Jewish children are jumping up and down and poor skinny goggle-eyed Simon Schaffer has managed to steam up his lenses. They've all begun to call out loud and each is more strident than the next.

'Miss! *Miss!*' they're saying. 'My mum says I'm not allowed copying out *ANY*fink about Jesus! *ANY*body as makes me copy out *ANY*fink about Jesus – that person's got to go to Mr Mynott!'

Mr Mynott is the school headmaster. He's a professional absentee. The school is being kept afloat by Mr Sparks with the assistance of an elderly Welshman whose name is Iain Davies. Mr Davies has a handicap in that he can't tell the black children apart.

'They all look the same,' he wails to Dinah, who hasn't ever encountered this particular affliction before because, while white South Africans may be dedicated to a particularly unpleasant racist caste system, they've been around black people long enough to tell that they don't all look alike. The black children in Dinah's school, having sussed Mr Davies's blind spot, are always ready with their alibis.

'Warrn't me, sir,' they say. 'Warrn't me who done it, sir.'

Mrs Potts, the school secretary, tells Dinah that she hates the Welsh.

'And now that they've gone and built the Severn Bridge,' she says, 'they'll all be coming here to take our jobs.'

Mrs Potts tells Dinah that she didn't see a real banana until the age of ten. This was because of the war.

'The greengrocers always had paper bananas,' she says. 'Strings of them across the back of the shop.'

Dinah's class is one-third Jewish and one-third Caribbean. Among the rest, some are recent Irish immigrants and the others are indigenous English. Of the English, half are not in the class when she first comes to take the register.

''Op-pickin', miss,' the children chant when she calls out the listed names.

Dinah hasn't a clue what they mean, because she's never heard of hop-picking. She's never heard of hops. She doesn't know anything much about beer, except that back home it's called Lion or Castle when white people are drinking it. And that, in the townships, strong-minded black women brew illicit beer in holes in the ground at the backs of their shebeens. That hop-picking is a form of traditional working holiday for London's East End poor sounds to her utterly, picturesquely yesterday – like something out of Laurie Lee. Plus another thing that baffles her is when the children in her class say 'indoors'. 'Left it indoors, miss,' they'll say – about their gym shoes, or their dinner money, or the library book that they ought to have brought in. Dinah thinks that the class-room is indoors, so she can't see why there's a problem. But indoors means at home, of *course*, so the children sigh and roll their eyes to indicate her singular stupidity.

'*IN*-doors, miss!' they say. 'Left it *IN*-doors, then, didn't I?!'

Again, she's puzzled that, for poorish children, they seem to have so many nannies. Dinah has always thought that it's rich children who are cared for by nannies – but these children, it materialises, are speaking about their grannies. Their nannies are their grannies. Their nans are their grans. Plus her reading of English social class is thick with innocent pitfalls. So one day she thinks it might be nice for the children to act out the poems from *Old Possum* and Isaac will read about Bustopher Jones: the smart cat, the cut-above cat, the cat who doesn't care to visit pubs and has several gentlemen's clubs.

Isaac pauses after reading the lines.

'My dad go to a club, miss,' he says. ''E go there to weave baskets.'

This is because Isaac's father is blind. Of all the children in her class, Dinah is the most intrigued by Isaac and his smaller twin brother, Menachem. Isaac and Menachem Isaacs are Indian immigrant twins. They are not only Indian but Jewish. They've been discovered living in direst poverty in a damp basement room. There is no mother. The boys' mother is dead. So they've been taken into care. Dinah has never heard of Indian Jews, but Sam is not that surprised.

'They've been there since the biblical diaspora,' he says. 'They practise a caste system based on colour.'

'*What?*' Dinah says.

The human species, Dinah sometimes thinks, is stark staring mad. People have no sooner got themselves born than they start to imagine the gods want them to flatten their heads, or perforate their genitals, or arrange themselves into hierarchies based on the colour of their skins. The gods require them to avoid eating hoofs, or to walk backwards in certain sacred presences, or to hang up cats in clay pots and light fires underneath them. The gods like them to slaughter birds and make incisions in their own skulls. The gods have put the banana on this earth so that the human species can apprehend that fruit as a miraculous revelation of the Holy Trinity. It has to do with their singular ability to think and dream in symbols. This is what makes the species so vicious. It's also what makes them great poets.

So Dinah is experiencing a mild form of culture shock – and that's in spite of the common language, in spite of all those Union Jacks planted in Durban's verdant gardens. Because, for all the Coronation mugs, for all the Beefeater costumes at the fancy-dress parade and the Authorised Version in morning assembly and the acres of Mallory Towers and the great Beacon Readers and *The Public School Hymn Book* and *The Barretts of Wimpole Street* – Dinah is finding that what she possesses is a settler construct of England. A construct in which no provision has been made for Isaac and Menachem Isaacs. Nor for the hop-pickers. Nor for the obsession with net curtains. Nor has it explained to her why the *English*-English, though they all have sinks, will always do the washing up in specially designated plastic bowls that they keep inside the sink. It hasn't prepared her for the bus conductors who bawl 'Inside only!' at her and then get furious if she goes upstairs because she thinks that upstairs is inside. It doesn't prepare her for those muddle-inducing telephone boxes that say she has to push button A as soon as she hears a voice. And then, if she doesn't hear any voice, she has to push button B. Otherwise she loses all her money.

But slowly Dinah is learning to love it. She's gradually making it her own. She loves the signs in the Underground, is always uplifted by them. 'To the trains', they say to her. 'To the trains'. And she's always disappointed by the ones that omit the article. Because 'To trains' is just not in any way the same. It's an awkward proofreader's error. It's a little bit like 'C. Argo' where she had to blink away the full stop. Because the first is a noble exhortation which is urging her to proceed, ever onward and onward. To the trains! To the trains! To the trains! It's like being in an Eisenstein movie. The second is merely, pragmatically, directing her to go this way or that.

She likes the launderettes. She likes the street markets where the vendors shout at her, ''Ow's about a bit o' ripe banana?' which always sounds a bit music-hall risqué. She likes the Anaglypta wallpaper that sits in baskets outside the DIY shops, because it looks a bit like stucco, or like some of the wood-carved coffering that Miss Byrd once taught her about. She likes the Belfast Linen and the fabric remnants in John Lewis. And she's especially drawn to any branch of the army-surplus shop. This is because of its shifting stock and its utilitarian chic. All that canvas with brass eyelet holes and those plain wooden boxes with rope handles; those galvanised wash tubs and plain donkey-grey blankets – it's like Muji before its time. Sometimes there'll be stacks of cheap white dinner plates. And sometimes – for reasons Dinah can't decipher – there'll be rows of monographed chamber pots and cut-price silver ice buckets.

She loves her walks on Hampstead Heath, because, on the Heath, all the trees are imitating Constable paintings. And then there's the light – that subtle, fluctuating English light that's forever imitating Turner. Camden Town is a place that she sees through the eyes of Walter Sickert. And on the Embankment at sunset she can see those kitsch orange dapplings on the water that are trying to look like Claude Monet. The Thames is always a turn-on for her, where those 'walls of Magnus Martyr hold,/Inexplicable splendour of Ionian white and gold'. Leastways, she's gone several times to take a look at the inside of the Church of Magnus Martyr, but each time she's found it locked. And she and Sam, on a trip to Greenwich, have wasted many minutes by the waterside waiting in the wrong queue. The boatman has been calling out 'Queue here!' repeatedly. But what he's really been calling out is '*Kew* here!' He means that passengers should queue there for Kew. And Sam and Dinah don't want to go Kew. They want to go to Greenwich.

Then there's the grass in Regent's Park which is always incredibly green.

'It's green because it never stops raining,' an English colleague reminds her.

And, yes, it's true that Sam and Dinah have experienced their first ever rainy picnic. The picnic has taken place in a bandstand in Wells where they look out, through the sheets of rain, on to the curious flat-topped towers of Wells's beautiful cathedral. A friend's mother has prepared the picnic. She's done cucumber sandwiches and sausage rolls and a simnel cake. Plus she's even brought along an urn so that the party can have freshly brewed tea.

'Well,' says the friend's mother, in a manner that indicates bags of good cheer along with several decades of character building, 'I must say, I've known many a *worse* bank-holiday picnic.'

Dinah likes it that the public holidays are called bank holidays in England. That's because they aren't commemorating an endless succession of brutal events in which white persons with gunpowder have laid waste to brown persons with spears.

Dinah is familiar with Camden Town because she and Sam are living there now – well, they're living on Primrose Hill. Because, along with Dinah's salary of forty pounds a month, Sam has now got a student award which adds another fifty pounds. So they've done their sums and they've found the flat: a small unfurnished affair. They do their shopping in Camden Town, mostly in Inverness Street. And sometimes, for a shop in the same little street, Dinah makes stuffed toys and children's clothes to supplement their income. She's got herself a part-time job due to start at the beginning of the autumn term. It's in one of the new comprehensive schools and she'll be teaching adolescents. This is so that she can sign up as a graduate student as well.

It's bliss for Sam and Dinah to be on their own in the flat. It's June and it's suddenly summer. Everyone is saying it's the best summer they can remember. Sam and Dinah spend the long evenings lazing in Regent's Park and sometimes they take themselves to the open-air theatre that's inside the park. They're enchanted by the length of the days, because in Durban the big orange sun will slide with speed behind those bottle-green hills and then it will be night. Whilst here, in London, people are still playing tennis at ten o'clock.

Between them, Sam and Dinah have once again acquired two cats. Two pale-gingers – Bart and Mattie lookalikes – so they're

306

happily playing house. Dinah's cat comes from a pet shop in Dalston Junction. Sam's cat is from Camden Town. And, because they've got a paragon of a landlady, she doesn't mind about the cats. She doesn't even mind when the cats have kittens. Which they do, because Dinah's cat, quite unbeknown to her, is a rare and precious thing. She's a female marmalade, when the proper equivalent of marmalade in a girl is tortoiseshell. So that when the kittens are born, not only are they all marmalade, but three of the four are girls.

'Well,' says the landlady. 'Three ginger girls! Why is that, do you think?'

But Dinah has no idea. 'I don't know why it is,' she says. 'It's just one of the wonders of the world.'

ACKNOWLEDGEMENTS

In being able to make sense of the racially stratified world in which Dinah de Bondt grows up, I have had the good fortune, first to have grown up in that context with parents who held dissenting views, and then to have spent the past forty years in the company of Stan Trapido, whose vast knowledge of South Africa's history, along with his astute and original takes on it, have not only inspired a generation of younger historians, but have always been of benefit to me in coming to understand the country of my past.

I could not have written this book without the enriching effects upon my early life of three remarkable women: Elaine O'Reilly, Suzanne Gordon and Frances McDonald. And on the subject of remarkable women, I have, throughout the writing, had the support and conviction of Victoria Hobbs, my agent, and that of my editor, Alexandra Pringle, in the face of whose special qualities words tend to fail. There is only one of her and not every author can have her, so I count myself particularly blessed. In conclusion – and I emphasise conclusion – my thanks to Iris Murdoch.

Barbara Trapido, Oxford, 2003.

TERMINOLOGY

In a world where terminology is a minefield, no term is more
problematical than Coloured because, while this is highly
offensive to any British person who isn't frozen in the 1950s, it
is inescapably the term used by certain groups of South
Africans about themselves: people who, culturally, ethnically
and historically, do not see themselves as black.

A NOTE ON THE AUTHOR

Barbara Trapido was born in South Africa and is the author of five novels – *Brother of the More Famous Jack* (winner of a Whitbread special prize for fiction), *Noah's Ark*, *Temples of Delight* (shortlisted for the *Sunday Express* Book of the Year Award), *Juggling* and *The Travelling Hornplayer* (shortlisted for the 1998 Whitbread Novel Award). She lives in Oxford.

READING GROUP GUIDE

A free six-page guide to *Frankie and Stankie* for reading groups
is available to all UK readers. The guide contains discussion
topics, background to the writing of the book and suggestions
for further reading.

To order your guide, please send an email to:
frankieandstankie@bloomsbury.com
or log on to: http://www.bloomsbury.com/barbaratrapido
or write to:
Frankie and Stankie Reading Group Guide
Bloomsbury Publishing Plc
38 Soho Square
London
W1D 3HB